I0761195

Tori Anne Martin

To Mr. Gevry, Dr. LaPlant, and Mr. O(gden)—thank you for allowing me to give you alternate identities.

And to Mr. Baker—without your encouragement, this book would probably not exist.

Printed and bound in August 2025 at Sheridan, Chelsea, MI, USA.

www.holidayhouse.com

First Edition

1 3 5 7 9 10 8 6 4 2

Library of Congress Cataloging-in-Publication Data is available.

ISBN: 978-0-8234-6035-9 (hardcover)

EU Authorized Representative: HackettFlynn Ltd, 36 Cloch Choirneal, Balrothery, Co. Dublin, K32 C942, Ireland. EU@walkerpublishinggroup.com

Chapter One

Lily

The night before her senior year of high school began, Lily Allerton meticulously readied her new backpack, laid out the perfect outfit, and unwrapped the black silk cloth from around her tarot cards. A hint of frankincense clung to the cloth like a stain, and Lily inhaled the incense's remnants as she surveyed her bedroom with satisfaction.

Her backpack (purple, because it was her favorite color) waited by the door. She'd already filled it with her laptop and a brand-new notebook, and she'd decorated it with seven pins from her enamel pin collection. The pins were attached in such a way as to appear haphazard, but in truth, Lily had contemplated their placement deeply to make sure they ended up in the most artistically pleasing formation, and the results were worth the time spent.

Her clothes hung over the back of her desk chair. Her outfit was new, and it was stylish without being overly trendy.

The shirt was a rich forest green that contrasted with her strawberry-blond hair and made her brown eyes seem like maybe, just maybe, they had a touch of green in them, too. They weren't witchy eyes, like certain girls had, but the green shirt made them more interesting.

Lily's hands clenched around her tarot cards and she took a deep breath, trying to dislodge that thought from her brain by sheer force of will and stale incense smoke, but it was no use. It, too, remained like a stain.

Witchy eyes.

Chrysanthemum's eyes.

Damn Chrysanthemum, damn her witchy eyes, and damn her stupid name. Merely thinking of her was like summoning a demon.

Who named their child *Chrysanthemum* in the first place? It didn't exactly roll off the tongue, and Lily refused to do her the courtesy of calling her Chrys, like she insisted.

Ella—one of Lily's two rabbits—nipped at her bare foot as though to remind her that she, too, was named after a flower.

"Well, okay," Lily said, setting the cards down on her altar and scooping up the brown-and-white ball of fur. "But mine's a *normal* flower name. She could have been Rose, or Violet, or Daisy."

Besides, there was nothing flowerlike about Chrysanthemum herself . . . unless, possibly, Lily considered blooms of the poisonous variety. Monkshood. Foxglove. Datura. Those names would have been more fitting for someone as bitter and spiteful as Chrysanthemum.

With another deep breath, Lily buried her face in Ella's soft fur, and the rabbit hummed contentedly against her ear. She needed to put Ella and her sister back in their castle before proceeding with her tarot reading.

Thanks to her particular witch talent, they'd probably stay out of her way if she asked them to, but while being able to communicate with animals was a nice gift, it was pretty basic. She couldn't hold a full conversation with them or command them to do anything. Her rabbits had minds of their own, and just because they understood her did *not* mean they cared to listen. Much like people. She certainly couldn't stop them from jumping onto her lap while she was trying to concentrate.

Or from eating her new sandals' straps.

"Cinder, no!" Lily gave Ella a light push into the rabbit castle, an enormous network of cage and tube that gave them plenty of space to wander unsupervised. Her brother, David, had helped her build it a few years ago, the summer before he left for college on the mainland. They'd decorated pieces to look like stone, and David had painted purple flowers along some of the walls. As annoyingly perfect as he was, he was also a good brother.

Lily hustled Cinder into the castle, lecturing her for the hundredth time on why she was not allowed to chew on shoes, and locked the door. Snippy, Cinder turned her back on Lily.

Whatever.

Lily turned off her bedroom lights and padded back to her altar, moonlight illuminating the way. She was lucky to have a large enough bedroom to do this is in, so she wouldn't be disturbed. Sure, it was possible her parents might knock on her door, but that was about as likely as Ella and Cinder starting to speak. Her mother was working a late shift at the ER, and her father was just always working. Lily didn't understand how there were enough houses on Thornhaven Island for him to constantly be selling something, but between his job and his volunteering on the Thornhaven Historical Society board, he was never around. And on the very rare occasions when her parents *weren't* working, they were fussing over her younger sister, Sara.

Lily would have to burn the house down for them to remember she was here.

In her irritation, she snapped her fingers with a bit too much force, and flames streaked from the five candles on her altar all the way up to the ceiling before settling back into place.

Lighting a candle with your mind was one of those spells that looked cool but was mostly useless. All young witches attempted it endlessly as they waited for their powers to develop, as success was often the first sign, but it lost its novelty quickly. Most days, Lily found it less tiring to use a match like a normie.

Anger, however, made it easier to draw on her power. Unfortunately, anger also made it harder to control her power, and control was what a witch needed to master to do anything worth bragging about. Lily knew she needed to practice that part more, if only she had time. In retrospect, that was how she should have spent her summer instead of hanging out by the pool or going sailing. Without a doubt, it was how Chrysanthemum had spent her summer, which meant Lily was going to regret her choice soon enough.

Focus, she commanded herself as she lit a fresh stick of incense from a candle flame. She was really not in the best headspace for performing magic, not even anything as simple as a tarot reading, but there was no way she was starting her senior year without magical guidance. Too much was at stake. She was neck and neck with Chrysanthemum for being named valedictorian, and with the number of report cards between her and the finish line dwindling, she had no room for error. If there was a way to use magic to help her, Lily was certain Chrysanthemum would do it, and as her witchy eyes would attest, Chrysanthemum would likely have more success. Whatever advantage Lily could give herself, she had to take.

She had to win.

Maybe then her parents would fuss over her a little, too.

Scowling, Lily closed her eyes and shuffled the cards. The key to tarot magic working was the same as the key to any magic working—intent. Cards were a tool, like the candles and the incense. They helped a witch focus, but magic always came from within. The most powerful witches, it was said, needed nothing but their minds.

Lily concentrated on her breathing, the feel of the smooth cards between her fingers, the scent of frankincense as the incense filled the air and mixed with the light sulfur smell of the burning candle wicks. She shuffled the cards five times. One for sea. Two for earth. Three for sky. Four for fire. And lastly, five for the magic they created.

When she opened her eyes, a shimmery purple haze surrounded the deck. (Her magic always took on a purple tint, one reason purple was her favorite color.) Although the tinge—as it was called—was faint and already fading, it was proof of the power she'd released, the magic that had guided her hands as she shuffled.

Lily peeled off the top cards, one by one, and laid them out left to right.

The present—the Knight of Wands.

The obstacles—the five of Wands.

The future—the two of Cups.

And atop them all, a fourth card. The binding thread—Death.

Lily blinked, thrown for a loop. She'd wanted insight into her year academically, but the cards seemed focused on anything but her grades.

The Knight of Wands suggested movement or change, but possibly in the form of a boy. The five of Wands meant conflict.

That was straightforward. Finally, the two of Cups usually represented deep, abiding love. And the thread linking this change of events? Death.

Contrary to its scary imagery, Death simply implied change, albeit big change. Bigger than the Knight of Wands, and since it was unlikely that change was both her present and the force connecting everything, that suggested the Knight was probably truly about a boy. That was strange, and Lily considered what she'd been focusing on as she shuffled.

She hadn't actually been thinking of academics specifically, had she? Her intentions had all been about what she needed to do to make her senior year perfect. She'd just assumed the universe would understand that *perfect* meant beating Chrysanthemum for valedictorian, winning the top prize at the magic fair, getting into her first-choice college, and basically everything academic or magical.

So. A boy?

Lily didn't believe high school was her last chance to fall in love and meet the person she'd marry. Her parents hadn't met until college. But maybe there was something to sharing the experience with someone you were close to that made it better. All the movies and TV shows about high school seemed to suggest it, and if nothing else, Lily had always assumed she'd have the perfect date for the prom—someone she could pose for beautiful pictures with, someone who would walk into the dance with her in a stunning entrance that turned everyone's heads, just like a movie scene.

There was only one problem with that prom scenario, a problem she hadn't thought about until this moment. Unlike most of her friends, Lily had never once believed herself to be in love. In fact, she so rarely felt even the slightest stirring of her pulse that she'd started to wonder if she ever would.

Most of the time, this didn't bother her. Between academics, witch school, and her extracurriculars, she didn't have time to be distracted by boys. It hadn't happened yet, and she was fine with it continuing to not happen. Or she *had* been fine. The more she contemplated the situation, the more the absence of a boyfriend stood out like a glaring hole in her social life.

Before she realized what she was doing, Lily bit down on her thumb. She'd started chewing on her fingertips after having trained herself to stop biting her nails, but it wasn't much of an improvement. It didn't leave behind as ugly a result, but it looked silly and childish and was unbefitting an Allerton witch.

Sighing, she occupied her twitchy fingers by writing the reading down in her tarot journal as the last of her magic's tinge dissipated like so much candle smoke. If pressed, she could admit that tarot readings were not her magical strength, but this one seemed easy enough to decipher yet disappointing.

To make the most of her last year, she needed a boyfriend.

The five of Wands suggested there would be some conflict along the way, but the two of Cups assured her of a romantically satisfying outcome—assuming she did what was required of her. Whatever that was. And Death? Death was likely the discovery that she was *capable* of falling in love, which would honestly be a relief.

Lily didn't think there was anything wrong with her, exactly, but the lack of a romantic life made her *different*, and everyone knew being different made life harder.

So yes, a boy. She would finally fall for someone and make that perfect-senior-year vision come true. After all, no matter what challenges the cards dealt her, Lily Allerton did not fail.

Chapter Two
Lily

"Have you seen the new kid yet?" Evan Cohen asked, coming up behind Lily and Sonia Kim as they entered Ms. LaPlant's math classroom.

"I haven't seen *anyone* yet." Lily tossed Sonia a disdainful look, and her best friend shrugged sheepishly.

Lily liked getting to school early, especially on the first day. But she'd given Sonia a ride, since Sonia didn't have her license yet, and she had basically dragged Sonia out the door and made her finish doing her hair in the car. They'd barely arrived on time. If they hadn't been inseparable since preschool, Sonia would be finding another method of transportation this year.

"Boy, girl, enby, or unknown?" Sonia asked.

"Boy."

Sonia's face lit up with interest, and Evan's fell a touch. Lily refrained from rolling her eyes. The two of them had been on again, off again since freshman year.

"Witch or mundane?" Lily asked under her breath. That was the most pertinent question, and she couldn't *not* think of her tarot reading from last night and the Knight of Wands.

There were only six witches in their grade and twenty-three in the whole high school. Thornhaven Island was one of a mere handful of witch enclaves in the States, its large magical population only large in the relative sense. Her brother had dated witch and normie girls both, and her parents had never seemed to care, but Lily suspected that was because they hadn't anticipated any of those relationships lasting beyond high school. Lily, however, expected her unknown boyfriend to be a witch, too. *Perfect*, after all, meant perfect in every way.

"Unknown," Evan said.

Normally, the odds would be against it, but witches were drawn to live in Thornhaven. Magic ignited magic. A witch's power shined brighter here, their magical flame flaring until it was as powerful as the midsummer sun. And the more witches who gathered in one place, the more powerful each of them became. Witches had huddled together on the island since the 1600s, and because of that long history, the air fairly shimmered with enchantment. Many witches who were born and grew up in mundane places never experienced the true extent of their power until they visited. Once they did, they moved.

The normies felt it, too, to a degree. In the summer, they mostly visited Thornhaven for the beaches, the sailing, and the pirate history. But in October, they came for the legends about witches. For the atmosphere of something being just a little wild, a little *off*, a little mysterious in a way that most of them would never be able to quite place, even if they saw something impossible. They didn't know it, but that was one of the island's defenses—non-witches could never quite remember the *real* magic they experienced.

The weirdness, though? That would remain with them. Or it would unless they stayed too long, at which point the weird would become their normal and therefore go unnoticed.

Since the classroom was starting to fill, there could be no more magic talk, and Lily scanned the chairs, assessing the seating options. She preferred to sit up front, which would annoy Sonia, and that was only fair since Sonia had almost made them late. But as Lily started toward her chosen desks, a vision in black set her backpack down on one of them.

Damn Chrysanthemum.

She was like a walking hex. How did she know where Lily was heading?

With that option gone, Lily led the way to a less satisfactory area, dropping into her suboptimal seat and glaring at the back of Chrysanthemum's head as she got out her supplies.

Despite the early-September warmth, Chrysanthemum wore sturdy black boots and black jeans with a rip in the knee that was probably not made for fashion. Her black shirt hung loosely off one shoulder, exposing a shockingly pale patch of skin, and Lily had the urge to take a black Sharpie to that spot and color it in until it matched the rest of her. Even Chrysanthemum's hair was black, and the memory of how it had gotten that way still burned Lily with a mixture of humiliation and rage.

It had all started back in ninth grade when Chrysanthemum had moved to Thornhaven. Lily hadn't paid her much attention at first; Chrysanthemum had looked like a soft goth who was trying too hard, nobody of consequence. If Lily hadn't *known* she was a witch, she'd have assumed Chrysanthemum was one of those poser normies who came to the island and claimed to *feel its power* while blathering on about ley lines and moon phases.

Then the unthinkable had happened. Chrysanthemum had beaten her in the witches' annual student magic fair that year. Beaten her *seemingly effortlessly* with a spell to turn her hair black. Not a glamour or an illusion, which was fairly simple as far as magic went. But permanent change. The kind of spell that even fully trained adult witches could struggle with. Lily, who had entered a glamour spell that she'd been extremely proud of up until that point, hadn't been so humiliated in defeat since she'd tripped during a ballet recital when she was ten. (Coincidentally, the last year she'd done ballet.)

Three years later, Lily remained vigilant when it came to competing against Chrysanthemum. She'd beaten her in the magic fair the following year, but last year the judges had proclaimed a tie, which was just insulting. Lily had worked on her spell for months—she'd charmed a pen so that when she wrote on one piece of paper, the words appeared on another piece. No one else in her year had performed such a complicated spell until Chrysanthemum had managed to charm a pen so that its writing could only be seen by the person *intended* to view it.

It was infuriating. Not only had Lily expected to win, but Chrysanthemum's spell was so similar it was like she'd chosen it on purpose. If Lily hadn't been determined to hide her anger, she would have accused Chrysanthemum of cheating.

The only thing that had lessened Lily's fury was that she'd won the school's academic award for having the highest GPA in their class that same spring. Chrysanthemum hadn't looked her way during the awards ceremony, but Lily had looked at *her* as she'd walked to the stage and taken great satisfaction at Chrysanthemum's stiff posture and barely concealed scowl.

Their rivalry burned hot to this day, and their mutual enmity was intense.

Meanwhile, Chrysanthemum had left her hair black, as if taunting Lily with the reminder of what she was capable of when she put her mind—and her magic—to it. That hair ensured that there was nothing bright or cheerful about her. Except for her eyes, which were like a crystalline arctic glacier. Lily had never met anyone with eyes like that before, such a pale, icy blue that they practically glowed.

Witch eyes, if ever there was such a thing.

"Good morning, everyone, and welcome back!" Ms. LaPlant swept into the room, her long skirt swinging and earrings jingling as she shut the door behind her.

Lily sat up straighter and smiled, Chrysanthemum forgotten for the moment. Ms. LaPlant was one of the only teachers at the high school who was also a witch, and she was going to be Lily's witch school teacher this year, too. The quintessential earth-witch type, Ms. LaPlant had always been kind and patient. Starting off the year in her class had to be a good omen. Her classroom windowsill was covered in greenery, and her room was decorated with discreetly disguised charms that ensured no one cheated on her exams.

Before Ms. LaPlant could speak again, the final bell rang and the classroom door burst open. Lily turned, ready to laugh at whoever was late on the first day, but surprise wiped away her amusement.

"Sorry I'm late. I went down the wrong hallway."

Lily had never seen the newcomer before, so he had to be the new student, and he didn't sound sorry at all. Rather, he carried himself the way most boys did—with total confidence, as though they knew they'd won the gender lottery and were playing the game of life on easy mode.

That kind of confidence could be attractive or obnoxious, depending on the situation, and Lily eyed the boy, curious as to which she'd find. He was tall and cute, with perfectly curled blond hair, and built like an athlete. Basketball, obviously, given his height. Nothing about him screamed *witch*, but nothing didn't, either. (Then again, Lily had learned the mistake of prejudging anyone's magical ability with Chrysanthemum.)

He smiled at Ms. LaPlant with just a hint of trepidation, as though he knew he was unlikely to actually get in trouble but thought he should act otherwise. When he did, a dimple appeared on his left cheek. Sonia inhaled sharply.

Poor Evan.

New Boy was objectively cute, but Lily's stomach didn't do so much as twitch in response to the dimple. (That was typical for her.) What was more important was that he bore a resemblance to the picture of the Knight of Wands in her tarot deck. Could this be him? The card wasn't just about a boy but about change, and it made far more sense for the boy in question to be new than someone she'd known for years. Where was the change in that?

Lily's heart beat faster.

She could already see how her reading was playing out. Sonia was smiling broadly at the boy, as were a couple of other girls in the room, and Isaiah Thomas had leaned forward with interest. By the end of the day, the competition for the boy's attention would be fierce. That could be the conflict part of her reading. She'd have to fight her way to the front of the pack.

If her interpretation of the cards was correct (and how could it not be when they were so clear?), then it was odd that she herself wasn't swooning already, but surely, true love could take time. Just because Lily wasn't losing her head yet didn't mean she wouldn't eventually lose her heart. She needed to have faith in her reading and follow through with the actions she could control.

Ms. LaPlant smiled patiently. "You must be Luke Goodman, our new student. Welcome to Thornhaven. No assigned seating in my class, so pick a desk."

There were still five empty desks in the classroom, and seventeen pairs of eyes watched Luke assess his choices. Lily wished she'd picked a spot that had left an empty desk next to her.

Luke bypassed the empty seat in the front row next to Isaiah and went to put his backpack down on . . .

This could not be for real. Lily almost choked on her own breath.

He chose the desk next to Chrysanthemum? Why, of all the options available, would he choose her? Was it her perma-scowl? The black nail polish? The boots that said, *I will step on your bare, sandal-footed toes and enjoy it*?

Chrysanthemum seemed as flummoxed by this as Lily, but the confusion on her face registered for only a flash before disappearing behind her usual indifferent mask.

"All right, let's get started," Ms. LaPlant said, and the class settled down, heads returning toward the front of the room.

Lily's did not, and she narrowed her eyes at Chrysanthemum. This was unfathomable. Was she truly a demon? Lily wasn't entirely sure demons were real, but legends claimed that a witch who cast too many hexes would be consumed by the evil they spread and become one. (Although you probably had to have been hexing people for a long time before that happened, so, you know, it was an unlikely fate to befall a seventeen-year-old.)

As if she could feel Lily glaring at her, Chrysanthemum glanced back, and Lily quickly fixed her gaze on Ms. LaPlant, her pulse speeding up. Stupid of it. She wasn't afraid of Chrysanthemum, and she had no reason to feel guilty.

She just didn't want Chrysanthemum to know she'd been looking her way.

With her potential Knight of Wands sitting so close to her enemy, Lily didn't dare antagonize Chrysanthemum right now and make the situation worse.

Honestly, having a nemesis was exhausting.

Chapter Three
Chrysanthemum

Chrysanthemum Quinn locked up her bike outside the Thornhaven Historical Society building and wondered if the first day of school was too early to start a countdown-to-the-end-of-the-year calendar. Possibly it was a bit like starting your Christmas countdown calendar on December 26—a sign of a disturbingly overeager and one-track mind.

But screw it. She needed something to look forward to, and five days a week of getting up before the sun rose, breathing the same air as her classmates (99 percent of whom were as obnoxious as they were rich), and having to do pointless homework was almost as intolerable as waiting tables for tourists had been all summer at the Pirate Shack.

Almost, because at least she didn't have to wear a ridiculous hat or address people as *matey* while she carried trays of fish and chips every day.

On the other hand, she'd gotten *paid* for waiting those tables and putting up with the indignity of it all. No one paid her to put up with the indignity of high school, and her mother had forbidden her from working during the school year, even though they could use the money. When Chrys had pointed this out, Samantha Quinn had told her that school was her job from September to June, and she shouldn't worry. As if her worries could be snuffed out of existence as easily as a candle flame when they roared inside her like a bonfire.

Despite the foulness of her mood, Chrys's shoulders released their tension as she entered the Historical Society building. Although she cynically thought of the organization as the Craft Country Club, it was the closest thing the island had to a coven—a shared meeting space for teaching, socializing, and when required, working magic together.

A tingling sensation washed over her skin as she crossed the threshold, thanks to the many wards poking and prodding her, assessing her for any kind of threat—whatever that might be. And a muddy brown tinge—the result of so many witches' magical contributions—permanently clung to the doorway. (The wards also magically repelled mundanes.)

The building's scents were muddled as well, but pleasingly so. Over the years, burning herbs had permeated the plaster walls and dark wainscotting, and their presence whispered in Chrys's nose like ghosts of magic long past—frankincense and myrrh, sandalwood and jasmine. Under the sweet smell was the scent of old wood and ocean salt and the mustiness born of centuries of use. Chrys liked the mustiness—drafty rooms, creaky floors, narrow staircases, and low ceilings included.

Many of her peers lamented that witch school didn't meet at someone's house or in one of the nice modern hotels down by the harbor, but that was one more thing Chrys didn't have in common with these people. She *liked* it here. History gave her a sense of place and belonging that she rarely felt in the present. History was a reminder that she was part of something bigger than herself, a legacy of witches . . . even if the witches she personally knew treated her like she was an interloper.

They could ignore her, but they couldn't deny her entry into this world.

Back when she and her mom had moved to Thornhaven, the possibility of belonging had been tantalizing. Her mother had lived the first twelve years of her life in Thornhaven, so Chrys had heard all about the island, including that she'd get to attend witch school. Crossing the water from mainland Massachusetts had felt magical itself. She was leaving her old life, and all the misfit feelings that had plagued her existence, behind. On Thornhaven, she'd be one of many witches, no longer the weird kid whose secret abilities made her feel like an outsider.

What a bunch of bullshit that had turned out to be.

Yes, Chrys had a few friends here, but none of them were witches. In some ways, they were like her—students who didn't quite fit. But in other ways, they were nothing like her, because she couldn't truly be herself around them.

On Thornhaven, the witches had rejected her just as surely as the normies had rejected her back on the mainland. But to hell with them. She'd showed them all that she was every bit as good as them her first year, and if they couldn't deal with it, that was their problem. She'd never forget the way Lily Allerton had whined about losing to her at her first magic fair—it was like Lily believed she *deserved* to win, just because her family's legacy was old and they were rich.

She could still hear Lily's tantrum as if it were yesterday. *This isn't fair! There's no way she could do that spell on her own when she's only been attending witch school for a year. She must have cheated. Who does she think she is?*

And then a man's voice—Lily's father, presumably: *Your competition, that's who. And the reason you'll try harder next year.*

Chrys was embarrassed to remember that she'd spent most of that year fixated on how pretty Lily was, and wishing Lily would notice her. Her fourteen-year-old self had needed better taste in crushes, but at least Lily's behavior had cured her of that one.

Exiting the stairwell, Chrys paused in the doorway of one of the third-floor rooms that had been turned into a classroom. Most of the other eleventh- and twelfth-grade witches were already here, and Chrys took a seat as far from everyone else as possible. Hopefully, witch school would be more interesting than regular school this year.

“When magic goes awry, we have a tendency to blame the magic,” Ms. LaPlant was saying ten minutes later. “You may have heard it’s wild and can’t be controlled, that spells are only suggestions. To a point that’s true, but if we couldn’t guide it, then no spells would work.”

At the front of the room, she sat on a table, her legs swinging beneath her. Brown boots dotted with silver buttons peeked out beneath the green fabric of her skirt. She’d worn the same outfit at school, but in the Thornhaven Historical Society’s classroom, it took on a whole new vibe, as did Ms. LaPlant herself. She was still an authority figure and a teacher, but she seemed softer and friendlier.

Following Ms. LaPlant’s instructions, Chrys pulled out her personal Book of Shadows and ran her thumb over the embossed black leather cover, enjoying the feel. For her sixteenth birthday last year, she’d used her gift money to splurge on the fancy journal from the bookstore downtown. Even though such extravagance wasn’t necessary and several of her classmates just used spiral-bound notebooks, Chrys liked the sense of importance the journal provided. Far more than a spell book, a Book of Shadows was a *workbook*, a chronicle of each witch’s journey into the secrets of magic and the discovery of their power.

Some witches, *cough,* Lily, color coded and indexed theirs. Chrys enjoyed watching Lily squirm with frustration every time she was forced to cross something out. Chrys’s book, on the other hand, was filled as much with doodles and song lyrics as it was with magical insights.

"By now, you all understand the basics of spell work. This year, we're concentrating on how to create and focus intent," Ms. LaPlant said. "I want you to think about the last time you attempted magic and it didn't work as planned. What were you trying to do versus what happened? Where was the disconnect?"

Chrys blew a strand of hair from her face. The last time? Who knew. *Most* of what she attempted didn't work—but that was probably her own fault for following her gut when she did spells, not instructions.

Her saving grace was that when her gut worked for her, it really worked.

The strand of hair returned to itching her nose, and Chrys wrapped it around her pen. She'd tried again before school started this year to change her hair color, and again she'd failed. She was starting to think she'd only succeeded in changing it once—and, even then, badly—out of pure luck.

"Chrys, could you stay a moment?" Ms. LaPlant called out when class broke up forty-five minutes later.

Chrys frowned, taking her time to put away her Book of Shadows. A sinking feeling in her stomach warned her what this might be about, and she didn't need anyone else around for the conversation. Luckily, at nine o'clock on a school night, no one seemed inclined to hang out, so they were alone when Chrys dragged herself to the front of the room.

"How was your first day?" Ms. LaPlant asked.

"Fine." Chrys tucked her hair behind her ears, realized she was still frowning, and forced her lips into a smile. None of this was Ms. LaPlant's fault. "Thanks."

"Wonderful." Her teacher's smile seemed genuinely delighted, but delighted was her default mood. "I'm excited to have one of the two most talented witches of your age group in both my classes this year."

Ignoring who the other person might be (Lily, she had to be referring to Lily), Chrys braced herself. Although she did consider herself one of the most talented witches of her age group, being flattered was never a good sign.

"I hate to bring this up," Ms. LaPlant continued, "but your mother forgot to pay her dues for the year. I wanted to let you know so you could remind her in case she missed the email."

All the island's witches paid dues to the Historical Society. The money covered upkeep on the building and maintaining a library filled with books and expensive supplies that could be borrowed, and it also enabled people like Ms. LaPlant to be paid for their time teaching students how to control and use their power.

The dues probably weren't a lot for the average witch family—the Historical Society also hosted a giant Halloween ball as a fundraiser every year—but *a lot* meant something different to the Quinns than it did to, say, the Allertons. Or even a schoolteacher. As Ms. LaPlant surely knew, judging by the sympathy in her eyes.

Chrys was thankful she'd already grasped her backpack's shoulder strap, and she squeezed it tighter. The only thing worse than people like Lily, who looked down on her for not having as much money, were people like Ms. LaPlant, who were kind about it. The former, Chrys could get angry at. The latter made her want to curl up and die.

"Oh, she's been really busy," Chrys said, hoping her voice didn't waver. "I'll remind her. Thanks."

Then she turned and raced out of the room before Ms. LaPlant could say anything else.

Shit. Her mom got paid on Friday. Odds were, there would be no money for dues until then unless she or her mom attempted some sort of money spell, and her mom would never do that. Money spells were risky.

Magic was very good at certain types of effects, especially the intangible and ephemeral. It could create fantastic illusions, manipulate thoughts and emotions, and protect people and things. With more effort, it could alter objects that already existed, like turning your brown hair black, fixing a broken glass, or swelling apples to the size of pumpkins. And, in talented hands, it could combine *all* of those effects.

But magic couldn't create something out of nothing.

For Chrys to magic an extra two hundred dollars into her hand, if she were even skilled enough to do so (which she was not), someone else had to lose it. Everyone knew a horror story of a witch who cast a poorly thought-out money spell and ended up with a loved one dying and leaving them an inheritance. Chrys had witnessed the Society's most powerful witches perform some incredible spells, but anything that wasn't a mere glamour—that is, anything that caused *actual change* in the world—carried risk.

Her mother would probably be in bed by the time Chrys got home, so she pulled out her phone and began a text to her about the dues. Since she was fairly certain there wouldn't be a spare two hundred bucks in the bank until Friday, she could have waited, but Chrys had no interest in having this conversation in person. Her mom would make it sound like everything was fine, and Chrys would have to pretend to believe it.

For a moment before she hit SEND, she considered not telling her mom at all; she could pay the dues herself with some of the money she'd earned over the summer. But Chrys discarded that idea as easily as she had the money spell. When her mom found out—and she would find out—she would insist on returning the money to Chrys, and Chrys would have succeeded only in making her feel bad.

Our luck will change now that we're in Thornhaven and have full access to our power, her mom had insisted when they first moved, and Chrys had believed that for a time.

In fact, *for a time*, it had seemed like her mom was right. Their apartment was small, but because they were witches, they got an excellent deal on the rent. They'd never struggled for food, although—as her mom joked—they weren't buying the gourmet cheese. And the old car that they'd inherited from Chrys's grandparents, which used to break down regularly, had (with some magical assistance) run without issue since the move. But money remained tight, and her mom hadn't yet figured out a way to get her business dream off the ground.

As for Chrys's friendship hopes, the less said, the better.

A hint of autumn brushed her cheeks in the breeze as she unlocked her bike. Soon, that crispness would be more pronounced, and as the cool weather rolled in, so, too, would the celebratory atmosphere. Thornhaven Island was pretty in the summer—flowers crawled up its white picket fences, sailboats filled the harbor, and the wild blackberry brambles that gave the island its name were in bloom.

But fall was when the inhabitants *partied*, and decorations were already beginning to cover the buildings downtown. Dried cornstalks and early pumpkins had sprung up around the Historical Society's doors. The Cauldron Supply magic shop had replaced its summery flag with a Halloween-themed one, and Black Cat Coffee was advertising autumn specials, including cranberry muffins, and—of course—everything pumpkin spice.

Lost in her thoughts, Chrys startled when she heard her name drop from Lily's lips.

"I can't believe he sat next to *Chrysanthemum*." Lily must be right on the other side of the row of parked SUVs. The Witch Princess of Thornhaven refused to call her Chrys for some stupid reason.

"Right?" And that was Lily's sycophantic best friend, Sonia. "He sat with her and her friends at lunch, too!"

Ah, they were talking about the new kid, Luke. As much as Chrys wanted to sneer at their incredulous tones, she couldn't argue with their skepticism. Luke's whole *everything* screamed that he belonged with Lily's crowd. That didn't mean he was a witch, but that he possessed the other source of popularity on Thornhaven—money.

Chrys had spent years perfecting her resting bitch face precisely to keep people like Luke away, and he'd been completely unfazed by it.

Almost as bad, she kind of liked him for defying her expectations. Not *liked* him, liked him, since she'd figured out a few years ago that boys didn't hold any interest for her that way, but he seemed friendly and funny, and it was pretty obvious that half the school had already developed crushes. Just walking into choir class with him this morning had drawn more attention Chrys's way than she preferred, but she hadn't been about to blow him off when he'd asked for directions after math class.

"You're taking choir?" She'd wished she hadn't sounded so surprised, but Luke didn't strike her as the musical type. Also, perhaps more to the point, she wasn't used to being the person anyone sought out for assistance.

His lip quirked in a way that suggested he was giving her the benefit of the doubt—that she hadn't intended to be rude. "If that's okay with you."

It had been a while since Chrys had wished, quite so strongly, for the floor to swallow her. When she finished full-body cringing, though, she thought she detected humor in Luke's eyes. "Um, yeah. Sorry. I didn't have enough coffee this morning. Isaiah and I are heading there, so just stick with us."

She hadn't dared turn in Isaiah's direction to see the way they were laughing at her stupidity.

"So, coffee impacts your ability to believe I might take choir?" Luke asked as they entered the stairwell.

Next to her, Isaiah snickered.

"Coffee impacts my ability to function," Chrys said, which was a bit of an exaggeration, but not an outright lie. "Don't take it personally."

"Yeah," Isaiah chimed in. "If Chrys wanted to be rude, trust me—you'd know. She'd just *glare* at you, and you'd feel your soul shriveling inside your skin. It's brutal."

Chrys tried to pretend that description didn't please her. "Wait till you meet Ms. McNeil, current choir director, former prima donna. Your soul hasn't shriveled until an ex-professional opera singer is disappointed with your performance."

"For real?" Luke looked excited about that, and Chrys's opinion of him moved another inch in the positive direction. "Does she have us sing opera?"

"Occasionally she's tried it," Isaiah said, "but that's where the disappointment usually shines. We do a lot of show tunes."

Luke's eyes lit up. "Modern or classics? I love them all. I was Seymour in my old school's performance of *Little Shop of Horrors* last year."

Chrys was so taken aback by this confession that she couldn't even manage a joke. Luke and Isaiah started comparing opinions about *Little Shop* and every other show their schools had put on. Her opinion of Luke slid even further toward the positive.

"I just figured . . . it has to be a mistake, right?" Lily said, and her voice drew Chrys back to the present like a blast of frozen air. "New school. He was nervous and glommed on to the first people who were friendly to him, but who looks at Chrysanthemum and thinks *friendly*?"

Chrys snorted and clasped a hand over her mouth.

"It makes no sense," Lily continued. "I told you about my tarot reading. If we're meant to be together, then it's up to me to help him."

Wait—Lily had done a tarot reading about Luke already and *thought they were meant to date*? That was hilarious. The first genuine grin of the day spread over Chrys's face.

"I was holding out hope that he might be a witch since that would make it easier," Lily said, "but since he's not, we have to run an intervention and save him from himself."

Chrys couldn't stifle her laughter any longer. Stepping between two parked cars, she emerged in their row, pleased to see Lily's cheeks turn red with the realization she'd been overheard. Sonia looked less embarrassed and more uncomfortable, and she glanced down at her sandals.

"An intervention?" Chrys was close to cackling, but standing so close to Lily, her amusement gave way to something darker. Irritation. These spoiled rich witches. "Save him from himself? From me? Did you ever think that not everyone in this town is interested in falling at your feet?"

Lily's cheeks continued to redden until Chrys wondered if her face would explode. "He deserves the chance to have normal friends, and not just"—her gaze flicked up and down Chrys's body as she clearly strained for her best insult—"Wednesday Addams."

Okay, that was almost too funny to get annoyed about. "Have you ever actually watched that show?"

Judging from the look on Lily's face, the answer was no. Same with Sonia. Probably the only things Lily watched were Disney movies.

Chrys placed a hand over her heart. "Why yes, I am a smart, sarcastic goth girl with no interest in your bullshit. A-plus powers of observation. What a *devastating* insult."

Not waiting around for a retort that would probably be every bit as ridiculous as that attempt at an attack was, Chrys returned to her bike and rode home. The whole conversation was absurd. Laughable. Lily really did expect everyone to worship at her altar.

When Chrys had moved here, Lily had taken one glance at her and dismissed her without a second thought, despite Chrys being an actual witch. Someone who shared a bond—theoretically anyway—with Lily. Someone who had actually wanted to adore Lily and, if nothing else, be her friend.

Chrys knew better now. Lily was shallow and obnoxious and spoiled. And Luke, who'd seemed genuinely nice, deserved better than that. Chrys didn't have to want to date him herself to also believe he deserved saving—from Lily.

So that was how it was going to be. After three years of being snubbed, the only thing Chrys had thought she wanted was to ignore Lily the way Lily ignored her. But the resentment that had been simmering in her blood wasn't ignorable any longer.

For a moment, she considered a dozen different hexes—spells to give Lily acne, to cause all her teeth to fall out, to simply make it so that no one would ever consider dating her for no other reason at all besides magic. But Chrys had never cast a hex, and the more she thought on it, the less she wanted to use one. It would be infinitely more satisfying to just show Luke what Lily's true personality was. Snobbish. Self-absorbed. Superficial.

It would hurt Lily more that way, too. To be rejected for who she was.

How hard could it be? Chrys had never set out to compete with Lily, but she'd already proven that she could beat Lily at magic, and she was going to beat her for valedictorian. Her GPA was behind by only one one-hundredth of a point.

In short, it stood to reason that she could protect Luke from Lily's greedy clutches, too.

Let the best witch win.

Chapter Four
Lily

After the confrontation at witch school, Lily's stomach had been in knots. All she needed was for Chrysanthemum to share what she'd overheard with Luke. Knowing how Chrysanthemum hated her, no doubt she'd try to make Lily sound like an obsessed stalker, and that could ruin everything.

Since he'd waltzed into her math class, Lily had become ever more certain that Luke was her Knight of Wands and a necessary piece of her perfect senior year. Even if the fact that he'd sat next to Chrysanthemum should have cast that in doubt. Or that he'd had lunch with her. Three days in a row.

That was all okay, because Luke had sat next to *her* in AP Physics, which was blissfully Chrysanthemum-free. (Chrysanthemum took AP Chemistry. Lily had absolutely *not* chosen a science course this year based on which one she'd overheard Chrysanthemum planning to take, but it might have solidified her decision.)

"So, is Lily short for Lilian?" he'd asked their first day. "I just met a Chrys that's short for Chrysanthemum, so I'm suspicious of people named after flowers now."

Lily's jaw clenched as she smiled. "No, I'm just Lily. Is Luke short for Lucas?"

"Nope. I'm just Luke. Lucky us with the four-letter names. I'm sure we had a much easier time learning to spell them." He grinned, and the dimple emerged.

Lily's breath didn't catch, but again, that was okay. She was very aware that other girls in the class were watching Luke smile at her, and maybe that meant she ought to focus on the conflict part of her tarot reading. The falling in love could come later, after she got to know him.

So Lily had peppered Luke with questions: Where did he move from (Tampa), why did they move (his dad got a job managing one of the large hotels on the island), how did he like it here (he was nervous about starting a new school, but so far everyone was really friendly)?

"Probably Spanish and choir," Luke said in response to her question about his favorite classes so far. "I didn't see you in choir, so are you in band or orchestra?"

"I had a year of recorder and a year of violin like everyone else." Lily pressed her fingers together, preferring to forget the classes where she hadn't naturally excelled. "I discovered my talents lay elsewhere."

Luke chuckled at that. "I bet you're class president or something instead. You have that look of being a popular overachiever."

Lily stared at him. "Did someone tell you that?"

"No. Wait, was I right?" Luke seemed to find that hilarious, and Lily couldn't help but laugh with him—even if she wasn't sure whether to be pleased or insulted that she'd been so easily categorized.

In the end, she'd decided on pleased. It meant Luke understood her, and that was obviously a sign that she was on the right track with her plan.

Even though it was promising to be her most challenging class, Lily began looking forward to physics. Luke was fun to talk to, and she liked the idea that he sang, since musicians were hot. Luke had plenty of true-love potential besides his cute face, although that cute face would look great next to hers in their future prom and yearbook photos.

One day, Lily expected, her pulse would catch up with these facts and start fluttering.

In the meantime, she had to wonder what was the deal with him hanging out with Chrysanthemum? Could she have cast a love spell on him? As much as Lily hated to admit it, she had to believe Chrysanthemum was powerful enough to perform such a spell.

Whatever the reason, Lily had to do something about it. If Luke was her Knight of Wands, then she'd identified the true source of her five of Wands—Chrysanthemum. Never mind that half the school was competing to capture Luke's heart. Chrysanthemum was the real source of conflict, and possibly Lily should have expected that.

After all, Chrysanthemum was the source of most of Lily's problems.

There was no time to waste. She had to go on the offensive, and that began today. Her intentions were so focused, Ms. LaPlant would be proud. But Lily wasn't going to cast a spell. Her plan was much simpler.

She was going to host a party for Luke.

It was perfect. Someone inevitably held a back-to-school bash every September, so why not her? The only hitch was that she couldn't do it this weekend, but that could work in her favor. Two weeks gave her plenty of time to plan and more time for the anticipation to build.

Strategically, she could make the party about introducing Luke to everyone and anyone who mattered on the island (ridding him of Chrysanthemum's influence), and she would come across as supremely thoughtful for helping him navigate the Thornhaven High School social scene. Which, really, she *was*. And if being a gracious hostess provided her with extra opportunities to spend time with Luke, even better.

All she had to do was invite him personally, to give it that extra touch, and Lily had a plan for that, too.

Lily had told Sonia there was no being fashionably late to school today, and by some miracle, Sonia had complied. After stopping at the library to exchange her damaged copy of *Pride and Prejudice*, which they'd just started in English class, Lily strolled down the hallway on a mission.

And almost groaned out loud when she discovered that Luke was talking to Chrysanthemum.

Lily considered being patient and hoping Chrysanthemum might go away, but Chrysanthemum glanced in her direction and caught her looking toward Luke, and it was too late. Avoiding Luke now would make Chrysanthemum believe Lily was avoiding *her*. Although she'd like to, she wasn't about to give Chrysanthemum that satisfaction.

Lily took a deep breath and instantly regretted it as her lungs filled with that indecipherable school stink. Old sweat combined with cheap perfume and decades of cafeteria food that had seeped into the floor. No wonder she wasn't all giddy around Luke! How was a person supposed to feel romance with that smell, the pressure of exams hanging over their head, and the cacophony of voices and sneakers squeaking on linoleum?

Head high, she marched across the hall. "Luke, I was hoping to catch you before class."

"Hey." He smiled at her, but Lily caught the brief glance he shot Chrysanthemum and the pinch of his brow that vanished as quickly as it had appeared. *He'd noticed that she hadn't greeted Chrysanthemum.* Unfortunate, but as long as it didn't make her look too bitchy, Lily didn't care.

He really was cute, too. Even up close, his skin was perfect, and his height meant her gaze landed on that hollow at his throat. She could totally understand why people were falling all over him, and yet her stomach wasn't spawning any butterflies. It was frustrating beyond measure.

For once in her life, Lily wished she were more like everyone else.

On the positive side, however, the lack of emotions meant her tongue didn't tie itself in knots, so maybe she should be thankful and save her confusion for another time.

If anything, it was Chrysanthemum's presence that Lily was keenly aware of, as though the other girl gave off some kind of aura that prickled against Lily's own and made her hyperaware of the blood flowing through her veins. Chrysanthemum must be glaring at her, judging her. But Lily refused to turn and find out.

"I'm hosting a back-to-school party the weekend after the equinox," Lily said. She was pretending so hard that she couldn't feel Chrysanthemum's disdain that she completely forgot the equinox was probably not as meaningful a date to Luke as it was to a witch. Ugh. "I wanted to personally invite you because I thought it would be a great way to introduce you to everyone. I hope you can make it."

She held out one of the cards she'd printed with her address and the date on them. Was it over-the-top to issue an actual invitation? Maybe a bit, but Lily liked the extra formality. Anyone could spread word about a party, and anyone could show up. But only the people she cared about got an invite. It was a way of showing who her friends were, and there was magic in the act, too. Whether a witch tried to or not, she sent out power with everything she did.

"That sounds fun. Thanks!" Luke's face brightened as he took the card, but then his eyes darted again toward Chrysanthemum.

Lily held in a scream. It was great that Luke was nice and considerate. Exactly the qualities she'd want in her true love. But being nice to her nemesis was *not* okay.

Of course, Luke had no idea that they were nemeses, and it wasn't like Lily could explain. Witches did not go around advertising themselves as such. The ocean separated them from Salem, but memories were long.

It also wasn't like Lily didn't know she was being rude. She didn't want Luke to form a bad impression of her . . . So, ugh again. What was the harm in inviting Chrysanthemum? She'd never attend.

Lily adopted a fake, bright smile and finally turned so that her back was no longer to Chrysanthemum. "Everyone is invited."

Lily didn't hold out an invitation, and Chrysanthemum didn't appear to expect one. She raised an eyebrow, and the corners of her lips twitched ever so slightly. "A party? Sounds deadly. Think I'd rather stay in and do an *Addams Family* marathon."

Damn it.

She would not flush. "Fine. Don't come if you don't feel like crawling out of your coffin and being sociable."

"Wednesday is not a vampire."

"Who cares about Wednesday!" Sheepishly, Lily realized she'd raised her voice and Luke wasn't the only person watching her with a confused expression. Several heads had turned in her direction. She could hex Chrysanthemum right about now. "Do what you like," she said at a more reasonable volume. "No one will miss you."

Shit. That was too rude. Luke looked like he wanted to say something, but before he could, Lily's copy of *Pride and Prejudice* reached out and bit her. Which was to say, the book shifted of its own accord in her hand, opened its pages like a mouth, and slammed down on her fingers.

Lily yelped in surprise and dropped it.

It was only a paperback, so it didn't hurt, but books were not supposed to do that. Not even books carried by witches.

Luke stared at it. Lily stared at it. The only person who didn't seem shocked by what had happened was Chrysanthemum, who continued to smirk at Lily.

She must have done that, but how?

Lily shook off the thought. Obviously, the how was magic, although she couldn't detect any tinge about the book. Lily didn't know exactly how Chrysanthemum had invisibly cast a spell in the middle of the hallway, but nothing else explained a book moving on its own. *Magic* barely explained a book moving on its own.

"What just . . . ?" Luke knelt for the book, regarding it like it was a wild animal.

"I dropped it," Lily said, furious as soon as the words left her mouth. Doing magic in public like this wasn't exactly forbidden, but that was because, with the exception of spells like glamours or candle-lighting, working magic was a process, and the results tended to manifest slowly. Once created, they might stick around for years or decades, but it took a lot more effort than a snap of the fingers to create them. No witch was going to stand in the middle of Main Street and perform an elaborate working to fix potholes, even if they could manage to concentrate well enough to try.

So why was Lily the one making excuses and trying to cover this up? Chrysanthemum was the one who'd done it. She had to be, and she knew better.

"Yeah, but . . ." Luke scratched his head. "It jumped in your hand. I saw it."

Lily glared at Chrysanthemum, willing her to say something, but Chrysanthemum merely sighed and shrugged innocently.

Lily wanted to strangle her, and she dug her nails into her palms.

Near her feet, Luke blinked, and his face went blank. Then he picked up the book and handed it to Lily. "Did you drop this?"

Behind him, Chrysanthemum tossed Lily a *duh* kind of expression. As if the fact that Luke couldn't quite remember what had happened made it okay for her to have . . . done whatever she'd done. (As Luke grew accustomed to strange things happening, he'd remember more, but his disinterest in unusual things would remain. Lily didn't know if the island's protective spell had been cast that way on purpose, or if people just acclimated to it, like people could acclimate to the ocean's briny smell.)

Lily tossed her hair back, ignoring Chrysanthemum's infuriating face, and took the book from Luke. "Yes, thank you. Anyway, I hope you'll be able to make the party. It's going to be loads of fun. We have a firepit and a pool, so if it's warm enough, bring your bathing suit."

Chrysanthemum frowned, and although Lily didn't know why, that made her happy, all things considered. Lily was annoyed with Chrysanthemum, so Chrysanthemum being annoyed with her simply made them even. The universe was temporarily balanced.

Lily said goodbye to Luke until first period and left before Chrysanthemum could do anything else to fluster her, pleased with how she'd handled the situation and more pleased with the outcome. It didn't appear that Luke was so under Chrysanthemum's demonic thrall that he wouldn't come to a party, and that meant there was hope. For both of them.

Chapter Five
Chrysanthemum

"Please tell me you're going to audition for the musical this year," Isaiah said at lunch.

Since the weather was nice, most people were eating outdoors, and Isaiah had snagged a table under a maple tree. It was a less-than-ideal situation as leaves would rain down into everyone's food, but it was better than sitting on the grass, which was damp from last night's rain, and it shaded them from thieving birds.

"*West Side Story*?" Chrys wrinkled her nose. "Can you picture me onstage singing 'I Feel Pretty'?"

Luke glanced between Chrys and Isaiah's hopeful face. "I've only known you for a week, and I would already pay good money to see that."

"Everyone would," Anushka Singh, the fourth person at their table, said.

"No."

Isaiah pressed a hand against their forehead dramatically. "Every year, she has an excuse."

Chrys squirmed, feigning concentration on her lunch. It wasn't that she didn't want to be in the musical; it was just that putting herself out there like that required a trust in her fellow students that she didn't feel capable of. And while Isaiah would be in the cast, and Anushka would play violin in the pit orchestra, there would be too many other people Chrys didn't know. It wasn't even like she knew Anushka and Isaiah that well. There was a whole part of herself she hid from them, and she tried keeping them at arm's length so as not to accidentally scare them away.

Anushka and Isaiah made it difficult, though. After a morning of not talking to anyone on her first day at a new school, Chrys had been surprised when a Black freshman with bright green hair had approached her in choir. Isaiah had taken one look at her appearance and determined that 1) Chrys would approve of their style, and 2) Chrys was the sort of person who'd appreciate a good ghost story. Isaiah had attached themself to her immediately so as to be the first to share the island lore. Anushka had been Isaiah's friend already, and her first words to Chrys had been *nice shirt*. Chrys had thought Anushka was being sarcastic (she'd been wearing a T-shirt for a Dutch symphonic metal band she'd recently discovered), but the next thing Chrys knew, Anushka was introducing her to more European metal bands.

"All right, forget about the musical for now. I'll bug you more later. But it's Monday." Isaiah leaned around Anushka and batted their eyes at Chrys. "Did you bring any gifts?"

Anushka snorted. "Subtle. Did you think we didn't see you sniffing around her backpack this morning?"

"Busted." They held up their hands. "But this is the only thing that makes Mondays bearable."

"What am I missing?" Luke asked.

"Chrys's mom is an amazing baker," Isaiah said, as Chrys pulled out a container of cookies.

It was true, and if only everyone in Thornhaven were as effusive about her skills as Isaiah, Samantha Quinn would be one step closer to achieving her dream of opening her own bakery. At the moment, however, Chrys's mom worked at the Shop-n-Go grocery store's bakery. Since she always had Sundays off, she often spent them developing new recipes or honing her decorating skills. Which was why Chrys often had treats to share on Monday.

Chrys had remembered to bring an extra cookie today for Luke—chocolate gingerbread with spiced frosting. Her mom was hoping to convince Black Cat Coffee downtown to place an order for them.

"Something I've been wondering about," Luke said after a moment. He looked a little embarrassed as he brushed away cookie crumbs. "This is going to sound stupid, but . . . is this island haunted or something?"

“Oh yeah,” Isaiah said, their eyes lighting up. “Super haunted. Tons of ghosts around here.”

Luke stared at them. “Are you making fun of me? Because I swear, I never believed in ghosts, but there’s something . . . off . . . about this place.”

“Not making fun of you,” Chrys assured him. She wasn’t so positive about hauntings herself. Not because there weren’t spells for summoning ghosts—because there were—but she’d never seen a ghost just hanging around without being summoned. She suspected most of what normies attributed to ghosts was actually magic they couldn’t quite grasp. But it appeared Thornhaven was catching up to Luke at last, if he was remembering more. “You’ve heard the legends about the island, right?”

“I’ve heard about pirates and that there’s supposedly some ship that sank nearby filled with treasure.”

“And witches,” Anushka said.

Chrys tucked the empty container away. If they were going there, then this was her time to talk. Not only was she the only witch at this table, she was the history geek. “The big legend is that pirates attempted to sack Thornhaven in 1706, but they didn’t count on a lot of witches living here. So, when the pirates were almost to shore, the witches got together and conjured a massive storm. The pirates were all blown out to sea, and their ships sank.”

“Thornhaven residents never got into that Puritan anti-witch propaganda,” Isaiah finished. “They were grateful to their witches, and that's why the island loses its collective mind around Halloween. Although I, personally, would not discount the possibility of pirate ghosts."

"Yeaaah . . ." Luke drew the word out. "Okay, things are making sense now. I noticed that the witch theme going on in town was as strong as the pirate theme. Figures you'd be the one who likes telling that story." He motioned toward Chrys's shirt.

"What?" Chrys pretended to be offended. "This is my happiest shirt."

Yes, there was a skull on it, but the skull was made out of sunflowers.

Although she'd done her best to cultivate a very specific image, Chrys secretly adored sunflowers. Her grandparents had filled their yard with them back in New York—short ones, tall ones, ones whose enormous happy faces stretched smiling toward the sky. But Chrys did not advertise this inclination. Once people discovered you liked something light and soft, they realized you must have inner light and softness yourself. And once they discovered *that*, they'd poke and prod until they found those soft spots and the source of that light. Then they'd dig in. Life would become an endless onslaught of fingers sinking into vulnerable flesh until she was bruised and bleeding and her glow was snuffed out like a spent match. All for their entertainment.

Chrys had learned that lesson long before coming to Thornhaven. No sunflowers, or flowers period, in spite of her stupid name. Black clothes were her armor, her lack of words was her shield, and the way she glared at everyone was her weapon.

Or it was supposed to be, anyway. Luke hadn't been scared. When Chrys had finally asked him why he'd opted to sit next to her in class that first day, he'd laughed.

You looked more approachable than anyone else is the room, he'd said. *Mostly because you were the only one who didn't seem to be sizing me up.*

She supposed that made some sense. He was wrong, though. Maybe he hadn't caught her, but if so, that was only because she'd sized him up the moment he'd plowed into the room and had already dismissed him as one of Lily's crowd.

Speaking of which.

And witches . . .

Chrys hadn't expected Lily's book to jump about in her hand the way it had this morning; she'd just wanted to startle Lily and make her drop it. But sometimes her power burst out of her and other times it whimpered, and Chrys couldn't predict the results. Either way, Lily had correctly guessed that Chrys was responsible.

But what Lily might *not* have guessed was that Chrys had declared war on her, and Chrys was merely getting started.

"Some families on this island can trace their ancestry all the way back to that time," Anushka said. "Like the Allertons can, and the Howlands. Lily's family is supposedly directly descended from some of those witches. If you look through the stuff in the maritime museum and on display at the town hall, you can see the Allerton name is everywhere."

"I did not know that," Luke said. "That's kind of cool."

Chrys forced down her scowl. She had every bit as much claim to that history as Lily did. But although you wouldn't find the name Quinn among those mentioned in the stories, one pair of Chrys's maternal great-grandparents were Langmores, a name as prominent in the witch tales as Allerton.

And yet *they* didn't have any buildings or streets named after them.

Chrys had always been told that the reason her grandparents had left Thornhaven was that her grandfather had gotten a job opportunity in New York that had been too good to refuse, but maybe there'd been more to it. Maybe her family had *never* been welcome here. Unfortunately, it was too late to ask. A car accident had taken her grandparents the year before she'd moved to Thornhaven. It was the incident that had spurred her mother into believing they would be better off if they moved back and had greater access to their magic.

"It is cool," Chrys admitted slyly, "but if you think there are unusual things going on around here, Lily's the one you should ask about it. Thornhaven's witches are real. You can't trust that they aren't magically messing with your head. Lily could be dangerous."

Luke scoffed, but Anushka and Isaiah both nodded solemnly, and a flicker of doubt crossed his face. "You really believe that?"

"This place gets strange sometimes," Isaiah said. "You said it yourself. Why believe in ghosts but not witches? I still remember this one time . . ."

The bell was about to ring, so Chrys stuffed her lunch remains away as Isaiah launched into a story she'd heard a hundred times about how, when they were seven, their dad had lost control of his car during a nor'easter and almost slammed into the side of the Bramble Lane B&B. According to Isaiah, the car had suddenly turned, stopped, and righted itself—and a moment later, their dad had forgotten all about the incident.

Was it magic? Chrys couldn't say for sure. From what she'd learned, normie kids were more likely to remember magic than adults, because kids accepted it better. And the Bramble Lane B&B *was* owned by a witch couple, so it was certainly possible they'd erected wards around their property. But regardless, it made a good story, and Isaiah loved telling it.

"You research it," Isaiah said as everyone headed back to class. "For that local history term paper we have to do this year."

Chrys smirked, but Isaiah's suggestion gave her an idea: Why not research her *own* family? She'd already proven that she could hold her own magically against any island witch her age, but if she could provide some historical basis for why she was every bit as much a Thornhaven witch as the others, even better.

In the back of her mind, she knew this wouldn't make any of them accept her. And more pointedly, some niggling itch suggested that this desire to prove herself to everyone must mean that she cared about their approval.

But that was stupid. She didn't care. She just wanted to rub everyone's noses in her presence. It was about being vindictive, not about being vindicated.

Huge difference.

"Luke, you should research Lily's family," Chrys mused aloud. "Find out the truth."

"We all know the truth," Anushka said, "and it's that *witch* is a euphemism."

Chapter Six

Lily

Lily couldn't believe it. It had taken a week, but Evan and a couple of other guys were trying to convince Luke to join the basketball team, and so for the first time, Luke had been roped into sitting with Lily's friends at lunch. This was such a fortunate opportunity that Lily couldn't let it go to waste, although it was unclear how to use it to her benefit.

She glanced Chrysanthemum's way to see how she took this change (badly, Lily hoped), but Chrysanthemum's back was to her, so Lily would have to assume instead.

"How can you be so tall and not play basketball?" Sonia asked, leaning over the table. She rested her chin on her hands and gave Luke a smile that was hard to misinterpret.

Lily seethed in frustration. *She* needed to be the one flirting with Luke, but flirting with him seemed wrong. She hadn't fallen for him, so trying to make him fall for her was a little cruel.

Taking a bite of her sandwich, Lily shoved these concerns aside. She hadn't fallen for him *yet*. That *yet* was important. Her cards had made it clear that she could eventually, and to make sure that happened and that her year would unfold successfully, she had to act like it was her only possible fate, since it very much was not. She could practically hear her father telling her that if she wanted something, she had to take action. At the time, he'd been encouraging her to run for student council her freshman year (back when her parents paid more attention to her), but the point held. If Lily wanted perfection, she needed Luke. And that required action. A party was a good step, but it couldn't be the only one.

"I did play in middle school," Luke said. "But the season overlaps with the fall musical."

"Forget the musical," Evan said. "You should play. We could use you."

Conversation delved more deeply into basketball, and Lily found herself tuning most of it out. As her mind often did when boredom took over, her attention drifted toward Chrysanthemum.

All these years, she'd suffered quietly as Chrysanthemum plotted against her. There was value in being stoic, of course, but mostly her reticence had been about not acknowledging that she knew Chrysanthemum was her nemesis. Her silence—hopefully—prevented Chrysanthemum from seeing the way her existence got under Lily's skin. It was seeming like that time had come to an end, though.

Strange that Luke would be the reason for it. As much as Lily liked his company in a friend kind of way, there was something irritating about her battle with Chrysanthemum escalating over a boy. It felt very anti-feminist.

"So what are you guys?" Luke asked. "The Thornhaven Witches or the Thornhaven Pirates?"

It took Lily a second to realize he was asking about the school mascot and not everyone's personal affiliation. "We're the Thornhaven Pirates."

"There's really no such thing as witches," Sonia added, a little too quickly.

"You have a shop downtown that sells magical supplies," Luke pointed out.

"Yeah, but . . ." Sonia took a drink from her water bottle, which was decorated in stickers of crystal balls, tarot cards, and the insignia from her aunt's psychic shop.

Lily kicked her under the table. "Witches aren't, like, evil hags cursing people or anything. You wouldn't have to be afraid even if they were real. And the tourists *love* that stuff—it's really good for the island. As for the Cauldron Supply, it just sells nice candles and incense."

The Cauldron Supply was owned by a couple of witches, so they also sold plenty of necessities for real magic, but the normies didn't know that.

Luke didn't look convinced as he reached for a potato chip. "Maybe you would say that. Chrys and Anushka said your family is descended from a bunch of witches. Are *you* a witch?"

He said it with just enough humor to allow anyone listening to interpret it however they wished. Like he didn't believe such a thing, yet he would totally appreciate some confirmation either way.

Lily would not scream. Her parents had raised her to have more decorum than that. An Allerton witch didn't lose her temper. She smiled in public and hexed her enemies in private.

But Chrysanthemum had talked about her to Luke.

Lily *wanted* to take satisfaction in knowing Chrysanthemum was thinking about her, maybe even *obsessing* over Lily's burgeoning friendship with Luke. Hopefully, it was irritating the shit out of her that her plans for keeping Luke to herself couldn't compete with Lily's plans to save him from her.

That didn't cool Lily's temper, though. The scream remained lodged in her throat, held down by two years of practice in suppressing her Chrysanthemum-related emotions.

"Please." Lily tossed her hair over her shoulder and gestured at Chrysanthemum. "Look at us. Which one of us looks like a witch?"

She was wearing a blue cardigan over a white sundress with blue and yellow flowers, living it up these last few days before the weather turned chilly. Chrysanthemum, with her witchy eyes, was dressed all in black. As usual.

Luke shook his head. "I don't know. You do have that hair. Isn't red hair associated with witches?"

"I thought the saying was that redheads didn't have souls," said Evan, which was so not helpful.

"That's all part of European folklore." Sonia waved around her water bottle. "It's related. Don't you remember? We studied that in—" She cut herself off before she could say *witch school.*

Groaning, Lily walked her lunch trash over to one of the bins. About thirty feet away, Chrysanthemum smiled at something Isaiah said, her strange blue eyes flashing, and Lily's irritation with the lunch conversation increased. She didn't want Chrysanthemum's creepy eyes; she only wished she had some outward sign of her own power. Proof that it was strong. And yet, when she'd ended up being told she had some proof (her hair), it had come in the worst possible way.

A seagull was picking at the grass near the trash can, and Lily's hands balled into fists. "Hey," she whispered, with only a brief check to make sure no one had crept up on her from behind. "See the girl over there in all black?"

Lily wasn't sure how well the seagull could distinguish between students, so she mentally formed an image of Chrysanthemum in her head. While she had not mastered her talent, trial and error had taught her a few tricks. One of them was that visual aids often helped.

"If you steal her lunch, I'll bring you a treat tomorrow," she said.

The seagull cocked its white head in her direction, and Lily held her breath.

Now that the words were out of her mouth, she wondered if she should have uttered them. This was crossing a line she'd never crossed before. Of course she'd thought of hexing

Chrysanthemum. Who wouldn't in her position? But while this wasn't a hex, it *was* a direct attack.

Or, well, she was asking the seagull to attack for her. That technicality didn't make much difference other than that the seagull could refuse.

Part of her hoped it would. This wasn't like her at all. Another part—the frustrated, stressed, and angry part—hoped it wouldn't. *An Allerton witch smiled and hexed her enemies in private*—and she was an Allerton witch. If she wanted to be powerful, she should own that power.

Besides, Chrysanthemum had started it. Whatever had happened with the book yesterday, *she'd done that* to Lily. Payback was only fair.

The seagull took flight, and Lily willed herself to toss out her trash and not watch it go. To not do anything suspicious at all. Using a talent wasn't like a normal spell—it didn't leave behind a tinge, so Chrysanthemum would have no reason to believe Lily had done anything. But her heart pounded, and her hands shook like she'd exerted herself on a real spell.

Composing herself, Lily returned to her table, and she was just sitting down when she heard a scream.

Chapter Seven

Chrysanthemum

Chrys wasn't much of an animal person. She didn't hold any dislike toward animals, but she'd never had pets growing up, not even fish. There had been a short period of time when she'd begged for a puppy, but that phase had passed, replaced by her *I want to be an astronaut* phase and then her *I want to perform in the community musical theater* phase, before she settled on her current phase, aka the *I will hate you before you can hate me* phase.

The seagulls that flocked around Thornhaven were the exception to her animal indifference. Chrys eyed them as warily as she might a nest of hornets. The birds had lived on the island longer than people had, and after several centuries of this joint arrangement, they were still pissed about being forced to share. Everyone knew that when the seagulls took off from a building roof in a giant feathery crowd, you ran for cover. To do otherwise meant you risked getting caught in a literal shit storm. It had yet to happen to Chrys, but it had happened to other students her freshman year, and it was as gross as it sounded. As a result, Chrys—like most sane people—gave the birds a wide berth.

That got harder to do when a seagull was homing in on her like a hawk aiming for a kill.

Chrys caught the blur of motion from the corner of her eye and had barely enough time to leap out of the way before the bird would have crashed into her.

Anushka screamed, and Isaiah let out a loud "what the hell?" But Chrys was too busy moving to yell, clutching her lunch to her body because she hadn't had time to set it down.

Her pulse pounded from surprise, and sweat beaded on the back of her neck. Without glancing around, she could tell every head in the lunch area had swiveled her way. It was exactly the kind of attention she did her best to deflect, and although she'd done nothing unusual or wrong herself, she knew a bird dive-bombing her at lunch was going to make her the laughingstock of the school.

Anushka, Isaiah, and others had also jumped away since the seagull was standing on their table, and they all stared at it, waiting for it to leave. Which it could do any day now, please and thank you. There was only ten minutes left before the bell, and Chrys had most of her lunch to finish because she'd been catching up on assigned reading first. It was a good lunch, too. Yogurt with the last of the gourmet chocolate granola she'd splurged on. If this stupid bird was going to . . .

The stupid bird seemed to hear her unspoken threat.

It took off in a violent motion, but it didn't aim for the sky. It came straight at Chrys. Again! Like it had some personal vendetta!

This time Chrys did scream, but she didn't get further than "what the fu—" before her foot hit a tree root as she backed up. She spun around, dodging the seagull and fighting for balance, and didn't quite manage both. Instead she went flying, and her container of yogurt did as well, hurtling from her hands like she was a champion discus thrower.

Chrys landed on one knee. Her lunch, including the last of her precious granola, landed all over one of the sophomores who had gathered around to gawk. The girl screamed, Chrys swore, and the seagull took off at last, clacking—*laughing*.

Wincing, Chrys stood, testing out the ankle she'd caught. She started to apologize for the yogurt, but the girl ran off, wailing to her friends. A few people clapped, and Chrys heard a smattering of laughter.

Assholes.

Still, it seemed like the worst was over as she shakily returned to her table with her mostly empty container. "What was that about?" she muttered, scraping out the few remaining bits of lunch.

"What was what?" Anushka asked.

Isaiah tore into their bag of chips. "Just the birds acting strange."

"That seagull . . ." Chrys trailed off at the unconcerned expressions on their faces.

That was what. Suspicion exploded in her gut like a bomb, and she scanned the area for confirmation. All around, people were returning to their seats. Some looked confused, but most looked bored, like the past couple of minutes hadn't happened.

Except . . .

A *few* people were snickering. A *few* people remembered exactly what had happened. They were witches, every one of them, which meant that seagull attack had not been a random act of animal insanity.

Someone had made it happen with magic.

Someone, as if Chrys didn't know *exactly who that someone was.*

She glared at Lily, who was giggling with Sonia, and Lily's gaze met hers for a moment before she snapped her face away. Chrys hadn't the faintest idea how Lily could have been responsible, but she had no doubt it was her. Guilt had flashed over Lily's face, just the teeniest, briefest amount. Just enough to confirm it had been her before she'd dissolved into new laughter.

Chrys's grip tightened on her spoon. This war was escalating quickly, but that was fine. If Lily wanted to laugh, Chrys would give her something to laugh about.

Unfortunately, vengeance was delayed.

Chrys was sent to afternoon detention for allegedly tossing her yogurt all over another student, because the normies couldn't think of another reason for how that might have happened. When she finally got home, eager to attempt her first-ever hex, fate intervened again. Chrys discovered that her mom had been promoted at work and Black Cat Coffee had placed an order for her cookies. Her mom was determined that they should celebrate, and faced with the need to choose between obliterating Lily and going out to dinner, Chrys chose her mom.

The delays didn't stop there.

Over the following week, Chrys's anger faded as schoolwork piled up and she assisted her mom with filling cookie orders. Lily fell further and further down her to-do list. She was coming to understand why wars were fought by professional soldiers. It was hard to maintain the necessary level of animosity when your mind was occupied elsewhere. If trying to best Lily over the years hadn't involved things that Chrys had already been motivated to accomplish—get good grades, excel at magic—then she wasn't sure she'd have been so successful.

Lily likely would have gotten away with her crime longer still, but hubris was a bitch, and so was she. Chrys had learned the first axiom from reading Greek tragedies in English class. The second was self-evident.

After their major history term paper was announced Tuesday morning, Chrys headed to the school library during a free period. With her earbuds in, she wandered down the stacks, her finger tracing the spines of the books in the history section. Tucked away in a dim corner, the section provided a sense of seclusion, and Chrys dropped her guard ever so slightly, allowing her talent to flow and help her with her search.

When she was younger, and her magic was developing, Chrys had initially been bummed that she didn't have a flashier magical gift. School had cured her of that, and it had made her realize how perfect hers was for her. Magic might be chaos, and a talent seemingly random, yet each talent fit its witch like a custom pair of jeans.

For Chrys, that was books. Old ones, new ones, thick ones filled with knowledge, cheap paperbacks bursting with stories—it didn't matter. Chrys loved them, and they loved her back. Sometimes her magic pulled her in the direction of whichever books she needed; other times, it pulled the books toward her. They responded to her intentions as she moved past, whispered their secrets indecipherably in her head. Every now and then, one would twitch beneath her finger, as though shouting, *Pick me! I have what you're seeking.* Chrys plucked those couple of books off the shelves.

Using the online catalog might be helpful in some ways, but her talent provided far more certainty that the book in question would truly be useful.

Lost in her own world, she turned at the end of the row and bumped right into the most loathsome person in the school. Lily startled, too, and she glared at Chrys, but Chrys was the one who dropped her books in surprise.

Furious at Lily and at herself for not being more aware of her surroundings, Chrys knelt to retrieve the poor tomes by her feet. If she hadn't been clumsy, she'd have smirked at the unintentionally hilarious expression on Lily's face. It was too late now, though. She was the one who looked ridiculous, and not Lily, who seemed incapable of appearing threatening. She was too wholesomely pretty for that.

Chrys yanked her earbuds out, growing ever more furious with herself—and with Lily, for reminding her that she was pretty. That her brain immediately went there was obnoxious of it.

She gathered the books with all the venom she could muster, which was probably not much with Taylor Swift providing a soundtrack from her clutched fist. Why couldn't she have been listening to one of her more typical playlists today?

To her surprise, Lily stepped closer, and Chrys found herself fighting the urge to take a step back. They were nose to nose, almost exactly the same height since Lily was wearing heeled sandals, and Chrys could smell her. She must have on perfume or use some kind of expensive shampoo like they sold in the fancy shops downtown. It made Chrys's skin tingle, so possibly she was allergic to whatever it was.

She narrowed her eyes and did *her* best to look threatening, knowing she could do a better job of it.

Lily took the smallest of steps back. "I can't believe you told Luke I was a witch."

Chrys rolled her eyes and used the opportunity to adjust the books in her arms, allowing her to move farther away. The air felt thick between them, as though she could sense . . . something. Magic? Anger? Even with the extra space, it was getting hard to breathe between these rows of books.

"So?" She shrugged. "You are."

Lily closed her eyes, and when she opened them, she regarded Chrys like she was gum beneath her shoe. "You're not supposed to go around talking about this stuff. I know you didn't grow up here, so you don't understand how it works, but someone must have told you that."

Yeah, yeah. The first rule of Craft Country Club was that you didn't talk about Craft Country Club. Like Chrys had needed to grow up in Thornhaven to learn that showing people you were different was bad.

"Stop being dramatic," she said. "All I did was fill him in on some of the island's history."

"It doesn't matter. You're not supposed to talk about *any* of it."

"If all the normies talk about witches, but the witches say nothing, isn't that going to make people suspicious?"

Her logic seemed to stump Lily, but only for a second. "Don't be stupid. Of course we can talk about it in a general sense. But we don't outright *say* that people are . . ."

"Witches?"

Lily groaned, and Chrys was surprised she didn't stamp a foot with it.

Why had she never tried antagonizing Lily before? Ignoring her might have been easier, and beating her was delightful, but this was *fun*.

"You should watch yourself," Lily said at last, tossing her hair with a haughty flourish. "Even the seagulls don't like your attitude."

Outwardly, Chrys made sure to hold her face perfectly still.

But inwardly, fury reignited in her blood.

That jab was her own fault, Chrys was forced to acknowledge as Lily spun on her heel and flounced away. Since she hadn't retaliated, she'd let Lily believe she'd won.

Tomorrow, Lily would rethink that assumption.

The first thing Chrys did when she got home from school was toss the note her mother had left, saying she had to run errands, into the recycling. Then she got to work.

Shutting her bedroom door, she took a deep breath. Lily likely had a walk-in closet larger than Chrys's bedroom, but this was her space to do with as she pleased. Three walls were painted lavender, making the most of the scant light that came in through her solitary window. The fourth was painted black. Rather than lamps, Chrys had strung lights around the ceiling—two strands, one that was pure white for general light, and one that was all purple for ambience. Her only furniture was her bed and the bureau she'd had since she was a baby, but even still, she barely had enough floor space to set down her backpack. She couldn't risk her mother returning while she was in the middle of a spell, though, so this cramped room had to do.

Chrys shoved aside the backpack and pulled the box with her spellcasting supplies out from under the bed. For once, she wished she'd been a bit more scrupulous about following rules and making detailed notes in her Book of Shadows. She had an idea of what she wanted to attempt, but not the recipe—such as it was—that most witches would use.

For Chrys, those tools had always felt more like suggestions than requirements. If she didn't need them, then why bother remembering which herbs promoted health and which oils were good for divination? What worked for one witch wasn't guaranteed to work for another. She had always felt there was no point in memorizing spells or ingredient properties when the magic came from within.

She closed the blinds on her window, which dimmed the light but left the room bright enough to see, and settled on the old beige carpet next to the bed. First, a black candle. That was obvious for any hex and would give her something through which to channel her power.

Second, some incense wouldn't hurt to focus her. More experienced witches would blend their own, carefully selecting herbs for their specific magical properties. Chrys, however, pulled out a premade blend she'd bought at the Cauldron

Supply. It wasn't one that was intended to be used for spell-casting, but that hardly mattered. The blend was called Masquerade, and its scent was dangerous and spicy. It made Chrys *think* of hexes, and that was what counted.

As for the rest, she was freewheeling it. Chrys got out her fancy red ink pen and a piece of crisp parchment paper. After a moment of inhaling the sultry smoke and focusing her intent, she distilled her plan into simple words. Her hand warmed with power as she wrote, and her vision blurred. When she finished, Chrys folded the parchment and spat on it. (Gross, yes, but nothing got contempt across better.) Then she stuck a corner of the paper in the candle flame until it caught fire.

It charred immediately as the flames devoured it, but not before the fire flared a deep royal blue with Chrys's tinge. Dropping the paper into her cast-iron miniature cauldron, Chrys watched the blue and black flames rise to the ceiling and vanish. A moment later, the fire extinguished, and so did her candle.

Chrys blew hair out of her face as she snuffed out the incense, her head swimming thanks to the smoke and magical exertion. *Something* had happened, but only time would tell what. She just hoped she got to enjoy it as much as Lily had enjoyed attacking her.

CHAPTER EIGHT

Lily

"Don't freak," Sonia said as Lily approached the stop sign at the end of her street, "but maybe you're taking this Luke thing too seriously."

Lily braked for the stop sign a little too hard.

"What are you talking about?" she asked.

"I'm just saying, I saw you talking to Chrys at the library yesterday." Sonia took a hesitant sip of coffee, correctly fearing that Lily might continue driving erratically under the circumstances. "I hope you're not planning another seagull attack. That was kind of scary."

It had been, and Lily knew it. She would never attempt another seagull incident after the first one had been way more violent than she'd expected. Guilt—irritating, unnecessary, useless guilt—had caused her to toss and turn the entire night afterward.

But the guilt hadn't stopped Lily from acting irrationally yesterday.

Luke had kept talking about Chrysanthemum's choir solo during lunch, and Lily had lost her temper. Not right then and there; not this time. But she hadn't been able to hold her tongue when Chrysanthemum had almost knocked her over in the library. No, she'd had to scold her and then goad her. She'd shown Chrysanthemum how much she got under Lily's skin, and that was not good.

"I was reminding her that she's not supposed to tell anyone about witches," Lily said, more to convince herself than Sonia that she'd acted wisely.

Sonia grimaced as Lily sped away from the stop sign. "No, you were just feeling pissy. Luke is friends with Chrys, and it is what it is."

"I hate that expression so much."

"Yeah, *it is what it is*. Listen, I'm worried you didn't come talk to me about what you did," Sonia continued, turning serious. "Attacking Chrys feels like the wrong way to handle this. Luke's cute, but if he likes Chrys, he's not worth the effort."

Lily gripped the steering wheel tighter. If it weren't for her tarot cards, Sonia would have a point. "Chrysanthemum had it coming."

"Why?"

"She's awful."

A long pause followed, too long for Sonia to just be sipping her coffee. "She's *weird*, maybe, and moody, and her sense of style is cringe, but what has she ever done that was awful?"

Did her best friend really not see how Chrysanthemum was trying to ruin Lily's life? Trying to beat her everywhere and at everything? But no, of course she didn't, because Lily had never talked to Sonia about that. She'd never complained. She'd only worked harder, practiced magic more dutifully, had stress dreams in which a pair of icy-blue eyes taunted her.

"Can we not talk about her before the sun has fully risen?" Lily asked. "She's half bat. She's probably flapping around and listening."

"Fine." Sonia sighed. "What about Luke?"

"What about him?"

"Can I talk about him?"

Lily shrugged. She didn't feel like any more conversation, but if it distracted Sonia from talking about Chrysanthemum . . . "Sure."

"I did a tarot reading last night, and it got me thinking about your reading." Sonia shifted in her seat. "Do you think you might have misinterpreted the cards?"

"You don't even know what cards I drew."

"No, but assuming Luke and you are meant to be together is kind of specific, like more specific than a reading usually is. The cards aren't that kind of magic. And you can't bend the universe to your will that way, either. I know you think you should be able to."

Lily turned into the school parking lot. While she was superior at spellcasting, Sonia had shown a knack for divination from a very young age, a gift she'd inherited. Her aunts were known as the best diviners in Thornhaven. If anyone else her age had been questioning her, Lily would have dismissed them immediately. It was harder with Sonia . . . but Sonia hadn't been there for Lily's reading.

As for the comment about believing she could bend the universe to her will, Lily wasn't going to dignify it with a comment. She worked hard and deserved to see results for it, and that was that.

"The cards were very clear," Lily said coolly. "It was super easy to interpret."

Divination is deceptive. She could hear the voice of Marina Kim—Sonia's aunt—in her head. Ms. Kim had been their witch school teacher two years ago when they'd focused on divination. *Divination is deceptive* was like witchcraft truism number two, right after *magic is chaos*.

"Okay, just asking." Sonia shrugged like it was nothing.

Lily shut her car off and buried the annoying doubts that Sonia had raised. She knew her friend was trying to be helpful, but this conversation was the opposite. She couldn't afford to have doubts when she had to focus on success.

"Thank you," Lily said. "I know you care about me. But I'm totally certain about this, and anyway, the Luke situation is starting to work itself out. He hangs out with us half the time now, and he's my physics lab partner. Things are looking up!"

She'd spoken too soon. Things went to hell in third period, which was, ironically, the last time Lily spoke at all for several hours.

Their English teacher had split the class into five groups, with each group assigned to discuss how one Bennet sister moved the plot of *Pride and Prejudice* forward with her particular personality. Lily's group was supposed to discuss Kitty, which, frankly, sucked. Kitty was ignored by her parents for good reason. She didn't even try to stand out or prove her worth; she just followed her younger sister around like a whining, coughing appendage. Lily despised her.

She was about to point this out, but something odd happened when she opened her mouth. Instead of saying, *The only thing Kitty does for the plot is tattle on Lydia*, Lily laughed.

She clamped a hand over her lips in surprise. No one in her group had said anything remotely funny, and Lily certainly wasn't amused by the task at hand, so it was no wonder the others looked at her in confusion.

Lily shook herself, playing it off like she'd been laughing at her own witty thoughts, and tried again.

Again, no words formed on her tongue when she attempted to speak. Just more laughter.

Lily's heart missed a beat or two as a chill slipped across her skin. These weren't dainty giggles, but hearty, body-shaking laughs pouring out of her when the situation was anything but hilarious. Every time she tried to speak, it felt like some external force was taking control of her body.

"Um, Lily, are you okay?" One of the girls in their group bit her lip in concern.

I don't know what's wrong. At least, that was what Lily attempted to say. What came out was a different story.

Oh, hell. How could this be happening? *What* was happening? The room swayed as Lily's breaths became shallow. She tried to speak again and again, but all that did was direct more attention her way as she laughed inappropriately.

"Lily, what's the problem?" her teacher asked.

How was she supposed to explain that when she couldn't talk? Gasping for breath, Lily darted out of the classroom.

The hallway was blissfully empty, and she sank to the floor, struggling to think through the panic. She hadn't felt any different this morning, and everything had been fine until a few minutes ago. But none of this was natural, and that could only mean one thing—she'd been hexed.

Lily's jaw clenched.

Obviously, Chrysanthemum was behind this.

She *knew* she'd made a mistake by goading her yesterday, but she hadn't expected Chrysanthemum would escalate with a full-on hex! To think she had felt guilty about the seagull, too. Oh, she was going to get Chrysanthemum in so much trouble.

Just, kinda, as soon as she could speak again.

The classroom door opened, and Sonia walked out, carrying Lily's belongings. "Are you okay?"

Lily shook her head, then nodded, then shrugged in defeat.

"Everyone but me and Stina forgot what happened already," Sonia said, referring to another witch in their class, "so I figured it was magic. I told Mr. Baker you were feeling sick this morning and must have run to the nurse."

Lily pulled out her phone and texted: Smart. SHE HEXED ME!!

"Who?"

Rather than type it out, Lily gave Sonia a *really?* sort of look.

"You think Chrys did this?"

Who else? Lily typed.

Sonia rubbed her hands together nervously. "What do we do?"

It was a good question. Lily had never tried removing a hex before, because witches her age were forbidden from messing with hexes, and this didn't seem like the sort of situation she wanted to test out her skills on. Even more experienced witches were advised to avoid attempting to remove hexes on themselves.

If something went sideways and you lost your ability to complete the spell, you could end up worse off than you started.

But that didn't leave Lily with a lot of options while she was stuck at school.

She would have to hope Ms. LaPlant was free this period. It was bad enough she was missing class because of this; getting in trouble for cutting would be a permanent mark on her school record, and who knew how that might impact her future class standing? If this was how she lost valedictorian to Chrysanthemum, Lily wouldn't be able to stand it.

She gestured toward the math hallway. Ms. LaPlant could both help her *and* keep her out of trouble for cutting class.

"Do you want me to come with you?" Sonia asked, apparently guessing Lily's plan.

Lily shook her head. She trusted Sonia, but some things were best faced alone or, barring that, with an adult who cared and wouldn't gossip.

Her father didn't count.

Ms. LaPlant had been free during third period when Lily had burst into her classroom and done her best to explain—with paper, pen, and an unfortunate demonstration—what was going on. But rather than cast a counterspell herself, Ms. LaPlant had insisted on calling Lily's parents. Something about her needing to teach next period and the fact that Lily's parents should be the ones to do the spell because of the risk involved. She'd promised that Lily wouldn't be in trouble for leaving school early, but Lily's hopes of making her afternoon classes were shot.

As was her mood. It shouldn't have been possible for it to get fouler, but as she huddled in a ball in the passenger seat of her father's Mercedes, she had to fight back tears.

He wouldn't even let her drive herself home in case the hex had more damage left to dole out. No doubt he was right to be cautious—Lily hadn't considered whether things could get worse—but it meant she had to listen to him lecture her during the whole drive.

"You should be better able to defend yourself from magical attacks," Donald Allerton said, drumming his fingers against the steering wheel. "Your teachers are always telling us how magically gifted you are, but being a witch is more than doing tricks in a classroom. Or are they not teaching you about warding in that school?"

Yes, they'd covered wards and the importance of maintaining magical protections last year. Good warding practice was to recast and strengthen those protections every full moon. Lily hadn't done that. She didn't know anyone who did, because who was going around casting hexes? Although she knew the Historical Society had resources about hexing, they weren't allowed to learn about them in witch school. That hadn't stopped anyone from sharing illicit knowledge on the down-low, but it wasn't anything anyone took seriously.

Of course, Chrysanthemum knew how to cast a real hex, though. Of course, hers were powerful enough to get past any weak protections Lily's crumbling ward had left.

The worst part about this was that Lily should have known better. With an unhinged, vengeful nemesis like Chrysanthemum on the loose, she should have taken everything about wards to heart. She should have been rebuilding and strengthening hers regularly since she'd learned how to cast one. But just as Lily had assumed there were some lines she wouldn't cross, she'd assumed Chrysanthemum felt the same. How naïve of her.

Reminding her father about her witch school lessons was as pointless as bringing up Chrysanthemum. He was upset and wanted to fume, not hear her rebuttals or accusations. And, oh yes, she couldn't talk anyway, and he couldn't read messages while he drove.

Normally, Lily would have been happy to have his undivided attention for several hours. But could she get it when she'd won the magic fair two years ago? Or when she'd been elected student council class president? No. She got it for being miserable and pathetic. The bar she'd have to clear to prove herself to her parents had been raised another several feet because she was starting off so much lower in their esteem. At least if her mother had been the one to pick her up, she would have been spared the lectures. She might even have gotten some sympathy.

Tears burned at the backs of her eyes, and Lily forced herself to hold them in. She couldn't afford another sign of failure.

"There it is, tilt your head a little farther."

She did as instructed, and her father took a picture of her tongue.

"Crude-looking thing, but I guess it was effective. Unfortunately, no sign of tinge anymore, so we can't identify the caster that way." His voice went cold. "*You should have been able to ward against this*. You are an Allerton witch, the beneficiary of an old, distinguished family's accumulated talents. A role model for magical excellence. Yet today someone made a fool of you because you're not living up that legacy. I'm disappointed."

Embarrassment mixed with anger flushed Lily's cheeks as she studied the photo on her father's phone. A hazy black mark, vaguely star-shaped, marred her tongue. Lily bit down on the organ, and the pain felt relieving.

She could do nothing except stand aside and watch her father put together a counterspell. Such a measure required the witch to either cast a spell strong enough to overpower the original spell, or for them to disrupt the original spell's power. That was usually the easier of the two options, assuming the original spell wasn't masterfully crafted. In this case, her father seemed to think Chrysanthemum's hex was weak enough to simply overpower.

Lily stood still while her father burned a broom made from sweetgrass to sweep away residual negative energy. Then she sat in the house's designated magic workroom—a sunny third-floor spot set aside specifically for this sort of purpose—surrounded by five white candles while he drew a banishing pentacle on her tongue with a special mixture of salt water and herbs. The taste made Lily gag, and she squeezed her eyes shut.

The tingling sensation that followed was almost worse. She cracked her eyes open, caught sight of black smoke drifting up in front of her face, and closed them again.

That smoke was coming off her tongue.

She was going to murder Chrysanthemum.

Well, dream about murder, anyway. Plot elaborate revenge fantasies that she would never follow through on, because *she* was a decent person. *She* had lines she wouldn't cross. But, oh, Lily was going to rub it in Chrysanthemum's snarky little face when she was named valedictorian. It didn't matter if she didn't sleep the rest of the year due to excess studying and practicing. She. Would. Win. It was the best revenge.

"Good," her father said, and Lily snapped open her eyes. "Try to speak."

Lily swallowed, afraid to try in case it hadn't worked. "Trying."

The word came out the way it was supposed to, and she let out a sigh of relief deeper than any she'd felt in a long time. Tears of gratitude threatened, but they were every bit as bad as the ones of frustration.

Her father nodded. "Then it's done. I expect you'll strengthen your ward before school tonight, and I'll be having a word with your teacher."

"What?"

"Someone attacked you, and you were unable to defend yourself." He screwed the lid shut on the jar of salt water. "Both these things are unacceptable, particularly when I'm positive you are more than capable of preventing it from happening. Do you know who did this?"

Oh no. The last thing this situation needed was her father throwing his weight around.

As if being hexed weren't embarrassing enough, he was going to make a scene. There was no way to hide what had happened from the Society, since Lily had already gone to Ms. LaPlant for help, and Stina had probably already spread the news around the school, but this was taking it to another level. And Chrysanthemum would love it, even if she got in trouble, which Lily intended to make sure of.

"Dad . . ."

He held up a hand. "Do you know?"

The air around his hand flickered a deep burgundy with his magic. Her father was very good with simple truth spells. He'd done it many times on her and her siblings.

Lily's stomach sank. The best she could do was make this easier on herself by not requiring the spell. "Chrysanthemum Quinn."

"We'll discuss this more later. I need to salvage the rest of the workday."

All Lily could do was hope that they would not, in fact, discuss it later. Hope that her father got so caught up in his work that he went back to forgetting she existed, leaving her to handle Chrysanthemum herself.

CHAPTER NINE

Chrysanthemum

There were days when Chrys wondered if her mother had pissed off another witch when she was pregnant and that witch had cursed her unborn child.

May she grow up bitter and lonely, doomed to walk the halls of high school in solitude. May she alone have to bear witness to the travesty of her peers' fashion choices, the shallowness of their pop culture opinions, and the tediousness of their requests for teachers to repeat simple information that they would have gotten the first time around if they'd only donated a couple of brain cells to the cause. And finally, may she suffer the indignities of adolescence without the blissful obliviousness of the empty-headed or the funds to purchase high-quality concealer for the occasional zit.

Maybe that was a bit dramatic.

But sometimes it felt like the simplest explanation for her terrible luck.

Like today, for example. The hex she'd placed on Lily might have worked, but Chrys didn't know for sure, and if it had worked, she hadn't gotten to experience the gloriousness of the effects herself. All she knew was that *something* had happened because Lily hadn't been at lunch, and a rumor had spread that she'd gone home sick with some mysterious illness.

Had it been too much to hope that someone could have caught whatever had happened on video? Apparently, the answer was yes. Lily was too popular to suffer such humiliation. Even the students who didn't know she was a witch could pick up on the kind of vibes that said, *You don't want to mess with this one.*

Still, as Chrys strode into the Historical Society building for witch school that evening, she hoped she might get some better information. Not being able to witness the hex's effects herself was frustrating, but she deserved to revel in the juicy gossip, and there had to be gossip if she'd been successful. If Chrys was really lucky, Lily wouldn't even be at school.

As for Lily, Chrys expected her to save face by laughing off the experience. Or, if not that, to glare furiously and defiantly, cowing people into silence.

Instead, when Chrys entered the classroom, Lily's face was red and she was staring straight ahead, refusing to make eye contact with anyone. Somehow that seemed worse. Anyone who checked on her had their questions about her health responded to with terse answers.

Chrys's hopes of discovering more information were essentially dashed.

She wondered if not wishing Lily well like the others marked her as guilty, but she decided acting so out of character would be far more damning. In the end, she kept her head down more than usual throughout class.

"Lily and Chrys, if you could both stay a few moments," Ms. LaPlant said when class ended. "Your parents should be waiting downstairs. They've been meeting with Mr. Stephens."

They what?

Dread filled Chrys's gut. She hadn't stopped to think whether anyone could prove she'd been behind the hex. They'd never been taught about hexing in school, so for all she knew, a hex could be traced. Shit.

She also hadn't considered whether Lily would get her parents involved, and that had been a mistake. This was no longer a battle between the two of them, and with this new move, Chrys was seriously outclassed.

The Allertons were not people to mess with. Lily's parents were rich and powerful, and they were heavily involved in running the Historical Society. If they could prove Chrys had hexed Lily, her life could get a whole lot worse. How, she wasn't entirely sure, but her concern was less for herself and more for her mother, who didn't need the grief.

The only upside to any of this was that Lily looked like she wanted to throw up, too. It made Chrys feel marginally better.

"Follow me," Ms. LaPlant said, gathering her keys and her tote bag. Lily started to protest, but Ms. LaPlant cut her off. "We will discuss everything downstairs."

The trip to the first floor was the longest two flights of stairs Chrys had ever taken. Her mother hadn't said anything to her about a call from the Society, so someone must have reached out while Chrys was in class. Chrys didn't like that at all. She'd had no warning, though possibly that was the point.

Ms. LaPlant led them into a comfy-looking lounge that Chrys had never been in before. Like all the rooms, it smelled faintly of herbs. It was filled with worn but plush chairs, framed old maps on the walls, and two men Chrys knew vaguely by sight.

The first was elderly, with gray hair and dark brown skin and a cane leaning next to his chair. She'd probably been told his name at one point, but she couldn't recall it, though logic suggested he was the previously mentioned Mr. Stephens. All Chrys knew for sure was that he was often in the building and therefore was likely someone important.

The second man she'd also seen around often, without giving him much thought. Now there was no question in her mind who he was. He bore no easy-to-identify resemblance to Lily, but the way he held himself was every bit the same—self-important and stuck-up.

Chrys's mother was there, too, her face drawn and tired. She and the men had been talking in low voices, but they cut off as Ms. LaPlant marched her and Lily into the room. Chrys caught her mom's gaze for only a second, but she couldn't hold it. She bit her lip and stared at her boots.

Lily's father immediately turned on them. "Why aren't these students being taught how to defend and ward themselves—especially when they're being taught *very well* how to hex each other?"

"All the students in this class were taught basic wards last year." Ms. LaPlant didn't sound intimidated by the bluster. "And no one is being taught how to hex. Not at school."

"There was a very clear hex mark on my daughter's tongue."

Mr. Stephens cleared his throat. "We are aware, Don. That's why we're here." He turned in Chrys and Lily's direction, and Chrys braced herself. "Chrys, Lily believes you were the one responsible for hexing her."

When Chrys cast a glance in Lily's direction, her intention to deny everything dissipated in a puff of smoke. Lily no longer looked surly or upset. She looked smug, like she was enjoying getting Chrys in trouble.

Something inside Chrys snapped. "Yeah? Well, I believe she was responsible for *me* being attacked by a seagull last week, but I didn't run off and accuse her of it without proof."

The smugness slipped off Lily's face. "You attacked me with a book first!"

"All I did was make you *drop* a book after *you insulted me*." Chrys crossed her arms.

"You've had it in for me since you arrived." Lily's eyes opened wide, and she sucked in a breath, like she hadn't meant to say that. Then she turned her back on Chrys.

What in the world? Chrys shook her head, confusion distracting her from her fury. "You've had it in for *me* since *I* arrived! If your stupid book snapped at you, I—"

"Lily, you did *what*?" her father asked.

"Chrys?" That was Chrys's mom, sounding bewildered.

"*Enough!*" Ms. LaPlant held up her hands. Chrys hadn't thought Ms. LaPlant had it in her to raise her voice, but she did. The adults fell quiet, too.

Lily turned slowly, her face going white.

"It appears this has been going on awhile," Ms. LaPlant said. Her voice was back to normal, but she sounded exasperated as she rubbed her forehead. "I don't know what the source of this animosity is, but it is a terrible time of the year to indulge in such feelings. Intent matters, remember?"

Chrys said nothing, but Lily flinched.

Taking that as a yes, Ms. LaPlant continued. "Today is the autumn equinox. Do you realize what that means?"

Chrys assumed it was a rhetorical question, but of course Lily had to jump in and answer like the teacher's pet that she was. "The veil between the material and metaphysical planes has started to fade and will continue to do so until it reaches its thinnest point at Samhain."

"Exactly. Which means negative energies can intensify. Entities of the otherworldly plane will be drawn to them and may be able to manipulate them—and you. It's the most dangerous *and* the most powerful time of the year to cast hexes. You both should know that."

Lily's fingers twitched at her side, distractingly, and Chrys had to resist the urge to grab her hand and hold her still.

"No more hexing will be tolerated," Ms. LaPlant said firmly. "That goes for both of you. I don't care who started it."

With the smallest of wobbles, Mr. Stephens stood and reached for his cane. "Since no permanent damage was done, I've discussed the matter with your parents, and the Society will handle this like we would any situation where a minor engaged in dangerous magic."

What did that mean? Did witch school give detention? Could she be expelled? Dealing with whatever punishment the school handed out had to be better than dealing with the Allertons, but the possibility of exclusion reheated Chrys's anger at Lily. She'd thought Lily would fight her own battles, but clearly she'd given her too much credit.

Lily's father huffed. "We've agreed, but if the matter isn't dealt with in a way that Irene and I find appropriate, I will call a board meeting to discuss the issue."

Mr. Stephens showed no signs of acknowledging the comment, continuing to focus on Chrys and Lily. "First of all, one word of any sort of negative magic, and you're both disqualified from the magic fair this year."

Chrys dug her nails into her palms. How was this a fair threat? The grade-level winners received token prizes—a gift card to the Cauldron Supply or the local bookstore—but the prize for seniors was scholarship money, and not an insignificant amount. It wasn't like Lily needed it, but Chrys could very much use it.

"Second of all." Mr. Stephens handed a key to Ms. LaPlant, and she beckoned Chrys and Lily to follow her.

Chrys shot Lily a discreet glance as they started moving, but Lily's face was stony. If she was relieved that this was all she was being threatened with, she didn't show it.

Chrys didn't trust that this punishment held any meaning for Lily, and if it didn't, she had to assume Lily would be out for revenge. Chrys was at a disadvantage, even if she anticipated as much. She kept her personal wards strong, but that hadn't saved her from whatever Lily had done to make that seagull attack her. Lily's magic was more powerful than Chrys had given her credit for.

Ms. LaPlant ushered them inside the Society's library and turned on the lights. Although high-ranking Society members (no doubt people who said things like *I will call a board meeting to discuss the issue*) had keys and could come by whenever they pleased, the building was officially closed by this time of the evening. People like Chrys were around only for witch school, so she'd never been in the library this late before.

Despite her love for the building, the library at night was depressing. The heavy wood appeared oppressive. The spaces between the rows of bookshelves were too dark to make browsing easy, and the dim, old-fashioned table lamps would make reading or studying challenging. The air smelled more like decaying paper than old herbs.

In the light of day, it was perfect. Even the dust lent it a stately mood. Darkness was another story. Chrys's nose itched, and she stifled a sneeze.

"Precisely," Ms. LaPlant said, wrinkling her own nose. "We've noticed that fewer people have been spending time here over the last several years, and even fewer of them are our youngest members. One of the projects on the Society's Building Maintenance Committee to-do list is to make this room more usable and inviting, and there's no better time for that than in preparation for the new year at Samhain."

"What's not inviting about it?" Chrys muttered sarcastically.

"It's morbid in here," Lily said. Her brow was pinched, and Chrys wondered what she was worried about. That Ms. LaPlant would lock her in here and ruin her clothes with dust?

Ms. LaPlant glanced between them both. "It's too dark at night, and the paint is dingy. Everything could use a good dusting, too. Any additional punishments are between you and your parents, but as for the Society, this is going to be your task."

"You want us to dust?" Lily sounded so appalled that Chrys almost laughed. Only relief, and a small amount of confusion, kept her from probably getting in more trouble.

"Dust and paint," Ms. LaPlant said. "The walls and all the trim. I expect it will take you several Saturdays of working together to get it done. Mr. Stephens is our librarian, and he'll supervise you. He and your parents have already agreed on it."

“Saturdays?” Lily sounded even more horrified.

“Together?” Chrys thought she was the only one focused on what was truly awful about this scenario. But then, she didn’t have a weekend social life to lose.

Ms. LaPlant sighed. “Witches need to stick together. Aside from increased power, there are *reasons* we gather in communities. You don’t have to be best friends with everyone, but our strength is in our ties to one another. You’ll start this weekend, and maybe you’ll learn to coexist by the time it’s finished.”

Not likely, but Chrys’s mind was spinning.

The threat of being banned from the magic fair hung overhead, but for a brief moment, far worse fates had seemed possible—being banned from witch school entirely or having her powers suppressed, if that was possible. Giving up her Saturdays to paint would be annoying, having to spend the hours in Lily’s presence would be irritating, and Chrys figured she’d have to do 99 percent of the work because the witch princess would be useless, but this was not bad. Chrys was no great painter, but she had helped her mom paint their apartment.

How many Saturdays could it take?

Chrys wasn’t sure how much of these thoughts showed on her face, but Ms. LaPlant glanced between her and Lily’s expression of despair, and she seemed satisfied. “I want you to take a minute to breathe, reflect, and apologize to each other. When you’re ready, come back to the study.”

As soon as Ms. LaPlant left, Lily let out a low, frustrated cry of agony. “My party is this weekend! I’ve been planning it for two weeks! How am I going to be ready in time for it on Saturday night when I have to be here all day with *you*?”

Between the survivable punishment and Lily’s misery, Chrys was feeling almost cheerful. “Maybe you should have thought about that before you tattled.”

“Maybe you should have thought at all before you hexed me. Although it’s actually kind of flattering that you’d go to so much effort.”

“It was hardly any effort. Your wards just suck that much.”

That shot appeared to have hit, because Lily twitched. “Maybe some of us aren’t *obsessed* with evil magic.”

Obsessed? Leave it to Lily to be overdramatic, to create a scene so she could star in it. Total popular-girl energy. “You have some nerve. After you had a seagull attack me!”

“That wasn’t a *hex*.”

“Oh, so that makes it okay? Are we cool if I punch you because it’s not magic?”

“That is not even remotely the same. Oh my god, why are you like this?” Lily grabbed a pen sitting on the table and threw it.

The pen bounced once against the table, hit Chrys in the arm, and clattered to the floor. Chrys stared at it, dumbfounded. It wasn’t clear if Lily had meant to throw it at her or had just thrown it in frustration and it happened to hit her, but either way, Chrys had tolerated enough. Power surged within her, sweeping away her better mood. "Like what? I never did anything to you!"

"You've ruined *everything* for me from the moment you arrived—"

"I never even spoke to you—"

"Please! You've been out to get me since ninth grade! It's some kind of twisted vendetta!"

Chrys was the one with a vendetta? Was Lily for real? "I can't believe you're serious right now! That is the most pathetic—"

"You're like some kind of *demon*—" With nothing else to throw, Lily's hands clenched into fists at her side, and the lights flickered.

The hairs on the back of Chrys's neck stood up. The power in the room was making her skin tingle, much like it often did when she got too close to Lily. But this time, she understood the reason, and the magic in her blood responded as though challenged. "You are so *full* of yourself, as if you *own* the island and valedictorian and—"

"I wish you'd never moved here! *You don't belong!*"

"*Fuck you!*"

She had no more retorts left, no more quality counterarguments. The *you don't belong!* unleashed a fury inside Chrys that couldn't be put into better words. She flung those two out, barely. With them came a burst of power—her talent lashing out, searching for a way to inflict pain.

The two closest bookshelves shuddered.

Shit. She had to get out of here before she damaged something she didn't want to damage. Something that didn't include Lily.

Without another word, Chrys stomped out of the library to find her mother.

Ms. LaPlant and Mr. Stephens had left, so there was no one to pester her about whether she and Lily had apologized. Chrys loaded her bike into the back of her mom's car, and they drove home in silence. Chrys wished her mother had yelled, but that wasn't her mom's way. In the silence, Chrys felt all her rage bottled up inside, tensing every muscle, scalding her veins, creating a pressure inside her skull that begged for release.

Days—weeks—ago, she'd have laughed if Lily had called her a demon. Would have laughed at how self-centered Lily was to believe Chrys had spent the last couple of years plotting against her. Now, Chrys was just pissed off. Lily thought *Chrys* was the one who was obsessed? What bullshit. Lily had painted a target on Chrys's back from the moment she'd set foot in Thornhaven.

Being ignored no longer felt like a slight. That *you don't belong!* was malicious.

It wasn't until they got home that her mom broke the silence. "What happened?"

Lily had happened. The move to Thornhaven had happened. Her grandparents had died. She was perpetually a freak. Everything crappy happened, and eventually it all happened to her.

Chrys tugged off her boots, wishing, as she often did, for a bigger apartment, for more than a cheap wood door and five feet of hallway to separate her from her mother's disappointment when she would finally be able to retreat to her bedroom.

"Chrys?"

Chrys scowled. "Lily Allerton is a stuck-up bitch who enjoys blaming me for her problems."

Chrys's stomach growled. The tension she'd been carrying all day because of the hex meant she hadn't eaten much. She needed food, only she didn't feel like eating.

"What was the part about a book?" her mom asked as Chrys got out a bowl for cereal.

"It was nothing. I made Lily drop a book she was holding while she was talking to some boy she likes."

"First you're accused of hexing the Allerton girl, and now I find out you're using your talent at school?" Samantha leaned against the half wall that divided the kitchen from the living room.

"It's not like he knew what happened."

Besides, there was magic everywhere on the island. What was a little more? Most of it was subtle—the way there were rarely traffic accidents, the fact that storms mostly passed harmlessly by, the plants that bloomed a little more fiercely and held their blossoms for a bit longer than nature intended. Some of it was less subtle, like the way drinks at Black Cat Coffee stayed the perfect temperature until you finished them, or how the item you fell in love with at Second Chance Romance—the thrift store boutique—always happened to be in your size. So the Society's rule that witches shouldn't use their magic at school? Chrys was realizing how hypocritical it was. But saying so wouldn't help her case, so she swallowed down the words with a mouthful of store-brand cornflakes.

"That's not the point." Her mother rubbed her hands along her cheeks. "And a feud with an Allerton? They might be the single most powerful family in Thornhaven, in every sense of the word. Not that I'd want you fighting with anyone, but of all the people around here whose bad side you don't want to get on . . ." She sighed, and Chrys would have sworn she felt that sigh in her own chest. "How long has this been going on, really?"

Chrys stifled a groan. "Just what you heard tonight."

"It has nothing to do with being upset that you tied with her in the magic fair last spring?"

Ugh. She hadn't thought about that in a while, and the memory prickled like a scrape across her brain. "It's not my fault Lily's been my only real competition for anything."

She wondered, though, for the first time, how much of that was true. She'd told herself time and time again that she wanted to excel to prove herself, but how much of proving herself was actually just about a desire to put a frown on Lily's beautiful-but-snooty face?

Had she *needed* to perfect a secret ink spell for the last magic fair? No. But when she'd learned Lily was doing a spell with ink, she'd known entering something similar would irritate her. Same with Chrys volunteering to take the yearbook photos for the music department the last two years. Sure, it was something she could put on her college applications, but Lily was on the yearbook committee, and this way Chrys got to insert herself in Lily's domain and exert some power. It was revenge for the cold, persistent exclusion from Lily and the witches who followed her.

These realizations only fouled her mood further. "I'm tired. Can we discuss this later?"

"This isn't like you. You've always been responsible."

"Maybe I haven't." Chrys turned for the hall and those pathetic five feet of space. "Maybe I'm a quote-unquote 'demon.' Lily thinks so." Still carrying the cereal, she closed her door tightly, hearing her mother sigh again.

"We'll talk about this tomorrow!" Samantha called out. "Don't think we're done, but we both need to get to bed."

Chrys closed her eyes, hating the exhaustion in her mother's voice. Her mom had worked today, and she worked tomorrow, too. Her alarm would be going off all too soon so she could be at the Shop-n-Go bakery by 6:00 a.m. That was the only reason Chrys was getting this temporary reprieve. And yet her mom wouldn't rest easily tonight. She'd be worried about

Chrys, wondering if she'd done something wrong in her raising and possibly fearing what the Allertons could do to them.

Damn Lily all over again. The last thing Chrys wanted was to make her mother's life more stressful. And yet she was being pushed and pushed and pushed to her limit.

Chrys had once felt rejected by Lily. Bitter. Sad. But she'd never truly *hated* Lily. Even after the seagull attack, when she'd been angry and wanting revenge—even then when she'd *thought* she hated Lily—that hadn't felt like this did. Like she might burst if she didn't let out her emotions. Like not even screaming would expel them.

But she tried because she had to. Before she broke. Not a scream but a whisper, a deep breath in and an exhalation of all her fury. "I hate you."

She didn't have to say Lily's name or that she hoped Lily would suffer. Every syllable of that simple sentence was backed by her intent.

A shiver ran down Chrys's spine. A kind of soothing emptiness followed, as though she'd really managed to release some of her rage. Chrys blinked in surprise, confused by this unexpected outcome. But she wasn't going to question it. If it meant she could sleep, or finish her cereal without her stomach in knots, all the better.

Because her room was so dimly lit, she didn't notice the cloud of blue tinge dissipating through her window.

Chapter Ten

Lily

Lily shut off the engine and listened to its cooling clicks as she rested her head against the steering wheel. Outside, the temperature had dropped with the sunset. It wasn't cold, not yet, but a distinct autumn chill had taken over, and it was most noticeable at night. Lily didn't expect the temperature inside the house to be much warmer. Her father had arrived at the Society separately and had therefore driven home separately, and if he hadn't already informed her mother about what had happened, he would have as soon as he got in the house.

Which was why Lily was delaying in her car.

She didn't need her parents telling her how much they did not approve of her behavior. Neither did she, honestly. She'd lost her temper and actually thrown a pen tonight. It was shockingly unlike her. How had she gone from pretending to ignore Chrysanthemum's aggression to lashing out in public? Why was she suddenly losing her composure?

Lily didn't know, but she had to get her anger under control. Yet, even as she thought it, her white-hot rage at losing her Saturdays threatened to consume her. She was the victim here, not the aggressor. The seagull hadn't been her best decision, but Chrysanthemum had started everything else. The hex. Talking about Lily being a witch. The book . . .

Lily frowned. The bookshelves in the library had shaken when Chrysanthemum yelled at her. Did she have some kind of talent with books? It was the only explanation Lily could think of. Whatever it was, one thing was clear: Chrysanthemum and books was a dangerous combination.

Her phone chimed with a text from Sonia: Are you ok? What happened at school?

Fury curled Lily's hand into a fist around her phone. Too much had happened. If she wrote back now, she'd never leave the garage.

With that in mind, Lily got out of the car and entered the house, prepared for the worst.

She longed to sneak off to her room and fill Sonia in on the unfairness of everything, and she considered doing exactly that as she passed through the kitchen and grabbed a banana. But Lily had never liked to delay the inevitable. Voices drifted out of the family room, so she decided to get her reprimand over with and headed for them.

Her father was pacing, which was no surprise, but Sara sat on the floor by their mother's feet, her knees pulled to her chest, and she didn't seem gleeful to witness Lily's dressing-down. Her sister actually looked like she might have been crying. A sliver of concern pierced through Lily's foul mood, but her mother raised her head before Lily could ask what was wrong.

"Your father filled me in," her mother said with that same no-nonsense voice Lily imagined her using in the ER. "Aside from anything you need to do for school or the Society, you are officially grounded."

Lily stared at her. That was it? No reprimands, no *we're disappointed in you* speeches? Just *here's your punishment, take one a day until your behavior improves, and call us if you experience any unusual side effects?*

Unless . . . maybe they were so angry that they couldn't bear to look at her? Surely that had to be the reason.

It didn't explain Sara's pink-tinted eyes, though, and Lily hesitated. "Are you okay?" she asked her sister.

Sara shook her head.

"We're having a small crisis," said her mother.

Her father glanced Lily's way. "Elena is moving to New Jersey," he explained, dropping the name of Sara's swim coach.

Sara's whining increased in volume, and she curled up into a ball. "She's the best coach. We need to move off this stupid island. No one wants to live here but us."

Lily's stomach sank. Her parents wouldn't actually consider that, right? There wasn't even a witch enclave in New Jersey. "We can't move. You know you won't swim half as fast anywhere else because your water talent won't be so strong."

That got Sara to look up, and she glared at Lily.

"Lily!" Her father raised a hand in a *stop it* kind of gesture. "You have already caused enough trouble for one day. Be thankful we have other things to worry about besides your behavior. Go to your room, reflect on what you've done, and under no circumstances expect to throw that party you were planning. Understood?"

Lily's jaw dropped, but her parents' attention had already been lost as her sister began plaintively detailing why the mainland would be so much better. She'd been dismissed.

The sparks of anger in Lily's blood roared into a wildfire.

She stomped up the stairs and barricaded her bedroom door, for all that mattered. No one was going to check on her. No one cared enough to be upset. No one thought of her at all.

No one except Chrysanthemum.

It was too much to tolerate. She was going to scream, to throw something. To break things before she broke.

Except, she'd already broken—she'd lost control, and she had vowed not to do that again.

She had to do something, though. She had to protect and care for herself, because no one else would. And that meant defending herself from Chrysanthemum. Chrysanthemum would keep hurting her, keep talking about her, keep hexing her, keep stealing successes from her, keep diminishing her in her parents' judgmental eyes. Lily needed her to *stop*.

And, clearly, the only language Chrysanthemum respected was aggressive magic.

Hands trembling, Lily had set a bloodred candle (the most violently colored one she owned) on her altar before she even realized what she was doing. She'd never attempted a hex before, and she didn't know how to do one, but the basics were clear enough. All spells relied on intent; everything else was mere theatrics. And Lily had intent seeping out of her pores, so what need did she have for props or ritual?

With a snap of her fingers, she lit the candle, and the flame streaked toward the ceiling. The effort didn't tire her at all. If anything, it had the opposite effect. As if a small leak had weakened the walls of her magical dam, the full force of her power strained for release. She was wide-awake and full of fire, magic crackling like lightning along her skin.

"I hate you." She whispered the words, pouring her intent into them. "May everything you feel about me be redirected back at you a hundredfold. May every bit of magic you work on me be turned against you. May . . ." Lily choked on her rage, unable to articulate her intentions, and she waved her arms to extinguish the candle.

Exhaustion overtook her as the flame went out, leaving her as burned out as the wick. She fell back on the floor and sighed. Despite the tiredness, something faintly like relief was washing over her. The hate in her gut, the anger boiling her blood, flowed away.

A purple mist rose from the candle smoke and dissipated with it.

Swallowing, Lily watched it vanish, and only then did the hairs on her neck and arms rise to attention. Without her anger, the air felt colder.

She should not have done that.

It was hardly a focused spell—just fury and bitterness strung together with some vague words. Not even all *were* words. That last *may* had been nothing but raw emotion.

It was exactly the sort of spell that no witch should ever cast under the best of conditions, and these were not those.

An unfocused hex cast between the equinox and Samhain was the most dangerous sort of magic.

She took a deep breath, then another, trying to shake off the cold dread. Her actions likely hadn't done anything besides create a little tinge and allow her to vent, she reasoned. She hadn't even known what she was doing, and while powerful witches could cast spells without tools, Lily was not powerful enough for that. Not yet. She needed instructions and the sort of external focus that candles and incense and detailed actions provided.

So yes, everything would be fine. All she'd done was make herself feel better.

And she *did* feel better, which was both a surprise and a relief. Better enough to know that her parents ignoring her was not Chrysanthemum's fault.

A scratching noise from behind shook Lily, and she gasped, spinning around before realizing it was only Ella and Cinder getting antsy in their castle. Great. She was going to be jumpy until she knew for sure she hadn't done anything irredeemably stupid.

"I'm coming, you two." Lily crawled over to the cage and opened the door.

Recalling the banana she'd taken, Lily peeled it and took a bite for herself (expending all that magical energy had left her ravenous), then broke off bits for the rabbits. They gobbled them up happily, conveying their pleasure through a stream of images into her mind. For a moment, she allowed herself to enjoy their contentment and let it push aside her lingering worries about the almost-certainly futile spell.

Chapter Eleven

Chrysanthemum

Chrys did her best to avoid Lily at school for the rest of the week. She couldn't in their shared classes, of course, but she spent Thursday's and Friday's lunch periods in the library, silently fuming and contemplating taking up journaling. She'd tried her hand at songwriting a few times in the past (Isaiah was constantly suggesting that they, Chrys, and Anushka start a band), but she needed a more immediate release for her emotions than trying to awkwardly cram them into lyrics that lacked satisfying rhymes and rhythms.

If only she had a friend she could talk to about the situation, that would help. But neither Anushka nor Isaiah was a witch.

Her first Saturday working on the Historical Society's library passed mostly silently and uneventfully. Mr. Stephens spent the morning going over the task with Chrys and Lily in more detail, and they spent the afternoon cleaning and prepping the room for painting. She and Lily communicated only when necessary, and then, only by glaring.

At three, she was released, and she couldn't bolt out the door fast enough, a mood that had little to do with the work and everything to do with getting out of Lily's presence. Chrys escaped to the town library to catch up on homework, and afterward, she went for a walk through the small park that connected the library and town hall. The first trees had begun to rain down golden leaves, but it was the bite in the wind that helped clear her head, a sharp smack straight to the brain.

She should let the whole thing with Lily and Luke go. If Luke decided he wanted to date Lily, then wasn't he getting exactly what he deserved? This way, Chrys could go back to pretending Lily didn't exist. Life had been simpler that way.

Life was always simpler when you could pretend other people, especially those who had hurt you, didn't exist. If you pretended hard enough, then no one could ever hurt you again. You could see right through everyone around you, like they were ghosts. Their words and actions became an inconsequential shimmer in the passing breeze.

Chrys's meanderings had taken her from the park down a short stretch of road to the old Thornhaven church and its ancient cemetery. Centuries-old tombstones and crypts rose from the grass like they'd been planted there, their faces worn down over many, many years by the sun and the Atlantic storms. Chrys loved it here. As with old buildings, her appreciation for the time-beaten cemetery gave her a sense of peace. Ancestors of hers were buried in here. Their feet had walked this dirt, too.

But today, the chill in the air left her uneasy. The headstones weren't monuments to people's lives but reminders that death marched relentlessly forward and that one day it would catch up to everyone. If she breathed deeply, she could almost smell it. The sweet scents of woodsmoke and earthy decay that she associated with autumn had been replaced by something sinister that she couldn't quite put a finger on . . . but it touched a memory, one that she also couldn't place.

A fresh shiver ran down her spine as she thought of the way she'd spat out her feelings toward Lily on Wednesday. Chrys pulled her hoodie tighter around her body. She didn't know why that memory had sprung to mind, but with it came the realization that there had been a slightly off smell at school the last couple of days, too. That was the familiarity—the connection—that was prickling her brain. But she didn't understand it.

She had to be imagining things, but this also had to be a sign that she was right to give up on this war with Lily.

Declaring Lily her mortal enemy wasn't worth her time. Any issues Lily had with her, those were Lily's problem.

She wasn't admitting defeat. Just moving on.

As far as Chrys was concerned, from now on, Lily was nothing but a dead leaf beneath her boot. She stepped on the nearest one, and it gifted her with a satisfying crunch.

Chrys wasn't exactly eager to go back to school Monday morning and test out her plan, but, to be fair, she was never eager to go to school, and least eager of all on a Monday morning. But she *was* determined to prove to herself that she could put this new plan of hers into action. Or rather, no action, since that *was* the plan.

Everything started off great. She studiously did not so much as glance in Lily's direction during math class, which was easy since Lily sat behind her. And if she flicked her pen faster around her fingers when Lily was talking, that was, no doubt, a coincidence.

The real challenge would come at lunch, because Chrys had decided she was done avoiding Lily, which meant it was back to the cafeteria. That might require some willpower, but she was confident she had it in her.

But, as it turned out, the day took a turn for the weird during choir, banishing all thoughts of Lily from her head.

"Good morning, everyone. Happy Monday. Get in your spots." Despite having retired from performing years ago, Ms. McNeil ruled her domain like a first-class prima donna.

Chrys, Isaiah, and Luke abandoned their conversation, each shuffling to their respective place on the risers before Ms. McNeil could start snapping her fingers and telling them all to *make haste*.

Satisfied with the scurrying, Ms. McNeil nodded in approval. "Let's warm up."

Class always started the same way. The same scale, the same flick of Ms. McNeil's wrist to get them singing. Only today, when Chrys opened her mouth, she didn't hear her voice or the voices of her classmates.

She heard a racket.

The noise was so loud, so jarring that she cut off mid-note, as did everyone else. As soon as the last student stopped singing, the cacophony died down. A few people giggled nervously.

Confused along with everyone else, Chrys searched the room for a cause without finding one. The choir had its own rehearsal room next to the band room, but that was definitely not the band. Not even on their worst day. And there was nothing in the room with the class aside from Ms. McNeil's music stand and an old whiteboard.

Hands on her hips, Ms. McNeil sighed into the ether. "Mondays. Let's start again."

Her baton moved, everyone started singing, and a second later, the racket returned. This time some instinct had prepared Chrys, and she attempted to home in on the source as best she could, but it wasn't coming from only one spot. The sound thundered and crashed from overhead and from the walls themselves. Half the class stopped singing, but Ms. McNeil urged them to continue for several more notes before the noise grew so loud, there was no way she could possibly hear them. Chrys could barely hear herself.

"I think it's the pipes," the girl next to her said.

That made sense. What didn't make sense was that the noise had stopped again as soon as the singing did.

They tried a third time to warm up, and a fourth.

Ms. McNeil's frown deepened with each failed attempt. "This is absurd. What on earth is going on with the building today? Give me a minute."

Chrys kicked at the risers with her boot, watching with a sense of foreboding in her gut as Ms. McNeil headed into her office and disappeared from view.

Around her, the classroom descended into a rumble as everyone discussed the situation. Pipes was the most common culprit suggested, but a sophomore boy joked about the ceiling collapsing, and Isaiah maintained that the island's ghosts were getting active early this year.

It wasn't until a soprano on her right—an annoying junior who thought she was destined for Broadway stardom—raised her voice above the din that Chrys had to acquiesce to what logic had been whispering all along. "What's going on? Where did Ms. McNeil go?"

Chrys jerked her head in the girl's direction. The junior's memory wasn't the only one fading, as was evident by the expressions of confusion on the faces near her. *Almost* all of them, anyway. Chrys caught the eye of another witch, Tessa, and the girl shrugged at Chrys, clearly as befuddled by this turn of events as she was.

When Ms. McNeil returned a minute later, she looked as baffled as Chrys felt, although Chrys would have bet anything that it was for different reasons—that is, she probably couldn't remember why she'd left the room in the first place.

Sure enough, their choir teacher raised her baton, blinking away a memory lapse she'd probably later fret about in private. "Let's begin."

They began again.

So did the noise.

In the fifty-minute period, Ms. McNeil left the classroom three times in total, and the normies who were more sensitive to magic, like Isaiah, were starting to express a strange sense of déjà vu. As for Chrys, she wrapped her arms around herself, making more eye contact with witches she wasn't friendly with than she ever had before, hoping one of them might offer a clue as to what was going on. If someone had cast a spell on the choir, it stood to reason that a witch in the class might be responsible, but no one seemed guilty.

In frustration, Chrys searched the room for sigils or tinge or some other indicator that a charm or spell had been placed on the classroom, but she found nothing of that sort, either. Nor could she make sense of what kind of spell could have caused such a specific effect, never mind why someone would have done it.

The news would travel fast, though, and the Society would look into it. Of that, Chrys was sure. She just hoped they'd be as fast in responding. Choir was the one class she actually enjoyed.

Chapter Twelve
Chrysanthemum

Tuesday morning began more normally. Nothing went afoul during choir, and Chrys breathed a sigh of relief. Either yesterday had been a fluke, or someone from the Society had gone to the school last night and cast some wards or counterspells under the cover of darkness. Either option was fine with her.

It had finally gotten too chilly to eat lunch outside, so Chrys flopped down at the table she shared with Anushka, Isaiah, and (every other day) Luke. She'd been wanting to talk about the choir incident with someone, and she was feeling her lack of witch friends acutely. The best she could hope for was to overhear something good at witch school tomorrow night, and that felt like forever away.

"What are you moping for?" Anushka asked, misreading her mood.

"I'm not moping."

Isaiah poked at the slice of pizza on their tray. They'd forgotten their lunch and had been left to the mercy of the cafeteria gods. "Sorry, no. That was a total moping face. And you're not even eating tomato-sauce-covered cardboard."

"Is it our English quiz?" Anushka asked. "It is, right? I hate English."

Chrys rubbed at the bruised spot on her apple. "The quiz isn't until tomorrow."

"Yes, but I'm *pre*-moping," Anushka said. "I'll be very prepared this way for when I get my grade."

"I'm not moping." Ugh, was Chrys wrong? *Was* she moping and misreading herself?

This was stupid. *She* was being stupid. Her week had improved since yesterday morning, and she wasn't someone who gossiped anyway.

Across the room, Lily laughed loudly. Every head at Chrys's table turned in her direction, but Chrys held her ground and took a bite of her apple.

"So, Luke," Anushka said, "I wanted to ask you . . . *What the hell?*" She jumped up midsentence, leaving everyone hanging.

Chrys was about to ask what had happened when one of the cafeteria's brown cardboard trays went zipping past the end of their table. "What the hell?" she echoed Anushka.

A girl shrieked, and someone yelled, "Who did that?"

"Knock it off!" another girl yelled back.

"Is someone really trying to start a food fight?" Luke asked warily. He also stood and was using his height to scan the room for the culprit.

Obviously, Chrys had been too optimistic about her week improving. She should have known better than to think it on a Tuesday. Another tray went flying, this one covered in food.

"Hey, that was my lunch!" a third girl called out, and the room erupted in more yelling.

"I didn't do it!"

"Stop it already!"

The voices grew louder and more numerous, and Chrys closed her eyes in exasperation. A food fight? What was wrong with these people? It occurred to her, then, that she'd better keep her eyes open in case she had to dodge any projectiles, and she opened them in time to witness a stack of unused trays by the serving lines lift into the air and whiz across the room like a deck of playing cards.

"Did you see that?" a boy asked.

In answer, another tray sailed by in the opposite direction. It hit the boy in the face and splattered the remains of indistinguishable food in all directions.

"You are dead, Cal!" the boy called out, pulling pizza crust off his shoulder.

"That wasn't me! It leaped off the table, I swear," came a response, presumably from Cal.

Not only trays were starting to fly. Chrys's lunch bag twitched in front of her, and she slammed her hand down on it, her pulse quickening.

Magic. Again. Different, but no less unpleasant or more logical than choir.

Wetting her lips, she glanced at Anushka, who, although she might not understand the cause of the ruckus, knew what the wise call was. "Let's get out of here."

The four of them grabbed their fidgeting food—Chrys's bag wasn't the only one developing a mind of its own—and rushed toward the cafeteria door as someone yelled out, "Food fight!"

"Oh my god, I hate people!" Anushka said, dodging as half a peanut butter and jelly sandwich missed her by inches and smacked the wall, smearing sticky goo everywhere.

"What has gotten into everyone?" Luke muttered. As the tallest, he was partially hunched over, trying to make himself a smaller target.

The normies couldn't accept that the trays were flying on their own, so they assumed someone was behind it. That much made sense. The who, the why, and the what of the spell—that was something else entirely. Like yesterday, it made Chrys's brain hurt. It was almost as if someone had hexed the school, but who would do such a thing? Chrys despised high school as much as the next sane person, but this did not seem like a good way to deal with emotions.

And hexing Lily was? an annoying voice whispered in her head.

Chrys scowled, refusing to second-guess her choices. That had been a very specific, direct kind of hex. It was nothing like whatever this was.

A memory of the venom with which she'd spat out *I hate you* about Lily last Wednesday night, and the feeling of release that had followed, nearly made Chrys trip over her feet as she exited the cafeteria. Okay, fine. *That* had not been very specific. But that also hadn't been a hex. It was just her venting. Totally different.

"Stupid," she muttered, and she shook her head at Isaiah, who'd heard her talking to herself. "Everyone is acting stupid."

They weren't the only ones who'd poured into the hallway, and, unable to help herself, Chrys glanced over her shoulder to see if Lily had made it out, something irritatingly like guilt gnawing on her gut. She was being ridiculous, and she knew it. No words spoken in a fit of anger could be responsible for anything bad happening to Lily. If that were the case, surely witches would be harming other witches on a regular basis every time someone lost their temper.

There was no sign of Lily, but Chrys blinked at the doorway, a fresh "what the hell?" forming on her tongue.

Black lines were creeping out from around the opening. No one else seemed to notice them, but to her, they were clear as day and very . . . *wrong* was the only way to describe it.

At first, Chrys thought they were cracks forming, that the whole wall was going to tumble down and they'd all soon be buried in the school's rubble. But she realized her error a second later as the tail end of the lines faded while the front snaked forward. They more closely resembled veins; they pulsed slightly, carrying their magical ichor to some unknown destination.

A cold dread swept over her, reminding Chrys of that momentary sensation she'd felt in the cemetery on Sunday. She couldn't detect any off-putting scent this time, but given all the off-putting food being tossed around, she wasn't drawing any conclusions. She'd also never seen or heard of magic like this, but there was no doubt in her mind that it was related to what had gone down in the cafeteria. How could it not be?

"Out of the way!" Some boy pushed past her as more students ran out of the cafeteria, and Chrys stumbled backward.

In the second when her gaze flicked elsewhere, the lines disappeared. Chrys squinted at the wall, reached deep inside herself for that well of magic that would open her third eye as though she were scrying, but it was impossible to focus with the chaos around her.

Anushka grabbed her arm. "Mr. Ogden is coming," she said, referring to the vice principal. "Let's get to the library."

Only half-aware of what she was doing, Chrys nodded and let Anushka pull her through the crowd. Something very creepy was going on at school, like she'd needed another reason to loathe this place.

Chapter Thirteen

Lily

More than anything, Lily wanted to believe that whatever magic was infecting the school had to be Chrysanthemum's fault. While she might not literally be the demon Lily had (regrettably) accused her of being, if anyone in school was going to cast violent spells, it had to be her, or so Lily told herself. Except someone else *had* cast a hex recently, and it wasn't Chrysanthemum. And considering Lily didn't really know how to cast a hex, the possibility that the week's unfortunate events were due to her spell couldn't be ignored. Especially not when Lily considered where the magic was manifesting—first in choir, a class Chrysanthemum took, then during Chrysanthemum's lunch period (which was, unfortunately, also Lily's lunch period).

The only thing Lily couldn't account for was the timing; she'd cast her hex Wednesday night, but nothing had happened until Monday.

Nothing you noticed, her conscience clarified.

Most of the school might not be able to remember lunch trays flying of their own volition, but they had no trouble remembering a food fight, so this topic dominated Tuesday afternoon's gossip. Nothing like it had happened as far back as anyone could recall; the last Thornhaven High scandal had been two years ago when a couple of seniors had been caught spiking the hot chocolate at the school's annual Halloween bonfires.

The excited conversations provided plenty of cover for Lily's distracted and anxious state of mind, but she had no choice other than to focus now. The student council meeting was after school today, and as president, it was her responsibility to run it.

Bitterness ruined what should have been excitement as Lily headed into the classroom where they were meeting, but it was better than anxiety. After three years of serving on the student council, first as a regular member, then as treasurer, and last year as vice president, Lily had thought being elected council president would earn her some of kind of respect from her parents. Instead, they'd barely acknowledged the news. Lily wasn't entirely sure they'd been aware of what they were congratulating her for at the time.

But it was fine. Whatever. She'd accomplished it, and without using any magic to help herself get elected. She could be proud. And once she'd led their school to their most exciting year ever, she could be even more so.

Just as long as *exciting* had everything to do with pulling off a spectacular bonfire celebration and nothing to do with magical chaos.

The rest of the student council arrived as Lily was putting her nervous energy to use, moving desks into a loose discussion circle. Their chatter died down as they helped, but as soon as everyone was seated, the same conversations she'd been overhearing all afternoon picked up.

"Can we please focus?" Lily asked. "We have actual things we're supposed to accomplish. I have an agenda." She also was sick of hearing about the cafeteria incident and stressed enough as it was, but that was beside the point. "The bonfire event is next month, and it's our job to plan it."

"You think there'll be another food fight at the bonfires?" a student named Hunter asked with a laugh.

Lily narrowed her eyes at him. "There had better not be. The first thing we need to do . . ."

Her voice was drowned out by a few people laughing in response to Hunter's comment. Naturally that encouraged him to run with the scenario until no one was paying attention to Lily again.

It was the story of her life.

"I heard something weird happened to the choir yesterday, too," said another student. "Is that true?"

Lily clenched her teeth. Some of the normies were sensitive enough to magic that they'd remembered *something* weird had happened, and that, combined with conversations they must have overheard among the witches, was creating all sorts of vague stories. Lily was only surprised she hadn't heard anyone connect the two events before.

"Talk about it afterward." She tried not to raise her voice. Nothing said you'd lost control over a situation like raising your voice—a lesson she'd been completely unable to put into practice with Chrysanthemum.

Lily took a couple of deep breaths. It felt like the room was spinning around her, and why not? They weren't a full month into the school year, and everything else was already spinning out of her control.

"Don't forget the frogs in biology class," Evan muttered.

"I heard they twitched," one girl said.

"Is it true someone fainted?" Hunter asked.

Lily lowered her head in despair and turned to Evan. "What happened?"

He kept his voice low, since they were the only two witches on the council, but it hardly mattered since the others were all shouting rumors back and forth. "They didn't twitch. They started moving, almost like they were dancing."

Something that might have been panic forced an unsteady laugh from Lily's lips. "Aren't they supposed to be *dead*?"

"Long dead. Embalmed." Evan turned a little green. "Something is very not right."

"Okay, right. No, wrong. Yes." Lily took a few more deep breaths, but the room was spinning faster. Her knuckles whitened as she gripped the desk in front of her.

Could she have been responsible for this? *How* could she have been responsible for this? This felt dark and scary, even terrifying.

"The Society will do something about it," Lily said, as much to herself as to Evan. Not at all as reassured by this as she'd like, she turned her attention back to the rest of the room. "Enough! Please, let's get to work before something else strange happens, okay?"

That finally got everyone's attention. But while the other student council members quieted, it was as if the school itself took her words as a challenge. A disturbing noise emanated from the walls. Half rumble, half groan, it raised the hairs on Lily's arms, and not only hers, judging from the expressions around her.

Fresh chaos broke out, and from around the doorway, directly opposite where Lily sat, something black began to seep over the wall. Lily gasped. At first, the blackness reminded her of fissures, as though the wall were cracking, but it was too silent and smooth for that. Sinuous almost. It was more like ink, Lily decided, like an invisible hand was drawing on the wall.

"Look at that," she whispered to Evan.

"Look at what?"

She swallowed through what was definitely panic, no mistaking it this time. "Those lines. The blackness."

Evan shook his head. "I don't see anything."

Lily would have sworn her heart missed a beat. No, that couldn't be right. Evan was a witch. If the normies couldn't see those marks, that would be one thing. But if *Evan* couldn't . . . *What did that mean?* Was this proof that this really *was* her fault?

"Is this whole building going to collapse or what?" Hunter asked. The humor in his voice had vanished as he glanced around at the walls, one hand clutching his backpack in case he had to run for his life.

"Meeting adjourned." Lily slammed her chair back. Losing control of the meeting was no longer her biggest problem.

A couple of the more industrious student council members suggested rescheduling somewhere off school grounds, and under normal circumstances, Lily would have appreciated their sense of responsibility. At the moment, though, she couldn't think straight enough for that. She exchanged some mindless words about the topic, then escaped with everyone else into the hallway.

The black lines followed her.

Lily didn't notice until she exited the stairwell, and she shrieked with surprise. Luckily no one else was in the immediate vicinity to hear her, and she darted down the hallway, unable to leave the building fast enough. The closest door was up ahead. Her heart thudded in her ears.

The lines moved as quickly as she did. They never quite reached her, but Lily could see them from the corners of her eyes. They flowed like water and hummed like her pulse. Or maybe this was all her imagination. Stress catching up to her—a hallucination. She'd never heard of magic behaving this way.

Wetting her lips, she fumbled for the door before throwing it open.

The lines didn't follow her outside. The blackness stopped several feet from the door, and before it swung closed behind her, she could see the lines retreating. The walls cleared until the school was the same as it had always been.

Lily stared in disbelief, barely aware of the chilly wind on her neck.

It wasn't until she heard an engine revving in the parking lot that she snapped back to herself, and then only barely. Her hands didn't stop shaking even after she got in her car.

She didn't know how she was going to force herself back into school tomorrow morning, but if there was a chance she was responsible, she had no choice. If her hex had created this mess, she had to do something.

But had it?

The signs of foul magic hadn't been aimed at Chrysanthemum. So what if it *hadn't* been her? But then, why had *she* seen the blackness and not Evan?

Lily stuck one of her trembling fingers in her mouth and bit lightly without realizing what she was doing.

Evan wasn't the most powerful witch. Maybe he wasn't strong enough to see the lines? Surely that was as likely as him not seeing them because he hadn't caused them to appear.

That meant the first thing Lily needed to do was discover whether the lines were visible to other witches, and if so, who. Step two was observing how the magic reacted tomorrow, because she was certain there would be more tomorrow. Did it target Chrysanthemum again? Herself? Some random biology students? Step three . . . that would depend on one and two.

It wasn't much of a plan, but any plan made Lily feel better, a little more in control. She finally caught herself chewing on her finger and yanked it from her lips.

"Step zero point five," she said aloud, starting the car. "Strengthen my wards tonight."

CHAPTER FOURTEEN
Chrysanthemum

Chrys hadn't seen the black veins again after lunch (nor had she smelled anything off), but she wasn't convinced they'd disappeared. Every now and then, while sitting in her afternoon classes, she thought she caught movement from the corner of her eye, like a shadow slinking over the walls. But whenever she turned her head, nothing would be there.

Still, it was eerie . . . and given everything going on (she'd heard rumors about dancing frogs), she was looking forward to school on Wednesday even less than usual. Which was saying something.

Despite that, she arrived early, determined to tell Ms. LaPlant what she'd seen at lunch the day before. Waiting until witch school that night was out of the question.

After she'd locked up her bike, Chrys's fingers toyed with the piece of quartz she'd stuffed in her jacket pocket. Last night, she'd performed a basic protective spell on it. If any negative magic in the school focused on her, the crystal should absorb it.

Or some of it.

In theory.

Chrys wouldn't know if her spell worked until it was tested, which she'd prefer it not be, and—logically—she had no reason to believe it *would* be. As far as she knew, there had been three incidents of abnormal, seemingly uncontrolled magic. Only two of them had happened around her, and neither of those had been solely directed at her. But it was better to be safe than sorry, especially when she still had to deal with her Lily problem. All her usual defenses—her aesthetic, her glare, her snark—had been calibrated for mundane attacks. It had never occurred to her that one day she might need to prepare for magical ones, and in retrospect, that had been shortsighted.

Even so early, the school was lively when Chrys entered near the theater hallway. Several music groups met before classes, and none of the normie students seemed at all deterred by the fact that magic was going haywire around them. That normality was comforting for all of a minute before Chrys noticed that something wasn't right.

The veins were back.

She hadn't seen them at first because they stretched across a busy expanse of wall, one that showcased student artwork and photographs of previous years' music and theater productions. But now that Chrys *did* notice them, she didn't know how she'd missed them initially. Like yesterday, something about them seemed vaguely . . . alive. She suppressed a shiver and removed the quartz from her pocket.

The crystal remained clear. With a sigh of relief, Chrys put it away before anyone saw her, and she stepped closer to the wall to inspect the veins.

There was something slightly iridescent about the blackness. It gave Chrys the sense that it had *split the wall open*—magic pushing its way into the material world from the metaphysical one. Chrys raised a finger toward one of the lines, wondering if she could touch it, and it shuddered as though sensing her presence.

Chrys jumped back. The vein she'd gotten closest to thrummed, but the others faded until the wall was whole once more. With a quick check to make sure she was still alone, Chrys pulled the crystal from her pocket again and shook her head in confusion. The quartz was clear. That could mean her spell hadn't worked as she'd intended, or it could mean the way the veins reacted to her was a coincidence, or it could mean . . .

The vein moved. Like an optical illusion that challenged her brain to keep up, it slid down the wall and stopped at the corner. In her pocket, Chrys tapped the crystal with her fingers.

Well, what the hell. She'd been about to touch it. Following it was no riskier.

As soon as she approached the corner, the vein took off a second time, picking up speed as it went. More confused than ever, Chrys chased after it. Down another hallway, up the stairs—the vein paused around corners, as though waiting to make sure she kept coming.

The rational part of Chrys told her that allowing some clearly chaotic—if not downright *evil*—magic to take her for a walk was a bad idea, but so far the vein wasn't leading her anywhere she didn't already want to go. The more information she could share with Ms. LaPlant, the better, and the vein was heading toward the math classrooms.

Chrys kept right up with it until it slithered through a girls' bathroom doorway. Ms. LaPlant's classroom was mere feet away, and Chrys considered heading straight there. Ms. LaPlant was not going to tell her she was smart or brave for following some creepy magic.

On the other hand, it was just a bathroom. What was she likely to find in there—a demon?

Chrys flung open the door and found something equally nauseating.

Lily.

A squeak erupted from Lily's throat, but she quickly stifled it, shooting Chrys an annoyed glance. Chrys barely registered it. She couldn't even find it in her to laugh at Lily's surprise; her own was too great.

The walls around Lily were covered in more veins, a whole spiderweb of them crisscrossing the bathroom's hideous cinder block walls.

Judging by the fear on Lily's face, she could see them, too.

Had the vein she'd been following ended up among that mess? And if so, why? Chrys strained to see if she could find it—as though she'd be able to identify one black line from another—and when she bent closer, what she witnessed caused her to shiver all over again. More veins were forming in the wall as she watched, spreading out around her body like another web.

"Shit." Chrys took a step closer to the center of the bathroom, to Lily.

"You can see them?" Lily whispered. She stood up straighter, haughtiness erasing some of the fear on her face, but her voice wavered, giving her away.

Chrys tried to smirk but couldn't manage it. Thanks to her crystal, she'd been feeling pretty sanguine about the situation a minute ago. She wished she could find it amusing that Lily was afraid, but there were *so many* veins. Lily wasn't wrong to be concerned.

For that matter, why were the veins fixating on Lily, too? Chrys swallowed, pushing down her questions and the worries that were gaining control over her muscles. "Of course I can see them. I *am* a witch."

Lily scowled and glanced away. Then she seemed to resign herself to something and sighed, facing Chrys again. "Evan can't see them."

"Oh." Chrys's fingers twirled the quartz more violently in her pocket. Her list of questions was growing, but she didn't feel like confessing her ignorance to Lily. Asking questions would give Lily one more thing to look down on her for.

Besides, the veins around Lily were multiplying, and that didn't seem great. Especially not when Chrys glanced over her shoulder and saw that the ones surrounding *her* were doing the same. The spiderwebs were stretching toward each other, and Chrys wasn't sure she wanted to be in the middle when they met.

"Um . . ." Chrys attempted to point this out, but the manner in which Lily was scrutinizing her was making her self-conscious. This was *so* not the time to regress to her fourteen-year-old self who got all flustered being in the same space as Lily, but here they were, here were the veins, and words were sticking in Chrys's throat. For lack of better coherence, Chrys pointed, hoping that would both divert Lily's attention and get the message across.

It didn't, not immediately, and Chrys finally managed to shout Lily's name as she gestured with increasing franticness toward the wall above the sinks. The veins had almost met.

Lily turned, but it was too late. Chrys tried to run for the door, but that was also too late and her feet felt stuck in place. Two of the veins melted into each other and . . .

Nothing happened. Chrys's shoulders sagged with relief, and she dropped her arm.

And then water *exploded* out of the taps.

Lily shrieked, and Chrys's feet remembered how to move. She dashed for the door with Lily on her heels as the spray drenched them. Lily slammed the door shut, and they both collapsed against the wall.

Chrys swore, pushing wet hair out of her face, and scanned the hallway with a pounding heart. No veins were anywhere in sight, but that did not make her feel much better.

Lily whimpered as she blotted water off her cheek with a tissue. Chrys could practically feel her hesitating, internally debating whether to say more about what had happened.

Unsure whether she wanted to hear more, Chrys dropped her gaze to her clothes, assessing the damage. It was just water, but until she dried off, she was going to be cold and uncomfortable. It was easier to focus on that than on what she'd seen, and it allowed her to ignore Lily. Or pretend to.

The first bell would be coming soon. The hallway was growing noisy, and it would be only a matter of time before someone approached them with questions about why they were wet. Lily must have been having similar thoughts (coupled with a desire to not be seen talking to Chrys). As Chrys more closely inspected her backpack's contents (all fine, luckily), Lily abruptly rose and strode away.

Chrys sighed, torn between relief, frustration, and—most disturbingly—a sense of disappointment.

Stupid. Lily probably didn't know anything more than Chrys did, not really. Therefore, nothing useful could come from talking to her about this, and Chrys had no reason for being disappointed about losing the opportunity. The only person Chrys should talk to was Ms. LaPlant, and she was running out of time for that.

Before she did, Chrys reached into her pocket and pulled out the quartz. It had turned a dull gray.

Chapter Fifteen

Lily

For only the second time in her life (and, coincidentally, the second time this month), Lily dreaded going to witch school. She couldn't even blame Chrysanthemum—although if Chrysanthemum weren't the demon she was, Lily would never have lost her temper and hexed her, and if that hex was responsible for what was going on at school, then, in a way, so was Chrysanthemum. That was the sort of twisted logic that Sonia would describe as *pitiful,* however, and Lily's conscience wasn't buying it.

Worse, all through math class, Lily could have sworn that Ms. LaPlant's gaze was boring a hole into her forehead. That every time there was a strange noise in the hallway, or whenever a chair squeaked, Ms. LaPlant turned her way.

It didn't help that other people *did* stare, but that was to be expected when her right side was soaked. She hadn't dared go in another bathroom before classes started, so she'd used her car mirror to fix her hair while she composed herself. Nothing could be done for the rest of her, and truth be told, Lily had barely noticed the wet clothes once she'd calmed down enough to think clearly.

Chrysanthemum could see the lines, too.

No one else had, or possibly no one else could, and Lily was starting to suspect it was the latter. After the bathroom incident, Lily had seen a couple of lines by the girls' locker room during gym class. They were nothing like what she'd experienced earlier, although still terrifying, but when she'd tried to show them to Sonia, Sonia hadn't known what she was talking about.

Without asking every witch in the high school, Lily could tell herself she was jumping to conclusions, but she wasn't buying that any more than her conscience was buying that this was Chrysanthemum's fault. In fact, the way lines had formed in the wall around her and Chrysanthemum in the bathroom struck Lily as pretty damning evidence that whatever was going on, it was somehow tied to them both.

So, yeah, witch school was the last place she wanted to be right now. As she took her seat while her classmates discussed the unusual magical events, she felt . . . well, it could only be called *dread*.

The ancient radiator in the Historical Society classroom rattled as heat began flowing through it, and Lily's brain rattled with it. The room alternated between too hot and too cold, and a few students were wearing charm bags stuffed with herbs (agrimony and garlic, among others, given the smell), no doubt hoping it would protect them from whatever was going on at the high school. (As for their effectiveness, Lily had no idea, but the pungent odors emanating from all the bags certainly repelled *her*.)

Everything in this room was giving her a headache.

Lily let her pen roll onto the floor so she had an excuse to twist around as she picked it up, sneaking a glance at Chrysanthemum. As usual, Chrysanthemum's face was a bored mask, her eyes far away and her lips slightly downturned. But under the desk, her feet shifted restlessly, as though the same nervous energy in Lily's veins were coursing through her own.

There was something oddly comforting about that, a relief to know that Chrysanthemum wasn't so magically superior that she was impervious to the situation.

Of course, Lily already knew that, too. Chrysanthemum had seemed anything but chill in the bathroom earlier. So whatever. Lily didn't know why she was fixating on Chrysanthemum's feelings.

She retrieved her pen and spun back around in her chair. What was Chrysanthemum *thinking*, though? Had the bathroom incident scared her as much as it had Lily? Was she angry? Did she suspect Lily had something to do with it?

"Lily?"

Damn. She hadn't heard the last five minutes' worth of instruction that had come from Ms. LaPlant's mouth. "Yes?"

Ms. LaPlant looked at her with concern, and that made her insides writhe with guilt. "I asked a question, but I don't think you were paying attention."

Her cheeks burned, and Lily shook her head. "Sorry. I'm distracted."

At least the reason why was so obvious that no one could fault her. Even the most magically obtuse normies knew something strange was happening at school. It was all anyone had been discussing tonight before Ms. LaPlant had called the class to order.

"Right." Ms. LaPlant slid off the table where she'd been sitting. "I know that what's going on at the high school is disturbing and disruptive. The Society is working to contain the problem, and everyone needs to stay calm until they do."

"Why haven't they yet?" Sonia asked. "Can't they put more wards around the school or something?"

Ms. LaPlant took a sip from her coffee cup and checked the time. "It's not that simple, unfortunately. Wards need to be put in place before a spell hits. Otherwise, it's like you're locking the doors after the thief has already broken in. The spell either needs to be revoked, which is impossible without knowing what it was, overpowered, or countered. Either of those last two options will be difficult but doable in time. For now, the best that can be done is to suppress the spell's effects, and that's in progress. It took a couple of days to prepare, but hopefully, tomorrow you'll have a normal day."

Lily tightened her grip on her pen. Revoked? If she was the one who cast the out-of-control hex, she was probably the best hope they had of revoking it. But everything she'd learned about revoking a spell made it sound extremely hard.

Magic did not like to be undone.

Think of a spell as blowing on a dandelion puff, her ninth-grade witch school teacher had said. *Those seeds are your intent. Your breath is your power that sets them free, and once you have, they're carried on the wind to plant effects. To revoke a spell is to inhale deeply and strongly enough to summon them all back after they've scattered, after they may have sprouted roots.*

A witch needed excellent control to do that, and Lily had to face it—if she'd had that, her spell wouldn't have turned into this catastrophe in the first place.

Possibly her spell. She had no definitive proof that she'd done it, although evidence was mounting.

Ms. LaPlant set out a white candle. "The best thing you can to do is to talk to any of your elders if you have information about what's happening or what might have caused it. The next best thing is to strengthen your personal wards to keep yourself safe. The magic seems to be getting more aggressive"—here, for the first time, Lily knew for sure that her teacher's gaze flicked toward her—"so being protected gives us all one less thing to worry about."

Lily started to point out that her wards hadn't helped her, but a new realization dawned. Perhaps Ms. LaPlant knew about the faucets, and that was why she'd looked at Lily. Her classroom was right across the hall from the bathroom.

And there was a good chance Chrysanthemum had talked to her afterward.

This epiphany, which could also explain why she thought Ms. LaPlant had been watching her during math class, was such a relief that Lily didn't bother to bring up her wards. After all, she could be wrong about them not helping. What if the incident could have been a lot worse?

Along with the rest of the class, Lily got out a white candle while Ms. LaPlant lit a censer filled with frankincense and myrrh. They'd gone off lesson, but more protection never hurt. Considering Lily's plan for after class, she might need it.

Chapter Sixteen
Chrysanthemum

Chrys stepped out of the Historical Society building and breathed deeply of the crisp night air. Woodsmoke overlaid the normal saltiness on the breeze, sweet and pungent and worlds better than the jumbled stink suffusing the classroom. Too many people had created their own charm bags. Plenty of herbs could be used for protective spells, but no one should be subjected to the scent of all the possible combinations at once.

While Chrys understood the urge—charging a crystal the way she had was more challenging, and herbs were cheaper to replenish—she couldn't approve. Who wanted to go around stinking like old socks? The joke was on her, though, because she had only a few more pieces of quartz left. Maybe she should give old socks a chance.

Although the stink wasn't the cause, Chrys was in a rush to get home. The rest of her day, post-bathroom, had been unexciting, but this morning's adventure had drained her. Part of her had stupidly hoped that by her telling Ms. LaPlant what she'd seen, the mystery would be solved. Ms. LaPlant would either know exactly what was causing the weirdness, or she would take the information to the Society, and they would know.

Funny how disappointment, even when your expectations were unrealistic, left you wanting a nap.

"I'll meet you at the car," Chrys overheard Lily saying, and that jostled her into moving faster. She'd seen enough of Lily for the day.

Yawning, Chrys walked down the stone steps to the parking lot.

"Chrysanthemum." Her name was a half whisper out of Lily's mouth, an obvious attempt to get her attention without ensnaring anyone else's notice. But even so, Chrys was not expecting Lily to call out for her, so while she heard her name, it didn't register that Lily was speaking to her until she heard it again. "Chrysanthemum."

A hand landed on her arm, and Chrys nearly jumped out of her skin. Lily was inches away, that same anxious and conflicted expression on her face from the morning.

Something inside Chrys twitched, a long-buried piece of her that once would have been gleeful to have Lily initiate a conversation. She scowled her displeasure at it. "What?"

"Can I talk to you for a minute?"

The *no* danced on Chrys's tongue, but curiosity won out (never mind the long-buried piece, which softened in the face of Lily's distress). Chrys raised her eyebrows in a *go on* gesture.

More people were leaving the building, and Lily frowned. "Not here." She started moving away, and Chrys rolled her eyes.

Following Lily, she decided, would be too enthusiastic. She didn't move. Whatever Lily had to say about the incident this morning—because that was what it had to be about—could be said with an audience. Chrys had already told Ms. LaPlant everything, and she didn't care if Lily didn't want to be seen talking to her.

"Please. Come on." Lily stepped toward her and grabbed Chrys's hand to pull her along.

The pure shock of Lily's skin on hers sent Chrys's feet and pulse flying. Chrys didn't touch anyone—she wasn't a hugger—and she certainly didn't touch Lily.

Of all that had happened today, that satiny skin contact had her mind reeling the most strongly.

Lily seemed to realize immediately what she'd done. She dropped her hand and looked at it as though she no longer knew what to do with the offending appendage. Chop it off, maybe, before it contaminated the rest of her. Blood rushed to her cheeks, and she stuffed her hands in her jacket pockets as though she'd like to pretend they didn't exist.

"Sorry," she mumbled. "Please, just come here."

Baffled, Chrys followed Lily around to the granite courtyard in front of the Historical Society building. Cauldron-shaped planters had joined the stone urns around the stairs for the season, each bursting with purple, orange, and yellow chrysanthemums that looked faded and ghostly in the building's lights. Below her feet, the only nod to the Historical Society's true mission were pentacles carved into the rocks, one centered in each cardinal direction. Above, a few streaks of turquoise clung to the sky in the west, velvety enough to almost touch.

Lily paused in front of a wrought iron bench and bit her lip.

Chrys waited. The jolt from Lily's touch had worn off on the brief walk, and irritable tiredness was overtaking her.

"We're the only two people who can see the lines," Lily said at last.

Before class had begun tonight, Lily had been asking the other witches if they'd seen *creepy black lines* around the school. But clearly, no one had, and Chrys didn't like the implications. "We don't know that for sure. They're not everywhere. They come and go. Maybe other people haven't encountered them yet."

Lily crossed her arms. "You believe that?"

Chrys didn't. "I just don't understand why it would only be us."

"Me neither!" But guilt flashed over Lily's face, leaving Chrys with the distinct sense that Lily *did* have thoughts on the matter. "I mean, it's obviously some kind of negative energy, and you hexed me a couple weeks ago, so . . . "

That was what this was about? Chrys's blood warmed. "A tiny hex that was quickly undone. I can't believe you're blaming me for *this*, except I also totally can. You are deranged. You know that? I . . ."

Chrys swallowed down the *I hate you*. Lily didn't deserve the satisfaction of knowing she'd gotten under Chrys's skin. It flew in the face of her Ignore Lily plan.

I hate you.

This time, the words came back to Chrys on the wind, a memory of spitting them out in her bedroom, and the feeling of relief and emptiness afterward. A feeling that was awfully reminiscent of releasing the power in a spell.

Anger's heat drained from Chrys's blood. She hadn't been *trying* to hex Lily, but if she'd done so, that was about as vague and dangerous a spell as could be cast.

Except she wasn't that powerful. She couldn't have done it.

Except she'd been full of rage. Strong emotions heightened power.

And that vagueness—it could explain why the effects had taken so long to manifest. Even the smell at school, the smell she'd noticed on the wind—those could have been early signs of the negative energy hovering around her.

Chrys closed her eyes. No. A thousand damn nos. She was not accepting the possibility that she might be responsible. It didn't make sense. More to the point, she refused. Completely.

These Thornhaven witches, and Lily first among them, had treated her like a second-class witch from the moment she arrived. Whatever was going on, it was their mess. If she couldn't be one of them, she was not taking responsibility for their problems.

"I'm not blaming you. I'm just . . ." Lily's fingers tapped along her lips, as though she hadn't even heard the venom in Chrys's voice. As though it were irrelevant. Just like she always seemed to think Chrys was irrelevant. "I'm only saying there's bad energy between us, and we've manifested it a few times, and maybe this is related. I'm trying to figure this out."

"Well, figure it out on your own. I had nothing to do with it." She shoved her hands in her pockets and stormed off.

Lily's feet pounded the stones after her, and she darted in front of Chrys so that they almost collided. Chrys took a step back as Lily's warm breath washed over her face. This close, it was easier to see how deep the worry in Lily's eyes was. The birthmark on her left cheek stood out against her skin, which seemed paler.

Again, Chrys softened a touch.

"Wait," Lily said, and her arm moved, but she wisely dropped it back to her side before getting closer. "If it concerns the two of us, don't you think we need to talk about it? Together?"

Chrys mentally clamped that irritating twinge of empathy and crushed the life out of it. If, and it was a big if, a spell she'd inadvertently cast had gone wrong, she would have to think about how to deal with it. Any so-called assistance Lily might provide would not improve that thought process.

"I told you—no," Chrys said, doing her best to keep her tone and her face blank of her conflicting emotions. "You heard Ms. LaPlant. Let the Society deal with it. I know you think you're the greatest witch to ever cast a spell, but trust me: you're not good enough to fix this on your own."

She yanked her hood up against the wind and huffed the rest of her way to her bike, and Lily didn't follow. That was good. But the possibility that Lily had put in her head, the memory of last Wednesday night, chased her all the way home.

Chapter Seventeen
Lily

Birds were going mad around the town hall.

Lily parked her car in the Historical Society's lot Saturday morning and stared, unsure whether she wanted to leave the safety of its confines. Everyone knew what happened when something riled up the seagulls, but these weren't seagulls, and this scene more closely resembled something out of *The Lord of the Rings* than a gross-out comedy.

At least a dozen crows flew in a circle above the building's clock tower. Mottled gray clouds covered the sky, making for a warmer-than-usual morning, but also contributing to the ominous display. Lily wouldn't have been surprised to see the clouds part, opening a portal to some other dimension, and a chill ran down her back.

Since the Society had cast dampening spells Wednesday night, school had been calm, but the way things had been escalating before that, an open portal didn't seem entirely impossible. Nor did it seem impossible that those spells had caused the magic to slither its way into town in search of new opportunities.

Or this could be her projecting a lot of anxiety. Lily was here for weekend two of her unfair, unjust, and undeserved punishment, and having to put up with Chrysanthemum all day did kind of negatively impact her mood.

She watched for a few more minutes, but despite her expectations, the clouds remained unchanged and the old brick building wasn't sucked into some kind of magical vortex. For the moment, the crows were just hanging out, acting creepy. People walked down the street without incident, although most were keeping an eye upward. Given her suspicions about her link to the magic, Lily questioned whether she'd get inside the Historical Society with its strong wards unscathed, but she couldn't sit in her car all day, either.

She needn't have worried. She slipped inside the Historical Society building without issue, and she redirected her thoughts to the more pressing matter ahead of her—dealing with Chrysanthemum after Chrysanthemum had rejected her suggestion to work together.

Her cheeks burned, and her mind had the gall to drift to the worst possible part of their whole interaction—when she'd actually grabbed Chrysanthemum's hand. Shock had frozen Lily before it had spurred her to move from embarrassment. It had fried the words she'd meant to say and left her without the strong argument she'd planned to make for cooperating. It was no wonder Chrysanthemum had refused.

But, in the end, maybe that was for the best. The suggestion that they work together had been born of desperation. On Wednesday, Lily had been afraid. (Okay, fine, she was still afraid, but she wasn't panicking as much and was therefore thinking more clearly.)

If this was her spell that had somehow gotten out of control, then she didn't need Chrysanthemum to fix it. If she needed anyone, it was a wiser, more powerful, and more knowledgeable elder, but Lily wasn't ready to confess to casting a hex. The trouble she'd get in would be immense, and there were too many unknowns for her to be entirely convinced this was her fault.

But she could figure it out without Chrysanthemum. It would be better this way. She wouldn't have to deal with Chrysanthemum's unsociable attitude. She wouldn't accidentally touch Chrysanthemum (ew) because she was stressed and not thinking clearly. Or look at her distracting eyes, eyes that seemed to see right through Lily's skin.

Eyes that met her gaze the moment Lily entered the library, causing a wave of heat to wash over Lily's body.

Chrysanthemum was dressed in a pair of faded black leggings, a plain T-shirt, and a flannel shirt over that. Even that didn't sport any color, merely more black and gray. Pathetic. But Chrysanthemum's hair was pulled back in a messy bun, and her irises more than made up for the blahness of her clothes. Lily took off her backpack as an excuse to glance away, trying to ignore the annoying flush.

Honestly, she was *not* scared of Chrysanthemum. Not even after the laughing hex. Less so, actually. Lily had rebuilt her wards after that incident, and they were stronger than ever. Nothing Chrysanthemum could send her way would get through, so it was frustrating beyond belief that her body insisted on acting like she was nervous.

Lily took a deep breath, wishing she'd grabbed a drink from Black Cat.

"Instructions and a note." Chrysanthemum pushed the paper she'd been reading toward Lily, then walked away.

Lily snatched it. Last weekend they'd managed to work without speaking to each other. She'd been hoping to continue that trend, but no one from the Society was here this morning to orient them and supervise. For the moment, all they had was exactly what Chrysanthemum had said: a set of instructions on how to proceed.

Grimacing, Lily read everything twice. These tasks could take all day and then some. Almost as infuriating was the fact that she was going to be exhausted by the time she got home, where she could mope around the house because she was freaking grounded.

Once Sara's crisis had passed, Lily had protested the unfairness of it all to her parents, hoping that they'd at least try to get her out of the library work. Spending every Saturday breathing in paint fumes and mildew took away from her schoolwork, and that had struck Lily as a winning argument. Her parents had disagreed. They'd seemed to think this whole working-with-Chrysanthemum deal was a good idea—witches needed to stick together and all—and since Lily was grounded, she'd have plenty of time for her assignments.

The wrongness of it stung like a slap, and the pain hadn't subsided over the last two weeks.

Four hours later, Lily was still ruminating on how far her senior year had gotten off track. Her tarot reading, which had seemed so clear, felt more like a burden than a glimpse of a path forward. She felt *nothing* for Luke, so she resisted flirting with him. Even if pretending that she liked him was the wisest course of action to kick-start a relationship, faking it felt wrong. And who was she kidding, anyway? She'd barely thought about him at all since she'd begun fighting with Chrysanthemum, which was a painful irony.

After a hasty lunch that she'd eaten while texting with Sonia, Lily hurried back to work. Last weekend, she and Chrysanthemum had been released before four o'clock, but their to-do list was longer this week. Plus, painting over the dark green trim with a fresh, bright white was tedious work.

Lily alternated between taping one window's worth of trim and painting another's to keep the task from being too monotonous. But there were several large windows, each with lots of tiny pieces of wood trim and muntins, and it was a painfully slow process if she didn't want to be sloppy about it. Which she didn't.

Unlike Chrysanthemum.

Chrysanthemum seemed to be taking the taping part as a suggestion. She'd started out doing it, but soon abandoned the task. As a result, Chrysanthemum had painted *herself* significantly more than Lily had. Not to mention the walls. But when Lily had pointed this out—the only words she'd spoken to Chrysanthemum all day—Chrysanthemum had snapped that they were painting the walls after they finished the trim, so who cared if some trim paint got on them?

No one should, that was who. The logic felt like another slap in the face, and Lily's cheeks still stung from the last ones.

"Intent matters," she'd snapped back. "Sloppy work makes for sloppy results."

She'd dug in after that, doing her best to be even more meticulous. Unfortunately, that meant she was working even more slowly than she had previously, but it would be worth it when someone came by to check up on their work and Lily's was praised and Chrysanthemum was told to be more careful. Surely that would happen.

Fortified by the thought, Lily slid her ladder another foot to the right. Through the window, she had a clear view into downtown, and it didn't help her mood. The trees were starting to rain down leaves, and the colors that were left were nothing short of spectacular. Crowns of fiery oranges, golden yellows, and cozy reds made it look like the streets were ablaze. The town had finally pulled out all the stops, and every storefront was a vision of black-and-orange Halloween vibes. If she closed her eyes, Lily could practically smell the air, filled with the scents of pine needles and woodsmoke.

She stretched her arm farther, hoping she could reach the last bit of trim above her head without moving the ladder again, when a flicker in the hard-to-reach corner startled her, and she grabbed the ladder before she could slip.

Every window and doorway in the building was warded, one reason Lily had felt safer the moment she'd stepped inside. The wards were old but constantly reinforced by her father and other board members, and the elaborate magical sigils they used remained visible for days after they'd been updated. On those days, it was possible to see how they moved as they reacted to threats.

Lily had always assumed that those threats were nothing more than normies poking too close to the Society for the building's comfort. That was why, although she was initially startled by a shadowy movement, she didn't think anything of it. By the time she realized it had been too long since the wards had been refreshed for her to see them anywhere else, something moved again.

Not a ward, but a thin, pulsating black line.

Lily's hand had been hovering inches above it, and she yanked it back.

Impossible. For a second, she refused to believe what she was seeing. Whatever had been going on at the high school couldn't have traveled here. The Historical Society was the best-protected spot in all of Thornhaven.

But before Lily could finish that thought, before she dared look behind her to see if there were more lines or to consider whether she should alert Chrysanthemum, the wall around the window lit up like a neon sign. The warding sigils (there were always three per window) flared with power, spinning and writhing.

And then they burst. Silently, in a flash of multi-tinge-colored light.

Lily screamed, and she instinctively reached up and shielded her eyes, turning away as she did. Her foot slid on the rung, but with only one hand on the ladder, she couldn't steady herself. This time, she lost her balance for good. Lily crashed to the floor, pulling the ladder—and the bucket of paint on its shelf—down with her.

The ladder landed partially on top of her, and white paint exploded everywhere. The trim. The windowpanes. The wall. The floor. The tables and nearest bookshelves, which were, thankfully, covered in drop cloths. It landed all over Lily, too, spattering her in the face and hair. The paint can clattered to the floorboards and rolled toward her, somehow vomiting up even more Avalanche White (such a hideously appropriate it name, it turned out) on its journey. How there had been any left inside had to be magic.

Lily lay there, too stunned by everything that had happened to notice she was in pain and too horrified to remember she wasn't alone until she heard Chrysanthemum's voice.

"Are you okay?" Chrysanthemum must have turned as the paint can hit the floor, because white flecks splattered one side of her face and clothes.

Lily almost laughed; Chrysanthemum would never be caught dead in white.

She was losing her mind.

"I . . ." Embarrassment flooded Lily's veins. After she'd been lecturing Chrysanthemum about being careful, she was the one who'd created a hellish mess. Lily looked like a fool, and she knew it.

Pride, or a sense of self-preservation, it was impossible to tell which, urged Lily to snap something nasty back. Her tongue itched with a *do I look okay?* retort, but something else, something Lily wasn't sure of, stopped her.

Chrysanthemum wasn't smirking, and there had been nothing mean in the way she'd asked the question. She looked genuinely worried.

Lily didn't know what to make of that, but it melted the snippy retort right off her tongue. "I think so. The wards, though, I think they all broke."

Chrysanthemum wet her lips, then seemed to realize they were splattered with paint. She grimaced, wiping her mouth on the inside of her flannel shirt. "I saw. The ones on the door, I mean. This seems bad."

That had to be a vast understatement, but Lily couldn't make fun of her for it. Lily's own brain, her emotions, and her mouth were struggling to link up. Although, she *did* feel the tiniest bit vindicated for having asked Chrysanthemum to work together on the hex problem, and she hoped Chrysanthemum was also feeling the tiniest bit of regret for refusing.

"Here." Chrysanthemum shoved the ladder over, making it easier for Lily to worm her way out from beneath it.

Lily's knees throbbed with a pain that she tried not to show as she sat up. Her palms, too, were scraped, or so she assumed. It was hard to tell beneath the layer of white paint. She must look a hundred times more ridiculous than Chrysanthemum. The paint spatter, combined with the mostly fallen-apart bun, softened Chrysanthemum's stark features. Or maybe it was that she wasn't acting evil at the moment. Whatever the reason, Lily had a hard time glancing away as Chrysanthemum set the ladder aside.

This was weird, and she had to snap out of this daze. The wards had broken. Black lines were slithering around the library walls. Of all the times for Chrysanthemum to distract her . . .

Lily closed her eyes and just as quickly opened them when something in the room went thump. Her heart thumped with it. "What was that?"

Chrysanthemum spun around slowly, and Lily couldn't fail to notice that she'd inched closer to her. Almost protectively. "There!"

With her gaze, Lily followed the direction Chrysanthemum pointed in and caught a book sliding off one of the shelves. Even though she watched it move, the sound it made when it hit the floor jostled Lily's frayed nerves.

Another book on another shelf followed. Then two.

Chrysanthemum started to say something, but she never got to finish because things escalated rapidly until the library resembled a book tornado—or, on deeper reflection, it was like the books were imitating the crows that had been circling the town hall this morning. One zipped by Lily, its pages and cover flapping in a poor imitation of flight.

Screaming for help, Lily crawled across the paint-sticky drop cloth and sheltered under a table. Chrysanthemum had started off trying to minimize the damage by grabbing for books to prevent them from flying around, but she gave up quickly and crouched next to Lily.

Then, just as unceremoniously as it had started, the chaos stopped. The books fell to the floor, and the silence that ensued was as loud as anything Lily had ever heard.

Warily, she inched out from beneath the table, surveying the lifeless books and empty shelves with dismay. Chrysanthemum climbed to her feet on the table's other side. She wore a devastated expression as she gently ran a finger down the spine of a book that had landed with its cover splayed open, paint oozing from between its pages like white blood.

Footsteps heralded the approach of Mr. Stephens, and Lily broke away from gaping at the mess to face the Society's librarian.

"Oh no." He rubbed his eyes. "Are you girls okay?"

"The wards," Lily began.

"The books," said Chrysanthemum.

Mr. Stephens nodded, somehow managing to appear even older than he was. "The wards broke all over the building. Luckily, this is the only room that appears to have been damaged by whatever did it."

Luckily, perhaps, but it wasn't a coincidence. As much as Lily wanted to believe that she and Chrysanthemum weren't involved in whatever was going on, this made it a lot harder for her to do so. She glanced over at Chrysanthemum, and her nemesis, who didn't seem especially nemesis-like at the moment, met her gaze. For once, Lily managed not to look away.

For once, she thought she and Chrysanthemum might be agreeing on something.

Chapter Eighteen
Chrysanthemum

What the hell had she been thinking by agreeing to this?

Chrys had assumed they'd be stuck at the Historical Society until all hours of the night cleaning up the mess, but Mr. Stephens had sent them away for their safety. Chrys wasn't at all certain that leaving the building was safer than staying, but she also hadn't looked forward to the extra work. So here she was, twenty minutes later, as cleaned up as she could get in a Society bathroom, walking to Black Cat Coffee with Lily.

She hadn't had any caffeine yet, but her hands were jittery, and it was only partially due to having witnessed a bunch of powerful wards burning out and surviving a book tornado. (Chrys's heart hurt when she thought of the poor damaged books.) She worried she might truly be somewhat responsible for what was happening and worried even more that if she admitted it, Lily would get her in such big trouble that Chrys could be kicked out of the Historical Society.

Trying to ignore these thoughts, Chrys glanced toward the town hall. The ominous clouds and the circling birds had vanished. The sky was a clear, sunny blue over Thornhaven's downtown. These blocks were stuffed with two- and three-story shops with their quaint historical New England facades, weathered brick abutting brick and brightly painted trim struggling to maintain its color in the face of the harsh Atlantic weather. Heavy wood signs hung above the doors—THE CAULDRON SUPPLY, THE BLUE MERMAID TAVERN, BLACK CAT COFFEE—and warmly colored leaves carpeted the cobblestone sidewalk beneath them. Chrys loved everything about the atmosphere, but given that flecks of dried paint she'd missed were making her cheek itch, the scenery and weather were of little comfort.

The bell over the door jingled cheerfully, and a warm, coffee-and-cinnamon-scented breeze brushed Chrys's nose as they entered. The shop smelled of perfection, the first calming moment of her day. As much as she loved coffee, she rarely allowed herself to indulge at Black Cat. Everything on the island was expensive, and the downtown catered to tourists as much as to the locals, which made it extra pricey. But Lily had suggested they come here to talk, and Chrys had decided she'd earned a hot drink. Not just for surviving the mess at the Historical Society, but also because if she had to deal with Lily outside of school multiple times in one week, she deserved to treat herself with some of that money she'd made over the summer. It might be the only way she could get through the conversation.

A few minutes later, she carried her pumpkin spice latte over to the secluded table where Lily was breaking off a piece of a very familiar-looking confection. Chrys considered telling Lily her mother had made those chocolate gingerbread cookies, then thought better of it.

"So?" Chrys asked, taking the chair across from Lily and really looking at her for the first time all day. Or, well, the first time when her mind wasn't clouded by panic.

Lily wore a deep maroon Thornhaven High sweatshirt that brought out the red in her hair. And in her lips. Chrys told herself that it made Lily look like one of the sugar maples outside, but that didn't explain why she stared at the bite of cookie Lily popped in her mouth. A couple of dots of white paint stuck to Lily's neck like birthmarks, and Chrys curled her fingers around her mug.

This was such a mistake. The need to have their conversation not be overheard warred with Chrys's desire to keep her distance.

Perhaps Lily shared her thoughts, because she took the lid off a ceramic mug that was sitting next to her drink, and suddenly the din of other conversations, the espresso machine, and the music drifting through the speakers vanished.

Chrys blinked. "You carry around a mug with a silence charm on it?"

"It's the shop's," Lily said. "You can rent them for private conversations."

"Oh." She'd had no idea, since she so rarely came here, but Lily's tone suggested she thought Chrys was painfully a normie for not being aware. Chrys bit the inside of her cheek and took a sip of her drink to cover for her lack of a scathing retort.

Lily wrinkled her perfect, tiny nose as she inhaled deeply. "Is that pumpkin spice?"

"Yeah?"

Looking confused, Lily tilted her head to the side and wrapped her hands around what appeared to be a giant mug of hot chocolate.

Chrys stiffened, the latte no match for her growing impatience. "What?"

"You didn't strike me as a PSL kind of person."

"What do you think a person like me drinks? Battery acid?" Wasn't it enough that she curated her entire aesthetic to convey a *back off* attitude? Did she have to watch what she ate, too?

Lily shifted. "I don't know. Black coffee? To match your clothes?"

There was some logic there, Chrys supposed. Then she wondered why she was giving Lily credit for insulting her and why the absurdity made her want to laugh. No wonder Lily usually ignored her. She was unintentionally hilarious when she tried to be cruel. The kids Chrys had known before she moved to Thornhaven could really have given Lily some lessons. It was almost like Lily was missing that killer instinct, but that couldn't be right.

Honestly, trying to understand the witch princess's brain had to be an exercise in futility. It was probably filled with pink glitter and singing animals and assumptions of her own superiority.

"I don't drink my clothes," Chrys said, fighting down her laugh.

"I guess not." Lily's fingers rubbed the notebook in front of her, and it dawned on Chrys that Lily was as anxious as she was. But why? She assumed Lily didn't want to talk to her any more than Chrys wanted to talk to Lily, but Lily was the one who had insisted.

Chrys took another sip of her too-hot coffee and let it burn her tongue. She did not care what Lily was feeling. She barely cared what Lily was thinking, but since that was why she was here . . .

"What's left to talk about that you didn't accuse me of on Wednesday?" Chrys asked.

To her surprise, Lily winced. "I wasn't accusing you of anything. Stop being so dramatic."

Chrys snorted. "I am hardly the dramatic one here."

"Sure, you don't dress in a dramatic fashion at all just because you look like you're always ready for a good funeral." Lily rolled her eyes, but she plowed on before Chrys could object. "I've been making notes about what's going on at school.

Since we're the only two people who can see the black lines, I thought it would be helpful to hear about where you've spotted them. I also still think we're connected to what's going on."

Be calm, Chrys reminded herself. Lily opened her notebook, and predictably, it was neat and organized. Chrys took back what she'd thought about Lily's brain and glitter. No way would Lily tolerate glitter; it was too messy. Pink sequins, on the other hand . . .

Still, part of her was impressed by the effort Lily was putting into this, and seeing pages of Lily's handwriting was making her more curious. If Lily had suspected Chrys was behind the magic, surely she'd have gone to Ms. LaPlant by now. That they were sitting here, that Lily wanted to share her observations instead, was suggestive. Of what, Chrys wasn't sure, but it couldn't be as straightforward as she'd assumed.

"Okay, go on," Chrys said, trying to hide her curiosity and the fact that she was the teeniest bit impressed by Lily's efforts.

Over the next few minutes, Lily described all that she'd observed throughout the week. Chrys had already heard much of it, gathered in bits and pieces if she hadn't been around to witness the particular event. But Lily had more details, as well as plenty of questions about what Chrys had experienced. Lily wrote everything down and chewed on her pen thoughtfully.

"Here's the thing," Lily said at last. "We can't count math class because Ms. LaPlant has wards around the room."

"As we now know, wards are not infallible," Chrys pointed out.

"True, so we should keep that in mind, but Ms. LaPlant's room is unusual. And if we ignore that nothing has happened during her class, there's a pattern. First, the incidents have always happened when one of us is present, except for the bio class. But I was in the classroom next door to the lab when it happened, and you were in the room almost directly above it. The bio lab was the midpoint between us. Most importantly, the incidents are always more violent when we're near each other—the cafeteria, the bathroom, and today in the library."

Chrys pulled her feet up onto the chair so she could hug her knees. The total number of incidents was small, and calling any of them *violent* was a stretch, but coupled with her and Lily seeing the lines . . . she hated to admit it, but she could see why Lily thought it was a pattern.

She searched her brain for an argument to refute the theory, but she could feel Lily watching her, and it made thinking difficult. Chrys wished she were wearing a hoodie so she could hide her head inside it. Instead, she tugged down her flannel's sleeves and buried her hands in them, wishing she could disappear completely.

It was ironic, after all that time she'd spent wanting Lily to notice her. Finally, Lily had, and Chrys longed to fade back into the shadows. She didn't know what was wrong with her. Besides the obvious—she didn't *care* if Lily noticed her anymore.

Right. Didn't care. Exactly why she was trying to hide in her shirt and escape Lily's very, very intense gaze.

Clearing her throat, Chrys dropped her feet back to the floor. She could figure out what was wrong with her later. For the moment, the trick was acting like she was fine.

And damn it—she hadn't found a serious hole to poke in Lily's theory. She wanted Lily to be wrong, and instead she was forced to acknowledge that Lily might be clever.

"I still don't understand why we'd be involved," Chrys said, since it was the best defense she had.

Lily cast her gaze to her unfinished hot chocolate. "The hex—"

"Was small, to the point, and thoroughly removed."

"Yes." Lily sighed heavily. "But what if, somehow, some of that ill intent lingered?"

"I've had lots of ill intent toward you. Don't see why that would make a difference now."

Shit. Chrys dug her nails into her palms, silently cursing herself for letting that slip. Lily wasn't supposed to know that she'd cared. She wasn't supposed to *have* cared—period. Chrys had bound up those hurt emotions from ninth grade and burned them during a waning moon. It was as simple and classic as a banishing spell could get.

Fine, maybe she'd missed some. Maybe her intent hadn't been strong enough and instead of releasing the hurt, she'd buried some of it in her chest. But she'd been able to ignore it for years. And it shouldn't matter anyway, because if Chrys was responsible, she knew what had done it. It wasn't merely ill intent and pain slipping out from the binding around her heart. She'd released it, purposely.

She expected Lily to look triumphant, pleased that she'd gotten Chrys to admit that she cared enough to harbor ill intent. But while Lily did look like she was feeling vindicated, she also looked miserable.

Lily closed her eyes and shoved her mug away. When she opened them, she kept her gaze focused on her thumbs, which she rubbed together over her notebook.

Chrys waited, angry at herself for her slipup and angrier for not hating Lily in this moment. For Lily *forcing* her to slip up by making her feel things. Lily seemed so fragile; not a sturdy and strong sugar maple at all, but a girl fading into the orange-toned wall behind her, swallowed by something bigger than she was. Chrys wanted to grab her hands and pull her back before she vanished completely. Instead, she tucked her own hands deeper in her sleeves.

"What if the problem," Lily whispered, "is that while you were putting out ill intent, I hexed you? And those two negative energies collided?"

It took a couple of seconds for the words to make sense, for them to shatter the moment of empathy Chrys had been having. "You what?"

"I'm sorry!" Lily's hands flopped to her sides. "I was furious about getting in trouble for something you did, and so I hexed you, and don't act all superior because you did it to me first, and—"

"Seriously?" Chrys was grateful for the silence charm. There was no way she could have kept her voice down. "After your whole ass-kissing moment with Ms. LaPlant about why this is a dangerous time of year for working negative magic?"

Lily scowled but said nothing, and although she hadn't meant it as such, her silence served as a rebuke to Chrys. She was a damn hypocrite to be lecturing Lily, wasn't she? But she hadn't intended to hex Lily that night. She wasn't even entirely sure she had. Yet Lily's theory made some sense. Not the way Lily was thinking of it, because Lily didn't know what Chrys had done, but overall. The veil was weak; magic could be hijacked or twisted. Two badly done hexes aimed at each other—it sounded like a recipe for disaster.

"What are you thinking?" Lily asked after a moment of uncomfortable silence. Then, when Chrys didn't answer, she pushed her advantage. "You think I'm right."

Chrys closed her eyes. Her blood was pumping quickly, yet still she managed to feel utterly deflated. It had to be guilt. "Not exactly."

Lily was staring at her, her face pale, making her lips redder and her eyelashes darker. Chrys's stomach twisted. Definitely guilt.

"I said something that night, too, and in retrospect, maybe it felt a bit like a spell." The admission had to be dragged from somewhere deep down inside her, and it left her mouth filled with the taste of acid.

"You just yelled at me, but you hexed me, too? Again?"

"It wasn't a hex." Chrys slid her chair back an inch as she caught a whiff of Lily's shampoo, the one that left her lightheaded. "It was just words said in anger. I don't think it should have done anything, but . . ."

But clearly something had happened, and it made more sense that verbalizing her loathing for Lily was responsible than any nebulous ill intent.

Lily swore. "It's fine," she said, waving her hands around. "I mean, it's not fine, but I guess we're even."

"If what I did is partially responsible, we're not, because I hexed you twice."

Lily paused mid-wave to consider this. "True. I appreciate your honesty."

Chrys shrugged. "Maybe I just like pointing out when you're wrong."

Lily blinked, and her hand smacked her mostly untouched mug. She stared at Chrys for a moment, looking seriously confused.

Oh shit. Despite everything, Lily's expression was too comical to resist, and Chrys's lips twitched ever so slightly. No, no, no! She fought down the smile. Why was she such an emotional mess today?

"Whatever," Lily said, but she seemed more confused than she had a moment ago, and Chrys had a bad feeling that Lily had seen the smile itching to break across her mouth and had misinterpreted it as friendliness. And if she'd done that, she might be thinking Chrys's comment was teasing instead of purely spiteful.

For the record, absolutely neither was true. Chrys was determined to be full of spite and empty of compassion. She dug her nails into her palms again, trying to focus on channeling her disdainful attitude. Normally it was easy.

"So," Lily continued, "we have a problem, and I think we need to be the ones to fix it. Remember, Ms. LaPlant said that the Society could work faster if they knew what had caused the magic to go weird. Since we're the ones who know, we need to figure it out."

"To be clear, this means we're not telling anyone what we think is responsible?" It sounded like that was Lily's point, but Chrys needed to hear her say it. She'd have thought Lily would want to run to the Society and tell the truth, trusting that her family would protect her from consequences. That she didn't was interesting. The witch princess wasn't as perfect as she pretended, and Chrys wasn't sure how to feel about that.

Lily's eyes opened wide. "We would get in so much trouble. You don't want to tell them, do you? Look at the trouble we're *already* in."

Chrys took a second to delight in the fearful way Lily watched her before she shook her head. Unlike Lily, she could deny placing a hex if someone wanted to cast a truth spell on them, and it might save her. But Chrys didn't really want to find out.

"I don't know how to fix this," she said. "Do you have any ideas for that in your notebook?"

"I hadn't gotten that far. But I do think the first thing we should do is plan to stay as far apart as possible at school. Agreed?"

Chrys let herself smirk this time. "Such a hardship. Agreed. Besides math and history, I think lunch is the only time that might be a problem, but I can hang out in the library."

Lily seemed to relax. "That works. Let me know if you want to trade off days."

"No, I'm good with the library." Books were always better company than people anyway. She'd just have to think of an excuse for ditching her friends.

"Okay, well . . ." Lily glanced down at the notebook like she was hoping it had filled with more information. "I also think we need to sneak into the Historical Society's restricted room and search their books. I doubt they'd leave anything with useful information about evil magic out in the main library for anyone to read."

Probably not, which was just as well, seeing what the current condition of the library was. Restricted books and other items, however, were located in a separate room in the back. Chrys had tried to check it out once, but the door had been locked.

"It might be a while before we can get into the library to get to the restricted room," Chrys said. "What would we look for, anyway?"

"Ways to undo hexes that have gotten out of control," Lily said, and her words were punctuated with an unspoken *duh* that Chrys thought was uncalled for.

"Is that the problem—an out-of-control hex or two? Or is it more complicated, like two hexes meeting in the night and pooling their power to create a mutant baby hex? Or is it hexes that were hijacked by malevolent spirits that are slipping through the veil? Or—"

"Okay, enough." Lily rubbed her head. "I don't know. I guess we're just researching hexes for now, unless you know all about them already."

"Because I dress in black?" When Lily said nothing, Chrys snorted. "I don't know anything about hexes. I made up the one I cast. I wasn't sure it would work."

"Fine," Lily grumbled. "I just meant it would have been helpful if you did."

Chrys sighed. This partnership was off to a great start. "So when do we try this? The building's crowded before witch school on Wednesday, but there's no way we can do it today. Half the Society's probably been called in to fix the wards."

"What about now?" Lily asked. Chrys could only imagine her face, because Lily rushed on. "Things seem to be getting worse, and I'm worried. Aren't you?"

Yeah, kind of, if she was being honest with herself. But Chrys didn't know if she could stand spending more time with Lily today. One minute, she was feeling empathetic and soft, and the next, she wanted to hex Lily all over again. "I just said we can't go back to the Society."

"We have some books at home that we could start with, if you want to come over."

Go to Lily's house? Be around Lily in her princess palace? There was not enough coffee in this shop that Chrys could reward herself with for enduring that kind of pain.

On the other hand, they were going to have to be very careful in their research at the Historical Society so they didn't get caught. Chrys could, unfortunately, see a reason for doing what they could elsewhere.

Was it possible to cast a spell to make yourself emotionally indifferent to someone? Banishing her feelings apparently hadn't worked all that great.

Not that she still had those kinds of feelings, Chrys clarified to herself. Lily's snobbery had taken care of them. This was about feelings in general so she wouldn't get annoyed with Lily. It would be hard work to undo a hex when she kept wanting to send another hex.

Chrys pretended to check the time on her phone. "I don't know. I could use the extra time today to do homework."

Lily groaned. "You're right. How are we supposed to do both?"

"If we worked on homework together, it might go faster. Then we could research." Chrys heard the words slip out of her mouth, unable to stifle her tongue. If they'd been a mug of coffee, she'd have tried in vain to stop it from tumbling over, her fingers flailing and catching only air.

This was bad, but Chrys assured herself it was also understandable. She was stressed, and Lily was stressed, and Chrys was not an evil person. Empathy was natural, and stress wore down the defenses. If any of these weird moods were indicative of feelings being revived in her chest, no one could blame her.

Besides, there was no reason to worry about her suggestion being taken seriously, because surely Lily hadn't been serious, either. She'd also want to take advantage of her extra Saturday free time. She was popular. Chrys didn't know what that was like, but she assumed popular kids always had busy social calendars, especially on the weekends. Lily would decline, and they could put this off to a reasonable time. Like never.

"That's a good idea," Lily said, and it took Chrys a second to realize what Lily meant, and that she wasn't reading her thoughts. "We can fit your bike in the back of my SUV."

Crap.

Chapter Nineteen

Lily

Lily cast a sideways glance at Chrysanthemum as she pulled into her family's driveway. After an intense discussion on how to best wedge Chrysanthemum's bike into the back of Lily's car, they'd gotten in and fallen silent. It had continued that way the entire distance to the Allerton home.

Every few minutes, Lily wondered what Chrysanthemum was thinking. Then she figured she probably didn't want to know. Had she lost her mind, to invite Chrysanthemum over? Desperate times called for desperate measures, and all that, but still.

Some part of Lily was terrified, and she didn't know why.

But then . . . Chrysanthemum had seemed unexpectedly human today. Lily had anticipated scowls and snark and judgment, and she hadn't been entirely disappointed. But Chrysanthemum had also struck her as *nervous* and *awkward*. (As nervous and as awkward as Lily herself had felt, perhaps.) She hadn't been friendly, exactly, but she had been a lot less abrasive than normal. When Lily recalled the way Chrysanthemum had pulled her shirt tight around herself, burying her hands in the fabric like she needed comfort, Lily had felt . . . something.

Like maybe they weren't as different as she'd always assumed. Like maybe there was something soft lurking beneath Chrysanthemum's harsh exterior.

It was ridiculous, and yet it was as though something sharp had been poking her in the ribs for a long time, and talking to Chrysanthemum had blunted it.

Chrysanthemum sitting next to Lily, though—that kept her tense. Chrysanthemum's closeness had every nerve in Lily's body firing for *absolutely no good reason*. At least Chrysanthemum was wearing sunglasses, sparing Lily the queasy feeling in her gut whenever she accidentally met that electric gaze.

Lily would never admit to Chrysanthemum that her eyes made her nervous. And maybe a bit jealous—of their beauty, of the way they announced her power. They were such an unusual color, blue like a winter sky. Cold and untouchable, fey . . . beautiful.

Lily jammed on the brake to bring herself back to reality, jostling them both. "Sorry."

Ten minutes later, and with a strong determination not to look at Chrysanthemum's face, Lily led her to her room. It was best not to risk being overheard by her sister or her father, who was in his home office. “Once we finish Ms. LaPlant’s assignment,” Lily said, “we can look at the books in the library.”

“You have your own library?” Chrysanthemum paused outside Lily’s doorway.

Lily made the mistake of turning around, and she realized Chrysanthemum was staring at her, those gorgeously eerie blue eyes unblinking. Discomfort made her skin prickle. “It’s just my brother’s old bedroom. My parents moved a bunch of stuff in there after he left for college.”

Chrysanthemum said nothing to that, but Lily got the distinct impression that she was thinking very hard.

Putting aside the question of what Chrysanthemum was thinking, for probably the hundredth time in the last hour, Lily opened her bedroom door the rest of the way. Her first priority on getting home was to let her rabbits out, and Chrysanthemum’s presence didn’t change that. “You can dop your backpack anywhere.”

“Your walls are . . .” Chrysanthemum was glancing around uncertainly.

“What?”

“Nothing. I was just . . .” Chrysanthemum shrugged off her backpack, looking sheepish. “I expected them to be pink.”

Lily had never worn pink since the day she’d been able to choose her own clothes, so she couldn’t fathom why Chrysanthemum would expect that. Though, to be fair, she’d made some strange assumptions about Chrysanthemum’s coffee.

And when did you decide to be fair? a voice in her head asked.

"I'm not a fan of pink," Lily said, since this was not the time to question herself.

A smirk teased the corners of Chrysanthemum's lips. "Let me guess—it clashes with your hair."

It did. Lily turned her back so she wouldn't be caught flushing.

"I was going to say your walls are almost the same color as mine," Chrysanthemum said.

How in the world was she going to avoid Chrysanthemum's face all day? It was impossible.

"Really? I assumed your walls would be black."

"My bedroom is too tiny. It would be like living in a cave."

"Oh." For the first time, Lily wondered where Chrysanthemum lived. Most of the island's year-round residents were clustered in one of two neighborhoods—Lily's own, with its large colonial homes and abundant trees, or the other, which was farther from downtown and comprised of more modest Cape-style homes. There were also a few apartment complexes and a row of enormous mansions high on the cliff side of the island, overlooking the ocean.

"I hope you don't mind them wandering around," she said as she knelt to open the rabbits' cage. She stepped back as Ella and Cinder poked their noses out, and she rubbed their heads. "Hey, sweeties. Did you have a good day? Do you need any water or food?"

Their responses came in flashes of insight, more emotion than words. *Not thirsty. Raisins, please.*

"One raisin each." Lily held up a single finger. "You know too many will make you sick. Okay, fine—*two*, since you asked politely, but I swear if you make a mess, no more until next week." As if the rabbits understood the concept of a week. Her talent wasn't great enough to convey that complex an idea.

She opened the bag on top of her dresser, and Ella and Cinder scurried to her feet. Lily held up one raisin in each hand, coaxing them to sit before they received their afternoon treats.

"I didn't know rabbits could be trained like that," Chrysanthemum said, and Lily almost dropped the bag. She'd temporarily forgotten she had an audience.

"Oh, um, yeah." Only her rabbits could have distracted her enough to make her forget that Chrysanthemum was in her room. Well, anything cute and furry could have. Cats. Dogs. Horses. Birds. Fine, anything that wasn't a fish. "It's my talent. I can communicate with them."

Chrysanthemum's face lit up, and the change was startling. Lily had never seen her look so absolutely delighted before. Smile sarcastically, laugh derisively—both, yes. But this was different, and the shock of it knocked something around inside Lily like a pinball was smacking into her organs.

This was alarming. Chrysanthemum looked entirely too human.

"Oh my god. You really are a Disney princess!" Chrysanthemum covered her mouth with her hand and doubled over in laughter.

Lily felt her cheeks burn. She floundered for a retort, but it was hard to think of something witty.

"Sorry," Chrysanthemum said, pushing hair out of her face. "I just wouldn't have expected that to be your talent, although maybe I should have, since it fits you so well. What are their names?"

Oh. Oh no. Lily winced. "That one's Cinder, and this one"—she nudged the rabbit nipping at her sock—"is Ella."

Chrysanthemum snorted.

"Fine. Laugh. Whatever." Lily willed the blood to leave her face.

"They even live in a castle," Chrysanthemum said. She was still grinning as she stepped over to the cage, box, and tube contraption.

Lily resealed the raisin bag and took a couple of deep breaths. Composure. She had to find some. But it was so unfair that Chrysanthemum always seemed to be the one getting the last laugh. "My brother helped me build that for them. It gives them a lot of space to run around while I'm gone."

"Did you paint it? Because if so, you're holding out on your skills at the Historical Society. It looks like a van Gogh. Or a Monet? It's one of those painters my mom loves. There's a print hanging in our living room."

“Van Gogh,” Lily said, thankful she could sound intelligent finally. Composure was found in dignity, and dignity was found in knowing stuff Chrysanthemum didn't. “My brother painted that, not me. David's talent is being able to replicate stuff he sees. He'd have made a great art forger, but he wants to go to medical school.”

“Boring, but I guess he's less likely to have legal troubles that way.”

“Yeah, and it makes my mom happy to have another doctor in the family.” Lily clamped her lips shut, not thrilled that had slipped out. The words were nothing special, but she was certain Chrysanthemum could taste the bitterness on her tongue.

Sure enough, Chrysanthemum's eyes flashed, some of their iciness thawed, and Lily dropped her gaze.

“I take it you *don't* want to be a doctor?” Chrysanthemum asked.

“I do, but a veterinarian.” Lily scooped up Cinder and buried her face in the rabbit's fur. Right now, she wanted to be a rabbit, but she'd settle for being part of the furniture. For anything that didn't feel like the center of Chrysanthemum's attention. That didn't have those eyes seeing inside her.

She startled, sensing Chrysanthemum's closeness before noticing how she was tentatively holding up a hand to Cinder's head. Of course Chrysanthemum wanted to pet the bunny. Everyone wanted to pet bunnies.

"She likes this spot on the back of her head," Lily said, showing Chrys.

It was extremely difficult not to twitch as Chrysanthemum brushed Cinder's head. She stood so close, smelling faintly of incense. Power seemed to emanate from her skin, making Lily's pulse quicken and her blood warm. Chrysanthemum must exude magic; it could be seen in her eyes and sensed in the aura around her. Lily could think of no other way to explain it.

And it put her on edge. Caused her gut to flutter with nerves, which was obnoxious of it because Lily was not—*would* not be—afraid of Chrysanthemum.

She wet her lips and focused on her breathing, hoping her reaction wasn't obvious.

"I think being a veterinarian who can communicate with animals is the perfect use of your talent," Chrysanthemum said, smiling at Cinder. "Much better than an artist who goes to medical school. That's a waste of a gift."

Lily waited a moment for the insult that had to be coming, but Chrysanthemum was cooing over Cinder, and Lily felt faint. "Thanks," she croaked out at last. "It's convenient that my talent aligns with what I like."

"I think talents usually do that. We might not realize it at first, but they fit us. It's just that people try to force themselves into being something they don't really want to be." Chrys scowled slightly at that, but didn't elaborate.

Lily longed to ask what she was thinking, or simply what Chrysanthemum's talent was, but Chrysanthemum's magical aura was interfering with her brain. Words were a struggle, and her head didn't clear until Chrysanthemum took a step back. Even then, Lily felt slightly dizzy.

Chrysanthemum, too, seemed disconcerted, but that much Lily understood. The rabbits had gotten to her. She was right to have guessed there was something soft in Chrysanthemum, and Chrysanthemum was clearly displeased to have revealed it. It should have felt good to find this weakness, but Lily was merely confused.

"Let's start homework," Chrysanthemum said. An edge was back in her voice, but Lily didn't miss the way she wrapped her fingers around her shirtsleeves. "We have a lot to do."

Lily couldn't agree fast enough.

They both had to deal with a history paper and an English group project, but Ms. LaPlant's AP Calculus homework was the most pressing and easiest to knock out together. Lily wasn't bad at math, but it wasn't her best subject. Working with Chrysanthemum, though, made it possible to fly through their assignment. In the time it took Lily to work out how to solve an equation, Chrysanthemum had already finished it. Lily was simultaneously impressed, annoyed, jealous, and concerned for her future valedictorian status, knowing this was what she was up against.

Still, in a much shorter time than she'd anticipated, Lily slid her chair back from her desk and stretched her arms. It wasn't a bad thing to have extra time to research hexes. Plus, seeing Chrysanthemum work was a good reminder to not to slack off academically because of everything going on. They were allies, but only temporarily and in this one task.

“If only all classes could be as easy as math,” Chrysanthemum muttered with a yawn. “Tests and homework. No papers.”

“I thought you liked books?”

“I like reading. I don’t like writing papers about what I read.”

Lily didn’t mind papers. She rather liked organizing information and planning out arguments to prove a point. This was another Chrysanthemum weakness. “Papers give you time to think about what you learn.”

Chrysanthemum shook her head, but her lips were doing that half smile again. “We are total opposites in everything. Just as I expected.”

“Except paint color,” Lily pointed out.

Chrysanthemum nodded, a little V between her eyebrows. “True. What’s your history paper on?”

Lily didn’t see the harm in sharing, and even if she had, Chrysanthemum smiling—even if it was a weak smile—was so disconcerting that she’d have blurted out the topic anyway. “What about you?”

“I’m researching my ancestors on Thornhaven.” Chrysanthemum’s tone was casual, but her smile slipped.

“Your ancestors? But you just moved here.”

"My mom was born here." She stuck her chin out, as though daring Lily to challenge her. "Anyway, hex time. Lead on to the library, princess."

"What did you call me?" Lily glared at her, but it was no use.

"Oh, come on. You talk to animals. You live in a palace." Chrysanthemum waved her arms around. "You probably have a tiara hidden in your closet."

She did. From her failed attempt at ballet, but no way would she admit it. "Ugh. I hate you."

The words came out limp and lifeless despite her frustration. The worst part of this day was that Lily couldn't generate the emotion behind the sentiment, even while she listened to Chrysanthemum laugh at her.

Chapter Twenty
Chrysanthemum

She and Lily pored over those books for hours, looking for any clues. Had she trusted her talent, Chrys would have known it was a waste of time, but the books belonged to Lily's family, so she'd figured they might have spells on them that blocked her.

They had not. And around six, when her mother texted to ask if she was coming home for dinner, Chrys decided to leave.

"Do you want to stay?" Lily asked, and Chrys dropped the book she was halfheartedly perusing in shock.

"Won't your parents care?"

Lily shrugged. "Not really. My mom has an ER shift tonight, and my dad . . ." She glanced at her phone, but it remained silent. "I'll probably just order food when I get hungry. We could keep reading . . . or watch TV if you're tired."

Chrys didn't know what to make of the offer except that Lily's house was big and empty, and it had gone quiet since Lily's sister had left for a sleepover. Lily must be desperate for company, but part of Chrys couldn't help but consider it. She loved her mom, and their apartment was nice, but everything at home was cramped. There was something luxurious about being able to sprawl on the floor and not have furniture pressing in on her from all sides.

Plus, Lily was acting strangely pleasant. She was incapable of coming up with good insults, so she'd taken to tossing things at Chrys whenever Chrys called her *princess*. Chrys had started doing it more and more, just to make Lily have to search for objects to throw—pen caps, paper clips, the popcorn they'd been snacking on, a little felt pillow with the Thornhaven High School insignia sewn on it.

Chrys panicked. A collaborative Lily was risky enough. A friendly Lily was worrisome. A Lily who hugged rabbits and forced down laughter as she tossed popcorn was downright alarming. If Chrys couldn't justify hating her, she might start to *like* her, and that could not be.

So Chrys lied and said her mom needed her home, and when Lily offered to drive her because it was getting dark, she refused. A long bike ride home ought to burn the *fun* right out of her body.

By the time Chrys arrived at the Historical Society on Monday afternoon for their break-in attempt, she'd picked off half her nail polish.

True, nerves about sneaking around where they didn't belong were part of it, but Chrys knew the rest was down purely to Lily. That made her angry. This getting-along stuff was a bad idea. She had to stay tough and keep her defenses up.

That turned out to be easier than anticipated.

Lily never showed.

After waiting an hour and sending Lily a series of increasingly pissed-off texts, all of which were ignored, Chrys stormed home. Her frustration did wonders for hardening her heart.

Tuesday morning, Chrys locked up her bike outside school, determined to hold on to her anger but also worried what it might do. Assuming she and Lily were correct and the hex was related to them, it didn't seem impossible that strong emotions would affect it. Although she *wanted* to yell at Lily, the best course of action would be to stay far away.

But before she could put that plan in motion, she heard Lily's voice behind her. "Sorry about yesterday."

Chrys took a deep breath. If only the frost in the air could cool her frustration into a chilly indifference. She was overheating, though, burning up with indignation.

Lily stopped several feet away. "Did you get my text?"

Lily had finally texted her around nine last night. A simple Sorry. Reschedule? that had only reignited Chrys's anger, and that she hadn't bothered to respond to. "I waited an hour."

"I'm really sorry." Lily picked at her fingerless gloves. Her cheeks were prettily flushed from the chill, and that only made Chrys more irritated. "I was meeting with Mr. Gevry, and it would have been rude to text you in the middle. I forgot we were supposed to meet."

"And it wasn't rude to ignore me while I was waiting for you?"

A bus pulled up to the school, and Chrys tugged her zipper higher despite wanting to rip off her jacket. People were going to get off that bus, see her and Lily talking, and gawk. Chrys loathed being the center of attention.

Lily, strangely, didn't seem to notice or care. She pulled on a loose thread on her left glove. "I got a B on my physics test," she said, as though that were some kind of explanation.

"So?"

"So!" Lily let go of the thread and stared at her, and when Chrys didn't respond, she let out a growl of frustration that provided Chrys with some small satisfaction. It was no longer just her who was pissed off. Good. "I had to meet with Mr. Gevry to go over what I did wrong and figure out how to make up the lost points. This could affect my GPA—although I'm sure you're thrilled about that."

"You couldn't have met with him another time?"

"I told you—*I forgot.* As soon as I saw my grade, I couldn't think about anything else. It was a B! What would you have done?"

"It's just a B. There's a whole other"—Chrys jabbed her finger at the school to indicate whatever was going on while she fumbled for the correct word—"*problem* to deal with."

Instead of looking abashed, Lily flung her hair back. "Well, I'm sorry I'm not as perfect as you. That everything doesn't come as easily for me, and that it stresses me out."

"What exactly do you think comes easily for me?" For that matter, what, exactly, was Lily's point? Chrys was having a hard time following her train of thought.

"Everything does." Lily waited a breath, as though Chrys could have a response to something so absurd. "The way you flew through the math homework on Saturday. The way you're so powerful that you cast a hex without even trying."

"So I'm better at math than you, so what? I'm sure you're better at other subjects than me. You think things come easily for me? What the hell do you know about easy? You live in a mansion. You drive to school every day in your own car. Easy is your normal. I work extra hard for my grades because I'm counting on scholarship money. When I'm not working a job over the summer, I'm practicing my magic. What are you doing—hanging out at your pool?"

Lily flinched, suggesting at least one of those shots had hit its mark, so Chrys went on, letting the anger pour out of her. But instead of emptying her, more sprang into existence with each word. "Why do you want to beat me so badly? Because of your ego? Because you were the best *until I showed up*? I'm sorry I make something about your life difficult, but I've never had it *easy* like you. You don't get to diminish how hard I work to throw yourself a pity party."

With that, she spun on her heel and stormed into school.

Chrys spent the morning stewing, wondering if she'd said too much. She didn't much care about the lashing out—Lily deserved that—but the stuff about Lily's house and Lily's car could give Lily the impression that she was jealous, and that would feed Lily's ego. Lily's ego was obviously big enough.

And anyway, Chrys didn't think she *was* jealous. Not really. The apartment she and her mom shared might be small and money might be tight, but there was a feeling of emptiness in the Allerton house.

If she thought about that emptiness for too long, her anger subsided, and Chrys didn't like that. It shouldn't be so hard to stay furious.

"You know," Luke said, as they sat down to lunch later, "I forgot to mention it yesterday, but I appreciate the town's dedication to Halloween. My last school did not go all out like this."

By *this* Chrys assumed he meant the decoration blitz that always went up the first day of October. The school currently looked like it had been turned into a pumpkin patch, after which one of those tacky Halloween pop-up shops had vomited all over it. (Only, in Thornhaven, those Halloween shops were open year-round and everything cost too much.)

In the cafeteria alone, black and orange crepe papers were strung across the ceiling, decals had been stuck on all the windows, and fake spiderwebs (studded with fake spiders) stretched across the walls. A skeleton sat in a chair at the end of the food line, too (an appropriate commentary on the offerings).

"You don't think it's a bit much?" Isaiah asked. "I'm good with streamers and skeletons and pumpkins, but the spiders should not be anywhere near food."

Chrys didn't hear Luke's reply as Lily, Sonia, and the rest of that group strolled into the cafeteria. Sonia was talking animatedly, but Lily hung slightly back, her face strained. She glanced at Chrys's table, and Chrys snapped her head back to her sandwich.

Shit. After lecturing Lily about forgetting things, *she'd* forgotten that she was supposed to be eating in the library. Chrys started to pack up her lunch to leave, but she paused as Anushka asked her a question: "Chrys, you there?"

Chrys blinked. "What?"

"We were telling Luke about the Halloween ball the Historical Society holds every year," Anushka said. "Your mom's selling tickets again, right?"

"Uh, yeah. They go all out for the Halloween ball. It's a real Thornhaven tradition. People from the mainland come over for it."

Normally, at this time of the year, the ball would loom big in her future, but current events had been a bit too distracting. Still, the ball was the *one* social event she enjoyed—for the spectacle, if nothing else. She didn't know if it was the thinning veil around Samhain or what, but it was also the one night of the year when Thornhaven truly let loose with its power. When the witches dared to be brazen and magic lingered in the air. Memories of the night would fade over time, but for a few hours (instead of a few minutes), the normies would see and believe.

The ball was always held the Saturday before Halloween, and since that was October 30 this year, it would be a bigger deal than usual. At the stroke of midnight, Samhain would officially arrive.

“Sounds fun!” Luke said. “Do you all actually go?”

“Everyone goes, even my family.” Anushka complained regularly about how strict her parents were, and she assumed Chrys didn’t have much of a social life for the same reason. Chrys had never had the heart to correct her. “Even Chrys goes.”

As a member, albeit a junior one, of the Society, Chrys didn’t have much choice. All members were expected to put in an appearance, and those fifteen and older were recruited as volunteers. The last two years, Chrys had been roped into helping collect tickets.

No one had asked for her help yet this year, though. Maybe getting in trouble had marked her as too irresponsible.

“See?” Isaiah said. “If Chrys shows up, you know it’s wild. The decorations alone are unlike anything you’ve ever seen.”

“If you think *this* is dedication, wait until the ball’s decor,” Chrys told Luke, gesturing to the cafeteria.

But whatever Luke did or did not think on the topic, she never found out. At that moment, a pumpkin exploded.

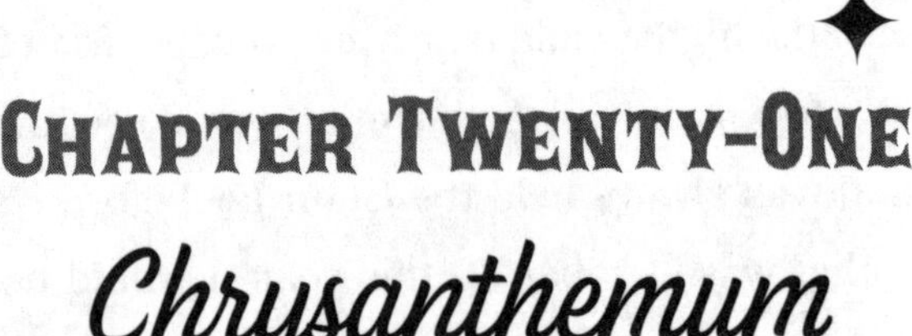

CHAPTER TWENTY-ONE
Chrysanthemum

After a week of magical nonsense, and a morning spent worrying that her mood might impact said nonsense, Chrys registered the chaos breaking out with surprise . . . but not shock.

Rather, her mood settled on *really?* and *again?* Both emotions were soon followed by *Why is it always during my lunch*?

Unfortunately, most of the other students weren't reacting with the same blasé attitude. Screaming got Chrys to her feet along with everyone else. But just as the third pumpkin exploded, even she began to lose her cool.

Because the plastic spiders grew to the size of baseballs and began crawling off their fake webs.

And then the fake skeleton stood up, stretched its limbs, and surveyed the pandemonium with its bony hands on its pelvis.

The screaming was losing its amused undertones. Baseball-sized spiders had a tendency to do that to people. Real screams of terror preceded a mad rush to the cafeteria doors as engorged arachnids dropped from the ceiling onto the student body. Some people were climbing onto the tables, and Chrys followed their lead, searching for a clearer exit path. A gust of cold air hit her face as students began shoving the fire doors to the outside open.

More screaming directed Chrys's attention toward the food line. The skeleton was on the move and . . . Oh no. So was the life-sized plastic grim reaper by the cafeteria checkout. Its scythe swung through the air, clocking the nearest boy on the shoulder. He let out a cry that would have been more fitting had that blade been real—but luckily, the hex hadn't gotten that violent.

Yet.

Chrys shivered. The floor was covered in pumpkin guts, and the air was full of yelling and cursing as shoes slid on the mess and bodies smacked the linoleum. Clearly, the magic-suppression spells the Society had cast on the school last week had worn off. Maybe if Chrys were as powerful as Lily seemed to think, she could stop this herself. But she wasn't, and people were getting hurt.

"Chrys, come on!" Anushka held her backpack in front of her body like a shield, following Luke and Isaiah toward the closest interior doors.

Slowly, so as not to slip and break a bone, Chrys hopped down and joined them. They broke through the press out into the hallway and ran, trying to get as far away as possible.

Black veins in the walls ran with them.

Ignoring Anushka, who was calling for her, Chrys peeled off and raced down a different hallway, and she didn't stop until the veins faded from view. She finally stopped and sat in a vacant stairwell, huffing. Bits of splattered pumpkin stuck to her sleeves, but nothing worse. Muttering to herself, Chrys plucked them off before they could dry in place.

After how she'd left things with Lily this morning, she didn't want to be the bigger person and suggest a second attempt at the Historical Society's restricted room. For that matter, she didn't want to deal with Lily again. Period. If she wasn't infuriating Chrys, she was making Chrys forget that she was, by nature, infuriating.

Still, Chrys didn't see a way around it.

She was pulling out her phone to text Lily when the stairwell door opened and Lily appeared as if summoned.

She hadn't fared as well with the exploding pumpkins. She'd clearly tried washing some of the bits off her clothes, but orange goo stuck to her hair. A traitorous part of Chrys longed to reach over and pull it out for her.

"You have pumpkin in your hair," Chrys said instead, knowing it would annoy Lily.

Lily made a whining noise and picked through her strands. "Look, I'm sorry about yesterday, but we need to work on this."

"Agreed. That's why *I* showed up yesterday. And now I'll meet you there *today*."

"I can't." Lily wiped her hands on a tissue. "I have to run a student council meeting. Tomorrow, before witch school."

Chrys sighed but didn't see the point in arguing. This was why so-called student government, besides being nothing more than a popularity contest, was bullshit. "Fine. You'd better show. We need to do something before blood gushes out of the supply closets."

Lily's eyes opened wide, and she glanced around as though Chrys had made a prophecy rather than an allusion. "Don't give it ideas. Why would you even suggest that?"

"It's funny? It's like a scene from *The Shining*. Haven't you ever watched it?"

"It's horror." Lily shook her head. "I don't like horror."

"It's a classic."

"Which is why I've heard of it." Lily's tone was a challenge intended to cut off any snarky remarks. "I don't like horror because I don't like seeing bad things happen to people."

Chrys shrugged. "Bad things happen all the time. How do you stand history class? Reading the news?"

"That's different. It's real."

"Isn't that worse?"

Lily stared at her like she was a dipshit. "Life is already full of people suffering. I don't understand why anyone would want to see more of it. At least with history, we can learn from the bad things so we can make the world better."

"Oh my god. You're . . ."

Disgustingly sweet. The words teased the tip of Chrys's tongue, and she clamped her lips shut until the urge passed. How could anyone be so arrogant and selfish and yet so . . . ugh, yes, sweet. Also infuriating. Chrys did not need these contradictions complicating her life.

"You really are a princess," she finished pathetically. "Totally ridiculous."

"Whatever. Excuse me for not choosing to make myself miserable. Maybe if I did that, I'd wander around dressed for a funeral, too."

"If we get out of this unscathed, I'm making you watch *The Shining* with me." Chrys heaved her backpack on. "Consider it punishment for standing me up."

"You're going to punish *both* of us?"

Chrys didn't realize what Lily meant until she'd walked away. Strange that she hadn't even been thinking about spending more time with Lily as a punishment. It had to be the stress.

Chapter Twenty-Two

Lily

The plan was simple, albeit not as detailed as Lily would have liked. Nor did it contain as many backup plans as she thought any sensible preparation should. Chrysanthemum did not do plans the way Lily did. Life with Chrysanthemum, apparently, was about hoping one didn't reach the *find out* stage of that whole *fucking around* business.

Arrive at witch school an hour early, break into the restricted room, hide anything useful they found in their backpacks, sneak it out after school, and pray they didn't get caught. That was it. Chrysanthemum had assured Lily she could pick the restricted room's lock. Where she'd learned to do that, Lily didn't want to know. She was discovering that Chrysanthemum was a lot more normal than she'd believed, but every now and then, she lived up (or down) to Lily's expectations.

Chrysanthemum arrived at the Historical Society a few minutes after Lily did, and Lily held out a to-go cup of hot chocolate she'd bought for her. Maybe it was an apology for standing her up, or maybe it was the fact that it was rude to buy herself a pre–break-in treat and not one for her partner in crime. All Lily knew for sure was that she'd wanted something to calm her nerves, and she wanted to give Chrysanthemum something, too.

Like Chrysanthemum was just another friend.

Chrysanthemum stared with a dumbfounded expression when Lily held out the second cup of hot chocolate for her, finally mumbling, "Thank you."

"They're in the good cups," Lily said quickly, referring to the ones the shop enchanted to keep the contents hot. "But the whipped cream will still melt if you don't drink it fast enough."

Chrysanthemum nodded and took a small sip. The heat pinkened her cheeks, and Lily wondered why she'd ever thought Chrysanthemum's face had a sickly pallor. Her skin did look extra pale thanks to how dark her hair was, but it wasn't an unfortunate contrast. It was . . . Lily tried to settle on a word and chose *interesting*. It wasn't the first word to come to mind, but it was the first that she could tolerate.

Clutching their drinks, they crept into the library. Several Society witches must have been hard at work since Saturday. The enormous mess was cleaned up. Since Lily and Chrysanthemum had been partially counting on that mess to keep people away, that was unfortunate.

"I am sorry about Monday." Lily felt the apology burst out of her.

Chrysanthemum paused midstride and stared. The silence compelled Lily on.

"You don't know what it's like at home. My brother is perfect—perfect grades, soccer team captain, debate club winner, got into every college he applied to. And my sister is a star swimmer. My parents have such high expectations for her. Everything is scheduled around what Sara needs. I can't afford to mess up, or I'll slip further behind. They barely acknowledged me even when I was elected student council president. I just . . ."

Her free hand had curled into a fist as she spoke, and Lily drew a deep breath, forcing it to unclench. She'd given Chrysanthemum a lifetime's worth of ammunition to use against her. Only, strangely, she felt lighter for letting all that pressure out. As if she'd been needing to tell someone for far too long. "Sorry to dump that on you. I just mean even princesses have problems."

Chrysanthemum looked a bit like someone had slapped her. "Yeah, I guess they do." The hardness in her face was gone. "It's fine."

It's fine wasn't *apology accepted*, but it was close enough. "I was thinking about it, and once this is over, I'll watch *The Addams Family* with you. Consider it part of my apology."

Chrysanthemum shook herself. "That's not even horror. It's comedy."

"It's a creepy comedy. I need to be eased into anything else. It's a compromise."

Chrysanthemum bit her lip like she was fighting down a smile, and she continued weaving through the shelves to get to the restricted room. In the silence, Lily's heart thudded in her ears. "Okay."

"That's it?" Lily asked as they set down their backpacks.

"What did you want me to say—no? You suggested it."

"I thought you were going to make fun of me. Call me a wimp."

Chrysanthemum swallowed more hot chocolate, then retrieved a couple of tools from her pack with a sigh. "I can't really call you a wimp when we're about to break into the Society's restricted room to research hexes so we can fight one. If we pull this off, we'll be pretty badass. And anyway, your reasons for not liking horror are fine. Understandable. If you were like, 'Ew, I hate fake blood,' that would be different."

Oh. Lily had to take a step back. Since when did she care what Chrysanthemum thought of her?

"Why do *you* watch horror?" Lily asked.

Chrysanthemum frowned as though she'd never thought about it before. "Real life can be pretty awful. It's a way of reminding myself that no matter how much things suck, it could be worse. I'm not dealing with vengeful ghosts or serial killers or something." In that moment, she seemed fragile and soft, and something inside Lily pinched in her gut. Then Chrysanthemum laughed ruefully, breaking the tension that Lily was positive only she was feeling. "I guess that's kind of morbid. Should've gone with 'I *like* fake blood.'"

"Because that wouldn't be morbid? I couldn't do it. But I get it. I think."

"Speaking of doing it." Chrysanthemum wagged her lock-picking tools and made a suggestive face. "Ready?"

Lily tried to fake a laugh at the innuendo, but she had gone hot. "What if there are wards on the door?"

"This whole building is lit up with tinge since the weekend." Chrysanthemum gestured to the nearest window. The old glyphs and their muddy-brown tinge were gone, replaced by fresh ones colored a golden yellow. Over time, those would also turn brown as different people strengthened them and the tinge colors blended together. "If there were wards on this door, don't you think someone would have strengthened these, too?"

Lily had to admit there was logic to this. Besides, the wards were about protection from outside threats. The Society was supposed to trust its own. "You're right. Let's do it."

While Chrysanthemum did . . . whatever she was doing, Lily took her hot chocolate and crept to the end of the row of shelves to keep an eye out for intruders. Chrysanthemum was quick, though. No sooner had Lily peeked around the corner than she announced she was finished.

Lily scurried back over. "Do I want to know where you learned this?"

Chrysanthemum stuffed her tools back in her backpack. "I had a friend in New York whose dad was a locksmith. He taught me. Most locks are scarily easy to pick." She gestured to the door. "After you."

Lily shot her an unamused glance that made Chrysanthemum grin. Lily's gut pinched again, but for some reason, seeing that grin made her feel braver. Bolder. She flipped Chrysanthemum off, and the surprised laugh that burst from Chrysanthemum's lips was like music.

All the nervous energy inside her was making her act silly and unlike herself, and she kind of liked it. She especially liked knowing she could be unexpected, too, and that she might be confusing Chrysanthemum as much as Chrysanthemum confused her.

Plus, all sniping aside, Lily trusted that Chrysanthemum wouldn't try to run if they got caught. They were in this together. When Lily had started trusting her, she couldn't say, but she knew it instinctively, and having Chrysanthemum at her back made doing something so stupid seem less risky.

Lily opened the door, and a light turned on automatically overheard. She held her breath a moment, searching for some telltale signs of a ward being tripped, but when no footsteps pounded down the hallway, she stepped inside.

The restricted room was small and had no windows (unsurprisingly, it smelled mustier than the main library). Lily counted three large bookcases, each stuffed full, and a set of wooden shelves filled with boxes. Some of the boxes were labeled with names or dates, and all were dusty. She reached a hand out, curious what was in them—but drew it back before she touched the closest box.

A shiver ran down her spine. "Can you feel that?"

Chrysanthemum did the same thing, and her face turned paler. "Is it me, or is there some *seriously* bad magic in there?"

Lily stepped away from the shelves without thinking, a move that pressed her against Chrysanthemum. This room wasn't much larger than her parents' walk-in closet, and the hairs on her neck rose, although this time she was certain it was because of her proximity to Chrysanthemum. The warmth of her body seeped through the fabric of Lily's shirt, and Lily's skin seemed to tighten.

"Let's go through these books and get out of here," she said.

"Yeah." Chrysanthemum's voice sounded strained.

Lily grabbed a book from the top leftmost shelf, not knowing what she'd find. The Historical Society had accepted a number of personal antiquarian collections from members over the centuries. And that was what Lily discovered: an old collection of hexes some witch back in the 1800s had gathered. The book was so fragile in her hands that she questioned whether she should be touching it, and flipping through the pages, trying to decipher whether it would be useful, was dicey. This was going to be a slow process, and they didn't have all night. Maybe only another thirty minutes until witch school began.

Lily put the first book back and tried a second. That book turned out to be a kind of index someone had put together in the mid-1900s, chronicling all the alleged hexes that had been cast on the island. Interesting, but unlikely to be useful. The third book she grabbed was some treatise on the nature of negative magic. Lily held on to that one, deciding it had potential.

Tucking that last book beneath her arm, she reached for a fourth, and her hand collided with Chrysanthemum's. Lily froze as something like an electric shock seized her muscles and her brain lost her entire train of thought.

This was so much worse than when she'd grabbed Chrysanthemum's hand without thinking last week. She wasn't sure why, as that had been weird and awkward and this was weird and awkward, too. Perhaps this was the result of standing side by side in such a confined area.

Chrysanthemum had frozen, too; she dropped her hand, and given their positions, her arm brushed Lily's arm all the way down to her side. Despite the sleeves protecting their skin, Lily felt that, too, and in far greater detail than she ought to have.

"Go ahead—"

"You can—"

Chrysanthemum tucked her hair behind her ears and glanced away. "Never mind. It's not useful anyway."

Lily thought she might suffocate. "What isn't?"

"That book."

She needed to breathe. She needed air. Lily stepped out of the room, clutching the book she'd found between them. "How do you know? You haven't looked at it."

While she was at it, why hadn't Chrysanthemum stuck to her end of the shelves? If she'd done that, that uncomfortable moment in the room wouldn't have happened, and Lily wouldn't be wondering if she'd caught blood poisoning.

"I don't need to," Chrysanthemum said, and that was when Lily noticed she was holding three books of her own. "It's my talent. Books, I mean."

Lily's jaw dropped. "Is that it? Is that how you make everything look so easy? You can just touch a book and know what's in it?" She wouldn't want to give up her own talent, she loved animals too much, but she couldn't help but feel jealous. With a talent like that, she'd never have to study for a test again.

"Not quite," Chrysanthemum said, easing Lily's mind a touch. "It's not like all the knowledge is dumped in my head. It's more like I touch a book while thinking of what I'm looking for, and the book will tell me if it has what I need. I still have to read it."

"Oh. I guess that's better."

Chrysanthemum snorted. "For you."

"Well, yes, I mean . . ." Lily shrugged. "That's a cool talent, but having everything dumped in your head would be an *amazing* talent." Another thought occurred to her as she tried to read the spines on the books Chrysanthemum had taken. "Wait. If you can do that, why didn't you tell me on Saturday that my family's books wouldn't help?"

It was Chrysanthemum's turn to shrug, and she clutched her books more closely. "I wasn't sure. I thought maybe your family might have done something to them to block me."

Like what? Lily wanted to ask. *Why?* But she didn't really care about the answer. Chrysanthemum would have left a lot earlier if they hadn't gone through every book together, and that would have been disappointing. As much as she hated to admit it, going through the books together had been . . . Well, *fun* wasn't the right word, although there had been moments that had almost seemed like it, moments where she'd laughed.

This was all extremely disconcerting. "Do you want to—"

"Someone in here?"

Chrysanthemum swore under her breath, and Lily's heart jumped into her throat. She shoved the book she'd taken behind her back and hoped Chrysanthemum would be smart enough to hide hers and the rest of the incriminating evidence as fast as possible. Then she walked calmly but quickly to the end of the row of shelves.

"Mrs. Cook, hi!" Lily smiled brightly. Mrs. Cook was a member of the Historical Society board, and as she was retired, she had too much time on her hands, making her the nosiest witch in the Society. If she heard anything suspicious—like Chrysanthemum closing the restricted room's door—they were screwed.

The older woman cocked her head to the side. "Shouldn't you be in class?"

"In ten minutes. I was looking around at the work that still needs to be done in here."

That had been the wrong thing to say. Mrs. Cook grunted and strode deeper into the room, holding her cat, Elspeth. Since her husband had died a couple of years ago, the cat went everywhere with her. Lily would have been more sympathetic about it if Mrs. Cook weren't always so condescending to the young witches. The last run-in Lily had endured with her, Mrs. Cook had told her that no one would ever take her seriously as a witch if she insisted on casting spells to make her nails change color.

"I heard about what you and that other girl got up to." Mrs. Cook clucked her tongue. "I expected better from an Allerton witch."

Lily backed up, wishing she were large enough to block Mrs. Cook's view through the shelves. Had Chrysanthemum closed the door yet? Lily hadn't heard it, and the hinges creaked something awful. Maybe she was waiting until Lily had chased Mrs. Cook off.

Elspeth squirmed in her owner's arms, and inspiration hit Lily. She casually took a few steps closer to the front library door, keeping her back—and the contraband book—away from Mrs. Cook.

Want some pets? she silently asked Elspeth. The cat seemed bored with being held, so if Lily could encourage her to act on it . . . *Down!*

That was all it took. Elspeth leaped from Mrs. Cook's arms and shot over to Lily.

"Elly, no! What are you doing?" Mrs. Cook bounded over and scooped up her cat.

Sorry, Lily tried to convey, as Elspeth meowed her displeasure at being confined again.

"Well, we've been working hard, and I think the room's coming along great, so we're definitely making amends," Lily said sweetly. "I should probably get going to class. I hope you'll be impressed when we're done."

Mrs. Cook didn't seem to hear her, trying to contain a squirming feline. "Yes, I should go, too."

Lily sighed with relief once she disappeared from the library, but it was short-lived. Doors were opening and closing, and voices filled the hallway. The previous class was getting out, and Lily's classmates were arriving. The noise provided the necessary cover for Chrysanthemum closing the restricted room's door, though, so that was good.

Lily stuck her pilfered book in her backpack, watching Chrysanthemum try to cram in her three. "Give me one. I promise I won't look through them without you."

Chrysanthemum handed over one of the books. "I'll be too tired to read them all tonight anyway. So when?"

The school had been quieter today, but Lily saw no point in waiting until the weekend. "Tomorrow after school?"

"Okay. That was good thinking, by the way. With her cat."

"Just putting my fairy-princess powers to use."

Chrysanthemum laughed. Lily wanted to laugh herself. Never having been much of a rule-breaker, Lily could only assume this was the adrenaline rush that came from getting away with a crime.

Chapter Twenty-Three
Chrysanthemum

Chrys knew she was in trouble.

First, Lily had apologized. Then she'd bought Chrys hot chocolate. Then they'd been squeezed in that closet of a room together. Not even the pungently musty smell of the Historical Society had been able to hide the delicious scent of Lily's shampoo.

And now, less than twenty-four hours after witch school, Chrys was back in a confined space with Lily.

Lily had insisted on stopping by Black Cat Coffee on the way to their after-school magical study session. Between finding a parking spot and waiting in line, the detour had so far added an extra twenty minutes to her time in Lily's company, and two coffee splurges in one week was more than Chrys should indulge in, but pride kept her mouth shut about the overpriced drinks. Besides, that overpriced coffee would go so well with the homemade cookies she'd brought for them to snack on.

Chrys glanced over at the very same cookies that were displayed for purchase in Black Cat's bakery case and reminded herself that she was sharing only because Lily had bought her a hot chocolate last night. Chrys had to do something nice in return or be forever in Lily's debt.

"Lily, Chrys!" Mr. Stephens's voice cut through the coffee shop's din as Chrys retrieved her PSL from the counter. "Glad to see you two getting along."

Presumptuous, Chrys wanted to retort, but she and Lily were standing close enough to each other that it was clear they'd been waiting for their orders together. And wait—since when did they *not* try to stand as far from each other as possible?

Chrys managed a polite nod, but Lily offered the Historical Society's librarian a pert smile. "Nice to see you," she said, and he seemed pleased.

Chrys waited until they were back in Lily's car before speaking again. "Were you born with that talent, or is it a skill you practice?"

"What?" Lily asked.

"Kissing people's asses."

Lily stiffened, her features turning brittle, and Chrys felt a twinge. She hadn't really been trying to be mean. She just didn't understand how anyone could make it to seventeen without becoming jaded.

"If you're referring to Mr. Stephens, I was being *friendly*," Lily said, coming to a harder-than-necessary stop at an intersection. "You might try it sometime."

I brought you cookies! Chrys wanted to snap back, but didn't. The pumpkin spice aroma had lost some of its appeal. "I like my way better. A scowl a day keeps the bullshit away."

"And the people."

"People *are* the bullshit."

"That's really sad, you know."

Probably, yes. But everyone had to do what was required to survive. "That's why you're the princess, and I'm . . ." The freak? The outcast? The loser? All those options were exhausting.

"The goth girly?" Lily suggested.

Despite the dip her mood had taken, Chrys couldn't help but snort. "How about the evil sorceress?"

"Please, you're not evil."

"You called me a demon," Chrys pointed out, as the light changed color and Lily began driving again.

"I don't think you're actually a demon." Lily paused. "Are you?"

"Do I look like a demon?"

"I don't know. A glamour spell could hide your forked tongue. There'd be no way to tell."

"Nah, a kiss would give that away." A glamour was just an illusion, after all. A kiss would reveal the truth about her tongue, and an image of kissing Lily popped into Chrys's brain, and *oh no*. This car, despite being so roomy, was too confined.

She could smell Lily's shampoo, practically taste the mocha on her lips, feel her breath against her cheek.

Lily was quiet. Had she been shocked into silence? Was she mentally gagging? Had her fingers always clutched the steering wheel that tightly, or was she silently freaking out?

Unable to stand it any longer, Chrys pulled her cookie container from her backpack. "Thank you for the hot chocolate last night. I brought cookies today. Would you like chocolate gingerbread or pumpkin white chocolate chip?"

She hadn't intended to share until they reached Lily's house, but desperate times called for distractions, and Chrys held out the container toward Lily.

Since Lily was driving, she gave it only a quick glance. "Are those from Black Cat?"

"They come from our kitchen first. My mom bakes the ones at Black Cat."

Lily sucked on her lip. "I didn't know your mom made them. Why didn't you say that the other day?"

Chrys shrugged. "I thought if I told you, you might spit out the cookie and complain to Black Cat's manager or something."

Lily gave her a funny look. "I would never."

"Okay." Chrys picked a pumpkin white chocolate chip, trying to sound nonchalant.

Lily narrowed her eyes, and nope—it still wasn't the slightest bit intimidating. But it was kind of cute. Chrys took a large bite of her cookie, hoping these thoughts were the result of low blood sugar.

"I think you can be demon-*ic*," Lily said after a moment. "There's a difference."

"Like, scary?"

"Hardly." She spat the word out too quickly and winced. "Just mean."

Being called mean was laughably hypocritical coming from Lily. Chrys opened her mouth to point this out—but shut it abruptly. Until this whole war over Luke had started, the meanest thing Lily had ever done to Chrys was ignore her (competing over grades hardly counted). To call Lily out for that would be to admit she'd noticed and been hurt.

"I brought you food," Chrys said. "That's friendly, not mean. Just like you wanted me to be."

"True." Lily sounded pained to concede it, and shock flashed over her face. "Oh no. If we're both being friendly, it's no wonder Mr. Stephens sounded so pleased at the coffee shop. Their punishment is working."

"Wow, I hope not."

Lily giggled. "Same. I refuse to be that easily manipulated. We should make a pact that once we solve the hex problem, we go back to fighting. Just on principle."

The very idea that they'd need to plan to fight when Chrys considered this only a temporary alliance made her laugh, too. "Do we need a pact? It'll happen naturally."

"You're right." Lily took a deep breath, her giggles subsiding. "I am not losing to you for valedictorian."

"Oh, you are." Chrys would make certain of it, as she would with winning the magic fair and its scholarship money. "You absolutely *are*."

The weirdness of the situation—she'd made Lily laugh, and she was laughing with Lily—hit Chrys like a paint can to the head. She felt like chaos in this moment. Nothing made sense anymore. And, oh, she was going to regret this, because making Lily laugh felt *good*.

"Are you sure no one's going to catch us?" Chrys asked as Lily pulled into the Allertons' driveway.

"Yeah, it's fine." Lily's tone was neutral, but Chrys sensed tension beneath it. "My dad's in Boston for some real estate conference, and my mom was supposed to be off today, but she got called into the hospital. Sara has a swim meet, and when that's over, she'll go home with one of her friends for dinner. We won't be interrupted."

Great. It would just be her, Lily, and a couple of rabbits. Her it's-not-a-crush-again problem aside, the privacy should have made her relieved, yet Chrys didn't feel it. She just felt sad, thinking about Lily's apology the other day.

"Do you have to cook your own dinner?" Chrys would never have imagined Lily needing to fend for herself.

"Sometimes? I know how to make stuff, but if everyone's going to be gone for a weekend or something because of Sara's swimming, I'll usually eat whatever or get delivery."

"Does that happen a lot—everyone being gone?" Chrys suspected she was being rude. Any moment, Lily would tell her to mind her own business.

"Only during swim season," Lily said. "The rest of the year, it's not as bad."

A princess shouldn't just have someone to cook for her; she should have a retinue, or whatever it was called. Although, Chrys supposed Lily did have that—at school. She was Miss Popular. But the important people, the ones who *should* be there for her, Chrys was less certain about them.

She knew what working odd hours was like. Her mom was out the door in the mornings before Chrys left for school, and most nights, she was in bed while Chrys was still doing her homework. But her mother tried to be there in between. They still ate dinner together every night. During previous winters, when witch school was in session, her mother used to stay up far later than she should so Chrys wouldn't have to bike home in the freezing weather. Chrys wasn't sure which of them had been more relieved when she got her driver's license so her mother wouldn't have to do that this year. They'd be sharing the one car, but it would help. In contrast, it was no wonder Lily had her own car. She had to be responsible for herself constantly.

Once Chrys's initial infatuation with Lily had worn off two years ago, she'd decided Lily was selfish and self-absorbed, but while her opinion wasn't entirely changing, she was beginning to understand. The people closest to Lily had left her to fend for herself. And, viewed that way, it wasn't hard to see why Lily thought she needed to be perfect. What other chance did she have of getting attention?

Unable to stomach any more of these softer thoughts, Chrys got out of the car, and instead of following Lily toward the house, she walked toward the yard. Leaves were piling up on the lawn, creating a thick brown blanket.

It was perfect. She needed to smash something.

"What are you doing?" Lily asked as Chrys set down her coffee and backpack on a retaining wall.

"Stomping." Chrys kicked a rough pile together near the driveway and jumped on it. It crackled nicely.

"That's . . ." Lily shook her head and disappeared into the garage.

"Spoilsport," Chrys muttered.

She kicked together another pile, grinding the leaves deep into the long grass. Lily was probably watching her from a window and rolling her eyes, and what had felt like fun a moment ago was starting to seem childish. Chrys turned to go inside, but before she could, Lily exited the garage carrying a rake.

"Don't do something unless you're going to do it right," Lily said, grinning. Chrys was too surprised to retort, so she stood aside as Lily swept up a decent-sized pile. "There you go."

"Are you laughing at me?"

Lily raised an eyebrow. "Do you care?"

No. Yes. Chrys warmed in spite of the chilly air.

Screw it.

She jumped, and leaves went flying with a delightful scrunch and flutter. Chrys had no idea why it felt so good, but it did. She scrambled up out of the pile, held out a hand for the rake—which Lily passed to her—and quickly raked the pile back together, even larger than before. The Allertons had several mature ash trees on this side of the house that sported partially naked limbs, so there were lots of browning yellow leaves to go around.

"Your turn."

She half expected Lily to turn up her nose, but Lily defied her expectations once again. Without a moment's hesitation, Lily jumped onto the mound. Chrys immediately began raking up the leaves that had gone flying, allowing Lily to jump again and again.

With her red hair, long brown boots, and forest-green jacket, Lily looked every inch a Thornhaven witch. Now that she had leaves sticking to her hair and clothes, it only made her look more magical—and it also made Chrys's stomach swoop like she was stuck on the free-fall side of a good jump.

"Jump with me!" Lily shrieked. She grabbed the rake from Chrys's hand and tossed it aside.

They took turns making piles and jumping, for how long, Chrys couldn't say. Lily's cheeks turned charmingly pink, and

Chrys laughed along with her. For a moment, nothing was more pressing than how loud a noise she could make.

A barking dog broke the spell at last.

Lily stumbled as they both turned to the sound. Instinctively, Chrys reached out to steady her. It wasn't a mistake, exactly, but all the anxious energy she'd burned off flooded her veins again with a vengeance.

She drew a deep breath that was filled with leaf dust and mold, hoping that lungful of death might kill off these feelings inside her chest. She hadn't wanted them before, and she didn't want them now.

Lily tucked her hair behind her ears, the most purely delighted grin on her face that Chrys had ever seen. But it faded into self-consciousness as she realized that the neighbor walking her dog was regarding them and their leafy mess with disdain. "We should get to work."

"Yeah, that's why I'm here."

"That was fun?" Lily almost made it sound like a question. "I haven't done anything like that in a long time."

"It *was* fun." Chrys grabbed her backpack and her coffee, which was still scaldingly hot thanks to the bespelled cup. "Who knew—*you* can have *fun*?"

"Me? *You're* the one who scowls all the time. I used to think you didn't know how to smile."

"Most people don't deserve my smile." They couldn't be trusted not to turn it against her. When you knew what made someone happy, you knew how to make them *un*happy. But wait. If Lily chose to interpret that comment as Chrys finding her more deserving of friendliness than most people . . .

She would simply have to hope Lily took it only as a friendly comment, not a flirty one. After all, she was 100 percent, absolutely, *in no way* ever going to flirt with Lily Allerton.

CHAPTER TWENTY-FOUR
Chrysanthemum

After playing with the bunnies, they spread out on the floor of Lily's room with more of Chrys's mom's cookies. One of the rabbits—Chrys couldn't tell them apart—had stretched out on Lily's foot, and Lily was absently petting her. Chrys found it a bit alarming, both how long the rabbit actually was (not a ball of fluff, after all, but more like a stretchy toy) and how sweet Lily looked scratching the back of the rabbit's head. The bunny's eyes had closed in contentment.

"Can you, I don't know, open the books to the right pages for us to read?" Lily asked.

"That's more specific than my talent gets," Chrys said, drawing her gaze away from Lily's fingers. "We need to do the legwork."

Lily sighed. "I suppose I should be glad your talent isn't *that* good. Then you'd just cheat your way to valedictorian."

"Like I need to cheat to beat you."

Lily stiffened, and Chrys regretted the joke . . . but then Lily shook it off. “Watch it, or I’ll tell Ella to chew your finger off.”

“Really?” Chrys snickered and opened the closest book. “I take back everything I’ve said about you being nice. You have a vicious streak.”

“Yes, I do.” Lily tossed her hair, but even she couldn’t pretend well enough to not break into a laugh. “Oh, shut up and read.”

Chrys shut up and read.

Only a few weeks ago, she’d discovered that antagonizing Lily was more fun than ignoring her. Only a few days ago, she’d discovered that antagonizing Lily was even more fun when Lily smiled as she shot back.

Knowledge was a dangerous thing.

“I don’t know if this helps,” Lily said sometime later. “But the person who wrote this book makes distinctions between hexes and curses.”

Chrys had rolled onto her back, and she turned her head. “That might explain why I’m getting confused by my book. What’s the difference?”

Lily sat up straighter, as if she liked being the first one to have found something useful. That should have made Chrys groan, but instead she found it kind of endearing. Undoubtedly part of that was developing an understanding of why Lily craved validation, but Chrys knew now that it was also much simpler—Lily was a geek. Learning new things made her happy. Just like it did Chrys.

This wasn't a total surprise. Chrys hadn't developed a crush on Lily three years ago just because Lily was pretty. She'd known Lily was smart. It was obvious in both regular school and witch school. When she asked questions in class, they were smart questions—frequently, the same ones in Chrys's brain. And when other people wasted class time by goofing off, Lily usually became as annoyed by their behavior as Chrys did.

"Apparently a hex is a specific spell. You know, like what you did to me." Lily shot her some massive side-eye.

Chrys made an innocent face. "I maintain you deserved it, but go on. A curse?"

Lily looked like she wanted to argue, but she returned to petting her bunny instead. "A curse is something altogether different. It lasts longer than a hex and takes on a life of its own. It almost sounds like you *can't* intentionally curse someone or something. The book talks a lot about how a buildup of negative magic is what leads to a curse."

Chrys chewed her lip. She still didn't entirely believe she'd hexed Lily the night Lily had hexed her, but it was true that she'd never felt any direct repercussions of Lily's hex. Possibly, Lily hadn't done it well enough. Or possibly, the negative energy Chrys had been giving off had collided with Lily's magic first and . . . created a curse?

"A buildup of negative magic that takes on a life of its own definitely sounds like what we're dealing with," Chrys said.

"It does."

"Hold on." Chrys picked up her second book. "I saw something in here about curses, too." Her hands were jittery with a toxic combination of caffeine, hyperawareness of Lily watching her, and growing anxiety about what they'd done.

As she searched, the other rabbit (the one not currently making a bed of Lily) came over and stuck her head under the crook of Chrys's arm, as if to offer herself up for petting stress relief. Coincidence, or had Lily noticed Chrys's tension and sent her over? Chrys rubbed the rabbit behind the eyes like she'd seen Lily do, and they both relaxed a bit.

"Okay, here it is." She began to read: "*All magic, while intangible on the material plane, contains mass on the metaphysical plane. Over time, if too much mass accumulates in a given location or around a specific object . . .*" Chrys stopped reading and skimmed ahead. "This is too long, but they're explaining how objects can end up having positive or negative magic associated with them. It's saying that the magic can break the veil separating the planes and manifest on the material one."

"Manifest?" Lily sounded like she might be ill. "Like, it's saying that the curse will be here physically?"

Chrys swallowed. The curses described were terrifying. Anything that could do what this book was suggesting would have to be a thousand times more powerful than any magic they'd yet encountered—or consciously performed.

"Yeah, there would be a physical manifestation somewhere, the center of the evil magic," she said, reading more.

"To destroy the curse, we have to find it and perform a ritual that destroys it."

"Oh, that's all?" Lily groaned and flopped to the floor next to her.

Lily's head was mere inches from hers, but Chrys tried to ignore that. "The ritual looks simple, but we'd have to know what energies the curse is made up of. Like, what motivated its creation."

"Seems obvious," Lily said. "It's that we hate each other."

Lily was right, obviously, but Chrys sat up, needing to do something to cope with the way Lily's words twisted up her insides. They hated each other. Simple.

"Here." She shoved the book at Lily's stupid, pretty face so she could read the ritual for herself. Lily shouldn't be allowed to have cute bunnies. She shouldn't be allowed to love animals or jump in leaves or buy Chrys coffee.

"So, yes, we need to find the curse's core manifestation," Lily said. "But we also need to gather some supplies before we can do this spell. The book makes it sounds like the manifestation is most likely to be where the effects are centered. That means school. You were right that the ritual doesn't seem too complicated . . ."

Not complicated wasn't the same as *easy*.

Lily was biting on one of her fingers as she set the book down. "Since we don't hate each other anymore, shouldn't half the work already be done?"

Oh.

This simple sentence sent Chrys's emotions spinning, and she fell back on her usual defense mechanism: sarcasm. "Presumptuous of you to assume."

Lily stared at her as if she couldn't tell whether Chrys was being serious or not. Chrys was torn between laughing and . . .

She had the strongest urge to kiss Lily. Her lips practically buzzed with anticipation.

But that was out of the question. The chasm between not hating each other and *other things* was wide. Temporary allies, acquaintances, even friends would have to do.

"I'm kidding," she said, flopping back to the floor next to Lily. Lily's eyelashes had a tint of red in them. She'd never noticed before.

"I know," Lily said, but she sounded relieved, and Chrys realized something more than the color of Lily's eyelashes: Lily was a shitty liar. "We should make a plan. Since the curse gets most violent when we're close together, we should wait until after school to look for its manifestation. We don't want anyone to get hurt."

"So, we'll search tomorrow?" Chrys asked, and Lily nodded.

Lily laced her fingers together above her head. "Saturday would be a good day to perform the ritual. No one around. So tomorrow, we find the curse, assuming it is at the school. This weekend, we gather supplies and practice the casting. And next weekend, we sneak into the school after everyone's left to do the spell."

Chrys imagined Lily color coding a calendar with a day-by-day breakdown of tasks. "I know you love plans, but overplanning stresses me out, just so you know."

Lily rolled onto her side, and holy shit—her face was even closer now, inches away, and every muscle in Chrys's body tensed.

"Look, I know we're apparently super powerful, but we can't wing this," Lily said. "Besides, doesn't having a plan make you feel better? We accomplished something."

Chrys sat up, casually (or so she hoped), wishing her brain could focus on the task at hand rather than the girl. "I suppose."

Lily rolled her eyes and also sat up. "Stop being negative. The Society recast their magic-suppression spells on the school, so we should be fine waiting another week. We deserve to relax a little. Let's do some homework."

"That's your idea of relaxing?" Chrys snorted.

"No, but it needs to be done, and tomorrow we're going curse-hunting, and Saturday we have to paint." Lily hesitated. "We could do homework together to get it done faster . . . then do something fun to celebrate."

Something fun. Together.

Lily had made a similar offer last week when she'd invited Chrys to stay for dinner.

Chrys felt less panicky this time, but still unsure. As an introvert, she didn't mind being alone (helpful when one didn't have many friends), but there was a difference between being alone and feeling abandoned, and Lily clearly leaned toward the latter.

Did Lily want *her* here, or just a warm body—someone she could talk to?

It felt ridiculous to think Lily wanted Chrys around for her own sake, but the idea held up better the more she considered it. After all, Lily had lots of friends. There had to be other people she could hang out with. But Chrys was the person Lily was asking.

"Okay," Chrys said, disbelieving the words coming out of her mouth. "Homework, then fun."

Chapter Twenty-Five

Lily

As she'd made the invitation, Lily had half expected Chrysanthemum to bolt like she had last week. She knew she should give up on thinking she'd ever had Chrysanthemum figured out, though. Similarly, she should probably give up on insisting she disliked Chrysanthemum.

The truth was, Chrysanthemum could be pretty likable when she tried.

Now Lily needed to stop feeling nervous around her for no reason. Perhaps spending more time with Chrysanthemum doing normal things like homework or watching a movie would help with that. She could train her body to stop seeing Chrysanthemum as a threat. Valedictorian competition, but not an enemy.

They worked in companionable silence over the next hour. Lily had another chapter of *Le Petit Prince* she needed to read and write about for French class, and

Chrysanthemum was taking notes on a book for their history term paper.

Around five, Lily's phone vibrated with a text from her mother:

Sara is going over to Ophelia's for dinner.

Okay

I think there's leftover chicken in the fridge.

Thanks

Sighing, Lily left Chrysanthemum to her reading and went downstairs to peek into the fridge. Sure enough, there was a container of leftover chicken parm.

It looked very unappealing.

"Pizza?" Lily asked, returning to the bedroom. It was early for dinner, but she was getting hungry, and it might take a while for her and Chrysanthemum to agree on something.

"Sure," Chrysanthemum said, although Lily wasn't sure at all that Chrysanthemum had heard her. "Listen to this. This is one of the books I'm reading for history, and it's going over reputed witchcraft on the island. It claims there was a feud between two families—the Allertons and the Langmores—in the early nineteenth century!"

Lily sat on her bed. "Okay? Why are you so excited?"

"An Allerton woman and a Langmore woman both mysteriously disappeared together. They had a friendship their families didn't approve of—hmm, wonder what *that* could mean—and so when they vanished, each family blamed the other. There were accusations of foul play, although no evidence of it was ever found. But soon after the women disappeared, fights broke out and—coincidentally, according to the book—there were crop failures, a roof that blew off a house, livestock that died . . ." Chrysanthemum tore through the pages. "This could help explain what's going on! There's a whole history of negative energy between us."

"Wait." Lily held up her hands. "How does this explain anything?"

Chrysanthemum stared at her for a moment. "I told you—my family is from Thornhaven."

"Yeah, but your last name is Quinn, so what does this have to do with us?"

"I'm also a Langmore—well, descended from Langmores. We haven't been Langmores in a couple of generations. But everything makes sense now! How could either of our hexes, even *if* they collided, been powerful enough to turn into a curse? They probably weren't. But if they built on negative energy that was already *there*, sleeping for a couple of centuries . . ."

Lily nodded, the pieces fitting together. "And because we did those hexes at this time of the year, when the veil between the material and metaphysical planes is already thin, it was enough to tear a hole and for the curse to manifest."

"What if we need to address the feud in order to destroy the curse?"

"But address it how?" Lily asked. She got up and started pacing. New information was good, but they needed more. "We can speculate about why our ancestors disappeared, but we can't really know what happened or why our families reacted the way they did."

Chrysanthemum flipped through a few pages. "There's nothing else here. But how do any of these things *really* start? There's probably no clear answer."

"How can there be no answer? Someone must have done *something* first."

"Really?" Chrysanthemum raised her eyebrows. "Why did we start fighting?"

Lily opened her mouth, then quickly shut it before something she didn't want out found its way into the air. "Luke," she lied.

Chrysanthemum slammed the book closed and tucked it into her backpack. "No. At the ninth-grade magic fair, you threw a fit to your friends when I won, and I decided I couldn't stand you."

Lily picked up Cinder. It was true—that hadn't been one of her finest moments—but she'd had no idea Chrysanthemum had overheard her. For the first time, she considered whether some of the nervousness she felt around Chrysanthemum was due to guilt. She should have been nicer to Chrysanthemum when she moved here. It seemed ages, now, although it had been only three years ago. She could console herself that she'd been less mature then, more judgmental . . .

Chrysanthemum had shown up that first day of school dressed all in black, and Lily had scoffed, because Chrysanthemum looked like she was faking it. A witch cliché. But if Lily was being 100 percent honest, that wasn't the entire truth.

The entire truth was . . . Lily had also been intimidated.

Chrysanthemum was different and she didn't care, and that took a strength, a power, that Lily didn't have. So Lily had ignored her, hoping that would help her ignore the jealousy and the something else—a kind of longing—that gnawed at her chest whenever she glanced Chrysanthemum's way.

She'd known the other witches would follow her lead; Lily had been on top of the social pyramid for too long for them not to. Ignoring Chrysanthemum was the only way she could stay there, and she *had* to stay there. Already her parents were growing less interested in her. David would be applying to college soon. Sara was beginning to shine as a swimmer. Lily was the unremarkable child.

None of that was Chrysanthemum's fault, but Lily had—because of her own insecurities—essentially ostracized her from the magical community. Lily was an Allerton witch, as people liked to remind her, a descendant of one of the oldest families on the island, and she should have been the one to welcome Chrysanthemum into the fold. They might not have had enough in common to become friends, but surely it had been Lily's responsibility to help Chrysanthemum feel like she belonged?

How could Lily take pride in being responsible if she couldn't do that?

All the times Chrysanthemum had teased her about being too kind to properly insult her, she couldn't have really meant *kind*, could she? Because Lily had not been kind. She wasn't good at insults; that was all.

Lily set Cinder down and sank to the floor next to Chrysanthemum.

"I'm sorry about that," she said. "About all of it."

Chrysanthemum froze, and in the perfect silence, Lily thought her heart was going to pound right out of her chest. "All of what?" Chrysanthemum asked at last.

Lily wished she hadn't pulled her hair back in a ponytail while they were reading because she wanted to comb it over her face. Without that option, she pulled in her knees. "For not being nicer to you when you moved here. For rejecting you. I knew other people would follow my lead." She gazed ahead, unwilling to see what was passing over Chrysanthemum's face.

"Why weren't you?" Chrysanthemum asked softly.

Lily didn't want to go into that—there was apologizing and then there was making a fool of herself—but she owed Chrysanthemum something. "It's complicated. But let's say that it's because I thought you were a tryhard. I literally thought you wore colored contacts."

Lily finally turned, let herself stare into Chrysanthemum's eyes. They did, still, strike her as an unnatural color, but there was nothing eerie about them. They were actually breathtaking, and that pinch of longing Lily had been trying to suppress for years expanded in her chest.

Chrysanthemum was, Lily had to admit, very pretty. Not just her eyes, but her thick eyelashes and pouty lips. Lily suddenly wasn't sure whether she was jealous that she didn't look like Chrysanthemum or upset that Chrysanthemum was almost certainly not thinking the same things about her. Although why should she care if Chrysanthemum thought she was pretty?

Chrysanthemum shifted, tugging her sleeves down over her hands, but it didn't hide the color creeping up her neck. She laughed, sounding a little nervous herself. "It's funny. I assumed you snubbed me because you didn't think I could be much of a witch, and I guess I was right. I really wanted to beat you at the fair that year to show you that I was—I am."

"You definitely did." Lily cringed. "It made me realize you were going to be major competition, and I became very . . . well, jealous. The spell you won with—the hair-color spell—have you ever thought about casting it again, changing things?"

Chrysanthemum doubled over, and for a moment Lily thought she'd burst into tears. She was shaking, her head pressed into the rug. But when Chrysanthemum raised her head, her eyes were watery, but only because she had been laughing silently. "Sorry."

"What?" Lily demanded. A pit had opened in her stomach.

Chrysanthemum took a couple of deep breaths. "I'm not laughing at you, I swear. Apparently that spell was a fluke. I've tried to change my hair back to its natural color so many times, and I can't. It wasn't even supposed to be black! I was trying to turn it *blue*, but I guess my intentions weren't clear, and . . . Well, you can see. I've never asked for help because I didn't want to admit that I screwed it up!"

Lily's stared at her in shock. A *fluke*? She'd been obsessing over Chrysanthemum's prodigy-level power for the past two years because of a *fluke*? She must have stopped breathing for a moment, her entire body too devoted to processing this information to remember how to sustain life. Then Lily gasped, and oxygen flooded her lungs. She was going to scream. Absolutely lose her shit.

She burst out laughing. "I don't believe this! Oh my god. I have . . ." But she had nothing, not even words. A few weeks ago, learning this would have filled her with triumph and relief. It was proof that Chrysanthemum was fallible. Lily was positive she'd have laughed then, too, but it would have been a very different sort of laugh.

Now, it all struck her as simply hilarious, and Chrysanthemum was laughing, too, and that made Lily laugh harder.

Before she could think better of it, she reached over and twirled a strand of Chrysanthemum's hair around her finger. Chrysanthemum's laughter disappeared abruptly, and she tensed.

Odd. A single strand of hair *could* be powerful if used in a spell (or a hex), but Lily had hoped Chrysanthemum trusted her.

Reluctantly, she dropped Chrysanthemum's hair, unsure what had possessed her to touch it in the first place. "You still cast a powerful spell. Even if it didn't go the way you intended. That's natural ability."

"True," Chrysanthemum said with a shrug. "On the bright side, black is better than blue."

"Did you just say 'on the bright side'?" Lily grinned, happy to put that momentary awkwardness behind them. "I didn't know you could think like that. I must be rubbing off on you."

Chrysanthemum clutched her hands to her chest. "Shit. I need to get out of here before it's too late!"

"It might be too late already," Lily said mildly, getting up. "You were the one who started *frolicking* this afternoon."

"I do not frolic. I was *smashing* those leaves."

Lily stood in her doorway and gestured for the rabbits to follow her. When no one else was around, they got to roam the house. "Call it what you want, but I know what I saw. Are you coming or not?"

Chrysanthemum glanced at the rabbits. "Are you talking to me or them?"

"All of you. You're not leaving before pizza, right?"

Chrysanthemum hesitated for a second; then she smiled. "I'd never leave before pizza."

CHAPTER TWENTY-SIX
Chrysanthemum

A smart witch would have spent last night and this morning reading more about how one would defeat a curse.

Chrys was not that witch. She'd spent last night, this morning, and 90 percent of the afternoon (until this very second) replaying in her head the time she'd spent with Lily yesterday.

The moment Lily had touched her hair (Chrys was still recovering). Hanging out on the sofa, eating pizza. Chrys had broken all her rules about not sharing more of her life than was necessary, telling Lily about growing up in New York, her grandfather's music career, her grandmother's sunflowers, and more. In return, Lily had told her about the trials of growing up with siblings and how one day she wanted to travel the world.

After the last bell rang, Chrys pulled out her phone, wondering where she was supposed to meet Lily, and as if summoned, a text from Lily popped onto her screen. Wait ten minutes for people to leave, then we'll meet in the main lobby.

Thornhaven High was built like a misshapen T, with the academic classrooms in the main building and two blobs coming off the western end—one for the performing arts rooms and theater, and the other for the gym and athletics rooms. The cafeteria sat on one end of the junction, nearest the academic classrooms, and the main lobby at the other by the theater.

There weren't a lot of places to sit in the lobby, so Chrys perched on a windowsill and brought up her latest library download on her phone while she waited.

"Oh, good. You're already here," Lily said, sitting next to her and startling her out of her book. "I have a plan, but I'm not sure it's going to work."

"Okay, good, yes. Yes. Great. I was wondering about a plan." Someone smack her. Looking at Lily, Chrys could barely string together a complete sentence.

Lily didn't appear fazed by Chrys's stammering. She was scanning the lobby, and she motioned to a spot above the large set of doors that led toward the academic hallway and cafeteria. Despite everything else going on in her head, Chrys caught on to what Lily was looking at immediately.

The black veins.

Over the past couple of weeks, they'd become a more constant presence around the school. Chrys could put them out of her head well enough to focus on her classes, but they trailed her like a shadow, appearing everywhere she went.

Lily waited for a few more students to cross the lobby and leave before speaking again. "Have you noticed that every time the black lines appear, they seem to move with us? They don't just fade in and out of existence."

"Yeah?"

"Have you noticed it's always from the same side?"

Chrys started to reply with an automatic *yeah*—she couldn't help that Lily's lips were distracting—but she snapped out of it and caught herself. "What do you mean?"

Lily bit her lip, thinking. "It's like a yo-yo string. They stretch one way, and then they pull back the same way." She demonstrated with her arm. "No matter which direction the lines move in, they always fade in and out from one side to the other. I noticed the other day. When I was in gym, the lines appeared and disappeared in one direction, and when I was in French, on the other side of the building, they did it the opposite way."

Chrys racked her memory for confirmation, but the truth was that she'd never paid close attention to how the veins moved. "You think they're moving in and out from the location of the curse."

"Exactly!" Lily grinned, and Chrys's stomach fluttered. "It's just a theory, but it's the only explanation I can think of. And I think the curse is always trying to pull us together. Lead us toward each other, you know?"

Chrys glanced up at the lines above the set of double doors. They were static now. She and Lily were sitting so close that their knees almost touched, and the air in that space between their skin felt charged with electricity. "Go on."

"I don't know if this will work," Lily said, although she sounded confident, "but what if we split up and start at opposite ends of the school? The lines should try to lead us toward each other, so they'll be moving, and when they move, we'll see the direction they manifest from. We head in *that* direction and see where it leads."

"Sounds like a good plan," Chrys said. It also sounded like their only plan, but flattery never hurt, and the way Lily's face lit up—as though a compliment from Chrys *meant* something—chased away her disappointment over needing to split up.

Since Chrys knew the theater wing better than Lily, they agreed that she would begin there while Lily would start at the far end of the academic wing. If the curse was located at one of the ends of the building where each of them was starting, it might confuse their search, but Chrys reasoned they would figure this out quickly enough based on the way the veins acted.

It took her a few minutes to get the hang of what she needed to do, but once her brain managed to focus, she moved quickly. Soon she was past the theater entrance and creeping right back to the lobby where they'd started.

Lily: Check in??

Chrys: Lobby. You?

Lily: Almost at cafeteria

Lily was moving faster than Chrys was. The performing arts wing was a convoluted mess of hallways, whereas the academic wing was a straight shot from one end to the other. Much easier to navigate.

Lily: I think it has to be here. Hurry up!!!

Chrys: Where?

The veins were on the move for her. They bypassed the doors leading to the gym and thrust straight toward . . .

Lily: Cafeteria

Chrys charged toward her. Lily stood on the far side of the room, near where the food service was located, and she spun around as Chrys flung open the doors. The veins streaked across the ceiling, leading her toward Lily.

"Did you find it?" Chrys panted.

"Not yet."

Chrys frowned at the grim reaper, which was once more a lifeless decoration, and suppressed a shudder. New pumpkins had replaced the ones that had exploded, although they were fewer in number, and the plastic spiders had long since returned to their fake webs. Perhaps it made sense that the curse would be located around the cafeteria. The biggest and most violent incidents had all occurred in this room.

"We're the only ones who will be able to see it, right?"

"Right." Lily wound a strand of hair around her finger nervously. "But we don't even know what it would look like."

"I'm guessing it's a you'll-know-it-when-you-see-it situation." For Lily's sake, more than her own, Chrys hoped it wasn't *too* nightmare-inducing. She figured she could handle a lot more ickiness than Lily could. Watching horror movies had to confer some sort of inoculation benefit. "Well, I don't see anything out here. What about in there?"

Lily turned sharply. "Where?"

"That's the kitchen where they store and reheat the food, right? Fewer people go in there." Some of the veins overhead *did* seem to be retracting toward that kitchen, which had only one door. But to really test the yo-yo theory, one of them would have to go in there while the other waited outside.

Chrys walked behind the food-service counter, swearing the stink of every meal the school had ever served blended together here. Pizza and mushy pasta and soggy hamburgers in foil pouches . . . Nausea roiled her stomach.

There was no lock, and the handle turned, so she inched the kitchen door open.

Behind her, Lily gasped. "The lines are all moving! It must be in there!"

Chrys swallowed, creeping inside. The main lights were out—school was over—but some safety lights provided a dim glow, enough for her to see the enormous industrial freezers and the long central stainless steel counter. The smell worsened, too. It wasn't old food now, but something earthy and rotting. She put her arm over her nose, amazed none of the normies who worked back here could detect it.

"It's here." Chrys knew it in her bones. That foulness could be caused only by something dangerous and unnatural. Chrys followed her nose, moving slowly into the kitchen, deeper and deeper. The smell was strongest at the center of the room.

“I think I’m going to vomit,” Lily whispered, coming up behind her.

“Please don’t. It smells bad enough.”

Lily scoffed and covered her nose. “Thank goodness the ritual for destroying a curse calls for ‘the burning of strong incense.’”

No kidding. Chrys wouldn’t admit it, but she was closer to gagging than she cared for, and vomit was one thing she really couldn’t stand.

The only thing that might be worse than the stench was the physical manifestation of the curse, or so Chrys decided as she squatted by the central counter and sucked in a sharp breath of surprise. Her stomach churned, and she breathed again through her sleeve, deeply and slowly, to settle her guts.

“You found it?” Lily darted over.

All Chrys managed was to raise one warning hand, hoping Lily would understand the gesture, but Lily was determined. She knelt next to Chrys—and grabbed her arm when she found what Chrys was staring at.

While Lily’s touch typically made her brain spin, today it steadied her. Made her stronger for Lily’s sake.

“Know it when you see it,” Chrys whispered.

The books they’d read had shown an example of a cursed tree—a sickly, rotting thing with withered leaves, peeling black bark, and an air of menace around it. But, while the tree in the drawing might have been cursed, Chrys was now certain the actual curse must have been buried *inside* it. Because the curse in front of them was something else entirely.

It clung to the underside of the central counter, over a stack of foil pans. At first glance, Chrys had assumed it was a nest of worms, but they were unlike anything she'd ever seen (or wanted to see ever again). They formed a mass that was vaguely heart-shaped, and despite its disparate parts, the curse pulsed as one organism to a slow, steady rhythm. Dark colors—purple and green—swirled over the inky, squirming surface like an oil slick.

With her free arm, Chrys retrieved her phone from her pocket and switched on the flashlight. Lily tensed. Chrys wasn't sure if she might disturb the *thing* with light, but she needed a better look.

In the flashlight's glow, the veins seeping out from the curse were obvious. As they had the very first time Chrys saw them, they once again reminded her of cracks, and she thought she understood why. They *were* cracks—cracks between the material and metaphysical planes. The curse sat in the middle of a nest of them, like a disgusting baseball frozen in time as it shattered a windowpane.

Nothing bad had happened the last time she'd tried touching the veins, so Chrys reached out with a finger, curiosity overpowering her better sense. She never made it. Lily yanked her backward, and Chrys landed on her butt.

"Please don't!" Lily scrambled to her feet. "We found it. That's all we came to do. Let's get out of here."

Lily's face was taut, and she had a point.

"Okay, okay." Chrys got up and followed Lily, who was already halfway out the door, holding it open and pleading with Chrys with her eyes. She was scared shitless—but she clearly wouldn't leave without Chrys.

They said nothing else as they returned to the lobby, gathered their belongings, and stepped out into the crisp autumn air. Chrys's lungs cleared, and her head with them. Maybe it was a combination of adrenaline and Lily touching her, but she hadn't felt this alive in a long time. She couldn't prevent a stupid grin from spreading across her face.

When she turned toward Lily, Lily was smiling, too. "I can't believe you!" She ran over and shoved Chrys. "What is wrong with you? Trying to touch it, shining lights in its face . . . Who knows what it might have done to you?"

"I swear there was a time when you would have been thrilled if something awful happened to me."

Lily's cheeks pinkened. "I mean, I never want something truly awful to happen to anyone. But . . . yes. There was a time I didn't like you. And I guess . . . I've started to enjoy having you around."

Was it possible to crack your face open from grinning? Chrys's cheek muscles hurt, and her pulse was pounding harder than it had been in the kitchen. "You're not so bad yourself. For royalty."

"Shut up." Lily shoved her again, and Chrys stumbled, laughing.

Not so bad yourself. Like she hadn't 100 percent fallen for Lily again.

Except this time it was both better and worse, because this time Lily wasn't some pretty but unattainable mean girl who didn't deserve her. This time, Chrys had gotten to know who she really was, and she'd learned that she and Lily weren't all that different. They were both messed up *and* messy. She couldn't be furious at herself for liking the real Lily.

So it was going to hurt a thousand times more when Lily didn't like her in return.

Chrys needed to do something about that, but she didn't know what.

"I don't actually like Luke as more than a friend, you know."

What the hell was wrong with her mouth? She might pass out. Honestly, that could be a mercy. She didn't know why she'd said what she did. Was it a confession? Did she think she should give Lily a hint about her own feelings?

If so, that was stupid. Lily liked Luke. Chrys knew this. Wasn't she essentially telling Lily that she would no longer stand in her way, then? So maybe it wasn't a confession at all. Maybe it was some kind of apology for trying to come between Luke and Lily in the first place. That would be fair, since Lily had apologized for snubbing Chrys.

Or maybe fairness had nothing to do with it, and Chrys was just a pessimist, so it was easier to stab herself in the heart now and get it over with rather than wait for the inevitable rejection.

Surprise turned to confusion on Lily's face, and no wonder. If Chrys couldn't figure out her own motivations, how could she expect Lily to?

As long as Lily didn't hear the unspoken second half—*I like you*—then Chrys hoped she could play her comment off like it was nothing.

"You don't?" Lily asked slowly.

Chrys buried her hands in her hoodie pockets. "I thought he was too pure and sweet for you, but you know, since I've decided you're not *that* evil . . ."

"Oh."

She didn't know what to expect from Lily, but she'd have thought a little more emotion would have been normal. Relief? Excitement? Eagerness to go claim the object of her affections?

"Thanks for telling me that," Lily said, although she sounded less thankful and more what-the-hell-just-happened than Chrys would have preferred.

Then:

"Do you want to go shopping?" Lily asked. Between the way she rushed her words and the change of topic, it took Chrys a moment to catch up. "For supplies, I mean? We could stop at Black Cat and get coffee, then head to the Cauldron Supply. It's such a nice day, and I have all this stress to burn off, and we could walk down to the harbor and see how the ball decorations are going." She paused. "If you want."

Chrys relaxed her hands in her pockets. "Totally. Let's do that."

Chapter Twenty-Seven
Lily

Lily couldn't shake the feeling that Chrysanthemum telling her that she wasn't pursuing Luke was somehow significant. She just didn't understand why, beyond the obvious. If Chrysanthemum was no longer standing in her way, then her biggest non-curse problem was solved. She'd conquered her five of Wands.

Next stop: romantic happiness and a perfect senior year.

And yet, Lily didn't feel happy. All through the drive into town, she considered bringing up the subject—her brain demanded clarification—but it wasn't like Chrysanthemum could explain Lily's hang-ups to her.

For that matter, Lily wasn't sure why she'd asked if Chrysanthemum wanted to go shopping and get coffee, either. Yes, they had to get supplies, but Lily had already volunteered to do that. She supposed she could chalk it up to celebrating another small victory, but she'd already used that excuse yesterday. And, if she was being honest, an excuse was all it was—today *and* yesterday.

It had to be the novelty, then. She'd known everyone else in Thornhaven practically her whole life. There were few nooks and crannies of their personalities left to discover, whereas everything about Chrysanthemum was different and exciting—her opinions, her sense of humor, all the stories she had to tell. Even being teased gave Lily a rush. Not only was Chrysanthemum more interesting than her other friends, she made Lily feel more interesting, too.

Lily had texted her parents that she was going to the library to work on her research paper. Although she was grounded, the library was on her "approved places" list, and she doubted they'd call up the branch for proof.

Downtown was bustling, which was no surprise considering it was an unseasonably warm day. Lily was forced to park a block away from the main thoroughfare, and a thought occurred to her as she shut off the engine. "Do you want to hit the Cauldron Supply first since we can't take drinks into the shop?"

If that happened to mean she and Chrysanthemum would hang out longer, because they wouldn't feel rushed to finish, that was just practical. Lily didn't want to be rushed.

"Sure. If you're really not sick of spending so much time with me." Chrysanthemum sounded dubious.

"I wouldn't have suggested it if I was." Despite everything she'd been ruminating on during the drive, it still surprised Lily to hear the words leaving her mouth. "Or wait—are you trying to politely say that you're sick of me?"

Chrysanthemum's ears reddened, much like they had earlier when they'd been talking about Luke. It was kind of cute. Lily liked this softer Chrysanthemum, one who didn't always seem disdainful and cold. The sight made Lily smile in spite of the wave of anxiety her half-joking question had caused.

"I told you—you're not so bad," Chrysanthemum said, and Lily's insides released their tension.

Yesterday, they'd made a note of everything they needed for banishing the curse. Luckily, between the two of them, they had many items covered already. For the rest, Lily had a list, and she and Chrysanthemum split it up as they wandered the cramped magic shop.

The Cauldron Supply had something for everyone, whether they were witches in need of real magical supplies or normies who didn't know better, in search of a witchy aesthetic. There were candles and beautiful candleholders; glass bottles filled with essential oils; dozens of jars packed with dried herbs; censers for stick or loose incense; books and jewelry; and so much more. Lily loved it in here, and if she hadn't been on a mission, she'd have taken the time to smell the various new incense blends, sort through the baskets of polished crystals and semiprecious stones, and covet the artwork in a lovely tarot deck that she didn't need. The Cauldron Supply's shelves stretched almost to the shop's open-beam ceiling, dark weathered wood that looked as old as the town itself. Dusty floorboards creaked beneath her feet as she strolled, and smokeless candles that had been bespelled to perpetually burn provided a cozy glow. The whole place had a timeless vibe to it—one that stretched from the seventeenth century into the modern age, depending on where you glanced.

As with the other witch-owned businesses and buildings in the area, faintly glowing wards surrounded the doorways and windows. And—like they all did of late—the wards gave off a recognizable tinge, suggesting they were being strengthened. The Historical Society had sent out an alert to all its members suggesting they remain vigilant.

After deciding the Peace & Purification incense blend would work for the banishing spell, Lily picked up one of the shop's empty paper bags labeled ONE OUNCE and placed it on one side of the old-fashioned balance scale. On the other side, she placed the jar of incense. Magic did the rest. As Lily watched, one ounce's worth of the incense disappeared from the jar and reappeared inside the bag.

"Thank you," Lily whispered, although she knew there was no point. It just felt impolite not to.

She stuck the jar back on the shelf with dozens of similar ones and taped the bag shut. Under better circumstances, she'd have created her own mix with the right herbs, but this didn't seem like the time to experiment.

Lily added the incense to her shopping basket and checked her list. Almost done. Chrysanthemum was supposed to be getting fresh frankincense oil, so Lily headed toward the front of the store, where the last supplies she needed were. There was a large selection of candles in all sizes and colors, and Lily began counting out the correct number of small white pillars for the banishing spell.

"Lily!"

Hearing someone greet her by name, she glanced up as Bethany Lord wandered down her aisle. Bethany was a junior, but Lily knew her. Thanks to the Historical Society, they had spent plenty of time together since they were toddlers. Lily considered Bethany to be better than averagely talented, but she had a mean streak that had gotten her in trouble on more than one occasion. She had even used magic to play cruel little pranks on normies. Lily kept as much distance as politeness would allow.

Bethany lowered her voice. "Watch out. There's some witch trash up front."

"What?"

"Chrys Quinn," Bethany said, as though Lily should have known. "Resident antisocial freak?"

Irritation flooded Lily's veins. She should have done more to stand up to Bethany all these years.

"Chrysanthemum has more power in her pinkie finger than most witches have in their entire bodies," Lily snapped. "I'd watch your mouth if I were you."

The shock on Bethany's face passed rapidly into disgust. "What the hell? I thought you hated her!"

The words *I don't hate her* formed on Lily's tongue, but she swallowed them down. It was time for something stronger. "We're friends."

As soon as she said it, her heart sped up with worry over what Chrysanthemum might think about that. But Lily meant it. Or at least, she wanted it to be true.

Bethany stared at her for a moment, caught off guard. "Okay. Fine. Very cool." Then she shrugged and sauntered off.

Lily stuck the last candle in her basket, walked around the row, and stopped dead in her tracks when she discovered Chrysanthemum had been on the other side of the shelf the entire time. She seemed to be debating between two jars of oil, holding each dark blue bottle up in turn toward the shop's low light. It was impossible that she hadn't overheard Lily's conversation with Bethany, but she was acting so engrossed by the jars that Lily could almost believe it and hope.

The studious expression on her face made Lily swallow. Serious, concentrating Chrysanthemum was fascinating to watch.

Chrysanthemum finally set one of the jars back on the shelf. "I wasn't sure which one would be better for the ritual."

"How did you decide?"

Chrysanthemum shrugged. "Gut feeling?"

They were partners, but that didn't mean Lily didn't have issues with the way Chrysanthemum approached magic. "I'm not sure that's—"

She didn't get any further, because a scream pierced the soothing music playing over the shop's speakers.

A second later, Bethany dashed past them. As she did, the store's dozens of candles extinguished, plunging the shop into a thick, hazy dimness as the charmed wicks began pouring out years of magically suppressed smoke.

Lily gasped, but before she or anyone else could ask the obvious question—*What is going on?*—the wards around the shop's windows and doors burst in a serious of pops, like a half dozen corks flying out of champagne bottles. The colorful glowing sigils fizzled into nothingness.

Bethany let out an anguished whine and threw open the door. "What is going *on* in this town?" She disappeared down the street at a run.

Chrysanthemum darted over to the door and held it open, coughing as she waved away some of the smoke. "Look!"

She was pointing at the flags that decorated the lampposts. One by one, coming from the direction of the Historical Society, they were being torn down, as though an invisible hand were ripping them away. Lily grabbed the door handle from Chrysanthemum and yanked it shut right before the closest flag went flying.

But whatever the curse was doing, it didn't pause at the shop. With her face pressed against the door's window, Lily watched the flags down the rest of the street being flung into the air.

"Prop that door open again, honey," Annabeth said from behind Lily. "Or we're all going to asphyxiate in here."

Chrysanthemum did as asked, and Lily turned while the shop lit up with muted electrical light.

Annabeth put her hands on her hips and coughed. "I just replaced those wards two days ago, and all these candles . . . The smoke in here!" She waved a hand in front of her wrinkled brown face. "Something foul is afoot in Thornhaven."

"Yeah." Lily glanced down at her basket of supplies and hoped it wasn't too obvious that she and Chrysanthemum might be responsible for it. "I don't suppose I can check out?"

"Still got electricity, so I don't see why not. Come on over so I can get to airing this place out."

Chrysanthemum was propping open the door with a large cast-iron cauldron filled with besoms for sale, so Lily grabbed the jar of oil from her and set it down with the basket on the counter. "You want to go grab a table at Black Cat while I check out?"

Chrysanthemum looked uncertain for a second, eyeing the street, but the moment of magical upset seemed to have passed. She nodded.

The smoke was already dissipating, and Lily glanced down at the display of random items for sale by the counter while Annabeth maintained a nonstop commentary about the magical weirdness infecting Thornhaven, interspersed with more coughing. Lily didn't want to be rude, but she didn't want to react, either, afraid Annabeth might see something reminiscent of guilt on her face if she did.

The store's display of enamel pins provided an easy excuse. As her backpack would attest, Lily loved a pretty enamel pin, and there was no shortage of designs to choose from. Pentacles and triple moons, trees and ravens, and there—a perfect yellow sunflower.

Chrysanthemum had told her how much she'd loved the field of sunflowers her grandparents used to have, one of many tidbits that left Lily desperate to know what other secrets Chrysanthemum was hiding.

Lily hesitated, then pointed to the pin. "Can I get that, too?"

Chapter Twenty-Eight

Lily

By the time she set the bag with her purchases down at the table Chrysanthemum had snagged, the coffee shop was packed with people discussing the afternoon's strong wind.

Lily couldn't imagine the kind of magic that worked on people's minds to make them believe a gust of wind could have blown away all the flags but left the baskets filled with flowers and the plethora of Halloween decorations unscathed. No doubt it was a good thing, though. This way, only 10 percent of the town might be on the verge of panic instead of all of it.

Not that Lily was panicking, oh no. She and Chrysanthemum could totally handle a curse capable of blowing the wards at the Historical Society and at the Cauldron Supply. No big deal.

To hold on to their table, they took turns getting coffee, and it wasn't until they were both settled with the supply bag by their feet that either of them finally addressed what had happened in the shop.

"Has the curse struck anywhere else around town?" Chrysanthemum asked.

"The school, the store, the Society . . ." Lily pulled out her notebook. "I heard my dad say something about an incident at the Bramble Lane B&B the other day, but I don't know if he was referring to the curse. If not . . . then it's only happening in places where we are."

Chrysanthemum nodded. "That means most of the island is safe."

"Yes. I don't want people to get hurt. But . . ." Lily tapped her pencil on the page. "It's basically proof that we're involved, if anyone's paying attention."

Chrysanthemum's eyes maintained their hold over her, emanating power. "I don't want anyone to suffer, either."

"You know," Lily said, "I would never have thought, before, that you cared what happened to Thornhaven."

Chrysanthemum set her mug down sharply, the ceramic thudding against the wooden table. A torrent of emotions swept over her face, too quickly for Lily to decipher them all, but she understood immediately that she'd said something wrong.

Remembering the pin she'd bought, Lily reached into the bag and grabbed it like a lifeline. "Forget I said that. Here. I bought this for you."

Annabeth had wrapped the pin, and Chrysanthemum's wounded expression turned to confusion and then to shock as she peeled back the black-and-silver tissue paper.

"I thought it would cheer you up," Lily explained.

Chrysanthemum held up the pin with wide eyes. "Oh, that's . . . that's . . ." She turned the pin around a few more times in lieu of words.

"Weird?" It suddenly dawned on Lily that randomly buying Chrysanthemum a gift was *very likely* weird. "You dress in black and scowl, but you like sunflowers, and that's also weird, so you don't get to judge. I don't mean *weird* in a bad way. It's weird, like it's interesting."

She was babbling. This was ridiculous. She didn't know what was wrong with her, but Chrysanthemum was turning the pin over in her fingers, and they were delicate fingers that ended in chipped black nail polish that Lily wanted to wipe off and repaint for her. And what the hell—*that* was a weird thought, too.

"Thank you," Chrysanthemum said quietly. Her cheeks had turned pink, and she was really pretty when they did that. "I was going to say, *that was very nice*." Then, more loudly, she added, "I can't believe I told you about the sunflowers."

Lily was relieved to hear that Chrysanthemum also had difficulty controlling her mouth sometimes.

Chrysanthemum didn't immediately attach the pin to her backpack, but she curled her fingers around it like it was a precious gem. "You weren't wrong earlier. I tried not to care about anyone here. I *wanted* not to care, because it's easier if you can turn that part of yourself off. If you don't care about anything, nothing can hurt you."

"That seems kind of depressing and lonely," Lily said softly.

Chrysanthemum rolled her eyes, but her smirk wasn't cruel. "Well, yeah." She reached for her coffee. "When my power started emerging, back in New York, I made the mistake of showing my best friend what I could do. We used to tell each other all our secrets. I thought she'd love it, but she freaked out. She stopped talking to me, told the rest of our friends that I was dangerous, turned them against me. It was awful, and I was so glad when we moved."

And when Chrysanthemum had arrived here, Lily had snubbed her, and as a result, all the other witches their age had, too. "I'm so sorry I wasn't nicer to you."

Chrysanthemum's cheeks flushed again, or maybe they'd never unflushed. Lily wished they would. It was . . . distracting.

"I actually wasn't trying to make you feel bad," Chrysanthemum said. "Especially since I heard what you said to Bethany. I, um, really appreciated that."

Lily had a sudden urge to wrap her arms around Chrysanthemum, and squeeze her, and maybe bury her nose in Chrysanthemum's hair . . . stroke her cheek . . . promise her that she wouldn't let her down again . . .

Lily drew a deep breath, belatedly remembering her own coffee, and took a large sip. "I *should* feel bad, though. And so should your ex-friend."

Chrysanthemum smiled. "In hindsight, showing her I could light a candle with my brain and thinking she'd be impressed was naïve. I blame TV for convincing me that people would find powers cool and not terrifying."

"They are cool," Lily said forcefully. "You are way cooler than she could ever hope to be."

Chrysanthemum looked very much like she was trying not to seem pleased by that—and Lily, in turn, couldn't help but feel pleased herself.

"Anyway," Lily continued, her voice becoming more serious, "I think we have everything we need now to undo this mess. Let's go over the list again . . ."

CHAPTER TWENTY-NINE

Chrysanthemum

"Chrys."

With a start, she realized her mother had said her name twice already. "Sorry. Yeah?"

Her mom scooped up more scrambled eggs on her fork, failing to notice them sliding off as she gazed Chrys's way. "I asked what time you would be home."

"Um, not sure," Chrys said. "I'll let you know if I have dinner with Lily."

Samantha Quinn was looking at her funny. It wasn't quite side-eye, but it came close enough for Chrys to lower her head and shove some eggs in her mouth.

"I'm glad you're making friends with other witches," her mom said at last.

Chrys would have choked on her food at the very idea of it a week ago, but Lily had called her a friend yesterday. Lily had stuck up for her and bought her a gift. *Lily, Lily, Lily.*

"Some of them are . . . tolerable," Chrys said between bites. *Some of them* being Lily.

She'd just finished stuffing her dishes into the dishwasher when a message popped up in her group chat with Anushka, Isaiah, and Luke.

Luke: Forgot to ask yesterday, but did I really see you and Lily leaving Black Cat together, or is this island making me hallucinate again?

It was so very tempting to let Luke believe he'd imagined it, but that was rude. Before Chrys could decide how to respond, though, more messages followed.

Anushka: WHAT???

Isaiah: Is this why you didn't audition for the musical? You've been sneaking around to hang out with Lily after school?

Luke: Maybe they're both witches.

Chrys: Ha ha.

Chrys: We have to work on a project together for the Historical Society.

Anushka: I'm sorry.

Isaiah: Project?

Chrys: Not a fun one, but it's fine. She's . . .

Chrys's fingers hesitated. Lily had called her a friend yesterday. Her description of Lily as *tolerable* was so weak in comparison. Worse, it felt like a lie. Lily was actually way better than Chrys had wanted her to be.

Chrys: I guess we've become friends.

Luke: lol! I told you she's nice!

Shaking her head, Chrys packed a container with baked treats to share with Lily—apple-cranberry coffee cake with hazelnut drizzle and more of the chocolate gingerbread cookies that Lily liked so much.

If only Luke had a clue that his arrival in Thornhaven had precipitated all this, but she could never tell him that. Maybe one day, if he and Lily dated and got married, Lily could cast a spell that would make him resistant to Thornhaven's memory-altering magic, and then Chrys could tell him the truth. Witches who married normies did it all the time.

But that was a big if. Lily and Luke weren't even a couple, not yet, and Chrys had a hard time imagining that the Allertons would approve of their daughter marrying a normie.

Speaking of Lily, Chrys's phone had been making lots of noise as more messages arrived, but the latest wasn't Anushka or Isaiah demanding an explanation for her change of heart.

Lily: I'm out in the parking lot, but idk which building is yours

Although Chrys had been to Lily's a few times now, the thought of Lily seeing *her* apartment was more than Chrys could handle. She wasn't worried about Lily judging her, at least she didn't think so, but the apartment was so small. Like, small-small. Having anyone over felt intimate in a way that Chrys wasn't prepared to deal with.

Chrys wrote a hasty talk later in the group chat, yelled her goodbye to her mom, and dashed out the door. The sky was mottled with gray clouds that were just starting to drizzle, and they rumbled as Chrys jumped into Lily's car.

Lily raised an eyebrow. “Sunflower earrings? I knew I got you the right pin.”

Chrys shrugged, feigning carelessness, and touched the tiny silver flowers dangling from her ears. She hadn’t worn them in years, and wearing jewelry while painting was probably silly, but if putting more thought into her appearance because she was hanging out with Lily was silly, then . . . yeah, she was acting completely silly. She’d picked out the earrings precisely *because* she was hoping Lily might comment on them.

“Maybe I’m trying not to be such a cliché,” Chrys said.

“You’re not a cliché. You only pretend to be.”

Chrys wanted to argue with that, but Lily wasn’t wrong, and she wasn’t sure how she felt about Lily having this kind of understanding of her. “I work *hard* to project a certain image,” she said, falling back on sarcasm to cover her confusion. “How dare you.”

“Excuse me for telling you that you’re more interesting than a cliché.”

Chrys’s confusion turned to something that warmed her from the inside. That was twice in two days that Lily had called her *interesting*. “Fine, but don’t tell anyone else. Only you’re allowed to know.”

Lily bit her lip at that, and she smiled.

Chrys got even warmer. She hadn’t been completely sure of herself when she put the earrings in this morning, but for the first time in a long while, the sunflowers felt like they belonged on her.

CHAPTER THIRTY

Lily

Wednesday evening, before witch school began, Lily arrived early because she and Chrysanthemum had to sneak back the books they'd stolen. They'd gotten lucky that no one seemed to have noticed they'd gone missing, but judging from the dust in the restricted room, perhaps that wasn't so surprising.

They could have attempted to return the books on Saturday, but Chrysanthemum had insisted it was worth it to finish reading them in case they found anything else helpful, and Lily had agreed. Besides, meeting early was another opportunity to spend time together and review their plans for the weekend, and she wasn't about to argue with that.

In fact, Lily was discovering that she would take any excuse to spend time with Chrysanthemum. After spending Friday and Saturday together, they'd spent hours chatting while doing homework on Sunday, too. At some point, Chrysanthemum had become the first person Lily thought of when she had something funny to share or needed to complain or just generally felt like talking. Chrysanthemum was very talkative when Lily got her started, and funny, and insightful, and . . . and . . . Lily didn't know what exactly, but thinking about it made her excited.

She felt a little bad, like she might be ignoring Sonia, but Sonia hadn't been as available since she and Evan got back together, so Lily told herself that Sonia probably hadn't even noticed.

Chrysanthemum met her at the Book Nook, the bookshop down the street from the Historical Society. She'd brought more of her mother's amazing cookies to share, and they ate while Lily ran through her to-do list for Saturday. It was not the fun, just-hang-out kind of conversation Lily wanted to have, but it was necessary.

Chrysanthemum made faces when Lily brought up her notes about who should do what for the spell, but she didn't put up any fights. Like Lily, she'd seemed more cheerful over the last week, like a blackberry bramble that had lost some of its thorns, making it easier (and less bloody) to find the sweet fruit it usually held out of reach.

It made Lily feel special to have gotten to know this other side of Chrysanthemum.

Sneaking the books back into the restricted room was far less stressful than obtaining them had been. The first break-in had clearly made them pros, and the second went off without a hitch. Now they had ten minutes remaining before class began, and they idled in the hallway together, looking determinedly innocent.

She and Chrysanthemum had no reason to spend time together again until Saturday, when they'd be stuck together the entire day, painting in the morning and tackling the ritual in the evening. Considering they would probably finish with the painting this weekend, it was likely the last time they'd see each other outside of school.

Unless, of course, she simply asked if Chrysanthemum wanted to hang out sometime.

Lily was contemplating how Chrysanthemum would respond to such a suggestion when the main doors opened and Sonia and Evan strode in.

Sonia's eyes widened, and Lily could see dozens of questions behind them—and she wasn't the only one to notice. Chrysanthemum turned and headed for the stairwell without a word. Lily deflated.

Sonia nudged Evan toward the stairs and cornered Lily before she could take off as well. "Together again?"

Lily shuffled into the library, stepping around the drop cloths and the neatly stacked cans of paint. "We were assessing our progress. I think we'll finish this weekend."

Sonia didn't look impressed by this attempt to evade, but she kept her voice neutral. "About time. I can't believe they made you two do all that painting, anyway."

Was she really going to get off that easily? Lily doubted it. "Right? The room will actually look usable."

"I'm confused, though." Sonia raised an eyebrow. "You hated her. You were *obsessed* with hating her, but I heard from Bethany Lord, of all people, that you're friends now? Why didn't I know first? I'm supposed to know everything first."

"I was not obsessed." Had she been that obviously obsessed? "She was my nemesis, and now she's not."

"Was? What changed?"

"I don't know," Lily said, closing her eyes. "Me, I guess. She's actually smart and funny, and . . ."

And trying to put her jumbled thoughts into words shouldn't be this difficult, should it?

She's clever and brave, and a lot sweeter than she pretends to be. She buries herself in her shirt when she gets uncomfortable, a bit like a turtle, and she scrunches up her nose when she's reading. I like being around her. She almost never smiles, so when I can make her do it, it makes me happy. I like *making her happy.*

Breath caught in Lily's lungs, and she exhaled slowly while her heart beat faster. This was all sounding mildly alarming. No wonder she was having a hard time admitting it.

"So you *are* friends." Sonia tilted her head. "Amazing."

Yes, friends.

Just friends.

Like she and Sonia were friends.

Only not at all like that, because there was something *else* about Chrysanthemum. Something that Lily had never felt around Sonia. It was in the way Lily was still obsessed with Chrysanthemum's eyes, and was constantly looking for excuses to touch her, and kept noticing how soft her skin looked and wondering what it would be like to nuzzle her cheek, and *oh shit*, the room was spinning around her.

Funny. This felt an awful lot like getting nervous in close spaces with Chrysanthemum, which made her skin tingle and her heart race and . . .

Lily grasped the doorframe.

Had that fluttering in her stomach, that electricity in her blood, *not actually been nerves*?

Oh no. She'd always thought attraction—from the way other people described it—meant something else entirely.

Lily had opinions on people's appearances, naturally, but they were rational, thought-based things. Not emotions. No different than the opinions she might have on whether a painting was pleasant or a dress was pretty. She'd certainly never looked at another person and wanted to kiss them, no matter how objectively attractive she believed them to be. Even admitting that Chrysanthemum had beautiful eyes, a disconcerting thing to acknowledge, hadn't made Lily think about kissing her. Although, now that the idea was in her head, she realized she wasn't opposed to it. It might be nice. And so would touching her hand, and making her laugh, and putting her head on Chrysanthemum's shoulder . . .

All this time, all these years of watching her friends develop crushes—Lily had thought she was too busy for it, too focused on more important things. But she'd never been focused on anything more important or daunting than the horrible curse, and here she was, fixating on a girl.

Was this just how *she* liked someone, then? Not with the *wow, the new boy is hot* lusty kind of attraction that Sonia and others seemed to feel, but with this quieter, *I want to be near her* craving that was taking over her brain?

It had to be, because Lily also liked hanging out with Sonia and their group of friends, but she'd never once looked for an excuse to touch Sonia's hair or felt the need to be the center of Sonia's attention. With Chrysanthemum, she almost couldn't stop herself. And now that this understanding was dawning on her, Lily could tell that this longing for connection had been buried inside her awhile. When it had started, she couldn't say, but over the past couple of weeks, it had sprouted like a seedling that had been waiting for the sun to shine on it.

"Lil?" Sonia snapped her fingers.

Lily startled and sucked in a deep breath. "Um, what was the question?"

"You're freaking out."

"I am not." The response was reflexive. They both knew it was a lie.

Sonia crossed her arms. "We've been best friends since preschool. Do you think I don't know what a Lily freak-out looks like? You panic more than any person I've ever met, including

Auntie Marina, and she loses her shit every time Mercury goes retrograde."

Lily covered her face with her hands. "Okay, yes, fine, I'm freaking out. It's just . . . I don't know if we *are* friends."

And I don't want to just be her friend. I want to be her sunlight. If she wants to kiss someone, I want to be the person she chooses. And oh God, why couldn't she stop thinking about what kissing Chrysanthemum would be like? Especially on her neck. Chrysanthemum had this beauty mark on the left side of her neck, and Lily was sure that spot would be soft and warm and smell of the faintly spicy incense that clung to Chrysanthemum's skin.

"I mean, I like her," Lily said, desperate to break this train of thought. "She's nice and funny . . ."

"You already said that." Sonia narrowed her eyes, scrutinizing Lily in a way that made her shrink. Then she gasped. "Oh wait, you mean you *like* her, like her? That explains so much!"

"What?" Lily glanced down in the hallway, but they were alone. Still, she motioned frantically for Sonia to lower her voice. "How did you figure that out?"

Sonia huffed. "You were always *obsessed* with her—shut up, you were—because she's every bit as nerdy and talented as you are. Spending so much time together, learning to appreciate each other, learning to talk and not to fight . . . It's only natural that you'd develop feelings for her. You're two sides of the same coin—day and night."

Lily didn't disagree, but she didn't like it, either. She'd managed seventeen years without developing feelings for anyone (or, well, feelings she'd been aware of), and it had made life simple. She did not want to be a Sonia and Evan, constantly stressing over the status of a relationship. That looked exhausting and took time away from the important things in life, like studying. "What do I do?"

Given Sonia's chaotic dating history, she might not be the best person to ask, but she was the only one Lily trusted.

"What does Chrys think?" Sonia asked.

"I don't know." *I don't actually like Luke*—Chrysanthemum's comment reverberated in Lily's skull. "How do I tell?"

"I think it depends on the person, the kind of signs they give off, whether they're trying to hide their feelings or not. If we're not talking about outright flirting, that is."

They were definitely not talking about outright flirting. Lily could no more imagine Chrysanthemum flirting with her than she could imagine trying to flirt herself. She'd never done it before in her life.

Unintentional flirting, though . . . ? Was that how she came across every time she found an excuse to touch Chrysanthemum?

Lily rubbed her eyes. "I never really looked for signs."

"Then you've got to start."

Right. Because splitting her attention when they had to *destroy a freaking curse* was such a wise move.

A chime snapped Lily's thoughts back to the present. She'd set a five-minute alarm for class. "We need to go. But wait." She grabbed Sonia's arm. "Is this weird? Are you okay with this?"

She wasn't even sure what she was asking, specifically. There was too much to wrap her head around. Did she only like girls, or now that she knew what the signs were, had she ever had these kinds of feelings for a boy? And for that matter, what else did that say about her—was she asexual, demisexual, something else? She vaguely knew what all these terms meant, but applying them to herself was going to be an ongoing project. Given her love of organization and clarity, Lily foresaw much frustration in her future.

Sonia's brow pinched. "Weird that you like Chrys or weird that you like girls?"

Lily just nodded, her thoughts too muddled to recall what she'd intended to ask.

"If Chrys deserves you, then it's all good," Sonia said, apparently deciding that was the only question worth responding to. She appeared completely unfazed by everything. Which made one of them. "If she hurts you, I will be first in line to kick her ass. But if she's your date for the Halloween ball, I'm officially pronouncing you two the oddest but most brilliant couple ever."

"Okay." She hadn't thought Sonia would be weird about it, especially considering Sonia's auntie Amelia was trans and married to another woman, but the reassurance was good.

"Honestly, I'm just mad I didn't figure it out sooner."

Lily rolled her eyes. "*I* just figured it out."

"You can't be smarter about *everything*. I'm the relationship expert."

"The frequency with which you and Evan break up and get back together is practically in sync with the moon phases," Lily said dryly, heading to the stairs. She didn't know what to do about her feelings for Chrysanthemum, but accepting them for what they were made it clear what she had to do in a more general sense, what she should have done from the beginning—make Chrysanthemum feel welcome at witch school.

"We do not break up thirteen times a year," Sonia said, just as dryly. "You wait. You'll learn that relationships are hard. It's why you need me."

"I do need you." With Sonia at her side, Lily felt stronger, more confident about what she had to do. Because what she was about to do would surprise a lot of people, Chrysanthemum among them. "And I need you to meet Chrysanthemum, for real."

Chapter Thirty-One
Chrysanthemum

It might have been her imagination, but Lily had been on edge since Wednesday evening at witch school. Possibly, it was because Lily had made a point to draw a wary Chrys into her conversations there after class—a gesture Chrys didn't want to be pleased by, but secretly had been. But that couldn't be all of it. Lily was the one who'd always set the expectations, so Chrys didn't think she had a reason to be nervous about the social repercussions.

Certainly, the curse was part of it, yet that didn't entirely make sense, either. Since the latest cafeteria incident, the Historical Society had been enlisting the help of every witch in Thornhaven to strengthen wards and recast magic-suppressing charms on a daily basis. As a result, the curse had been quieter over the past week, with only one minor incident involving a gym class. Plus, thanks to Lily's meticulous planning, the two of them knew exactly what they were going to do tonight to destroy it. Even Chrys, who didn't work well with plans, felt she had this one down. Lily had been barraging her with texts to make sure of it.

While Chrys bided her time after a light dinner, she scrolled through their most recent conversation.

Lily: Have you been asked to help out at the ball this year?

Chrys: No. You?

Lily: No. Do you think that's part of our punishment?

Chrys: Not being forced to work?

Lily: They think we're irresponsible.

Chrys: We are irresponsible.

Lily: Rude

Lily: But seriously, do you think they're going to keep holding this against us?

Chrys: No idea. Maybe they didn't ask bc if we hadn't finished painting in time, we'd be busy that day

Lily: Makes sense . . . Are you going?

Chrys: Yeah

Lily: With someone?

Chrys: My mom. Did you ask Luke?

Lily: No

Lily: How many times do we walk counterclockwise while sprinkling the water?

All their conversations over the past few days had been like that. Something normal, then boom—pop quiz. If Lily had been making sure Chrys knew her shit, she'd succeeded. So why was Lily acting so twitchy? It wasn't as though Chrys was totally devoid of anxiety herself, but Lily had been looking like she saw a ghost every time Chrys had talked to her.

Chrys stuffed a bottle filled with amethyst-infused water into her backpack and hoped Lily got over the worst of her nerves quickly. Anxiety could make a witch lose focus, and worse, it could bring negativity into the spell. They couldn't afford that when that was what they were trying to banish.

"I'm heading out with a friend," Chrys reminded her mom as she breezed through the living room.

"Okay, I remember." Her mom cocked a funny look at the overfilled backpack but chose not to ask, which was a relief. Chrys had an explanation, but she preferred not to use it. "Have fun. Text me if you're going to be out past eleven."

"Promise!" Her mom was surprisingly easygoing about all the time Chrys had spent with Lily recently, no doubt relieved that her daughter hadn't shunned all human contact.

Sitting on a bench in front of the apartment complex, Chrys scrolled back further through her and Lily's conversation history while she waited, her breath exhaling in white puffs. When the temperature on the island dropped, the salty ocean breeze accentuated the cold.

Across the parking lot, a string of orange lights blinked in someone's window, and the wind blew dried leaves about Chrys's feet. The air felt extra crisp; the evening sky, especially dark. Downtown and the harbor would be bustling—it was Saturday night, after all, and there were plenty of bars and restaurants to entertain people. But in her tourist-unfriendly corner of the island, the night seemed desolate, and the wind muttered to itself as it meandered through the barren trees. Even the moon had vanished, its sliver swallowed by patchy clouds.

Maybe, Chrys considered, she wasn't as calm as she liked to believe.

She took a deep breath, sharp air filling her lungs. A waning moon was *good* for the type of spell they were doing. That was a *positive* sign, and she should concentrate on it. Not the faintly ominous atmosphere of approaching winter.

Before she could give herself a pep talk, headlights flashed over the tree branches by the bench. Lily pulled up to the curb, and Chrys climbed into the SUV, eager to be gone. Her patience was short at the best of times, and doing this spell reminded her a lot of the advice Ms. McNeil had given her when Chrys had been selected to perform a concert solo last year—the best way to deal with nerves was to jump in and belt it out.

"I brought you coffee," Lily said, indicating the to-go cups in the central cup holder. "I thought we might need the caffeine, but you seem . . ." She looked Chrys up and down. "Perky."

Chrys picked up her cup and inhaled the pumpkin spice–scented steam. "Just cold. Are you sure you should be having caffeine? You've been jittery all day."

Lily made a whining noise in her throat as she put the vehicle back in drive. "Caffeine helps you focus, right? I might need that."

"You're the most focused person I've ever met. You're like a human laser beam." Which was why it was so unexpected that Lily hadn't asked Luke to the Halloween ball yet, considering that her million-kilowatt focus on him was how they'd gotten into this mess.

But . . . after they were successful tonight, she'd probably do it.

Way to go, brain, reminding me of that. Now Chrys was going to have a hard time focusing, too.

"Thanks for the coffee," she said, and took a sip, hoping it was hot enough to burn her tongue and distract her from soppy visions of Lily and Luke dancing.

"You're welcome." Lily's voice squeaked a little. "I wasn't sure if you'd want something different for a change, and I thought about texting you, but then I thought it might be nicer for it to be a surprise, so . . . Um, I hope it's okay."

"It's perfect." In truth, she'd have happily drunk whatever Lily brought her, even if it were something blah like chamomile tea. The idea that Lily wanted to surprise her with something nice made it taste wonderful and warmed her better than the SUV's heaters.

The rest of the drive passed in silence, and Lily parked just outside the school property. It would be a pain to lug their supplies, but she explained that she didn't want her car sitting in the lot in case people noticed the school had been broken into.

No cars were in the high school lot, and no lights were on in the building. Keeping to the shadows, they crept up to a single door by the theater. People involved in the school shows or music performances used this door during after-school rehearsals, and unlike the other entrances, it was secluded and lacked the bright lights that shone down on the lobby and cafeteria doors. The lock was sticky, but Chrys got them in after a couple of minutes of trying.

Since they'd never discussed what would happen if she couldn't, so far, so good.

Chrys gently helped the heavy door close behind them, but the click of the latch reverberated in the dark, empty space.

"Here," Lily said, and Chrys reached out into the darkness and found the candle Lily was offering her. Their fingers brushed, and Chrys pushed aside the fluttery feeling in her gut to focus and conjure a flame.

Chrys had figured normal flashlights would do for navigation, but Lily had argued that they didn't want the glow to be visible from outside. She had insisted they use charmed candles for light. The small flame from Chrys's candle lit the immediate vicinity better than it should have, but that was what the magic did. Often called a thief's candle, it gave off light only to the witch who lit it, and that light was more intense than a normal candle's. Lily had one, too, and she led the way.

By the time they made it through the hallways to the cafeteria, Chrys was dimly aware that her stress was getting the better of her, and she took a deep breath. Lily was counting on her to be the reckless one who courted danger instead of fearing it, and Chrys refused to disappoint her.

The kitchen behind the food line was exactly as it had been last week—dim, clean, and foul smelling. While Lily began unpacking their supplies, Chrys peered under the counter. The curse, too, didn't look any different. It still reminded her of pulsing, oily worms, and Chrys's gaze didn't linger on it. It made her feel *wrong*.

Lily handed Chrys one end of a tape measure as Chrys stood. "This is four feet. I think we need to go for eight."

Chrys stepped away until they'd pulled out eight feet of tape. The curse had chosen its spot under the counter well. Their positioning would be awkward, but an eight-foot-diameter circle fit in the kitchen and gave them room to move, which they'd need. As Chrys helped Lily center the curse in the middle of the circle, she couldn't shake the sensation that this was overkill. Were all these rules and steps truly necessary? A witch's power came from within, but the spell had been *very* specific about what to do, and since neither of them had ever attempted anything requiring so much power . . .

With the circle's diameter set, they spread eight white candles out evenly along the circumference and stuck another in the center on the counter, above the curse. Lily had already prepared those candles, rubbing them with anise oil and pressing sprigs of rosemary and thyme into the wax, as per the spell's instructions.

Lily nodded at her, and Chrys held her hand above the westernmost candle. Here went nothing. *"One for sea."*

She drew on her power. The candlewick flared to life.

Lily did the same over the northernmost candle. *"Two for earth."*

They took turns. *"Three for sky."*

"Four for fire."

Then together, over the central candle: *"Five for the magic they create."*

The fifth flame shot up high, thanks to their combined power, and Chrys snatched her hand back, palm stinging. Not only were they both tense, making it perhaps *too* easy to draw on their magic, they hadn't practiced casting together. Maybe that had been a mistake.

Chrys lit the remaining four candles with a match, reserving her energy, while Lily ignited the incense. Whoever entered this room on Monday morning was going to wonder why it smelled like a spice shop.

Like Chrys, Lily had pulled her hair back so it didn't get in the way, but a few strands had fallen free of her ponytail, and she tucked them behind her ears. "You remember your part?"

"You wouldn't let me forget." Chrys rolled her eyes, but in this moment, she was thankful for the way Lily had drilled her. With incense filling her head, the candlelight flickering, and the anticipation of the unknowns to come, it would have been too easy to forget. It had been a while since she'd felt this kind of pressure.

She pulled out the jar with the amethyst-infused water and unscrewed the lid, and Lily poured a premeasured quantity of sea salt into it. In spells, water usually signified movement, amethyst peering into the metaphysical realm, and salt purification. Chrys understood the purpose of the ingredients, and she focused her intention on them. That complete, she set the jar aside while Lily retrieved the final object from her supplies: the vial of frankincense-infused oil.

Here was where they'd had to get creative. To destroy the curse, they had to negate the magic that had caused it to form. As best they could figure, there were two parts—their own poorly directed hexes, and the hexes their ancestors had cast. Lily had found some language in one of the borrowed books that she'd adapted for them to say, and Chrys had suggested adding the oil. Anointing another witch with an appropriate type of oil was a common method of showing trust in a variety of ceremonies, from coven initiation to marriage. Frankincense was the usual choice, as it aided with protection and power.

In the end, none of the actual words they spoke or actions they took would make a difference if their intent wasn't strong and focused. They both knew that.

Lily turned to face her, and Chrys tried not to twitch. Shadows danced over Lily's face in the flickering light, and her eyes seemed darker. She looked beautiful and powerful.

"I, Lily Ellen Allerton, descendant of the Thornhaven Allertons, declare an end to the rift between my family and the Langmores. I disavow any negativity that remains, and I banish any remnants of discord between myself and Chrysanthemum Quinn. In this endeavor, we are one."

She dipped her finger in the frankincense oil and drew two lines on Chrys's forehead—an *L* and *C*, conjoined, to show they were united in purpose. Chrys held her breath the entire time, her eyes closed so she wouldn't have to stare into Lily's eyes.

Lily's finger left a tingling sensation behind on her skin—and when she inhaled again, Chrys tasted electricity in the air as well. It wasn't just her crush on Lily that was giving her a charge; power was growing thick around them.

Chrys's hand trembled as she took the vial from Lily. "I, Chrysanthemum Leigh Quinn, descendant of the Thornhaven Langmores, declare an end to the rift between my family and the Allertons. I disavow any negativity that remains, and I banish any remnants of discord between myself and Lily Allerton. In this endeavor, we are one."

Lily closed her eyes as well when Chrys traced the sigil on her forehead, and Chrys tried to ignore how close she had to stand to Lily to do it. Their faces almost touched. Their lips were inches apart, and she could practically count Lily's eyelashes.

Chrys swallowed and stepped away. What greater proof was there that they had put aside their animosity than her wanting to *kiss* Lily?

"Okay, done." Her voice came out in a low, tremulous whisper.

Lily carefully poured the salt water from the jar into two glasses and handed one to Chrys. "Here we go."

They stood across from each other, Chrys by the western candle and Lily by the eastern. On Lily's signal, they walked in a counterclockwise direction, letting drops of water fall from their fingers onto the floor.

Think banishing thoughts, Chrys told herself.

It was easier said than done when she was also trying to keep track of the number of rotations around the circle.

At the end of the fourth circuit, they stopped across from each other once more. The air around her felt close, voltaic, charged with power, but she couldn't detect anything beyond that (certainly no sign of distress from the curse), and she wasn't sure if she should. The book had spelled out the ritual, but not what to expect.

Kneeling, Chrys checked on the curse again. It pulsed and squirmed, but it didn't appear to register their presence. All of that was either about to change, or they were going to have to come up with a plan B.

Lily recited the chant they'd found in the book. "*As these words are spoken, this curse's power is now broken. As these words are spoken, this curse's power is now broken.* ***As these words are spoken, this curse's power is now broken.***"

She dipped her fingers in the water and flung droplets at the curse.

It flinched—that was the best way Chrys could describe it. As soon as the water touched it, steam hissed, and it twitched, writhed, seemed to draw in on itself.

Chrys quickly wet her own fingers. *"As these words are spoken, this curse's power is now broken. As these words are spoken, this curse's power is now broken.* ***As these words are spoken, this curse's power is now broken."***

Power rose in her throat as she spoke, although she hadn't consciously drawn on it. Chrys had felt stirrings in herself before, but not like this. Perhaps there really was something to these rituals.

Again, the curse reacted to the water, which sizzled on it. It shuddered more noticeably than last time.

Chrys met Lily's gaze, and Lily nodded. Together, they chanted in unison, and in unison, they flung more water. Again and again, until the words poured out of Chrys's mouth without her even trying. Her fingers delved deeper into her glass, grasping more water and tossing it with more force.

The curse thrashed. The louder and more insistent their voices grew, the more steam rose into the air, mingling with the incense smoke. A white haze enveloped Chrys's face. It was far too much smoke and steam for the water they'd used. It stank, burrowing into her lungs.

"As these words are spoken . . ." She coughed through the chant, clinging to Lily's voice for guidance.

A scream cut through their words.

Its force knocked Chrys backward, almost off her feet, and she only barely managed to hold on to her glass and keep the remaining water from spilling. On the other side of the counter, Lily cried out. She must have been hit with that burst of magic, too.

That alone was enough to propel Chrys back into position, and the power in her rose accordingly. That thing had hurt Lily.

Fuck. This. Curse.

"*. . .* ***this curse's power is now broken!***" She had so little water left, but she threw the drops on her fingers with the sort of force one reserved for softball tryouts.

Lily's voice rejoined hers. The curse lashed out a second time, once more sending Chrys sprawling backward, but this time she was prepared. Her chanting didn't stop, though her voice wavered from the magical punch to the gut. With each hit, her power surged with her determination. Her head felt like it was detaching from her body. Her hands shook.

She and Lily were screaming the words together, and the curse's magic was hot and strong, like a meaty hand, pressing down on her. Its slimy, wormlike fingers strained for her mouth, trying to shut her up. Its smoke attempted to choke her.

"*. . .* ***BROKEN!***"

Chrys had no idea how long they'd been chanting, but the pressure on her body stopped all at once. A final gush of power blew through her lips, and she collapsed to the floor. Lily must have experienced something similar, because her voice had stopped.

The smoke dissipated as quickly as it had formed, leaving nothing behind but sweet-smelling incense.

And the curse . . . Chrys's nose detected its absence before she could search for it. It was gone. The spiderweb of cracks remained, but the slithering, pulsing heart had vanished.

Belatedly, she realized there wasn't just salt water on her face, but sweat rolling down her neck.

Across from her, Lily's face was shiny with it, too, and she breathed heavily. "It's gone?"

Chrys wasn't sure whether that was a question or merely surprise that they'd done it. "I don't *see* it anymore."

"Or smell it." Lily wrinkled her nose. "But there's still pieces."

Chrys peered at the veins under the counter. "Are they part of it, or are they cracks that need to heal?"

Lily shrugged, but her face lightened. "Let's hope it's that."

"Yeah." Chrys climbed to her feet and surveyed the burning candles. Done. They'd succeeded. She felt dazed as she snuffed out the nearest candles.

Lily, too, acted a bit like she was coming out of a dream as they cleaned up. It wasn't until they'd finished and were sipping the remains of their coffee and eating the cookies Chrys had brought that they started to emerge from their stupor.

"It's really done," Lily said, when they finally stepped outside.

Cold air slapped Chrys's sweaty cheeks, and she took a deep breath, letting the chill fill her lungs. It was invigorating. At last she was waking up to the enormity of it all, and she let out a whoop of triumph. "We did it! Holy shit, *we did it*."

Lily shushed her, glancing around at the empty lot, before apparently deciding that it was okay to be happy. She burst out laughing. "It was choking me at one point! Like, what the fuck? I was *not* ready for that."

"It kept punching me. But you know what?" Chrys grinned. "We punched harder."

"Hell yeah, we did." Lily's cheeks were already flushed, either from the exertion or the cold, but under the streetlamp's glow, Chrys would have sworn they turned redder. Then Lily threw her arms around her. "We make such a good team."

Lily's hug landed awkwardly since they were both wearing backpacks filled with supplies, but Chrys didn't care. Now that her momentary daze had vanished, giddy elation replaced it. And Lily was hugging her. Good sense and rationality had no place here.

Before she knew what she was doing, she kissed Lily's cheek.

Lily's skin was soft and lightly tacky from sweat, and for once, her hair didn't smell of fancy shampoo but of incense. Chrys inhaled the remnants of frankincense and sandalwood, and they kick-started her brain once more. Oh shit, oh shit. What had she done?

She pulled back, heat rushing up her neck, begging the night to hand her an excuse.

"A very . . . yes, very good . . . team." She stumbled around the words, her grin plastered to her face with shock and panic.

She had to get away, and she picked up her pace toward Lily's car. Riding in the car together after what she'd done would be a problem, but she'd worry about that when she got there.

The SUV's locks clicked, and Chrys dumped her backpack in the back seat as Lily's footsteps grew louder. But although she'd put her bag in there, Chrys was finding it hard to bring herself to open the passenger door and climb in. A door on the driver's side shut, and she stiffened. Lily was walking around to her side, and Chrys forced herself to turn her way.

She'd been pretending to be brave all evening, so what was a few more uncomfortable minutes?

"I'm—" Chrys didn't get a chance to finish her sentence or judge Lily's expression, because Lily moved too fast.

Her lips touched Chrys's cheek, not forcefully but not lightly, either. With just the right amount of pressure to suggest she meant to do it but wasn't entirely sure how it would be received.

To be fair, Chrys wasn't entirely sure how she received it. Her spiraling thoughts came to a screeching stop. Her heart was beating so hard that it might burst.

"Um . . ." Chrys thought she might be hyperventilating. She could still feel Lily's breath on her face, and Lily wasn't breathing too steadily herself. "That was . . ."

"Revenge," Lily said, looking anything but vengeful as she bit her lip.

Oh, okay. Words. Thoughts. For goodness' sake, she had just destroyed a curse. She was capable of powerful magic. And yet at no time during that spell had Chrys felt so completely and utterly unmoored, not even when her head had been so suffused with power that she'd felt like she was floating.

"You should be careful," she said, her voice far steadier than she'd have assumed possible. "What if I feel forced to retaliate? This could escalate."

It was the right thing to say. Relief swept over Lily's face, and she smiled tentatively. "You wouldn't dare."

And yet a dare was so obviously what those words were.

Chrys cupped Lily's cheeks with her fingers and pressed her lips against Lily's mouth.

Lily froze, and for a half heartbeat, Chrys thought she'd made a terrible miscalculation. Then Lily melted against her, her hands closing on Chrys's arms, her lips parting slightly to bring their mouths closer. Breaths and heartbeats mingled in the chilly night, and all Chrys felt was warmth.

When she'd use to think about kissing Lily, it had never been like this—with the scent of frankincense oil and incense on her skin, the taste of coffee and chocolate on her lips. With the satisfaction of knowing it wasn't *just* this moment that joined them. That they were a team, more powerful together than apart.

Nearby, headlights flashed and an engine crescendoed, then faded, as a car drove by. Chrys had all but forgotten they were standing in the road. Hell, she'd nearly forgotten anything but Lily.

She withdrew her hands from Lily's cheeks, but Lily didn't let go of her arms. They stared at each other for a moment, and Chrys found it funny that Lily was as stunned by this turn of events as she was, but she wasn't able to laugh.

Then Lily released her and pushed loose strands of her hair around. "So, um . . ."

"Yeah."

Lily laughed nervously. "That was okay?"

Was she serious? Was Chrys's chest the only one that felt like a series of fireworks were going off inside it? "That was perfect."

Lily sighed with relief. "I'd never done that before."

"You never *kissed* anyone?" Who was she to talk? She'd never kissed anyone before, either. Shit. Should *she* be asking if she did it okay?

"I've never kissed a girl before," Lily clarified. "Or, well . . . anyone I wanted to kiss at all. I had to play a stupid kissing game at Sonia's fifteenth birthday party, and I didn't like it."

Oh shit. "Did you like this?" Chrys asked, suddenly terrified.

"Yes!" Lily must have sensed her anxiety. She grabbed Chrys's hands and kissed her again, and the anxiety couldn't maintain its hold over Chrys's body—it dissipated.

"I just needed to know I didn't screw it up," Lily said when they broke apart. "I didn't want to do it badly."

Chrys snorted. Lily was going to be Lily. "You have to be the best at everything you do, don't you? All the time."

Lily tossed her ponytail, but she was smiling sheepishly. "I'd think you'd like that in this case."

She had a point, and Chrys's heart danced inside her. "I kind of like *everything* about you."

"Yeah?" Lily looked very pleased about that. Her beautiful smile might kill Chrys yet—she was fairly certain this kind of irregular heartbeat was incompatible with life.

"You know, the only way to get better at kissing is to practice."

Lily jabbed her. "Then you better get in the car. I refuse to *practice* in the middle of the street."

With a perfect flounce, Lily strode to the driver's side, and Chrys got in the SUV, grinning. She couldn't think of a better way to celebrate their victory.

Chapter Thirty-Two

Lily

The day after she kissed Chrysanthemum, Lily had a hundred things she *should* have been doing. First on that list was probably not referring to the day as "the day after she kissed Chrysanthemum" when "the day after they destroyed a curse like a couple of badass witches" was right there, but there was no denying which of those events had taken priority in her brain. Just like there was no denying that she was agonizing over things like this when she should be delving into homework that had been neglected, but Lily was having a hard time stressing about any of it.

Last night had been out of a dream. Shock had rooted her feet in place when Chrysanthemum had kissed her cheek, then hope had blossomed in her chest. If she hadn't been so giddy with relief after their victory, Lily didn't know if she'd have had the courage to run after Chrysanthemum and kiss her. But she had been, and she'd told herself she could play the "revenge" comment up if Chrysanthemum reacted badly.

She was very, very glad she hadn't needed to.

Her plan to invite Chrysanthemum over so they could kiss again, however, hadn't gone as well. Adrenaline and joy had kept them both going long enough for Lily to drive back to her house. Then exhaustion had set in. In retrospect, they should have expected it. Intense spell work was known to be tiring, and neither of them had ever drained their power in such a major way before. They'd collapsed in the living room with hot chocolate and popcorn, mindlessly watching TV and snuggling on the sofa until Lily's parents had found them half asleep.

Today was a do-over. Lily's mother, having been the one to find them with Lily's head on Chrysanthemum's shoulder, had promptly invited Chrysanthemum over *for dinner tomorrow.* That had been unexpected. Sunday was the rare day when everyone was usually at home for a family meal, and Lily wasn't sure if she wanted Chrysanthemum to witness the Allertons in all their dysfunctional glory. She worried, too, about Chrysanthemum being given the third degree.

But Chrysanthemum was on her way, and Lily had tossed half her wardrobe on her bed, searching for the perfect outfit.

Ridiculous. She saw Chrysanthemum every day at school, and Chrysanthemum had seen her looking her worst with the painting. She was being all kinds of ridiculous . . . and she was too happy to care.

Around four o'clock, not long before Chrysanthemum was supposed to arrive, her mom called Lily into the kitchen. Her father had started a pot roast a couple of hours ago, and the house smelled delicious. It was one of the only dishes he cooked, but he did it well. He'd left it on the stove, and now only her mother was in the expansive kitchen, making buttermilk biscuits to go with the meal.

Lily retrieved the biscuit cutter from the cabinet above the fridge without being asked and handed it over.

"So tell me," her mother said as she rolled out the dough, "were you and Chrysanthemum *really* doing homework before we got home last night?"

"What?" Lily squeaked.

"It's a fair question. You are supposed to be grounded, if you remember."

Lily pressed her lips together, unsure of the best approach. She hadn't forgotten.

"I can't believe you'd doubt me," Lily mumbled with what she considered to be an appropriate amount of resentment.

"And I can't believe you'd hex someone," her mother retorted. "If I didn't trust the Quinn girl, you wouldn't have been going out at all. Your father needed persuading."

Lily leaned against the kitchen island, struggling to process this new information. "You only let me go out *because* I was with Chrysanthemum?"

Her mother shot her a look that suggested she knew Lily was trying to twist her words and wasn't going to get away with it. "We thought it was good that you were spending time with the girl you hexed. That you were getting along. We're a very small community, Lily. Witches need to stick together."

"Oh." Lily felt a flush creeping up her neck and hoped it stayed hidden beneath her shirt. "Yeah . . . we've been getting along better."

Her mother smiled. "I noticed. You spent the last two weekends together."

"I didn't realize you knew I was with her all the time."

"You're not as sneaky as you think."

"I don't think I'm sneaky. I think—" She cut herself off before *I think you don't care* could spill out. "I thought you were too busy with Sara to notice what I do."

The rolling pin ceased moving, and her mother turned her way. "Oh, baby, no. I'm sorry if that's what you thought. Your sister's swimming takes up a lot of time, and you were always the responsible one. I guess we figured you didn't need us interfering because you were doing fine on your own." Her mother sighed. "That was our mistake. The situation with the hex—it was partially our fault, I know that. We should have been paying you more attention, and I'm sorry."

I am doing fine. I am responsible.

Frustration roared in Lily's head. How long had she wanted to hear this? But she squeezed the island's granite top, not feeling the release or gratitude she expected. Could they really bury the past year of neglect with one brief conversation?

Maybe, in their own way, her parents were trying to make up for ignoring her.

"If my behavior was partially your fault, does that mean I'm no longer grounded?" Lily asked with forced levity, and her mother flicked flour at her.

"I will talk to your father about it," she said. She seemed to be fighting down a fresh smile.

There was so much more Lily wanted to add to this conversation that wasn't her joking around, trying to earn concessions, but the doorbell rang. Another day, then. The topic had been broached; it was a start.

"We can continue this later," her mother said, reading her thoughts.

Lily dashed to the front door. When she opened it, she found Chrysanthemum carrying a cake.

Chrysanthemum shrugged in way of explanation. "From my mom."

"Another test bake?" Lily asked, ushering her inside.

"Yup, but she decorated it for tonight. I thought we deserved to celebrate with cake."

Decorated it was an understatement. The bottom tier was shaped and frosted to look like a basket, and the second tier was its overflowing contents—bright orange pumpkins, yellow and red sunflowers, and a bumblebee whose spun-sugar wings shimmered with an effect that Lily could tell was magical in nature. Every now and then, the wings fluttered so quickly that it looked like a real bee.

A gorgeous cake could distract Lily for only so long, though. Her stomach fluttered along with the bee's wings as she smiled at Chrysanthemum. Her eyes were such a pure, clear blue that Lily could get lost staring into them, almost as if they were a scrying crystal. She wanted to push Chrysanthemum's long bangs out of her face for a better view, press their noses against each other until their lips melted together.

Sara shrieked something in the living room, and Lily shook herself. "Sorry about the noise. My sister and her friends are working on their group Halloween costume. Come into the kitchen and drop off the cake."

Chrysanthemum seemed relieved to stop carrying it, and after dropping it off, they headed toward the living room, too. Sara took one look at them and fled, carrying her phone in front of her face so she could keep up her video chat.

"Your sister is going trick-or-treating?" Chrysanthemum asked.

"Yeah. She has friends on the swim team that she goes with. I think she's getting old for it, but whatever."

Chrysanthemum poked her arm. "What? You're too mature to dress up and go begging for candy? I'm not—I miss trick-or-treating."

"Really? It doesn't seem like a *you* thing." Lily had never much cared for it. Her parents had never been particularly clever with costumes when she was younger, and witch families didn't typically put much energy into it, since they had Samhain to attend to. As for Lily's own attempts to create a costume, they never came out the way she envisioned them. She was glad this was the first year that she'd be able to participate in the Historical Society's Samhain celebration instead, with rites to honor the dead and spells for ushering in a healthy and prosperous new year.

Chrysanthemum tugged at her cuffs. "I always liked being something else for a night. Something better than what I am."

Lily snagged Chrysanthemum's hands before they could disappear up her sleeves. "Better than the powerful witch you are? Is that possible?"

"I thought we had this conversation about me not being super powerful, just super lucky that one time."

"What I *heard* was that you're super powerful, but your *control* needs work. I maintain that you are actually kind of amazing."

Chrysanthemum's cheeks turned pink, and she leaned over and kissed Lily so quickly that Lily didn't have much time to enjoy it. Then she glanced toward the doorway. "Should I not do that?"

Lily craned her neck, but her mother was busy in the kitchen, her father was nowhere to be seen (probably in his office, where he'd been dealing with preparations for the Halloween ball), and Sara was undoubtedly hiding in her room now that Chrysanthemum was here. "I think we're safe."

Before she could overthink it, she yanked Chrysanthemum closer for a kiss, but she yanked too hard. They flopped onto the couch, Chrysanthemum on top of her, and Lily was tangled in her limbs, Chrysanthemum's hair falling in her face like a cascade of black silk.

"Okay, relax?" Chrysanthemum lips quirked with amusement as she propped herself up.

Lily laughed nervously. "I do suck at this."

Chrysanthemum was having a hard time fighting a smirk. "I think that depends on what 'this' refers to."

"Romance. I was just trying to kiss you."

"You still can." Chrysanthemum didn't have to dip her head very low for their mouths to meet.

Lily forgot all about the fact that they were lying on her sofa. There was nothing else but Chrysanthemum's lips, the light tease of her tongue, the way her body was pressing into Lily's own. She still couldn't relate to the way everyone talked about attraction—*explosions* and *urges* and *fires shooting down her core*—but being this close to Chrysanthemum was thrilling and pleasurable in its own way. Even the uncomfortable bits—like Chrysanthemum's knee being too close to Lily's thigh and digging in—were perfect. She'd discovered last night that Chrysanthemum's skin was every bit as soft as she'd imagined it to be, and she never wanted to stop touching it.

How something could be so soothing when it also made her heart race was a mystery. But then, how she'd ended up falling for Chrysanthemum was a mystery, too, and it was one mystery that Lily was okay not understanding.

"Girls, you in here?" Lily's mother called out.

Chrysanthemum jerked away in alarm and toppled to the floor.

"Yes?" Lily answered, trying not to laugh and panic at the same time. She couldn't bear to look her mother's way, so she had no clue what her mother saw, if anything.

"Can you come here and set the table?" Was there a hint of humor in her mother's voice? Lily wished she could crawl between the couch cushions and hide.

"Okay!" Lily looked down at Chrysanthemum, who had curled into a ball and was laughing silently. How could she once have thought Chrysanthemum never laughed?

Luckily, Lily's parents were too polite to grill Chrysanthemum the way Lily had feared, and even Sara was in a good mood. Sunday dinner conversations usually revolved around swimming, and it might have been Lily's imagination, but her sister seemed relieved to not be the center of attention for a change.

"This cake looks amazing," Lily's mother said, once the dinner dishes were cleared away. "I almost don't want to cut it."

"Chrysanthemum's mom is an excellent baker," Lily said. "She makes the stuff they sell at Black Cat."

"Does she?" Lily's mom turned Chrysanthemum's way. "Does she happen to take commissions? Adele Cook's granddaughter is getting married next year, and I know they'd love to have another witch make the cake. Something like this, with just a bit more magic in it."

"She's looking to start her own bakery, actually. So I'm sure she'd be happy to talk to them," Chrysanthemum said eagerly. "She's been working on infusing magic into the decorations—keeping it subtle enough that normies sense it, but don't get scared."

Lily's father's face lit up. "She should bring that idea to the Society board. A bakery that caters to the magical community could be a big draw for tourism. The possibilities . . ."

Lily's face glazed over while her father rattled off the business opportunities, but Chrysanthemum appeared to pay attention. Her ability to maintain a blank expression in the face of pretty much anything was a useful talent. But Chrysanthemum also seemed to think some of what Lily's father was saying might be of real use to her mom. Lily believed her when Chrysanthemum said she would tell her mom to get in touch with Mr. Allerton for his guidance.

"What are you celebrating, by the way?" Lily's mother asked. "I heard you say something earlier."

Oh shit. Lily glanced at Chrysanthemum, hoping she would know better than to say that they'd battled magical wits with foul magic—foul magic *they'd* created.

"Oh." Chrysanthemum smiled, and Lily understood her well enough now to see the way her eyes crinkled in the corners and know it was a mischievous sort of smile. "It's for Lily, to celebrate her being elected student council president."

Lily gaped at her. She remembered telling Chrysanthemum that her parents had never acknowledged her election, but she hadn't thought Chrysanthemum was paying much attention to her then. It was one of those things she'd blurted out.

The same sort of painful longing she'd felt last night when Chrysanthemum had first kissed her cheek squeezed Lily around the chest. She was barely aware of what else Chrysanthemum was saying or the way her parents reacted to the news as though it were the first they'd heard of it (which maybe it *was*, since they hadn't paid attention before). She wanted to throw her arms around Chrysanthemum's neck and bury her face in her hair. Squeeze her the way she felt squeezed.

Since she couldn't do that, she smiled at Chrysanthemum as she accepted her parents' belated congratulations.

CHAPTER THIRTY-THREE

Chrysanthemum

"Found it." Lily held out an oval pumpkin, slightly larger than a basketball. "It's the perfect one."

A full week had passed since they'd destroyed the curse attacking Thornhaven. Saturday had come around again, and Chrys was slightly bewildered to find herself back on the mainland at a farm, surrounded by crates of pumpkins, baskets of apples, crowds of loudly chatting normies—and Lily.

Also Sonia and Anushka, although Chrys wasn't sure where they'd wandered off to among the crowds and piles of pumpkins and gourds being picked over.

"You sure?" Chrys asked. She scanned the pile of pumpkins before her, their stems of varying length and their shades of orange, until she found one similar to the one Lily was holding, and she pointed. "That one looks pretty good, too."

Doubt flashed over Lily's face, and she shifted her prize to another arm in order to take a better look at Chrys's discovery.

Chrys laughed, adjusting her hold on her own perfect pumpkin. According to Sonia, Lily took her pumpkin selection way too seriously, and Chrys couldn't resist the urge to tease her. Fortunately, they weren't in competition for pumpkins. Chrys preferred hers round, not oval.

Lily let out a deep breath after a moment of contemplation. "I think the one I have is better."

"As long as you're sure. You can't have regrets on the way home."

Finally catching on to what Chrys was doing, Lily poked her in the shoulder and glared.

Chrys grinned. Lily could still not look mean.

"Should we go find out where everyone else went?" Lily asked. "I want some hot chocolate and donuts."

Hot apple-cider donuts sounded good to Chrys, as did putting down the five or six pounds of pumpkin she was carrying. "Let's pay for these outside and then go in the store. I think I see Anushka."

Sonia's aunts had given them each a canvas bag to put their pumpkins, apples, or whatever else they bought in, and Chrys looked forward to carrying the weight on her shoulder and freeing up her hands.

Once that was finished, they went inside the packed barn that also served as a storefront, where Lily bought a hot chocolate and Chrys bought mulled cider. She took a sip immediately before the October air cooled it off. This was no Black Cat Coffee; there were no spells on these cups to keep the contents hot.

Despite having grown up in this world, it was disconcerting to feel her magic's absence. Access to her power had faded as they left Thornhaven's shores, imperceptibly at first, but now with her feet planted firmly on mainland dirt, Chrys could tell how much harder it would be to use magic. She hadn't left the island many times since she and her mom had arrived, and none of them had been in the last year. As her power had grown, so had her ability to detect its loss.

That loss was made up for by other things, though. The air was heavy with the scent of hay and autumn decay, and the farm was open for apple picking and fall festivities. There was even live music provided by a band near the barn entrance.

And then there was her company. Coming here to buy pumpkins had been Lily's idea. Pumpkins could be purchased on the island, but buying them at the Shop-n-Go wasn't the same as picking one out from the hundreds—if not thousands—for sale at this farm.

Lily had first suggested that just she and Chrys go, but Lily had also been nervous about driving off the island, and Chrys had been feeling brave and suggested inviting friends. She knew it was a little sad to think inviting people out with her was an act of bravery, but Lily understood. Or, if nothing else, Lily had agreed that getting to know Chrys's friends—and Chrys getting to better know her friends—was a good idea.

In the end, only Anushka and Sonia had been able to join them, but Sonia's aunt Amelia had offered to drive, and they'd all packed into her minivan. Chrys was bewildered but happy, and she was doing her best not to show how happy she was because she was convinced that it was also weird to be happy about something so mundane.

The truth was, though, she'd been happy all the past week in a way she couldn't ever remember being happy before. The pessimistic voice in her head tried to caution her that nothing good could come of being happy—it led only to disappointment. But she was trying, so very hard, to let go of some of her anxiety.

"How are things with your parents?" Chrys asked as they navigated their way outside.

"Well, I'm not grounded anymore." Lily ran a finger over a set of wind chimes that were tinkling in the breeze. "My mom's been working a lot this week so she can take off next weekend for the ball and Samhain. But she's also been texting to check in with me a lot more. Which is nice . . . except when it's annoying. She keeps sending me these stupid Halloween memes."

Chrys snorted. "What about your dad? He's been talking to my mom about a bakery and helping her with her business plan."

"He's suddenly very focused on me going off to college. He went through the same phase with my brother a few years ago, so the timing could be a coincidence, or it could be that my mom reminded him that I exist and I'll need to apply very soon. But it's . . . a lot."

"What do you mean?"

Lily shrugged. "Just the pressure. He expects me to go to the same place where he and my mom went, where my brother goes, where my grandmother went. It's this small liberal arts school in New Hampshire that lots of witches go to, so there's community and access to power—not like Thornhaven, but better than here. Better than most places." She waved her hand around. "But it's really hard to get into. It was bad enough when I was just thinking about competing with you for valedictorian. Now I keep thinking about all the other people out there I'll have to compete against for admissions."

Chrys cringed internally. Their own competition aside, they both deserved some time to de-stress—Lily especially. "What's the school?"

"Harvey College." Lily's face perked up slightly. "We could both go."

Chrys had heard of it, probably from other witches talking about applying. A college with a significant enough witch population to impact her power did sound ideal. But, academics aside, Chrys was sure it was expensive.

Plus, after three years of not feeling like she belonged in Thornhaven, the last thing she wanted to think about was leaving just as it was starting to not feel so awful.

Librarians and historians needed degrees, though.

"I'll look it up," she said finally.

"There you are!" Anushka draped an arm around Chrys's shoulder. She was also carrying a cup of something warm, and the cold had flushed her tan cheeks. After expressing horror over Chrys's choice in crushes, she was slowly softening toward Lily. Chrys understood. Anushka's history with Lily was longer than her own had been, but she was trying. "You two lovebirds wandered off to be together, didn't you?"

"We were picking out pumpkins," Chrys said, feigning indignance. "In plain sight of everyone."

"Likely story." Anushka removed her arm and stuffed her free hand deep into her fleece's pocket. "Sonia's aunties bought donuts for all of us. Come be all cute while the food is hot. Just not too cute, or the rest of us won't be able to eat."

"Sounds like a challenge," Chrys said.

Lily grabbed her hand, and Chrys's feet practically lifted off the ground. "More donuts for us."

"Did I ever mention how much I like it when you get devious?" she asked.

Anushka groaned in an exaggerated manner. "Too much cuteness. I'm so disappointed in you both." Then she ran off toward the picnic tables.

Lily giggled. "Never thought I'd hear anyone describe you as cute."

"Shut up, princess. She described *us* as cute, not me. That's all your bad influence. I'm still morose and morbid."

"Delightfully morose and morbid," Lily said, and she kissed Chrys on the cheek, leaving her grinning too hard to argue.

Chapter Thirty-Four

Lily

"I really don't want to ride to the ball with Evan's parents," Sonia was saying as they exited the cafeteria on Wednesday. "But there's not a lot of time to get ready otherwise. Do you think we'll be done setting up by four?"

Chrysanthemum must have been correct that the reason she and Lily hadn't previously been asked to assist with the Halloween ball was because they'd been busy painting. Now that their punishment was complete, they'd been asked to volunteer by Ms. LaPlant. (They'd been volun*told*, really, but whatever.) Lily had gotten herself on decorating duty, but no matter how much she'd tried to get Chrysanthemum there, too, Chrysanthemum had been stuck helping collect tickets. It was infuriating, but Chrysanthemum had promised she'd leave as soon as she could, and Lily planned to spend extra time hanging around the check-in table.

To be fair, over the past one and a half weeks, she had been spending plenty of time with Chrysanthemum already. At least, she had outside of regular school. *During* regular school was a different story. The past weekend's outing with Sonia and Anushka aside, the only person who seemed truly comfortable moving between friend groups was Luke. Everyone else had too much history not to feel like an intruder.

This was fine, or so Lily told herself. She didn't want to be clingy or one of those people who drifted apart from their friends when they began a new relationship. She and Chrysanthemum texted constantly, and although not everyone at witch school seemed ready to welcome Chrysanthemum (Bethany among them), Lily and Sonia had made their feelings on the matter clear.

Chrysanthemum, Lily knew, didn't entirely trust everyone's friendliness yet, and Lily couldn't blame her. Over time, though, she hoped Chrysanthemum would forgive the others for not making more of an effort, much the way Chrysanthemum had forgiven Lily for her rudeness.

And really, it made sense not to be too absorbed with each other at regular school. The curse had sucked time away from Lily's academics, and she needed to refocus. Just because she liked Chrysanthemum and they were together (whatever that meant exactly, which was something they'd never discussed), it didn't mean that Lily was ready to abandon all plans for becoming valedictorian. She would just be less bitter if she lost to the one person who deserved it as much as she did.

"We have what—four days to the ball?" Lily asked, adjusting her backpack. "We'll figure it out."

She and Sonia parted ways, and Lily slipped into physics class, eager for the day to be over. AP Physics wasn't just her most challenging class; it was her least favorite.

Lily waved to Luke, who took the seat next to her as usual. Not feeling like she needed to force herself into liking him was nice. She could enjoy his company as a friend and not worry about anything else. Thank goodness she'd never attempted to flirt with him.

"Hey." Luke smiled back, but his face was strained.

In fact, the classroom mood was quiet and tense, and Lily was beginning to worry. But when Mr. Gevry entered the room with a pile of papers, a memory clicked in the back of Lily's brain, and it was so much worse than she could ever have imagined.

She'd completely forgotten they had a quiz today.

Cold numbness washed over her as Mr. Gevry called the class to order and handed out the tests. This was her *worst* subject, and she was totally unprepared. Last night, when she should have been studying, she'd been texting nonsense back and forth with Chrysanthemum. Saturday, when she should have been reviewing the principles of motion, she'd been out picking pumpkins and kissing.

There was no question she was going to fail. Even a B would ruin her GPA beyond redemption. No valedictorian for her. No college acceptance letters. She was failing herself, and, once again, she was failing her family.

Tears, sharp and prickly, stabbed her eyes. Lily glanced left to where Luke was writing furiously, his blond hair curling around his ear.

Her Knight of Wands.

Her tarot reading.

How could she be so stupid? She had no romantic feelings toward Luke, which meant if she'd just *pursued him* like the cards had suggested, she would never have been distracted from her schoolwork. He was the ideal boyfriend in that way—nice to talk to, cute for pictures, and unable to impede her focus.

But Chrysanthemum? She was *never* supposed to fall for Chrysanthemum.

Chrysanthemum was her conflict. The cards didn't lie. *She* was the distraction Lily couldn't afford.

She closed her eyes, forcing the tears down. An Allerton witch did not cry in public.

Lily knew what she had to do to salvage any hope of good grades for the year. But it only made the threat of tears stronger.

Chapter Thirty-Five
Chrysanthemum

Something was wrong. Lily ignored her at lunch. They didn't talk before class. They hadn't texted at any point over the last few hours.

Chrys refused to show her anxiety, so she'd kept her distance, taking her cues from Lily's behavior, but her gut twisted all the same. Lily had arrived at witch school right before class started (late, by her standards), and she'd done nothing more than mumble "hi" before dropping into her usual seat.

Then she'd proceeded to not look Chrys's way once during class.

Half of Chrys wanted to pull her close and make sure she was okay. The other half—the half that had played with fire before and been burned—recoiled at the idea of showing concern and exposing feelings. Chrys spent the entire class internally debating what to do.

Had she misread everything between them?

Was she disappointing Lily by not taking the initiative and reaching out?

Should she back off and assume that if Lily wanted to talk to her, she would?

Chrys had no experience with relationships, but her experience with other people told her one thing clearly—to brace for the worst.

Was it pessimistic? Probably. But that expectation was why Chrys wasn't blindsided when Lily approached her after class. "Can we talk?"

She *wanted* to be hopeful as Lily gestured her into the library, but she wasn't. "What's wrong? Is there anything I can do?"

The expression Lily turned on her was miserable. "Kind of? I think . . ." Lily struggled for words, and Chrys waited, gnawing on her sense of dread. "I think we shouldn't go to the ball together. We can't keep doing whatever it is we're doing. It needs to stop."

Expecting it hadn't dulled the slap those words gave her. But it did help her recover more quickly than she might have otherwise. "Stop what—texting, making plans? Being . . ." Being what? "Friends?"

"Yes, all of it." Lily closed her eyes. "I don't want to be enemies, but I can't do anything more than that."

From within the hollow pain inside Chrys's chest, a spark of anger ignited.

"So we pretend nothing ever happened?" Never mind the kissing. Chrys was supposed to forget the coffee and the teasing and the doing homework together? The late nights texting? The sunflower pin Lily had bought her and that she'd stuck to her black backpack, completely ruining her aesthetic for the sake of a girl?

"Yes." Lily still wouldn't look at her. "Obviously, we saved the town together, and that was wonderful . . . but everything else was a mistake. I made a mistake. I'm sorry." She rushed out of the library before Chrys could say anything else.

So that was what she was to Lily—a mistake.

She should have known, but there she'd gone, giving someone the benefit of the doubt and having her heart stomped all over. Chrys had thought that maybe she'd misjudged Lily, but no. Lily was exactly who she'd shown herself to be in ninth grade. She thought she was too good for Chrys.

Chrys felt cursed, as she so often had, but worse than usual. Maybe there was a curse inside her, wormy and pulsing and full of negativity and pain and vileness, turning her blood black and foul, poisoning her heart with bitterness.

When was she going to learn: *Never drop your armor*? Why did she so stupidly want people in her life at all? If only she had Lily's talent, maybe she could give up on this need for human companionship.

Chrys dug her nails into her palms, willing down tears. Like hell was she going to let any of these Thornhaven snobs see her upset. Chrys would make sure Lily saw that she would never even think about her again unless she was forced to.

She just needed a moment to compose herself. Lily would be long gone if she took enough of them.

How long she took, Chrys wasn't sure, but approaching footfalls warned her to get it together. Chrys adjusted her backpack and turned to leave, surprised to see Sonia in the doorway wearing a tentative smile.

"Excuse me," Chrys said, trying to push by her. Her plan to make Lily believe she didn't care was off to a wonderful start.

"Wait, Chrys!"

She stopped. Nothing Sonia could say would make tonight any better. Chrys knew this, and yet her curiosity was too strong. Carefully fitting her mask of indifference back in place, Chrys faced her.

"I don't know what Lily told you," Sonia said, glancing behind, as though searching for the girl herself, "but I know that she's really upset. I think something happened at school."

And she wanted to make Chrys's day bad, too? What was Sonia's point?

"So?" Chrys asked, glad she'd stuck to monosyllables. It made her voice sound steadier.

Sonia winced. "What I mean is that she's not thinking clearly, and I'm sure she didn't mean whatever she said. You know how Lily gets when she's stressed." She paused. "Right?"

Yes, Chrys had gotten to see more than one Lily freak-out over the past few weeks, but that changed nothing. If Lily was stressed about something, then she should have come to Chrys for advice or comfort. Not pushed her away. Lily had made her priorities clear, and Chrys wasn't one of them. She'd called their whatever-it-was a *mistake*.

"She really does like you," Sonia continued, and Chrys was certain that there was no type of armor she could don that would protect against such a direct attack. "A lot. She talks about you all the time. Like . . . constantly."

"Bullshit," Chrys said, fighting to keep all traces of hurt from her tone. Her words would sound far worse if she didn't appear to care. "Look, Lily isn't my problem anymore. She just made that *very* clear."

Then she spun around and hurried away.

Outside, the frosty night air was cleansing. But the breeze, sweetly tinged with woodsmoke and biting with the ocean's brine, was only a momentary respite. No wind could carry away the pain. No fire could burn it, nor water drown it, and she couldn't bury it in the earth.

Yet, ironically, as much as this sucked, she knew this territory well. This pushed-to-the-outside territory, this alone-again territory, this angry-at-the-world territory. The uncertainty of happiness with Lily had always been a little uncomfortable, or so Chrys consoled herself. Now she once more knew what to expect from life and how to act. That had to count for something. She *was* morbid, just as Lily had said, but what people like Lily never understood was that they were the cause.

Her phone vibrated, and Chrys silently cursed the flash of hope that sprang to life with it. Even if it was Lily saying she'd made a mistake, Chrys wasn't going to respond.

It wasn't Lily, though. It was Luke.

Hey, can we talk? I want to ask you something about the Halloween ball.

Chapter Thirty-Six

Lily

The pre-Halloween bonfires the student council hosted were perfect. Despite the curse interfering with meetings, and despite it wreaking havoc on Lily's time and mind, they were everything she had intended them to be.

Four blazing fires lined Southcove Beach, one for each class, sending fragrant smoke into the velvety blue night. Strings of golden lights encircled the booths where representatives from each year were selling hot dogs, hot cocoa, s'mores kits, and more as a fundraiser. (Each class was in competition to see who could make the most money.) A long table glowed a fiery orange, decorated with dozens of entries in the annual jack-o'-lantern carving contest, and the path from the parking lot down to the rocky sand was lined with lamps, flooding the beach in a warm glow that defied the October chill.

It was beautiful. If Lily closed her eyes, the scent of burning wood and the ocean's steady, ceaseless breaths soothed her completely. That was, when she could hear the ocean over people shouting and laughing.

The bonfires were held each year on the Friday before Halloween. Lily had been excited to put her own personal touch on the event this year, as student council president. She'd done a simple glamour spell on each of the fires, giving the freshmen's a touch of green, the sophomores' a hint of blue, the juniors' a blush of pink, and the seniors' a purple hue. Four spells at once, even easy ones, was more than she was used to casting, but her and Chrysanthemum's triumph over the curse had convinced her to push herself harder. She could do more than she believed.

Except hold on to Chrysanthemum.

Or make valedictorian.

Or not ruin everything.

That was why this evening—with this event that she'd been looking forward to for so long and was so proud of putting together—was not actually making her happy. In fact, she was pretty *unhappy*.

Lily wasn't so naïve as to think she'd get over Chrysanthemum immediately or force her life back on track instantaneously, but she'd thrown herself into school (including last-minute bonfire prep) and *hoped*.

It hadn't helped. How was she supposed to focus when she was in pain? When thinking about the ball reminded her of holding Chrysanthemum's hand, of the way her skin smelled? It made her chest constrict.

She was taking her break from helping out at the senior class's booth, so she decided she should seek Luke out while she could. She didn't believe she was ever going to fall for him at this point, but he was the missing ingredient for success. And success was all that really mattered.

Lily grabbed a hot chocolate and headed onto the beach. Salty wind whipped at her face as she walked toward the purple-tinged fire, carrying the sounds of voices and laughter. Never had Lily felt so disconnected from everyone else. Even as she waved to people and made meaningless small talk. She was a piece of driftwood that had washed ashore.

There, a blond head caught her eye—Luke. Standing around talking to Chrysanthemum and Anushka?

It wasn't like Lily could go over there now.

She backed away, just enough to disappear into the fire's shadow. She shouldn't watch them, but she couldn't tear her eyes away, either. Had Chrysanthemum ever gone to the bonfires in the past? She didn't recall seeing her, and Lily was certain she'd have remembered. It just figured that Chrysanthemum would choose to go this year, another way to torment her.

Firelight danced over Chrysanthemum, making her into something wild and wondrous—something fey. But she and Luke were laughing, having a perfectly normal time from the looks of it.

Apparently, Chrysanthemum wasn't hurting from what Lily had done. How was that possible? Lily had seen pain pass over

Chrysanthemum's eyes that night. It was why she'd had to look away.

Chrysanthemum had cared about her, she was certain, but maybe . . . not very much. Or maybe she'd done what Lily didn't dare to do—cast a spell to make her feelings go away.

Luke leaned over Chrysanthemum. Although their faces didn't meet and their lips didn't touch, it was clear they were having an *intense* conversation. An *intimate* conversation. What? Why? How?

The hot chocolate curdled in Lily's stomach. That should be *her* there. In Chrysanthemum's place. Or in Luke's.

"Would you please go talk to her?" Sonia said, and Lily jumped.

"Don't startle me like that!"

"If you weren't pining over Chrys, you'd have heard me coming."

"I'm not pining." She was totally pining. She was a mess. "How long does it take to get over someone? Maybe my expectations are unrealistic."

"Longer than two days." Sonia took a bite of her s'more with an untoasted marshmallow in the center. Normally, Lily would make fun of her for her refusal to toast them, but she didn't have it in her. "Why are you so determined to *be* over her? I know you think you should date Luke, which is utterly ridiculous, by the way, but this kind of thing can't be forced. You can't study or practice your way into a perfect relationship. Not even you. You have to follow your heart."

"But what if it's wrong? What if it wants something that's bad for me?"

"I don't think it does. But your brain might."

"Excuse me?" Lily started to tremble.

"I ask you again: Have you considered that you read the cards wrong? Divination is deceptive."

Sure, Sonia was talented at divination, but Lily's reading had been clear. The question annoyed her no less the second time. Still. *Could* she have been wrong? Life *felt* wrong, just now.

She could sense panic coming on again, every muscle tensing, her pulse quickening.

Sonia must have seen the doubts creeping over Lily's face. "Tell me the exact reading again."

Lily nodded and wandered over to one of the benches that lined the edge of the beach. Farther from the fires, it was colder, but also quieter. She huddled in on herself for warmth. Sonia sat next to her.

"My present was the Knight of Wands. The obstacles were the five of Wands. The future was the two of Cups. And the binding thread was Death." She'd gone over it again and again in her journal since blowing her physics quiz. It was impossible to forget. "Chrysanthemum is the conflict. She's always been the conflict."

Sonia didn't say anything. Lily tried to be patient. It was easy to discount Sonia's advice about relationships, considering her constant *mess* with Evan, but her advice about a tarot reading would be a lot harder to discount. Perhaps that was why Lily hadn't wanted to hear it previously.

"I can see why you came to the conclusion you did," Sonia said at last. "But I think you let your assumptions guide the reading instead of letting the cards be your guide. Have you considered that you turned your reading into a self-fulfilling prophecy?"

"What?"

"Rookie mistake."

"Shut up!" Lily smacked her arm. "We *are* rookies!"

Sonia laughed and stuck out her tongue. "Speak for yourself. I am a Kim. I was reading the cards before I could read a book without pictures."

Lily groaned. "Fine. I'm ready to listen. Actually listen. What's your take?"

"Well, it's hard to say what it would have been two months ago, but . . ." Sonia brushed graham cracker crumbs from her hands. "Luke's arrival was the inciting event to spark a change in your relationship with Chrys, but the conflict isn't Chrys herself. The conflict was your war with each other. You resolved that, and it brought you two together—happiness and love as signified by the two of Cups. Death is a big change, symbolically, so it could be many things—maybe it was about discovering you and Chrys are compatible or that you like girls. Maybe it was falling for someone for the first time. There are many ways to interpret that spread."

Lily chewed on her fingertips as she contemplated this. Sonia's interpretation fit as well as her own had. Given the past, it fit better, but that gave Sonia an unfair advantage. "I mean, it sounds very easy after everything has already happened."

"Or possibly none of it has finished happening." Sonia shrugged. "'Divination is a bitch' is Auntie Marina's second-favorite saying after 'Divination is deceptive.' But it all makes good sense to me. If you'd wanted my *untainted* opinion, you should have asked for it in September, instead of shutting me down."

"You're right. And I'm sorry." Lily put her hands over her eyes. "But it doesn't change the fact that spending so much time with Chrysanthemum was affecting my grades." Wasn't that the real issue here?

Sonia gave her a hug; then she zipped her jacket higher and stood. "There's more to life than tests and GPAs. I say this lovingly, but honestly: Fuck your parents for making you feel there's not. Now—are you going to the fire with me? I need to warm up and find Evan."

Lily didn't get up immediately after Sonia jogged toward the concession stands. It was occurring to her that she was making the same mistakes over and over.

When she'd done her reading, she'd noted that she hadn't defined what she meant by *perfect*. She'd assumed *perfect* was obvious, but it was an undefined ideal in her mind, and vagueness and magic were a dangerous combination. So the cards had defined *perfect* in their own way, and instead of trying to see that, she'd made the most basic and uncritical assumption—that she needed a boyfriend. That she needed to be normal. That she needed Luke.

Not even finding happiness with Chrysanthemum had opened her mind to other possibilities. In fact, one single setback was all it had taken for Lily to retreat to her original flawed assumption—that a perfect year meant perfect grades, a perfect boy, and a perfect mask.

Despite everything the cards had been telling her, she was still trying to bend them to her will. She wasn't just acting irrationally; she was being a terrible witch.

Her grades were important. She wanted to be valedictorian and to go to a prestigious college. But did perfect scores make her happy . . . ? Not really. Not like Chrysanthemum had made her happy. Did she even *want* to go to the same college as the rest of her family? Maybe, but maybe there was another she'd like better.

Maybe Death was about reevaluating her outlook on life.

Maybe Chrysanthemum was the true key to a perfect year.

Ugh, she was so stupid, she didn't deserve to be valedictorian.

Lily took out her phone. She might be able to redeem her grades, but could she redeem herself? She hadn't done a very good job of explaining her decision to Chrysanthemum because she'd been too upset. If Chrysanthemum was angry at her,

Lily couldn't blame her. Although, to be fair, Chrysanthemum didn't seem angry tonight, and that was worse—she seemed indifferent.

That was a lie, though. It had to be. Lily had learned that Chrysanthemum covered up her feelings better than anyone she knew.

She typed out a message to Chrysanthemum, asking her to talk.

She had five minutes before she had to get back to the booth and let someone else take a break. Five minutes to stare at her phone and hope for a response.

None came. Chrysanthemum probably hadn't heard the text given the noise. That was all. She'd read it later, or Lily would seek her out before the party ended.

But by the time Lily was done helping with the cleanup, midnight had come and gone, and Chrysanthemum had disappeared, too.

Chapter Thirty-Seven
Chrysanthemum

Lily had tried to get Chrys added to the decorating committee, and for many reasons now, Chrys was glad she'd failed. She liked working the check-in table for the ball. The job took less time than decorating, and while it was probably a lot more boring, it enabled her to avoid being sociable. Most years, that was all Chrys had wanted. This year, it was still kind of what she wanted, but it came with a problem—Lily arriving with friends and needing to be checked in. If Lily approached her, Chrys couldn't run away.

The text Lily had sent her last night burned like a fire in the pocket of Chrys's black tulle skirt. She hadn't discovered it until she'd gotten home, and then she'd stared at it for a minute before throwing her phone at her bed in frustration.

Almost twenty-four hours later, Chrys still hadn't responded. Curiosity was killing her, but she had to have some self-respect. She needed to prove to Lily that nothing Lily had to say would interest her.

Speaking of, here she came, looking like an autumn fairy, reminding Chrys of the day when they'd stomped on leaves in Lily's yard. She wore an emerald-green dress with asymmetrical straps. Her shoulders were dusted with gold glitter, and her reddish-blond hair was swept back and held in place by golden leaf-shaped clips. She was so pretty, it made Chrys want to toss more things, including her stomach contents.

Lily was surrounded by the usual crowd—Sonia and Evan, and more witches who'd never acknowledged Chrys's existence until the last couple of weeks.

In her desperation to not look at Lily, Chrys accidentally met Sonia's gaze, and Lily's best friend smiled cautiously at her and motioned her head toward Lily as if to suggest Chrys be the one who did the approaching.

That could only mean Sonia was delusional.

Chrys took a step back from the table, wondering if it was too late to ask for a bathroom break, but if she did, she'd have to walk past Lily to get there. Since running wouldn't help, Chrys surreptitiously crept down to the far end of the table, toward the *Z* side of the registrants.

"Alina Young." One of the witches who'd entered with Lily held out her ticket so Chrys could mark her off the guest list.

Chrys snatched the black-and-orange card stock. As if she didn't know the girl's name after being in classes together for the past *several years*. She stamped the back of Alina's hand harder than necessary, and the inked cat (made of bespelled ink) growled at her before resuming its normal position on Alina's pink-freckled skin.

"Did you get my text?" Lily's voice froze Chrys in place.

"Yes." Chrys added Alina's ticket to the pile and became very busy straightening it so that all the edges lined up perfectly. It was a very Lily sort of thing to do.

"Can we talk?" Lily asked.

Chrys thumbed through the tickets, pretending to count them. "I'm busy."

"Later?"

Maybe later she would leave.

"Please?" Lily pressed.

Chrys shrugged. Bored indifference remained her preferred defense.

She was saved by a familiar voice. Anushka, dressed in a luminous pink gown with butterfly wings on her back, hurried across the lobby, her younger sister skipping on her heels.

Chrys hadn't been able to stop herself from sharing with Anushka that she and Lily were no longer together. Anushka and Isaiah could tell she was upset, and so for only the second time in three years, Chrys had accepted an invitation to go to Anushka's house after school on Friday. Letting out her feelings had been strangely helpful. Anushka had been ready to murder Lily on Chrys's behalf. They'd spent the evening listening to angsty music and plotting ways to convince Anushka's parents to let her travel with Chrys to Boston over winter break to see one of their favorite bands.

It was no surprise, therefore, that Anushka was glaring daggers at Lily's back as she approached.

Perhaps sensing that rage, Lily stepped aside. "I'll find you later."

Please don't, Chrys thought. She couldn't stand to hear whatever Lily wanted to tell her, and she was wearing makeup tonight. If she got too upset, she could smear it.

Chrys checked in Anushka and her family, but once they disappeared, she couldn't stop looking toward the ballroom, half hoping Lily would come back out to find her.

She was so weak.

Struggling to hold herself together, Chrys glanced above the ballroom's open doors and frowned. There was a *crack* in the wall, one she could have sworn hadn't been there the last time she'd looked that way.

As if it noticed her staring at it, the crack faded.

No.

Chrys swallowed, blinked, and scanned the rest of the lobby while her heartbeat picked up the tempo. Everything else seemed normal. The ball had opened an hour ago, and new arrivals were thinning out. Clusters of people stood around chatting, and hotel staff scurried by as they worked.

Clearly, no one else had noticed anything amiss.

Chrys told herself to relax. She had enough problems to deal with. Maybe stress was causing her to hallucinate?

When the new guests finally stopped coming altogether, Chrys was informed she should head into the ball and enjoy her evening. That seemed *highly* optimistic, but sitting around outside the ballroom was getting too boring to endure.

She should poke her head inside, check out the decorations, and figure out what to do. Leaving early actually wasn't that simple. Her mom would stay for a few more hours, and most people hung around until midnight, which the Historical Society marked with its most fantastical displays of magic. It was too far to walk home, and Chrys's black lace-up boots precluded that anyway. As it was, she'd be thankful not to end the night with any blisters.

If nothing else, she should wander the ball to convince herself that the thing she'd seen earlier wasn't real. That no black veins had somehow invaded the hotel.

Every year the witches' decorating committee transformed the Haven Harbor Hotel and Resort's ballroom into a Halloween fantasyland, and this year was no exception. The entire ceiling was filled with smoke. Lights cascaded down within it, dripping gold and purple, their colorful hues evaporating into the air in time with the music. More lights swirled up black walls, rising off strategically placed cauldrons that bubbled and overflowed with steam. Tables had been pushed to one side of the room, each covered in black cloth and lit with candles. The bars and food stations along the far wall were lined with mirrors, and the bartenders and servers working behind them were skeletons—real people, Chrys knew, but subject to a glamour spell that would create that illusion for anyone who stepped within its confines. Every now and them, amid the smoke above, more illusions—bats and ghosts—swept through the artificial sky. Finally, pumpkins sat everywhere off the dance floor, some carved and some not, filling any voids so that anywhere someone looked, there was a reason to marvel.

Once, the decorating committee had gone with a harvest theme; another year, they'd turned the entire ballroom into a haunted cemetery. The upside to this year's dark, almost psychedelic theme was that it would make being spotted by Lily more difficult, especially since Chrys had inadvertently dressed to match the color scheme: black skirt, black boots, lace gloves, plum satin bodice.

Chrys grabbed a couple of mini-quiches and some soda from a helpful skeleton (which was disconcerting despite her knowing how the spell worked) and headed toward the patio, keeping as close as she could to the walls. At one point, she thought she saw a flash of Lily's green dress moving across the dance floor, and Chrys ducked behind a bubbling cauldron until the vision passed.

The smoke rising from it smelled ever so slightly of rot, and Chrys jerked her head back.

That was wrong.

Almost all the spells that would have been used to decorate were glamour spells. They were, relatively speaking, simple things. Illusions, mainly. None should have a foul odor about them, and while it was possible someone might have thought it cute to burn some incense in the cauldrons to make the smoke more interesting, surely they wouldn't have chosen to make *interesting* mean *unpleasant*.

Chrys's stomach twisted. The curse had stunk of rot, too.

After another sip of her soda, she headed outside to clear her nostrils and her head. Fires blazed around the patio, though the air itself seemed to have been warmed by a spell, as there was no way the fires were generating so much heat. Hay covered the patio stones, and golden lights in the shape of an elaborate spiderweb hung of their own accord in the sky, creating a glowing canopy. More pumpkins and jack-o'-lanterns were piled everywhere she looked. The mood was less intense, and the number of revelers fewer, and both those changes were welcome.

Chrys breathed deeply, trying to relax, and she wandered through the maze of hay bales until she found a semisecluded area to rest. But as she sank onto one of the chairs scattered about, the weight of her phone brushed her thigh, reminding her of Lily's unanswered text. Did she text back and tell Lily what she'd smelled? Although she wanted to avoid Lily, she had a reason to respond, one that didn't involve giving away her feelings.

Or was she merely looking for an excuse?

That possibility forced Chrys to grasp her soda glass with both hands. No. She only *thought* she might have seen the veins, and the cauldron smoke could have smelled funny for any number of reasons. There was no need to jump to conclusions and therefore no need to alert Lily. Without another sign—a stronger one—that something was amiss, it was best to stick to the plan: She'd find her friends, avoid Lily, and figure out a way to leave early.

Chrys nodded at the smiling jack-o'-lantern across from her, as though they'd reached this conclusion together.

The jack-o'-lantern frowned in response.

Startled, Chrys almost dropped her glass, and she swore silently at her jumpiness. Someone had obviously bewitched the jack-o'-lanterns to change expressions. Frowning seemed rude, but clearly it was supposed to be playfully creepy.

She assumed too soon. The carved expression on the jack-o'-lantern's face turned uglier as it sneered. Once cheerful, the golden light glowing from within took on a greenish hue that made the expression more sinister.

More alive.

Chrys was gaping at it, wondering if it was somehow responding to her thoughts, when a worm emerged from the snarling mouth. The wiggling black-and-green thing was smaller than Chrys's tiniest finger, but a second one soon followed. Then another and another, until the pumpkin's face was vomiting worms, pouring them through its glowing eyes and nose. In seconds, a mass of slimy creatures that reminded her of the curse's pulsing heart swallowed the jack-o'-lantern.

Chrys jumped up, sweat breaking out on the back of her neck. As the worms trailed off, black smoke began to pour out of the jack-o'-lantern—stinking, gag-worthy smoke. Then it laughed, an evil, prickly sound that made the hairs on Chrys's neck stand on end and her stomach sink to her ankles.

Yet no one else seemed to notice anything amiss.

No one turned in her direction. No one exclaimed over the magic.

Chrys backed into the chair and stumbled. In case she hadn't put the signs together before, black veins spread across the straw beneath the pumpkin, removing any doubts about what was happening.

They shot right toward her across the patio.

Chrys darted aside, panic spreading throughout her body. She couldn't shake the idea that if they'd reached her feet, they'd have opened wider. That she'd have fallen through and they'd have swallowed her up.

Only a couple of hours remained until midnight. During Samhain, the veil would be at its thinnest. For all Chrys knew, it *would* be possible for her to disappear through it that way, trapped forever in liminal space.

A few people finally turned her way. Chrys was conscious of the confused looks they gave her, making it clear that it was her own behavior that had drawn their attention and not the jack-o'-lantern's. The pumpkin's carved face had resettled into its former smile. The black smoke had dissipated. The candle inside once more glowed a soft yellow.

Ignoring the stares, Chrys decided that the time had come to jump to some damn conclusions. She was reaching for her phone to text Lily when Lily burst into view around the nearest firepit.

"There you are," Lily said, catching her breath. "It's back!"

Chapter Thirty-Eight

Lily

"No shit," Chrysanthemum muttered, and Lily flinched.

Why did Chrysanthemum have to be so prickly? Even now? Yes, Lily had screwed up and she was determined to make it right, but if Chrysanthemum had just answered her text earlier, then she could have apologized and explained and . . .

Ugh. This was not the time to fret over their relationship issues.

Lily closed her eyes briefly, forcing herself to concentrate on the more pressing problem. Chrysanthemum's face was paler than usual, and her hands were shaking. She looked like someone who'd had the spit shocked out of her. Since Lily was feeling the same thing, it would have been nice to share a comforting hug and feel the reassurance of warm skin.

But they couldn't. (Her fault. No—time to focus.)

It shouldn't have, but Chrysanthemum's obvious anxiety relaxed Lily a bit. It meant she was taking this seriously.

"Was it a pumpkin?" Chrysanthemum asked.

"A . . . pumpkin?"

Chrysanthemum motioned toward the jack-o'-lantern sitting on a hay bale nearby. The patio and ballroom were filled with them, most with more interesting designs than smiles carved into their faces.

"There was smoke coming out of it," Chrysanthemum said. She sounded like she was making an effort to sound calm. Seeing as she'd been much more chill than Lily about everything that had happened up to this point, this didn't bode well. "Smoke and worms. You know what kind of worms I mean."

Lily shuddered. "What about the black lines?"

"Those, too." Chrysanthemum warily moved her gaze from the jack-o'-lantern to Lily, but she seemed unwilling to turn her back on it. "I was about to text you."

"Oh, finally. So this is all it took?" Lily tried to make it sound lighthearted, but she could hear the hurt in her voice, and no question Chrysanthemum could, too. She held up a hand, cutting off whatever Chrysanthemum was about to say. "Sorry. Not the time, I know. I think something is really wrong."

"No shit," Chrysanthemum said again. "What happened to you?"

"Nothing *to* me, but there are lines—cracks—appearing in all the mirrored surfaces in the ballroom. No one else can see them. I've been looking for you—I even went into the bathroom looking, and the mirrors in there all have cracks, too." Lily wrapped her arms around herself. "I've never seen so many. They don't fade away like they used to, either. That's how I found you—I followed them to you. And they're bigger than they used to be. Wider?"

Chrysanthemum's eyes opened wide themselves in response to that. "I had the creepiest premonition that they would get so wide that I could fall into them. When midnight comes . . ."

She didn't have to finish the sentence.

Lily didn't know if it was possible for living people to slip into the Other Side, but every witch knew that energies and spirits could. Widening cracks . . .

The veil wasn't merely thinning anymore; the curse was actively breaking the barrier.

What that would mean for Thornhaven was a question Lily didn't want answered.

"We have to banish it again," Lily said.

Chrysanthemum threw her hands up. "Yes, sure, great plan. Because we did it so well the first time."

"Obviously we missed something."

"Or we screwed something up because we don't know what we're doing."

"Or that." Lily spun around, fighting the urge to bite her fingertips. "But what's our other option? It's still about us. That means whatever has to be done, it needs to come from us."

She half expected Chrysanthemum to continue arguing for the sake of arguing, but Chrysanthemum's shoulders slumped. "We don't even know where it is. I think you're right that we have to be involved, but maybe it's time for help. We need more powerful people."

Although she remained convinced that Chrysanthemum had way more power than she was giving herself credit for, Lily sighed.

"Let's find it first," she said, putting a plan together as she spoke. "We know how to do that, and we don't need help with it. Once we've found it, I can go home and gather our supplies while you find Ms. LaPlant. We'll let her decide who else to involve. She'll know who the right people are."

That seemed reasonable to Lily, and Chrysanthemum nodded. Good. Plan accomplished. Lily wished it made her feel better like plans usually did.

"Do we start searching here or at school?" Chrysanthemum asked.

In vain, Lily tried to recall everything she'd read about curses. Could they move once they'd taken up residence somewhere? But her memory was foggy with fear, and her brain was spinning with Chrysanthemum's closeness and the emotions that aroused. She was certain she'd read something, but the words on those weathered pages wouldn't materialize.

"You said you trust your instincts," she said to Chrysanthemum. "What do they say?"

Chrysanthemum looked a little queasy. "I don't know how smart that is, but . . . my instincts say we kicked it out of the school, and since the school's been covered in spells by the Society, it would have a hard time returning. Last time it manifested, its magic was mostly focused on where it was located, so . . . here?"

Lily nodded. Everything Chrysanthemum was saying was conjecture, but hearing it calmed Lily down enough to recall some of what she'd read. "The hotel's been the focus of a lot of magic with all the decorating, but it's never been warded because it's not owned by witches. Magic attracts magic." Lily offered up a tentative smile that Chrysanthemum returned with something more akin to a grimace. "I knew *my* instinct to trust *your* instincts made sense."

"My instincts say your instincts suck," Chrysanthemum replied, deadpan.

"They can't possibly. My instincts allow me to talk to rabbits."

Chrysanthemum rolled her eyes, but her grimace faded into a more familiar expression. Lily had missed that sarcastic smile. "Okay, well, tonight we don't need princess instincts. We need *final girl* instincts so we can survive the last act and stop the killer. Er, curse."

"If this is what scary movies are like, I take back what I said about watching any with you," Lily said, before remembering that she and Chrysanthemum hadn't lasted as whatever they were long enough for films. "This is enough horror for me."

Chrysanthemum's smile dissolved into a scowl; then her face hardened into (what Lily was suddenly certain was) false indifference. "Yeah, I think you already took that back."

In spite of everything, Lily's face crumpled at the sharp pain in her chest. But Chrysanthemum didn't pay her any mind. She stalked past, heading toward the ballroom.

"Wait!" It took Lily a second to recover from the emotional punch, but she caught up quickly. "We should split up like last time. How do we want to do this?"

"I don't know, but it's too loud to talk in here."

It was true that the music had gotten louder and livelier as the night had gone on, but Lily sensed that the mood inside the ballroom was changing, and not just because the drinks were starting to catch up to certain guests. The decorations were taking on a sinister tone. Lily wasn't sure what, exactly, it was about them, but the colors looked off: Reds were too red, purples too purple, and suddenly there was too much lurid green. The cauldron smoke had a sickly smell, and the candlelight had dimmed. They strode past Mrs. Cook, who was talking to Lily's father, and both adults wore confused expressions. Lily considered scrapping her own plan and telling her father what was happening, but another member of the Society board joined his conversation before she made up her mind, and then another.

So, on second thought, no. She couldn't drag the Allerton name through the mud like that—so publicly, so irrevocably, screaming and crying in front of half the board. Patient, kind, discreet Ms. LaPlant, and only Ms. LaPlant, would do.

Lily pressed on.

They'd almost made it beyond the ballroom doors when one of the magical bats swooped down on them. It was just an illusion, a glamour spell, or it was supposed to be. But this spell had taken physical form; it grazed Lily's head.

"Did you—" She didn't have time to finish asking before the bat circled around for another pass. Astonishment froze Lily's feet in place as the bat aimed for her again. This time, its talons snagged a strand of her hair, and the shock and pain broke her stupor. With a cry, she swatted the bat, and it flew off.

Lily stared into the ballroom. Beneath the smoke and glittering lights, other decorations were going rogue. Most people hadn't noticed yet, but some were pointing, and they looked less awed by the magic and more disturbed. Chrysanthemum, having heard Lily cry out, had spun around, and their gazes met. As one, they dashed through the rest of the ballroom as fast as Lily's heels could take her.

Outside, Lily blinked as her eyes adjusted to the light in the lobby, and she glanced up. There were no more bats or other magical decorations, but the lines she'd spotted earlier had expanded. As she'd feared.

She rubbed the sore spot on her head and fixed the clip holding her hair back. The hotel was large, and aside from the main lobby's path to this particular ballroom, Lily wasn't familiar with the layout. She doubted Chrysanthemum was, either, which meant that choosing appropriate starting locations for each of them to follow the lines would be more difficult than it had been at school.

"Look." Chrysanthemum grabbed her arm.

For a moment, she wasn't sure what Chrysanthemum was motioning to; Chrysanthemum was gesturing all around. But that was because the cracks were all around. All around and all doing that yo-yo disappearing-reappearing movement from the same direction.

"Convenient," Chrysanthemum said.

"What does that mean?"

Chrysanthemum stuffed her hands into pockets hidden in the volume of black tulle she wore, and despite everything, Lily couldn't help but be slightly jealous that Chrysanthemum's dress had pockets.

"I was going to say we shouldn't split up," Chrysanthemum said. "That is a classic horror-movie mistake. But it looks like we don't need to. It's beckoning us."

That was the opposite of what it had been doing at the school. Or was it? Had the curse beckoned them all along? Lily didn't know what to think, and she whimpered as Chrysanthemum took off in the lines' direction.

"Are you coming?" Chrysanthemum asked.

No, absolutely not, Lily wanted to scream. But they needed to. This was *her* plan. She had to hold it together. "A quick look to see where it goes. Then you get Ms. LaPlant, and I get the supplies. We're just confirming it's actually here."

Chrysanthemum nodded. “We don’t engage. If it leads to a dead end, we turn around and don’t hunt for it.”

“Right.” She fought the urge to grab Chrysanthemum’s hand as they started down the hall, away from the main lobby.

The music and general din from the ballroom faded as they walked, and so did the lights. During the day, Lily imagined this hallway must be brightly lit. One side was all windows that would show off a view of the ocean. But at night, those windows were nothing but darkness encroaching on the hotel. She could barely see the cracks spreading out before them.

Only, there . . . a single light flickered in the blackness beyond the glass. Then a second. Finally, three of them emerged, vaguely human shaped and glowing as though lit by an invisible flashlight.

Lily gazed, mesmerized, trying to figure out what she was seeing. Ball guests outside, holding candles? But something deeper, something magical and primal within her, understood that wasn’t true. Soon enough, the figures were practically at the glass, so close that she could make out details.

They seemed dressed for a costume party: tattered shirts and short jackets and canvas pants, some in silks and scarves, with unkempt hair and . . . wounds. Wounds leaking *brighter* light. And weapons.

Chrysanthemum had paused, too. “Is that . . . ?”

Sailors, Lily started to say, but they weren’t just any sailors. “Pirates.”

"Ghosts."

Instinct told Lily to flee, but fascination grounded her in place as the pirates suddenly charged—that was to say, floated—through the window glass without a sound. A sensation of ice water rushed over Lily. Next to her, Chrysanthemum sucked in a breath. The ghosts paid them no mind. They swept right by and down the hallway toward the ballroom, their ethereal swords raised, their pistols bobbing at their bodyless sides.

"Have you ever seen a ghost before?" Chrysanthemum asked. Her breath expelled in a white puff about the color of her face.

Lily shivered. "Not even on Samhain proper."

Her gaze landed on the cracks beneath her feet, and she glanced up at Chrysanthemum. They were running out of time. Without a word, they took off again.

The hallway ended down a short flight of stairs in a quiet, dimly lit foyer. To their left was an exit door. To their right, a set of double doors that probably led to another function room. Lily wasn't sure whether to be relieved that the lines withdrew beneath those doors, but it meant the curse was definitely in the hotel.

"What are you doing?" She reached out for Chrysanthemum, but Chrysanthemum had already moved toward the doorway.

"Seeing if the doors are unlocked, or if we'll need to get someone from the hotel to open them."

"Okay, right. Makes sense." Lily stepped forward, too, pretending to be braver than she felt. Chrysanthemum had once told her that they were badasses, but Lily didn't feel like that. If it were her alone, she'd have let someone else check the doors, but she wasn't about to let Chrysanthemum do it by herself. She'd been stupid and pushed Chrysanthemum away, and all she wanted now was to pull her close. So Lily would stay close, no matter what.

They each grabbed one of the handles, the doors swung open, and an invisible hand shoved Lily inside the darkened room.

CHAPTER THIRTY-NINE

Lily

Lily screamed. Chrysanthemum screamed. The doors slammed shut behind them with a boom louder than them both.

Lily found herself on her hands and knees, staring into the hotel's hideously patterned industrial carpet. Its golds, blues, and reds were just discernible in the moonlight seeping through the tall windows against the far wall. It felt like it took an eternity to collect herself and scramble to her feet, but she was only a second behind Chrysanthemum.

Lily raced back to the doors, and together they yanked on the handles, but it was no use. The doors that had opened only too freely a moment ago refused to budge.

"Emergency exits!" Lily pointed at the faintly glowing red sign above a set of doors and dashed across the enormous room. Those doors didn't budge, either.

Lily threw her whole body into it, refusing to believe they wouldn't open. They were emergency doors, for goodness' sake. Weren't they supposed to be openable at all times? She stopped when she realized Chrysanthemum hadn't joined her. Like Chrysanthemum had known it wasn't worth her energy to attempt it.

"*Really?*" Lily shouted, although she wasn't sure if her frustration was directed at Chrysanthemum's fatalism, the curse's audacity, or the universe in general.

"You think the curse cares that it's violating the fire code?" Chrysanthemum asked.

Lily kicked a door in frustration. "It should. This is cheating."

The emergency doors were nestled between two enormous windows whose bottom sills were about even with her head. Lily eyed them, uncertain whether she and Chrysanthemum could reach high enough to attempt breaking the glass. Even more uncertain whether they'd be successful.

"What?" she asked, spinning around because she thought she heard Chrysanthemum say something. Chrysanthemum was looking at her, but it was too dim to read her expression from this distance.

"Nothing."

"You think I'm ridiculous, don't you?" Lily crossed her arms.

Chrysanthemum shook her head. "I think you're . . ." She turned away. "Motivated. Determined."

Lily's brain stumbled over those words, but before she could ask what Chrysanthemum was getting at, Chrysanthemum had pulled out her phone and turned on the flashlight. That seemed like a better, and possibly less futile, use of Lily's time, so she did the same.

Wordlessly, they shined light around the room. Lily assumed that, like her, Chrysanthemum was searching for the curse, although what they would do when they found it remained to be seen.

While the room was large, there weren't actually a lot of spots for the curse to hide. Chrysanthemum poked around some chairs that were stacked along one wall, and Lily found light switches near the door that had slammed on them, but unsurprisingly, none of them worked. She tried them all twice anyway. She was *motivated* and *determined.*

She was checking around a water station when Chrysanthemum's voice rang out.

"I found it!"

Lily followed her phone's glow to the room's enormous central chandelier. Perched among the dripping crystals, the curse sat like a shadowy blister, squirming and writhing in its own foulness. Cracks spread out along the ceiling, an intricate web of black lines that made Lily's feet itch to run toward the door, despite knowing it was pointless.

The whole ceiling looked ready to cave in on them.

Lily shuddered, then let out a cry of triumph as it dawned on her that she was holding the key to getting help and was just using it as a flashlight. But her triumph was short-lived. Her phone had no signal.

This time, when she glanced Chrysanthemum's way, she could see the *duh* expression Chrysanthemum was giving her. "I suppose you already checked," Lily said, hating the flush creeping up her neck.

"I did while we were searching." Chrysanthemum jerked her head up at the curse. "It's so typical. Just shitty, shitty behavior from that thing. Horror-movie cliché nonsense."

"It's . . ." Lily floundered for a word that didn't sound totally stupid. "Obnoxious."

That did sound stupid. But Chrysanthemum didn't disagree.

Lily tucked her phone away. It was time to plan again, and there was no sense draining what was left of her battery. "We have no candles, but we do have water." The water station's container was half full, and there were paper cups next to it.

Chrysanthemum turned her flashlight off, too. "We don't have half the things we need, and I don't remember half of what we did."

Lily took a deep breath. She had a plan, but it was a plan that went against every fiber of her being. What else was there to do, though? "You're right, but the last time we followed my scrupulous instructions, we failed. I think it's time we try your methods. We wing it."

Chrysanthemum stared at her. “Has the curse possessed you? Do I need to threaten to harm your hamsters to see if you’re still in there?”

“Funny. You know I have rabbits.”

“That was a test.”

“Oh.” Lily snorted. “It wasn’t a very good one. The curse could be reading my memories.”

Chrysanthemum was already running over to the water station. “I’ll keep that in mind. Look, we also have an amethyst.” She pulled a ring off one of her fingers. “It’s what I used to infuse the water last time.”

“Okay, and this will sound gross, but we have salt, too,” Lily said, filling a cup. “I don’t know about you, but, um, I’m sweating with nerves, and sweat has salt in it. So if we rub our necks or something and dip our fingers in the water . . .”

Was that too gross? Should she not have suggested that?

But Chrysanthemum grinned. “Super gross. I like it.”

“Thanks.” Lily smiled. “If you want, I can go second so you don’t have to dip your finger into the cup with my sweat in it.”

“Please. It’s not like we haven’t swapped fluid before.” Chrysanthemum averted her gaze, and Lily wondered if she was also remembering the last time they’d kissed. “Besides, we both need to fling water. We can each have our own cups of sweaty, amethyst-infused liquid.”

Right, of course. She’d been so proud of her own idea that she hadn’t thought it completely through, and it didn’t help that

Chrysanthemum was standing close to her again as they filled the tiny cups of water. Fear might be making Lily uncomfortably warm, but Chrysanthemum's presence made her brain fuzzy and her body aware of every breath she took.

As for the swimmy feeling in her stomach, that was probably a result of the combination of the two.

Despite the way Chrysanthemum's closeness threw her off, Lily kept one eye on the curse as they worked. It didn't make any more moves against them, but neither one of them wanted to risk wasting time. Without cell signal and being so far from the ball, it was impossible to know what else was going on in the hotel. Not to mention, the curse had used magic against them for just thinking about banishing it. Lily didn't know why it had stopped now that they were trapped, but she wasn't about to take this reprieve for granted.

Chrysanthemum dug the amethyst ring out of the second cup of water and stuck it in a third. Then she reset her phone's stopwatch.

"Why thirty seconds?" Lily asked.

Chrysanthemum shrugged. "That ritual you found said it's supposed to sit overnight. I figure sunset to sunrise is an approximation for half a day, so half a minute will be our substitute."

Lily decided not to question this logic. The faster they moved, the better.

Once Chrysanthemum had infused four cups, she stuck the wet ring back on her finger, and they carried the cups to the center of the room. The curse remained quiet, but Lily's heart beat harder with it hovering overhead.

"Good thing you were so unwilling to trust me about the ritual last time," Chrysanthemum said, scrolling through her phone. "You texted me the words we said."

Lily swallowed. "It's not that I didn't trust you would study. I was . . ." She closed her eyes. "I was looking for excuses to talk to you. I didn't think you'd want to talk to me except about the curse."

"Oh." Chrysanthemum's brow pinched. "I would have rather you just talked to me."

"Yeah, well." Lily scrolled through their conversations, searching for the messages she'd sent Chrysanthemum about the ritual. It was a good excuse to keep her head down. "I didn't know."

They'd anointed each other after speaking last time, but without supplies, that was out. Given they didn't have properly spaced candles, herbs for purification, or anything else, it seemed like a small thing to worry about. *Especially* considering the words they were supposed to say. Words that were no longer true.

How was the curse going to respond to that?

"Ready?" Chrysanthemum asked.

Hardly. But here went nothing.

Lily's voice shook as she spoke. "I, Lily Ellen Allerton, descendant of the Thornhaven Allertons, declare an end to the rift between my family and the Langmores. I disavow any negativity that remains, and I banish any remnants of discord between myself and Chrysanthemum Quinn. In . . ." The lump in her throat caught her. Lily paused; then she tried and failed a second time.

In this endeavor, they were definitely not one.

Lily attempted the line once more, but the words tasted like a lie on her tongue, and when she glanced up, Chrysanthemum was biting her lip. Maybe it was the shadows splayed across her face or fear wearing her down, but Chrysanthemum's nonchalant mask had slipped. Lily had known she must have hurt her, but seeing it was something else. Seeing it, there was no way she could force out the ritual's last line with any conviction.

Her own composure broke.

"We might be united in fighting this curse, but we're not in anything else. Because I pushed you away. And I'm sorry." Lily squeezed her eyes shut against a sudden rush of tears. "I did this whole tarot reading, and I should have done a better job of explaining everything to you, but it hurt so much, and I should have known that meant I was doing the wrong thing, and . . ."

She was babbling. She could confess her stupidity about the tarot reading another time. "The point is, I was so happy with you that it distracted me from school. I forgot a *test*, Chrysanthemum. *Me*. I was terrified of changing like that. I panicked. I wanted a perfect year. I wanted to be a perfect daughter. I wanted to be a perfect Allerton so someone would give a damn about me." She inhaled shakily. "But I've realized

I can't have a perfect year without you in it. And I'm sorry if I made you feel like I didn't care about you, because I *know* how that feels. I'm not as smart as I want to be about this—this sort of thing. But I do care, and I like you. A lot."

She'd said her piece. And because of that, she finally became brave enough to meet Chrysanthemum's gaze.

Chrysanthemum's eyes had never been bluer. Even in the dim light, they took Lily's breath away. But she looked like she'd been slapped. "That's . . . Shit. I don't know if I wanted to hear that." She turned away, rubbing her hands along her arms. "I'm just so tired of being hurt by people."

"'People.' You mean me. I keep hurting you." The truth of it stabbed Lily in the gut. She was an awful person. She didn't deserve Chrysanthemum, and Lily couldn't hold back the tears any longer. "You're right. You deserve to protect yourself from me."

That was that. She'd apologized, explained, and whether Chrysanthemum decided to accept her apology was out of her hands. All Lily could do was promise herself that she wouldn't bring it up again. She would keep her distance. Do whatever it took to not hurt Chrysanthemum a third time, no matter how much that hurt herself.

Chrysanthemum glanced back over her shoulder. "I—"

Whatever she was about to say got lost as Lily went flying to the floor.

Chapter Forty
Chrysanthemum

Chrys didn't think. She lunged.

Something black and inky was about to land on top of Lily's head. Chrys didn't consider whether it might land on *her* if she jumped in the way. All she knew was that her heart, which had surely stopped as Lily apologized, burst back into action. She had to protect Lily.

As a result, they both crashed to the floor. Lily screamed. Rough carpet dug into Chrys's knees. Her forehead smacked Lily's shoulder, and Chrys retained just enough of her wits to roll them out of the path of the curse's tentacle—or whatever it was.

Lily's cry of surprise cut off, and Chrys craned her neck. The blackness was retreating. Only then did Chrys realize she was tangled in a heap of limbs with Lily, her head mere inches above Lily's chest, her hands around Lily's arms, their legs . . . Chrys had no idea where those were. She was twisted and trapped in a mound of black tulle.

"What happened?" Lily shifted, and Chrys climbed off her, feeling as dazed as Lily sounded.

Her cheeks burned with the realization of how close Lily was. "It was about to . . ." She had no idea what, so she gestured vaguely at the inkiness creeping toward the chandelier, uncertain whether it was real or another illusion, like with the pumpkin.

Lily shuddered. "Um, thanks."

"You're welcome?" She should get up, get the water, finish banishing the wretched thing.

But Lily was so close. And she'd apologized. Chrys hadn't been expecting that. Not really, not the way Lily had done it. At best, she'd thought Lily might apologize for the way she'd dumped Chrys. Worse, Chrys had feared that Lily might suggest they try being friends, something Chrys wasn't sure she could handle. So she'd ignored Lily's text and done her best to avoid Lily and any more misery she might bring. She'd told herself she was strong for doing it.

But she'd never felt strong. Just sad and empty. It was strange—only because of the curse had she begun to acknowledge to herself that she did care what happened to everyone at school. To the people here at the hotel, too. In fact, she was more scared for what might be happening to everyone outside this room than she was for herself.

It didn't feel great being worried, but it did make her feel more whole.

Lily was right. She deserved to protect herself. But what

was she protecting—a hard shell of a person? That didn't seem very worth it. She had been happiest when she'd made herself vulnerable. When she'd let Lily in.

This wasn't the time to be having these epiphanies, and it sure wasn't the time to say any of this to Lily. Not with that writhing mass of evil magic hovering over their heads. But . . . it might be now or never.

Chrys started to speak, but the curse had other ideas. The magic that came for them this time was invisible. Like the hand that had shoved them through the hotel door, a gust of frigid, putrid wind sent her flying farther from Lily. Hair whipped Chrys about her face, and her skirt knotted around her legs, tangling her far worse than the tumble she'd just taken had. Lily screamed again, but Chrys could barely see her. Dark smoke began filling the room.

"The water!" Chrys yelled. They'd set the cups down nearby. She had to find them before she couldn't see at all.

"Chrys!" Lily's face appeared through the smoke. She was crawling along the floor, struggling to reach the cups, like something was pushing her away.

It was the first time Chrys had ever heard Lily use her shortened name, and it could have given rise to a thousand questions under other circumstances.

Chrys stretched for Lily's hand and pressed a cup of water into it. Her cup? Lily's? It hardly mattered. Water sloshed over the sides. There wouldn't be enough, *couldn't* be enough, but it would have to do. She turned and grabbed a second cup, swaying under the force of the magic that tried to pin her down.

"This curse's power is now broken!" Wait, that wasn't right. "As I speak these words?" How could she have forgotten when she'd read the chant a few minutes ago? Fear, like smoke, clouded her brain.

"As these words are spoken, this curse's power is now broken." Lily remembered (of course she did), but she couldn't seem to stand, and her attempts at flinging the water were worse than Chrys's own. Droplets sprinkled the floor, but neither of them could reach the curse high above in the gaudy crystals.

Chrys tried again, timing her voice with Lily's, but the cups were tiny. She ran out of water without being confident she'd hit the curse at all. She should have tried harder to talk Lily out of trusting her intuition, but then, what choice had they had? Lily's elaborate ritual had been impossible to replicate. Their innate power was all they could use.

"Lily?" Smoke choked her, stinking and thick. Lily had all but disappeared within it, and so had the remaining two cups. Chrys felt blindly around for them, and her fingers brushed one. Badly. She knocked it over, and she swore.

"Chrys?" It sounded like Lily used her full name, but her voice disintegrated into a coughing fit after the first syllable.

Giving up on the cups, Chrys scrambled to where she could barely make out Lily's outline. They'd made a valiant attempt, but this wasn't working. More water wasn't going to help. The pessimist in her had been right, which meant the only thing left to do was talk to Lily before it was too late. Crack her chest open and let her heart bleed out of its own accord. Spilling her guts was painful, but it was better than letting the curse end her.

More to the point, intuition was telling her she needed to do this. That they'd failed last time because neither she nor Lily had truly let go of the issues between them.

"Lily?" Chrys snagged her arm and dragged herself closer until she could see Lily more clearly.

She was *all* Chrys could see—reddish hair, warm eyes, an autumnal fairy of a girl. When Chrys glanced down, the carpet had disappeared. The floor seemed to have opened up beneath them. They were falling into a black void. Into the cracks.

Chrys pushed down the terror that streaked through her and focused on Lily's stupid, perfect face. "I'm sorry I didn't respond to your text. I didn't want to hear whatever you had to say because I thought it would rip me apart."

"I'm so sorry I hurt you." Lily was crying.

Oh shit. Lily was *crying*. Chrys couldn't handle tears. Her own eyes were getting misty, and if she was falling into a void or about to die, she did not want to do it with tearstained cheeks and smeared mascara. She wanted dignity. She wanted to go down fighting—if not against the curse, then for Lily. For herself.

The thought made her laugh, but the laugh didn't stop tears from pricking her eyes. "As you should be," she said, unable to resist one more dig. "But I'm sure I'll do something stupid and hurt you, too. And I'll try to learn from it, like you are. Lily, you . . . you made me happy. Happier than I've been in a long time. I think the truth is . . . if I can't let myself be hurt, I also can't let myself be happy."

Lily blinked, and confusion seemed to have stopped her tears. "Are you saying you forgive me, or was that some kind of inappropriately timed philosophy lesson?"

To be fair, she had rambled a bit. And maybe had forgotten to actually say she forgave Lily. So, possibly, they both could work on communication.

Chrys started to explain and decided to hell with it. The smoky darkness was encroaching on Lily's face.

Chrys reached out and grabbed Lily's cheeks, and she kissed her.

Lips against soft lips, eyes closed, Lily's warm skin beneath her fingers—the room or the void or whatever was around her—faded from Chrys's consciousness. There was nothing else but her and Lily, and she finally felt like they were moving past the hang-ups that had gotten them into this mess in the first place.

It just *figured* that it was too late.

Lily's hand tentatively touched the back of Chrys's neck, and her lips parted wider. Sweet and salty with tears, warming her from the inside out. Chrys could barely breathe, but when she did, all she inhaled was Lily. The scent of her perfume. The very air from her lungs. It was like they were becoming one person, and Chrys could sense that Lily felt the same. Some magic in their blood linked them. Some power pulled them together. They could have been unstoppable. One day, they could have created their own Thornhaven legend.

A bang like thunder broke the spell, and Chrys's eyes opened in spite of herself.

She could see.

Chrys caught her breath, inhaling the scent of Lily's shampoo, but the heady rush it gave her was nothing compared to the dizziness she felt about the sights around her. The smoke was fading. Moonlight once more poured through the tall windows.

"Lily?" The heaviness on Chrys's back was gone, too. She could breathe more easily. Hell, she could run a marathon, powered by her shock and the taste of Lily's lips.

Lightning flashed outside the room, and Chrys remembered her phone in her pocket. She had signal again, and when she turned on the flashlight . . .

"It's gone." Lily gasped. She stared at the chandelier with Chrys, but she hadn't removed her arms from around Chrys's neck. "We banished it."

Chrys swallowed. She didn't want to get too excited, but thinking rationally was a challenge when Lily was holding on to her for dear life. She dropped her phone to her skirt and wrapped Lily in a hug. "For good this time?"

"I hope so." Lily smiled. "I think we had, um, issues to work out."

That was exactly what Chrys's intuition had been telling her, and she grinned, her confidence growing since Lily had arrived at the same conclusion. "A few, I suppose."

Then she kissed Lily again.

At some point, they toppled over, and only when Lily's phone started making noises did Chrys remember where they were and that they needed to find out what was going on outside this room they weren't supposed to be in.

"It's my mom," Lily said. "She's frantic because she can't find me."

Lily sounded happy about that. Chrys, however, was not happy to discover that she also had frantic messages from her mom.

"We need to go," she said, jumping up.

Lily nodded. "Do I look okay?"

"You look like you just did battle, but since no one's going to suspect that, you look like you were rolling around on the floor with your girlfriend."

Oh. Presumptuous of her to use the G-word.

But Lily preened as she finger combed her hair. "Well, we *were* just rolling around on the floor, so I guess that's accurate."

Warmth flooded Chrys's veins, and she couldn't help but smile at that, too. She held out a hand to Lily. "Let's go see what happened."

Chapter Forty-One

Lily

Lily squeezed Chrysanthemum's hand as they exited the function room. Kissing Chrysanthemum had given her a second wind, a rush of energy and power as thrilling and fortifying as the elation of their success. But that feeling was fading, along with the tingle of Chrysanthemum's mouth, although Lily could still sense a whisper of it—a ghostly sensation—if she chased the memory.

Thoughts of ghosts forced her into the present. Had they faded, too?

As the sounds of the ball grew louder, her heart raced with the oddest mix of trepidation over what they might find, triumph over the curse, and elation that Chrysanthemum had forgiven her. Forty-five minutes remained until midnight. They still had time to experience the Halloween ball the way she'd meant to—dancing with Chrysanthemum.

Assuming there was still a ball in progress.

Everything sounded promising, though, and it looked even more so. They both kept alert for any black lines, but they didn't find anything amiss until they reached the ballroom lobby. Then it wasn't the lines that were alarming but the number of witches talking in hushed voices, confusion and worry written over their faces.

"Chrys!" Chrysanthemum's mother appeared through the crowd and pulled her daughter into a hug. "Where were you? Things got"—she lowered her voice and glanced around—"strange."

Chrys shot Lily an *oh shit* kind of look.

"We saw weird things," Lily said, settling on a version of the truth that she hoped wouldn't be incriminating. "Lines in the hotel. We followed them, and our phones lost signal."

Chrysanthemum's mother contemplated this, but whether she bought it or not in the face of how disheveled Lily and her daughter appeared, she didn't say. "Lily, your parents have been searching all over for you."

It shouldn't make her happy that her parents were worried, but a small thrill shot down Lily's spine. It wasn't nearly as strong as the other emotions coursing through her, but she couldn't shake it, either. They'd noticed her enough to realize she was missing when things went wild. That was, honestly, more than she'd expected, although that might be a touch unfair of her. They'd been trying lately.

"I should go find them," Lily said. The words were no sooner out of her mouth than Sara was plowing through the chaos, dragging their mother behind her and yelling, "I see her!"

Lily found herself squished into a hug in a way she hadn't been squished in a long time. Peering behind her mom, she caught Chrysanthemum grinning at her. Lily grinned back.

"I was so worried when I couldn't find you, and you weren't answering your phone," her mom said. She released Lily and began fussing with her hair. "Are you hurt? Where were you? You're a mess."

"That's what happens when you're magically attacked."

It was the wrong thing to say. In a heartbeat, her parents and Chrysanthemum's mom were demanding to know what had happened, and she and Chrysanthemum had to cobble together a story that didn't implicate them in any nefarious magic while under pressure. They succeeded, mostly, but sometime during Lily's second recounting of events, Chrysanthemum was dragged away by her mom to get magically checked out by one of the Society elders.

Not long after that, Lily's father returned to an emergency meeting of the Society board that was happening by the registration desk. Lily wanted to go as well, to find Chrysanthemum and be done with her mother's fussing, and she was aware of how ironic that was. For once, she had her mom's full attention, and she had other priorities.

Instead, over the next twenty minutes, Lily pieced together what had happened after she and Chrysanthemum had left the ball. In a word, chaos.

The same smoke that she and Chrysanthemum had experienced had filled the ballroom. The food had rotted at the serving stations. Decorations had come to life, much like they once had at the school. People had panicked in the darkness as they were chased by bats that weren't supposed to be real and pirate ghosts that definitely *were* real. They were swatted by broomsticks that shooed the humans around the room like they were tidying up the dirty floor. A lucky few had escaped, but for everyone else, the ballroom had become an endless darkened tomb, filled with cell service but no doors by which to leave.

And then, everything had returned to normal, as though none of it had ever happened. The normies' terrified memories were fading, if they weren't already gone, by the time Lily and Chrysanthemum were finally free to reenter the ballroom together. The band was playing again. The bar was reopened. More food had been brought out. Only the witches remained shaken, and they were trying to hide it. No doubt, the Historical Society would investigate and eventually conclude that the mysterious magic was linked to whatever had been going on at the high school and around town. What would become of her and Chrysanthemum, and their role in causing and stopping it—of that, Lily was unsure. For the rest of the night, she didn't want to think about it.

"We deserve to win the magic fair this year for everything we did," Chrysanthemum said for what was probably the hundredth time.

They'd made a restroom stop to fix their hair and clothes, and Chrysanthemum had reapplied a deep ruby lipstick, so dark that it was almost black. It was totally Chrysanthemum, and at one point, Lily would have rolled her eyes. Now she wanted to see how much would stick to her if they kissed.

"I had that same thought," Lily said, snagging them both a glass of the ball's nonalcoholic punch, which was being served from a giant cauldron. She couldn't figure out what was in it, but it had to be spiked with magic. Drinking it made her less tired and eased the aches in her feet. "We'd get in so much trouble, though."

"I'm sure there are ways around it. We could say we researched it on our own, after the fact."

Chrysanthemum nudged her, and Lily turned to catch Ms. LaPlant smiling in their direction. Like most of the witches, Ms. LaPlant appeared frazzled, but she also seemed delighted to catch the two of them together.

Lily waved, cringing as she did so. "You're right. We have to do something. I can't stand the elders thinking their plan to make us get along worked when it really backfired so spectacularly that we almost took out the whole island."

She didn't *know* they could have taken out the whole island, but it sounded better than the whole hotel, and who was to say the curse wouldn't have kept spreading? Legends had to start somewhere, and Lily was already envisioning how hers might go.

"I like it when you get all rebellious," Chrysanthemum said. "The princess isn't so perfect after all."

Lily choked on her punch. “I think it’s clear I’m far from perfect.”

“Not totally far.” Chrysanthemum’s cheeks turned nearly the shade of her lips.

“Did you just compliment me?” Lily clutched her chest.

“Don’t let it go to your head.”

“Too late. A compliment from you is . . .” Lily tried to think of something not totally cheesy and failed. “It means a lot.”

Chrysanthemum nudged her again, but she looked as pleased as Lily felt.

“Do you—” Lily started to ask if Chrysanthemum wanted to dance, but the music faded, and a hush swept through the ballroom. Whether by magic or simply some sense of what was to come, Lily quieted with everyone else.

A moment later, she gasped as the cascading purple and gold lights shot upward. They dispersed across the room, chasing away the decorative smoke and setting the ballroom ceiling ablaze.

The fake bats and ghosts, and all the other decorations, vanished, swallowed in this new display of magic. Above, the lights swirled like the cosmos, a thousand glittering stars and meteors in a thousand different colors. Then, one by one, the stars fell gently from the ceiling, and a single light landed on the palm of everyone present, twinkling like a jewel. Witches and normies alike clapped and shrieked with delight.

Lily tucked hers into her barrette. The lights would glow for hours after the ball ended, a piece of magic the normies could take with them that would be gone by sunrise.

"Midnight," Chrysanthemum confirmed with a glance at her phone. She stuck her light atop the amethyst on her ring. "Not a bad showstopper spell, considering people must be exhausted from everything that happened, but I liked last year's pumpkin tree better."

Lily had enjoyed that one, too. That spell had created a giant gnarled tree that rose from the ballroom floor. Instead of leaves, the limbs had been covered in tiny glowing jack-o'-lanterns, and the tree had presented each guest with one of them. The jack-o'-lanterns had turned out to be delicious cupcakes.

"Can't eat lights," Lily agreed, realizing how hungry she'd gotten.

As she glanced around the much more brightly lit ballroom for food, she spotted Sonia and Evan dancing, as were Anushka and Isaiah. Next to them, Luke was dancing with a group of friends.

"You never actually liked him," Lily said, partly to herself. She still couldn't believe she'd gotten so much wrong, but the whipped cream on her pumpkin éclair helped console her.

"Did you?"

Lily shook her head. "I thought I should. It was confusing—the whole misreading-my-cards thing. But I also thought you were a walking hex, out to torment me. So I've made some mistakes."

Chrysanthemum licked apple tart off her fingers. “I can still torment you. Don’t worry. We never had that horror-movie fest you promised me.”

Lily whined. “Can I take that back?”

“No.”

“I’ll just bury my head in your shoulder the whole time.”

Chrysanthemum smirked. “You’re giving me more reasons to look forward to it.”

“Well, in that case, we should go practice that move.” Lily wiped her hands. “Let’s dance, and I’ll rest my head on you.”

The look of terror Chrysanthemum shot her made Lily grin, and she ignored Chrysanthemum’s protests of “I don’t dance!” and pulled her onto the floor.

“It’s way too late for that,” Lily said.

Chrysanthemum didn’t dance, and Lily didn’t do horror movies, but they’d taken down a curse. Midnight had come and gone. It was officially Samhain, and that meant it was time to celebrate a new year and everything it brought.

Starting now, they could, and would, do anything and everything together.

Acknowledgments

Every book is a challenge, but at least I can say *No Charm Done* was a fun one. As with all my books, this one got its start thanks to an enthusiastic endorsement from my agent, Rebecca Strauss. I'm so grateful for her essential edit notes on earlier versions of this story. Not to mention the cheerleading, hand-holding, and every other task that I (thankfully) don't need to know much about but that's required to sell a book.

Thank you to my wonderful editor, Mora Couch. I'm so glad Mora loved this story, and I'm thrilled at how her insightful and meticulous feedback helped shape it into its best possible form. Additional thanks to all the behind-the-scenes team members—the marketers, designers, and more—at Holiday House for their assistance in making this book a reality. I also want to thank Siobhan Keenan for the gorgeous cover illustration. I actually gasped when I first saw it.

I need to give special shout-outs to the following awesome people. To Alicia Thompson, for reading over early chapters and not only assuring me that I could still write YA, but also giving me the encouragement I needed by providing the best (i.e., ego-boosting) comments. To India Holton, for helping me with Lily's tarot spread when I was twisting myself into knots by unnecessarily complicating things (as I so often do). And to Logan and Laurelle Ogden, who probably don't remember it, but for answering several stupid pop culture questions.

I am always grateful for the support and silliness of my writing groups—the Berkletes, the Y-Nots, and the Purgies.

Standing thanks to my family for always encouraging my book addiction when I was growing up. (I'm going to have to answer more questions with this book, aren't I?) And to Al, who was forced to watch TV alone some nights while I was trying to write and who is perpetually owed a sci-fi novel (sorry, dear). And finally, thank you to the two newest additions to our household—Allecto and Belladonna—for not decreasing my stress while I worked on edits, but for distracting me from it by creating different stress. (And for the cuddles, of course.)

Author Note

Different as they are, Lily and Chrys are probably the most like me of any characters I've ever written, and I was very stressed about getting them just right on the page. Lily's asexuality in particular was something I struggled with for all the reasons Lily struggles to understand herself in the book. So often, as writers and readers, we rely on some very standard "tells" to convey romantic attraction—with physical attraction being the obvious and most common one. I've certainly done it in every romance I've written prior to this book. As someone who doesn't experience attraction like that, it's fun to write about it and imagine it! But physical attraction is not a cue that works for Lily, and so conveying her feelings was a challenge.

Did I succeed? Well, I think I conveyed my personal experience through Lily, but there is no one way to identify as asexual, just as there's no one way to identify as anything. Everyone's experience is unique, and asexuality exists on a spectrum and in many forms.